Karin Baine lives in Northern Ireland with her husband, two sons and her out-of-control notebook collection. Her mother and her grandmother's vast collection of books inspired her love of reading and her dream of becoming a Mills & Boon author. Now she can tell people she has a *proper* job! You can follow Karin on X, @karinbaine1, or visit her website for the latest news at karinbaine.com.

Louisa Heaton lives on Hayling Island, Hampshire, with her husband, four children and a small zoo. She has worked in various roles in the health industry—most recently four years as a community first responder, answering 999 calls. When not writing Louisa enjoys other creative pursuits, including reading, quilting and patchwork—usually instead of the things she *ought* to be doing!

Also by Karin Baine

Mills & Boon Medical

A Nurse, a Pup, a Second Chance

Royal York Hospital collection

Winter Nights with the Midwife

Mills & Boon Love Always

The Tycoon's Festive Houseguest

A Pact Between Tycoons collection

The Trouble with Italian Millionaires

Also by Louisa Heaton

Mills & Boon Medical

The Surgeon's Relationship Ruse
One Night to Twin Miracle
Nurse's Night Before Valentine's

Royal York Hospital collection

New Year to Nine-Month Surprise

Discover more at millsandboon.co.uk.

SURGEON'S SECOND TIME LUCKY

KARIN BAINE

ONBOARD AND OFF LIMITS

LOUISA HEATON

MILLS & BOON

All rights reserved including the right of reproduction in whole or in part in any form. This edition is published by arrangement with Harlequin Enterprises ULC.

This is a work of fiction. Names, characters, places, locations and incidents are purely fictional and bear no relationship to any real life individuals, living or dead, or to any actual places, business establishments, locations, events or incidents. Any resemblance is entirely coincidental.

Without limiting the exclusive rights of any author, contributor or the publisher of this publication, any unauthorised use of this publication to train generative artificial intelligence (AI) technologies is expressly prohibited. HarperCollins also exercise their rights under Article 4(3) of the Digital Single Market Directive 2019/790 and expressly reserve this publication from the text and data mining exception.

® and TM are trademarks owned and used by the trademark owner and/or its licensee. Trademarks marked with ® are registered with the United Kingdom Patent Office and/or the Office for Harmonisation in the Internal Market and in other countries.

First published in Great Britain 2026
by Mills & Boon, an imprint of HarperCollins*Publishers* Ltd,
1 London Bridge Street, London, SE1 9GF

www.harpercollins.co.uk

HarperCollins*Publishers* Macken House, 39/40 Mayor Street Upper, Dublin 1, D01 C9W8, Ireland

Surgeon's Second Time Lucky © 2026 Karin Baine

Onboard and Off Limits © 2026 Louisa Heaton

ISBN: 978-0-263-41989-4

04/26

Printed and Bound in the UK using 100% Renewable Electricity
at CPI Group (UK) Ltd, Croydon, CR0 4YY

SURGEON'S SECOND TIME LUCKY

KARIN BAINE

MILLS & BOON

For Sheila xx

CHAPTER ONE

'I'VE NEVER SEEN anything like this in Las Vegas.' Nurse Ruby Jones watched as the casualties were wheeled into Clover Hospital. Paramedics shouting to be heard over the hubbub of the walking wounded to get help for the most seriously injured on the stretchers.

'It's all hands on deck tonight. A gas explosion means not only burns, but crush injuries from falling debris and collapsed buildings.' Nell, one of the doctors in the department, wrapped her stethoscope around her neck, then rushed over to assign herself to one of the patients being stretchered in.

Ruby took a deep breath and did the same. In major incidents like this the patients were assessed as they came in with the most urgent cases treated as soon as possible. The emergency department was ground zero and it looked, and felt, like a battleground.

People filling every available space were clutching damaged body parts. The once pristine bright corridors now splattered with blood and debris from those staggering in off the street. The air was thick with the smell of smoke, drifting in through the open doors. Even the noise was almost unbearable. The injured screaming and crying in pain. Medical staff shouting to be heard trying to treat the patients. It was overwhelming. Claustrophobic. Frightening. Yet there was no room for thoughts of herself when people's lives were literally in her hands.

Ruby worked quickly and efficiently helping to assess the injured and prioritise the most serious cases.

The sight of a little boy seriously burned stopped her in her tracks. So small and vulnerable, he immediately pulled at her heartstrings. He couldn't be any older than her daughter, Aimee. Who, thankfully, was at home being fussed over by her grandmother. Safe.

'Ten-year-old boy, Eugene Collins. He was in the apartment block where the explosion happened and found under the rubble. Extensive second-degree burns, crush injuries to the abdomen. Unresponsive at the scene.' Wyatt Logan, one of the paramedics she saw regularly in the emergency department, reeled off the boy's injuries and the treatment he'd been given since. Now it was down to Ruby and her colleagues to make sure he came through this.

'Okay, let's get an IV set up and oxygen started,' Nell instructed the medical team as they transferred the boy from the stretcher.

It was hard to look at the small body, covered in soot and dirt, raw wounds needing attention. But this was Ruby's job. To save lives. She could get emotional later once she knew little Eugene was stable.

As expected, Nell's preliminary exam determined that along with his other injuries, he was suffering from smoke inhalation. His lungs struggling, and his throat swollen, making breathing difficult. 'I'm going to intubate him to help him breathe, then we'll look at those burns.'

They inserted the plastic tube down his throat to assist with the boy's breathing, and Ruby wondered what had happened to his parents. If they were being treated elsewhere in the department, or if he'd been orphaned by the blast.

Her heart broke for the child. Aimee's dad hadn't wanted to stick around the moment he knew he was going to be a father, but at least she had a mother to care for her. There had been no way Ruby was going to let the chance of being a mother slip through her hands again. Not after losing a baby at the age of eighteen. A trauma which not only devastated her but showed the cracks in her fledgling marriage. She and Harrison had been high school sweethearts and their future plans for marriage had been pushed forward with the discovery that she was pregnant. Her new husband working and studying hard to give their family a home and the best start.

In hindsight, they had been too young to fully understand the commitment they'd been making. Or, at least, Harrison had been. Proving he was too immature to deal with the emotional complications of a miscarriage. Grief had driven Ruby back home to her parents, but Harrison hadn't followed her. The separation, combined with the loss of the baby, had driven them apart permanently. Eventually, she'd returned to her studies and qualified as a nurse, plunging all of her energy into her career.

Then, four years later, she'd met Chad. She'd thought

she'd met the real 'one.' The pregnancy hadn't been planned but that was no excuse for his behaviour. In the end, he'd done a runner, leaving her as a single parent. She only managed to juggle her career with raising Aimee because she had her parents' help. Hopefully, Eugene would have the same level of family support to get him through this traumatic time.

'We have a new burns specialist transferred from St Michael's in Boulder City. I'll give him a call,' Nell suggested.

'You would think with the scale of this emergency he would have checked in already.' It irked her that someone so clearly needed on a night like this wouldn't step up simply because they weren't rostered on. As far as she was concerned, being a medical professional wasn't just a job, it was a vocation. More than a paycheck, this was about saving lives, and those who didn't think about that first weren't right for the job, in her opinion.

'Sorry about that. I got caught up helping with the injured out on the street. I'm Dr Blake, the new burns specialist. Now, where do you need me?' It was the voice behind her which sent chills along the back of her neck, before she turned around to face him.

Time had chiseled his features into that of a handsome, mature man, from the teen she had known, but the swoop of dark hair, deep brown eyes and full smile hadn't changed that much. Harrison. Her ex-husband. Father to the baby she'd lost. The love of her life who hadn't loved her enough to stay. And now he was here, in front of her.

It took a moment for Ruby to compose herself, not

wanting to give away the nature of the relationship they'd once had to any of her colleagues. No one here knew of her life before she'd qualified as a nurse, and that was the way she wanted to keep it. Especially if she and Harrison were apparently going to be working in the same hospital from now on.

She saw the moment too when he recognized her, the almost imperceptible sharp intake of breath, and flare of recognition in his eyes. Before he could say anything which might have given away their secret, Ruby jumped in.

'Here. For the boy, I mean. He will have to get an X-ray to see what internal damage there might be, but he's suffered some serious burns over his body.' She was doing her best not to appear flustered, maintaining her professional demeanor, even though her heart was beating so fast it felt as if she'd just run a marathon.

He'd always had this effect on her. It didn't matter that they'd grown up together in high school and she'd seen him practically every day, he'd always made her heart race. Her body apparently hadn't processed the fact he'd abandoned her when she'd needed him most. Traitor.

Harrison looked at her for a moment as though there was something he wanted to say. A blink, and it was gone as he turned his attention to the young boy on the bed. She couldn't help but wonder what was going on in his mind. Regret? Nostalgia? A wish to be anywhere else than here near her? Ruby supposed she'd never know, but she had a million questions of her own running around her head. All based around what he'd been doing for the past fifteen years, and why he hadn't come back for her.

But he wasn't here for her now either.

'I won't know exactly what we're dealing with until we're able to clean and debride the wounds, removing any dead tissue. At a glance, I'm afraid he's going to need skin grafts.' Harrison frowned. 'It's going to be a long road back to recovery.'

'As long as he does recover. We'll have to keep him sedated and give him pain relief until we're able to patch him up properly.' With those sorts of wounds, the little boy would be in a serious amount of pain otherwise. At least whilst he was asleep, he might be spared the worst of it. Ruby brushed the matted dark hair from Eugene's brow. The children were always the most difficult for her to deal with.

Not only did they make her think of her own daughter in serious jeopardy, but also of the child she'd lost. Harrison here beside her amplified that feeling of loss. Wondering if their child would have been a little dark-haired boy like his father, or fair like his mother. Aimee took after her with her long blond hair and blue eyes. Thankfully she didn't look anything like her ex, so there was no permanent reminder of the other man who'd let her down so spectacularly.

When Ruby glanced up, Harrison was watching the interaction intently and she wondered if he was thinking about the child they'd never been given the chance to parent. Probably not, since once his responsibility was over, he'd disappeared from her life altogether. Until now.

'I'll do my best for him, Ruby. You know I will.' He gave her that devastating smile she'd forgotten could wreak so much havoc on her insides.

'I know.' Although she hadn't seen him in so long or witnessed him in action as a fully qualified medical professional until now, she was sure he cared about each and every patient. He'd always had a good heart. That was why it had been so hard to come to terms with the way things had ended between them. Cold and completely unlike the man she'd known and loved.

Ruby caught the other members of staff glancing between them, probably bemused by the familiarity between them when they were supposed to be recently introduced strangers.

'Yes, well, welcome to the hospital, Dr Blake. Once we get Eugene stabilized we'll get you back to take a look at the burns. Perhaps in the meantime you could check on the other patients and see what you can do for them too.' Ruby made sure to put that distinction back in their roles here. They had much to discuss, and though she didn't know if it would happen, or even if she wanted it to, that conversation needed to take place outside of a busy emergency department.

'Of course, Nurse...' he took a look at her name tag but didn't bat an eyelid when he saw she'd reverted to her maiden name, 'Jones. Although, I'm sure we'll be seeing a lot of each other in the future.' The twinkle in Harrison's eyes as he said it let her know that he wasn't just talking about meeting in a professional capacity.

The thought of it, of being alone with Harrison Blake, the love of her life, was something she knew she wasn't going to stop thinking about for the foreseeable future. With their painful history, it shouldn't be something she was looking forward to either, but she was. If only to give him a piece of her mind and get some closure. At least, that's what she was telling herself.

Seeing Ruby again out of the blue made Harrison feel as though someone had just delivered two thousand volts of electricity to his heart. She was the last person he'd expected to run into here. If he'd known, he mightn't have entertained the idea of a transfer from Boulder City, never mind moving. This was supposed to mark a change in his life. Moving forward. Not having to face the past. Especially when it had taken so long to get over what had happened to him and Ruby, and the grief he'd carried with him for so long. Now it seemed he was going to have to confront it all over again.

It was always going to be difficult facing her again. That's why he'd avoided it for so long. Until things were so broken between them there was no way to fix things again. Of course they were different people now, with different lives. Virtual strangers, but with a history he doubted either of them had ever been fully able to forget.

That meant finally telling her why he hadn't been able to comfort her, to be the husband she'd needed. Because losing the baby had destroyed him too. It had reopened old wounds. Reminding him of when his big brother had died. His hero. His world. They'd call it post-traumatic stress disorder these days. He hadn't understood at the time. Thought he was being selfish in wallowing in his own misery and that Ruby would be better off without him. She was young enough to start her life over again and forget about him, along with the child they'd never know.

It had taken a decline in his mental health and subsequent recovery for him to realise he'd been wrong, but by that time it was too late. He had no choice other than to try and move on too by finishing medical school and becoming the doctor he was now. Finding out that Ruby had completed her nursing the way they'd always planned was a surprise, but he was nonetheless proud of her.

In that moment of seeing her again, recognizing her despite the sleeker blond mane and more angular features than he remembered, he'd been transported to his teenage self. That instant flare of attraction before regret and guilt had set in for how things had ended between them. His love for her had never died, but he'd let it all slip away in the haze of depression and grief which had consumed him for too long. Making him weak and vulnerable and barely able to function, never mind be a good husband. Hopefully he'd get the chance to try and put things right, even if he could never hope to make amends or reconnect with the only woman he'd ever truly loved. That time might have passed. Unfortunately.

He could see Ruby out of the corner of his eye, rushing between patients and taking care of everyone. If this was her as a nurse, he could only imagine the mother she would have made to their baby. As always, the thought brought sadness with it. That feeling of loss and what could have been.

He guessed he'd never know because since then he'd made sure never to put himself in that vulnerable position again. No one else had ever claimed a piece of his heart the way Ruby had because he didn't stick around long enough for that to happen. As for ideas of a family, that notion had been well and truly quashed. He could never go through that kind of grief again. So, he'd lived the bachelor life, casual relationships a low priority next to his work.

Now, however, his personal life and his professional one were about to collide spectacularly. With such emotional ties to Ruby already, he had no idea how things were going to pan out. He only hoped neither of them would get hurt again along the way.

CHAPTER TWO

RUBY HAD BEEN aware of Harrison's presence all night. She knew the rest of the staff were pleased to have him on board, advising on the more seriously burned patients, and in most cases, taking over their care. Treating them personally and showing a compassion for all. It was difficult not to ask herself why he hadn't been able to do that for her when she'd desperately needed his support.

'I'm glad things have begun to calm down. Hopefully we'll get back to the usual status quo where all we have to deal with is the aftermath of drunken confrontations and tourists who've had too much sun.' Nell was yawning, reminding her that it had been a long night. An emotional one too, for various reasons.

'There's never a dull moment, is there?' That had been part of the attraction for Ruby. Always keeping her too busy to dwell on the past. Working somewhere that made her feel needed, appreciated, less lonely. She hadn't accounted for ending up as a single mother along the way. Aimee satisfied all of those criteria for her too. Ruby had been born to be a mother as much as a nurse. It was simply a shame she'd had to experience so much trauma before finally getting there.

'We'd worry if there was,' her colleague chirped much too heartily for the time of morning, apparently getting a new wind as she lifted a new patient file from the desk.

Ruby, on the other hand, was beginning to feel the strain of being on her feet all night and into the next morning. She rubbed at the back of her neck absent-mindedly, looking forward to spending the rest of the day in bed whilst Aimee was at school. Thank goodness for doting grandparents who were able to mind her overnight when her mother was working night shifts.

'You only feel it when you stop, don't you?' Harrison appeared beside her, furthering the tension already in her body.

'I didn't know you were still here, Dr Blake.'

'I'm just about to leave. I have to say, it was quite the introduction. Not how I imagined spending my first shift here.' He was smiling, doing his best to make things easy between them, but Ruby couldn't help but bristle every time he was near.

'Strictly speaking, this isn't your department, but we appreciate you helping out.' It was her attempt to put him in his place and make sure he was under no allusion that they were going to be friends. That would be too much to ask of her when he'd broken her heart and walked away, leaving her to deal with her grief all on her own. She wasn't going to simply forgive and forget because he was back in her life and wanted to carry on as though nothing had happened.

'Ruby, we don't have to keep pretending. There's no one around to hear. I think we need to talk.' Harrison took her hand, and though he was gentle with her, she was trembling nonetheless.

'I don't think so. Fifteen years ago was the time to do that.' She snatched her hand away again.

'Please, hear me out. If we're going to be working together in future, it's important that I explain things to you.'

'I don't want to hear it.' Ruby didn't want to be drawn back into memories of that time. It was still too painful to revisit.

'Please.' If he'd said anything else, looked at her with anything other than pain in his eyes, she wouldn't even have considered relenting. However, that same hurt she felt every day remembering their past was so evident in Harrison she'd be heartless to ignore it. Besides, he was right. She couldn't work here, seeing him all the time, and not address it. If she didn't get some kind of closure, it was going to open that wound every time their paths crossed.

However, she was too weary, too emotionally exhausted by the night's events to take this on now. She needed time to build her defences back up before confronting their painful past. A good sleep, some food and some time to think over the implications of having Harrison back in her life were needed before that conversation. Not necessarily in that order.

At the very least, he might tell her some things she wasn't ready to hear. That he hadn't loved her. That losing their baby had been for the best. That he'd met someone else. Any of those scenarios would crush her when she was already feeling vulnerable at being ambushed here at work by him.

She huffed out a sigh as she faced the inevitable. 'Fine, but not here, not now. I'm going to need some time.'

He looked relieved. As though she'd taken a load off his shoulders. A guilty conscience, perhaps? Good. He should feel bad about leaving her to grieve on her own the way he had.

See? That's exactly why she needed a little time and space. Otherwise she'd end up lashing out.

Harrison held his hands up. 'Of course. Sorry. This has come as a shock to me too.'

Ruby supposed seeing one another again like this must have been hard for him too. Albeit for different reasons. Being confronted by a painful past wasn't easy for anyone.

'You must have considered it a possibility when you moved here?' Okay, so he would never have known she was a nurse, or that she'd be working here, but Spring Valley, their hometown wasn't that far away. The last place he'd known her to be.

'It crossed my mind, but it's a big city. I thought the chances were slim.' Otherwise he might never have considered the move…she could read between the lines.

It wasn't a surprise that he never had any intention of seeking her out, accepting responsibility for the hurt he'd caused. Not when he'd been content to leave her on her own so soon after the miscarriage.

'Sorry to disappoint you.' She wasn't. He deserved his comeuppance in having to face his failure as a husband.

His sudden smile was alarming in the circumstances.

'Are you kidding? I'm so proud of you. Thankful that you finished your studies too and became the nurse I always knew you could be.'

If it had come from anyone else, the sentiment could have been construed as patronizing, or condescending. Except Ruby knew he meant it. They'd spent so long discussing their dream careers, and worked hard to achieve them, until circumstances had steered life in another direction. With her doubting herself every step of the way, and Harrison championing her. In completing her studies, and qualifying, it had felt as though she was showing him she could do it without him. Deep down knowing he'd want it for her, regardless of what had gone on between them.

That didn't mean she was going to make this easy for him when she'd been carrying this burden of rejection, abandonment, and feeling of not being good enough for so long, thanks to Harrison.

'Well, it was either that, or carry on haunting my parents' house like some wailing ghost of an abandoned wife who couldn't move on from the past.'

She had a lot of sympathy with those spectral figures rumoured to haunt old buildings, replaying traumatic events forevermore. It had been incredibly hard to pick herself up and start over, but there had always been that sense of having unfinished business as well as the sense of injustice. If nothing else, perhaps seeing Harrison again would finally give her that closure she didn't get first time around.

The flicker of shame which crossed his face gave her some satisfaction. He should feel ashamed of what he'd been able to do to someone he'd professed to love forever.

'I'm sorry. Of course I didn't expect you to sit around waiting for me, or my approval. I just…yeah… I'm glad you're doing well.' The half-smile could have weakened another woman. One who hadn't been fooled by this handsome man before into thinking he cared. But Ruby was a little older, wiser and more cynical to take him at face value anymore.

He was likely just trying to make his own life easier by trying to get her onside rather than being confronted by a still furious ex-wife. Which, as of right now, she still was. This wasn't simply about a bad teenage breakup she should have just got over. It had been the most traumatic time of her life. A mixture of grief and loss compounded by Harrison's betrayal of her trust and the subsequent dissolution of their marriage.

A smile, no matter how endearing, was not going to get him off the hook.

'I am. Now. However, it did take time to pick myself up again after everything that happened. Once I realized that I was on my own.'

Ruby didn't want to be impressed by him, or think about how handsome he looked, even more so now. The only emotion she wanted to associate with Harrison Blake was hate. She'd even take blind rage. Anything except liking him, because she needed closure. A reason to put him from her thoughts forever. Once she knew exactly why he'd abandoned her she could hopefully put it all behind her and finally move on.

Ruby was certain that Chad had been her second

mistake because she'd been desperate to replace Harrison in her life. Perhaps he'd felt that she didn't truly love him and he'd seen the pregnancy as an excuse to leave. Although she'd been content these past years with just her and Aimee, it might not be such a bad thing to finally close this particularly painful chapter of her life.

'I know nothing can excuse my actions, but I would like a chance to explain myself, Ruby. I've just moved into a new house nearby. Perhaps we could have a chat there after work.' Harrison's suggestion, regardless of her curiosity about what he had to say to her, was still a little too much too soon for Ruby. She wasn't sure she was ready for whatever he had to say.

'If I was prepared to hear you out, I'd prefer to have that conversation somewhere more neutral.' And public. She knew nothing about this man anymore, and being alone with him, on his own turf was a step too far. Although, it was possible he had a wife and children at home and it might not be just the two of them. A notion that didn't sit well with her either.

How would she feel if she found out he'd gone on to father another child with someone else? Being supportive to another wife and leaving her behind would be a double betrayal.

'Okay. You decide and let me know. It's on your terms, Ruby.' He sounded sincere, as if he actually cared about how she felt and what she wanted. Which only made the memories of those days and nights, spent sobbing for the loss of her husband and baby, hurt even more. Wondering why he couldn't come to her. Hug her and tell her everything was going to be okay the way he usually did when she'd needed his support.

'I'll let you know,' she said, making no firm commitment. Not knowing if she'd ever be ready to have that discussion, but hoping that would be enough to drop the subject for now. At least until she got her head around the situation and came to terms with the fact Harrison was back in her life. If even on the periphery.

He nodded, and finally walked away from the nurses' station, apparently content with the small concession. Ruby couldn't help but wonder if this unexpected run-in would have as much impact on him as it was already having on her. It was clear that he'd never wanted, or intended, to see her again. She had thought about it over the years, and how she'd react to seeing him again. In her mind she'd blasted him over how selfish he'd been, cursed the day she'd ever met him. All the while suspecting she'd end up a sobbing mess because despite everything she'd loved him.

This low key interaction wasn't what she'd expected. She put it down to the fact she was at work, and they'd been dealing with a large-scale emergency. Trying not to think about the other emotions she'd never dreamed she'd have upon seeing him again. Like thinking about how much she'd missed him. Or how her heart still skipped a beat every time she looked at him.

Ruby shook her head. She needed to get out of here and clear him out of her thoughts altogether. Hopefully their paths wouldn't cross again until she was better emotionally equipped to deal with him again.

She was just about to pass on her nightly report to the next shift when she caught sight of her mother rushing in through the doors of the emergency department, carrying a near hysterical Aimee in her arms. Her heart dropped into the bottom of her stomach.

'What is it? What happened?' She ran over, immediately searching her daughter for signs of injury.

'I'm so sorry, Ruby. I only took my eyes off her for a moment…' Her mother was clearly in shock too, her face pale and eyes wide with panic.

'What happened?' she asked again, reaching for Aimee.

The little girl wrapped her arms around her mother's neck, transferring between the two women, and clinging to her like a baby koala.

It was then Ruby saw the bandage on Aimee's arm.

'She said she wanted to make me breakfast. The coffee went all over her. I'm so sorry. I tried running her arm under the cold water but she was screaming. Your father's at work so I thought it best to bring her down here.' Ruby's mother was babbling, but she could just about make out what had happened.

'Why didn't you call me?' she asked, whisking her daughter to an empty cubicle so she could get a better look at her injury.

'I tried, but it just kept going to your voicemail. I thought it would be quicker to bring her down.' It was only now Ruby could see that her mother was in her pyjamas and slippers under her overcoat, and had obviously driven here in a hurry.

'Sorry.' Ruby pulled her phone from her pocket to

see that she'd turned it off and forgotten to turn it back on. 'We had an emergency with the gas explosion.'

'I heard about that on the news. I hope everyone is okay.' Her mother took a seat whilst Ruby set Aimee down on the gurney and began to unwrap her arm.

'I don't know the full extent of the damage yet, but we were full overnight. That's why I'm just getting off now.' If she'd left on time she might have been able to prevent this, but Ruby could never promise a set time when she had a duty here to her patients. Sometimes though, she wondered if she was compromising her role as a mother in the process. It wasn't easy being the only parent in her daughter's life and she often thought about whether or not Aimee was suffering as a result. This morning the answer was a resounding 'yes,' and impossible for Ruby not to feel guilty over it.

'Now, baby girl, Mommy's going to take a look at your arm and fix it all up, okay?' Ruby carefully peeled away the dressing her mother had placed on the wound, doing her best not to react to the angry red burn marring her daughter's otherwise smooth skin. At least Aimee's heart-piercing cries had dwindled down to a whimper as she sniffed through her tears. Hopefully, it was a reaction to the shock rather than the actual pain.

'Is everything okay in here, Nurse Jones? I saw you rushing in here.' A concerned-looking Harrison stepped into the cubicle, assessing the scene before him.

Great. This was all she needed. Her life now spectacularly clashing with the past.

Ruby's mother and Harrison exchanged glances, and

she held her breath as recognition and confusion registered on their faces.

'Mommy, it hurts.' Aimee drew everyone's attention back to her as she dissolved into pitiful tears. It was all Ruby could do not to sweep her up into her arms, but she needed to treat the wound before it became infected. There would be time for cuddles and treats once they got home.

'I know, sweetheart, and I'm going to make it all better for you.' Ruby could feel Harrison's eyes glaring into the back of her head. If it was a shock seeing her again, finding out she had a daughter would be a double whammy. Though she didn't owe him anything, she wished she could have broken the news a little easier. Certainly, if she'd discovered he'd had children after they'd lost their baby, it would have come as a gut punch to her. Then again, he hadn't seemed to be too overwrought at the time…

Harrison cleared his throat. If he had something to say, or questions to ask about her family, it appeared he was going to save them for now. 'Is there anything I can do?'

'I don't think we need your help,' Ruby's mother snapped.

Ruby had forgotten she wasn't the only one to bear a grudge over the way things had ended. After all, it was her parents who'd had to mop up her tears and prop her up again when the divorce was finalized and he'd decided to stay out of her life on a permanent basis.

'Mom. This is Dr Blake. He's just transferred here as a burns specialist so he's the right person to be here.'

Ruby hoped the warning look she shot her mother was enough to quieten her for now. Aimee took priority over everything. Including old wounds.

Her mother grumped as she folded her arms, but put up no further resistance.

'May I?' Harrison looked to Ruby for approval to approach Aimee and she nodded.

He crouched down so he was eye level with Aimee. 'I'm Harrison. What's your name?'

'Aimee.' Her daughter watched him through lowered lashes, already enamoured with the handsome doctor.

Ruby sighed. Apparently her offspring's taste in men was as ill-judged as her own.

'Well, Aimee, I'm just going to take a look at your arm if that's okay? Then your mother and I will try and make it all better.'

Aimee bit her bottom lip and nodded. She wasn't a child who trusted easily and it said a lot about Harrison that she was letting him intervene without a fuss. Though, as far as Ruby was concerned, it only proved he was only someone who could be trusted short-term. Any sort of long-term, emotional commitment, was apparently beyond the man, as she'd found out to her cost. A distinction she wanted to keep hold of even all this time later so she didn't forget what he'd put her through, regardless of who he might be these days.

Harrison gently cleaned the wound, murmuring soothing words anytime Aimee flinched. Ruby sat down beside her and took her other hand to offer some comfort whilst Harrison assessed the extent of the burn. Although she'd dealt with this kind of injury on many occasions herself, it wouldn't hurt to have an expert's opinion. Especially if it meant limiting any permanent damage or scarring to her daughter's skin.

'Well?' Her mother's impatience got the better of her.

'I'd say what we're dealing with here is a partial thickness burn, so it shouldn't leave any permanent scarring.' He smiled at Aimee. 'That doesn't mean it isn't painful. I'm going to put a dressing on it and give you some pain relief, Aimee. It might get itchy, but try not to scratch and make it worse. Mom can put some emollient on it so the skin doesn't get too dry.'

Ruby sighed out her relief. It was good to get a second opinion when it was her own loved one she was dealing with. 'Thanks, Harrison.'

She watched as he carefully dressed the affected area, by which time Aimee's tears had dried up altogether. A dramatic end to an arduous shift. Ruby was physically and emotionally drained.

'I think Miss Aimee deserves some ice cream for being so brave.' Harrison ruffled her daughter's hair. It was surreal watching the interaction, but also made Ruby think about the child they'd lost, and what kind of father he would have made. It was difficult to tell when he seemed so involved here, yet had disappeared out of her life completely once he was off the hook.

'Mommy?' Aimee looked at her with pleading eyes that she could never say no to.

'I guess there's no school for you today, anyway.' They were both going to need some sleep after everything that had happened.

'Don't expect me to babysit. I have to go to work

myself. I'm going to be late as it is. Thank goodness I've got a clean uniform in my locker at the store or I'd be in real trouble.' Her mother was gathering her things, and Ruby couldn't blame her for being upset in the circumstances. Hopefully they'd get to have a chat later and she could smooth her ruffled feathers.

'Thanks for bringing her in, Mom. Can you give us a lift home before you start?' Ruby was looking forward to falling into bed, and hoping Aimee would do the same for a while at least.

'I'm sorry, Ruby. I told you, I'm already late. You'll have to take a cab. I'll see you later, Aimee Bear.' Her mother dropped a kiss on Aimee's head before disappearing out of the cubicle and leaving Ruby open-mouthed.

She really didn't relish the thought of trying to get her injured daughter onto a bus or a cab at this time of the day.

'I can give you a lift if you want?' Harrison's offer was generous and unexpected. Even if it did present a new dilemma. As much as she wanted to get home as soon as possible, she didn't want him to think this was any kind of reconciliation. An acceptance that all was forgiven. Far from it.

'Then we can all get ice cream!' Aimee's injury was forgotten at the exciting prospect, making it even more difficult for Ruby to wriggle out of this. She didn't want to upset her daughter any more than she already was. Even though Harrison didn't deserve any sort of second chance with her, Ruby had to put Aimee's happiness before her own.

'For breakfast?' she asked in a last-ditch attempt to get everyone to see sense.

'Why not? Ice cream is an anytime food as far as I'm concerned.' Harrison grinned at her.

Ruby should have known better than to challenge his sweet tooth. This was someone who'd insisted on celebrating every occasion with sweet treats. It was a wonder he wasn't the size of a house by now. He must really look after himself to be in such good shape.

When she realized she was trying to assess the body beneath the lab coat, she had to admit defeat. 'Fine. Ice cream for breakfast it is.'

'Yay.' Aimee high-fived Harrison with her good arm and Ruby got the distinct impression that there was more than her waistline in trouble with this new alliance.

CHAPTER THREE

'Why don't you go and help yourself to some toppings. If that's okay with your mom?' Too late, Harrison looked to Ruby for approval, suddenly aware that he might have overstepped the mark.

'I guess so,' Ruby said through thinned lips, and Harrison knew he'd messed up. Again.

Sorry, he mouthed to her, as a happy Aimee skipped over to the topping station with her bowl of ice cream.

'That's all right, I'll send her home with you so you can watch her bouncing off the walls on her sugar high later.' There was a hint of a smile playing on Ruby's mouth now so he was able to relax a little, even though this was a strange situation for both of them.

'I'm not used to being around children outside of the hospital, where ice cream is always the answer. I don't stick around for the consequences.' His choice of words drew raised eyebrows from Ruby and he knew exactly why. As far as she knew, once they'd lost their baby he'd disappeared from her life, because he'd never explained why. Perhaps if he'd been able to express his feelings of loss and grief, and how they'd overwhelmed him, they might have been able to save their marriage. Easy to say in hindsight, but he'd never really know because he'd internalized everything until it had destroyed him, along with their relationship.

'I'm sure the parents love you,' Ruby muttered, taking a sip of coffee. The adults having opted for caffeine over sugar after their long night.

'Well, the young patients do at least.' Although they were glossing over the obvious elephant in the diner, Harrison was also struggling with finding out that Ruby had become a mother after all. He supposed he shouldn't have been surprised, given how happy she'd been when they'd discovered they were going to be parents, regardless that it hadn't been a planned pregnancy. And how devastated she'd been too after the miscarriage.

He was happy for her, Aimee was a lovely little girl. But he was also sad that he'd never got to see their baby grow up. It had been too early in the pregnancy to even know if it would have been a son or daughter when she'd still been in her first trimester. Not that it would have mattered, but that loss had ensured he'd never get the chance to be a father. He couldn't handle losing another loved one. So once a relationship seemed as though it was getting serious, he backed away. Before he ended up getting hurt again.

'I think Aimee's a fan already. She's hardly bothered by her arm at all since you appeared, even though I just lost a couple of years off my life through the stress.'

'There's always ice cream to make you feel better. You can have anything you want. It's my treat.'

'I'm good with the coffee, thanks. I'll take an IV full of it if you're offering,' Ruby said with a yawn.

Despite the playful back-and-forth, there was an

awkwardness between them which grew as they slipped into silence. Both watching Aimee scoop candies and sprinkles onto her breakfast ice cream, and hoping she'd return to the table soon.

The owner, who'd been surprised at having customers asking for ice cream so early in the morning, until they'd explained what had happened, was currently plying Aimee with crayons and colouring books. The middle-aged woman clearly felt sorry for the little blonde girl in her pyjamas who'd been in the wars and had a large dressing on her arm to prove it.

'She looks like you.' Harrison said it without thinking. He had no clue what Aimee's father looked like, but the resemblance to Ruby was uncanny. The blond hair, blue eyes and even the little dimple at the corner of her mouth when she smiled.

It was visible now in her mother. 'Yeah. She hasn't inherited much from her father, thank goodness.'

'Oh?' His curiosity was piqued. Of course he'd been interested to know who Aimee's father was but it hadn't seemed appropriate to ask. Harrison had no right to know anything about Ruby's life since their split, but it did appear as though the relationship hadn't ended well.

'Yeah. Turned out he wasn't the man I thought he was either.' It was a thinly veiled dig which Harrison couldn't begrudge her when he knew how badly he'd let her down. He had hoped that she would have found happiness with someone, even if it hadn't been with him.

'I'm sorry. I didn't know you'd remarried.'

'I didn't. Aimee hadn't been planned and fatherhood proved a commitment too far for Chad. What about you? Have you got a wife or kids?'

He shook his head. How did he ever begin to explain why not? Therapy had shown him how important it was to talk, to open up and not keep things to himself, so not having the chance to explain to Ruby why things had ended the way they had was killing him.

'Listen, Ruby, I know I said I'd wait until you were ready, but I really need to talk about what happened between us.' All he needed was a chance to finally give her some answers, and then perhaps it mightn't be so awkward between them. If they had the opportunity to talk things out, maybe it would make working together a little easier. Even if being with Ruby, seeing her with her daughter, was a reminder of everything he'd lost.

'Harrison...' Before she was able to stop him from saying anything more, Aimee returned to the table and did it for her.

'This is yummy.' Aimee had chocolate sauce all around her face and hands as she spooned some of the sugar-laden breakfast dessert into her mouth.

It wasn't a conversation they could continue now that Aimee was in listening range. Harrison had lost the moment to tell Ruby that it hadn't been her fault, nor had he been a coward and run away. Losing the baby had devastated them both, but he hoped they could still come back from it to be civil with one another, at work at least.

'Don't get too used to it, missy. This is a special treat.' Ruby took a napkin from the table and started wiping her daughter's face.

It was strange to watch their interaction: so natural and endearing, yet painful too. In another life he might have been part of this scene as more than an outsider.

Would he have been the one still pushing ice cream for breakfast with their own child, or the strict parent who would want their offspring to grow up on a healthier diet? He had more than a suspicion he would've been the pushover spoiling their little one, leaving Ruby to do the disciplining.

Mostly because that was how his big brother, Joey, had been with him. A ten-year age gap between them meant Harrison was the little brother trailing along after Joey when he wanted to be with friends his own age. Joey could easily have pushed him away, but he'd taken him very much under his wing. Buying Harrison anything he wanted once he got his first job, and treating him to days out and afternoons at the ice cream parlour. That's where he'd learned what it was like to be loved when their parents had been too busy working, trying to keep the family afloat, to pay their sons any real attention.

Harrison was only eleven years old when Joey had been hit by a drunk driver. His life extinguished on one dark, rainy night. He could still hear his mother's screams even now as the police had delivered the news. His own grief had been immeasurable. The void left behind was something he thought could never be filled. Until he'd met Ruby.

After Joey's death, they'd moved house to try and start fresh as a family. Although they'd all been too locked into their individual sadness to ever really come together again. Their parents had divorced a couple of years later, and Harrison had stayed with his mother.

Ruby had been his lifeline. He was the new kid in town, and she'd been appointed in class to show him around and they'd hit it off immediately. Best friends until teenage hormones had made it more. Even fifteen years later, he'd never loved another woman the way he'd loved Ruby Jones.

He'd never told her about his brother. Even now he found it difficult to talk about Joey, because that choking grief crept slowly back to consume him every time he thought of everything his brother had missed out on. His own life without Joey in it. That was why the miscarriage had such an effect on him. He'd been transported back to that all-encompassing feeling of loss, and how life could never be the same again. Worse, he'd been right. Everything he'd known had been taken away from him a second time in the aftermath of a loved one's death.

'Harrison? Are you okay? You seem a little zoned out.' Ruby was watching him intently across the table and he realized he'd been lost in the past. Never a good place for him to visit, though it was understandable after his many shocks over the course of these past few hours.

'Yes. Sorry. I guess everything is just catching up with me.' He drew back from the darkness and into the light of today, where he was having breakfast with Ruby and Aimee. An infinitely more pleasing place to be, regardless of what she might currently think of him.

Ruby nodded towards a drowsy Aimee, whose head was nodding dangerously close to the half-eaten bowl of ice cream, eyes closed and spoon still in hand. 'I think we could all do with going to bed. I mean, going home. Our own homes.'

Harrison smiled as she fumbled her words. The pretty pink tinge to her cheeks a sign that she wasn't as cool, calm and collected as she'd presented thus far. 'I think you're right.'

Ruby extracted the spoon from Aimee's sticky hand and the child turned and clung to her mother as she scooped her up. They made their way back to the car and he had to help extricate Aimee so they could strap her into the back seat.

Again, it struck him how this looked like a typical domestic scene, but one he had no right to be a part of. Aimee wasn't his daughter, and Ruby was no longer his wife. He'd forfeited any opportunity to have some version of this when he'd let her go without a fight. Having this with anyone else was off the table too when the shutters had come down around his heart the second his baby had died.

Harrison got into the front of the car and Ruby sat beside him in the passenger seat.

'Thanks again for doing this, Harrison. I know it's probably the last thing you feel like doing.'

He didn't tell her it was probably the highlight of his week. Despite all the memories of the bad which had come flooding back the moment he'd laid eyes on her again, he was enjoying being part of her life for a short while, and meeting her daughter. Finally finding out what had happened to her after he'd gone from her life.

It was bittersweet to discover that she hadn't been permanently wounded by events. Although he was happy for her that she'd been able to move on, and had her family around her, he was full of regret and sadness that he hadn't managed to achieve the same.

The move here had been an attempt to inject some

life into his days, realizing that he'd been stuck in a rut. Focusing on work, and leaving little room for any existence beyond that. He hadn't expected for everything to change all so dramatically, so quickly.

'It's not a problem. You're on my route anyway.' When she gave him her address, he realized Ruby's place wasn't too far from his new house. Only time would tell if that was a good thing or not. He certainly hadn't moved here with the intention of even seeing her again. At least, not consciously.

'I'm sure you're busy with moving in.'

'I've had a few days to settle in. I don't officially start work until tomorrow, remember?' So much for one last relaxing day to do a bit of sightseeing and maybe even a hand of poker at one of the casinos. He'd thought he'd have time to do the tourist thing before becoming a resident, but as usual, life had thrown him a curve ball. At least this time it had brought someone back into his life instead of taking someone else away from him.

'Oh, yes. Welcome to Las Vegas, I guess.' Ruby gave him a bright smile that was still capable of undoing him. In the old days driving together, she would have laid her head on his shoulder and held his free hand in hers. It seemed absurd, not to mention sad, that they were sitting here as strangers now, her daughter, who he had absolutely no ties to, sleeping in the back seat. It wasn't the future they'd planned together.

'Thanks.' Harrison had no idea how things would turn out for him here but he'd figured he'd needed a new start. Who knew that would entail finally confronting his past? Something he realized had to happen if he was ever going to move on from Ruby Jones. Even if that meant having her back in his life whilst no longer being a part of hers.

'I'll just open the door.' Ruby hopped out of the car to unlock the apartment. It wasn't much, but it was home. A small rental with a communal pool and garden, it had everything she and Aimee needed. They were happy here. Especially with work and family living so close by. And now, Harrison. A complication she'd never expected but perhaps a reconnection that was overdue.

He seemed so desperate to talk to her, and perhaps she owed it to herself to hear him out so she could stop torturing herself about their past and why she'd got him so wrong.

When she turned around, the sight of him carrying her sleeping daughter in his arms just about stopped her heart. This was the man she'd been married to. The Harrison who bought ice cream to fix everything, and was there when she needed him. Who'd made her feel safe and loved. Not the man who'd so coldly left her to deal with her grief on her own, making her feel abandoned and unwanted. A pattern in her life she could have done without.

'Where shall I put her?' Harrison asked.

Ruby moved aside. 'Straight down the hall, first room on the left.'

As he walked into her home, Ruby couldn't help the feeling that this marked a turning point of some kind as her past and present collided. This was the home she'd created for her and Aimee once she'd finally moved out of her parents' place. A new start. Seeing Harrison in it, the reemerging feelings of admiration and something more she didn't want to acknowledge, felt like some sort of home invasion. Leaving her fearful that she would forever associate him with somewhere that used to be her safe space.

She had to blink away images of their first place together. Where she'd been the one in his arms being carried to the bedroom in very different circumstances. They'd been so young, so in love, and so naive about what they were getting into. Everything had seemed easy then. Love was the answer to everything. Until it wasn't. It hadn't been enough to save their marriage. Or their baby.

The reality, that life sometimes steamrolled right over you, had come as a shock. One she'd had to deal with on her own whilst Harrison had apparently chosen denial. She wondered if anything had changed in him over the years. Ruby had definitely become stronger, emotionally. She didn't put up with weak men who didn't deserve her or her daughter, and though that meant she was single, she didn't regret it. There was more than her heart at risk now and she certainly wouldn't invite a man into her daughter's life who could cause her the slightest pain.

Since Harrison was on his own, starting a new position, she guessed commitment still wasn't high on his list. She didn't know if that meant the fact he'd even married her made her privileged, or unfortunate. A mistake he'd eventually realized and rectified.

'She must be like her mother. Sleeps like a log.' Harrison gently placed Aimee onto her princess bed decked with a tiara-shaped headboard and sparkly covers.

He looked so out of place in here, tucking Ruby's daughter into her bed. A masculine presence in a world of pink unicorns and fluffy rainbows. Yet, at the same time, he seemed quite at home. As though this was a role he could easily have fitted. If they'd been given the chance together.

'She snores like a warthog.' Talking about her sleeping habits seemed like a very personal thing to do with a man she hardly knew anymore. A stranger now, yet someone she'd laid beside many nights.

'Just like her mother.' Harrison grinned, and for a moment they could have been that young loved-up couple. Comfortable enough with one another that he could tease her about something so personal.

'I do not snore.' A debate which had run between them for the duration of their relationship, though she'd never been accused by anyone else of the crime. She'd convinced herself he only said it to annoy her. Teasing had been their foreplay once upon a time. Winding one another up until the only way to end the argument was with a passionate kiss, with both declared the winner.

Or perhaps, being with Harrison was the only time she'd felt safe enough to drift into a deep, deep sleep.

Aimee murmured and rolled onto her side. Ruby made sure she wasn't lying on her injured arm, dropped a kiss on her forehead and backed quietly out of the room. She closed the door carefully after Harrison made his exit too.

'She's had quite the day,' he whispered as they moved away from the bedroom.

'The ice cream did manage to take her mind off her arm. So thank you for that.'

'My pleasure.' Harrison followed her into the living area which had an open plan kitchen.

'Can I get you a drink, or something to eat?' It didn't seem polite to rush him out the door when he'd treated her and Aimee at the diner, and given them a lift home. Despite all of the red flags about having him here in her home.

He hesitated before saying, 'I wouldn't want to inconvenience you.'

Which was Harrison code for, 'I'm hungry.'

It put a smile on Ruby's face. Some things never changed. 'It's fine. Neither of us has eaten for hours. Besides, I know how cranky you get when you're hungry.'

'Do not.' He frowned, drawing up a chair to the breakfast bar.

It was tempting to keep the teasing going, but knowing where it used to lead to was sufficient for Ruby to end it there and concentrate on cooking. She had to remember the lonely nights crying herself to sleep, bereft by his absence. Not the ones where they were cuddled up in bed. Or doing more than cuddling...

If this was the one and only time they were going to be alone in her home, she was beginning to think now was the time to finally deal with the past. At least hear what he had to say, and take some time and distance to process it before she had to see him again. Better here in private than being ambushed again at work.

After breakfast though. She was hungry, and she had a feeling that she'd lose her appetite once she heard his excuses for abandoning her.

'Would you like some help?' Harrison asked as she

cooked up some bacon and eggs and placed slices of bread into the toaster.

'You could get some plates for me.' She pointed towards the cupboard on the wall which housed them, thankful that he had something to do other than watch her.

It was unnerving feeling his eyes on her, wondering if he was assessing the changes in her over the years, as she had with him. If he found her lacking in some way. Regardless that he'd broken her heart, somewhere deep down inside her, it still mattered what he thought about her. Perhaps if she got the answer as to why he'd left her the way he had, she would no longer care.

She dished up breakfast and took a seat at the other side of the counter. There was a sense of anticipation in the air between them as they ate. Perhaps both considering what they would say next to one another after the small talk ran out, and they'd have to engage in a more meaningful conversation.

Once they'd finished eating, she cleared away the dishes and sat down again, her procrastination finally running out of steam. It was time for her to finally face Harrison, and whatever it was he had to say. She only hoped she could get through this without making a scene. Be it tears or anger, whichever dominated her reaction.

Ruby leaned forward, her hands clasped on the counter. 'Okay, I'm ready.'

She wasn't. All of a sudden she felt more vulnerable than she had in years. Since raising Aimee on her own, she'd steeled herself against any further hurt, determined to put all of her energy into protecting her daughter. This was opening old wounds which had been present before her precious baby was part of her existence. She didn't want the failings of the old Ruby to undermine the strong woman she was now.

Harrison's eyes opened wide. 'Ready, ready?'

Ruby nodded, swallowing the ball of anxiety suddenly rising to her throat.

He took a deep breath, at least showing that this was a difficult subject for him too. This wasn't a matter he was taking lightly and she had some admiration for that at least. He could have brushed the whole thing off as ancient history. Indeed, in some of the scenarios she'd run in her head over the years of confronting him, that was one of the reactions she'd tried to anticipate. So it wouldn't hurt just as much. Except she was realizing now that in this moment, and how she felt about the past, if Harrison had told her it was time she moved on, she would have been devastated. She didn't know if it was better or worse knowing that this seemed as important to him as it was to her.

'Where to start...' He rubbed his hands over the stubble beginning to show on his face, suddenly looking as tired and anxious as she was.

'You could tell me why you left me to grieve for our baby on my own.' It came out sharper than she'd intended, but she'd been waiting for fifteen years to say it. To get some answers.

'It's not that easy. There are many reasons why I didn't follow you to your parents' place.'

As tempting as it was to say something sarcastic and

ask him to start naming them, she wanted to keep this as civil as possible and remained silent. Waiting a few minutes more for an explanation wasn't going to hurt her any more than the fifteen years of silence.

A long sigh, as though he didn't know where to begin. 'Losing the baby was tough on both of us. I know that maybe I didn't show you how much it affected me but I was devastated.'

'It was tough.' The understatement of the century.

'I wanted to be there for you. To be strong enough to hold us both up, but in the end I couldn't even manage myself. When you left to go to your parents, I had every intention of following you. But, everything caught up with me at once and I could barely even get out of bed.'

'I'm so sorry, Harrison. I had no idea.' She'd been so wrapped up in how the miscarriage had affected her, she hadn't stopped to consider what he was going through too.

'I didn't tell you. I didn't tell anyone. Thinking I just needed to get on with things. But I couldn't. Even though you were calling and begging me to come, to tell you what was wrong, I just couldn't. It was easier just to walk away. You had your parents to look after you. I would only have brought you down further.'

'But we could have been there together. Gone through it leaning on one another.' She hated to think of him suffering as much as she had, but on his own. He was right. She'd had her parents fussing over her, feeding her and making sure she was okay. Harrison wasn't close enough to his family to seek that kind of support even if his pride would have let him.

Harrison shrugged without showing any conviction in what she was saying. 'Perhaps. Though I don't think it would have made any difference. I was so lost in my own grief, the loss of our future as a family, I don't think I could have been there for you the way you needed.'

Ruby wished she'd had the chance to find out. If she'd known he'd felt anything other than relief that he wasn't tied to her forever, it could have changed everything. Even if they hadn't stayed together, it might have saved her some of the heartbreak she'd gone through. At least then she would have known it wasn't her fault. That he'd cared too. Maybe too much.

'I wish you'd tried. Or at least told me how you felt.' Finding out now wasn't doing anything to make her feel better, only worse, knowing he was grieving on his own too. That he hadn't felt secure enough in their relationship to confide in her, if no one else.

In hindsight, she supposed everyone's condolences and support had been focused on her, but Harrison had lost the baby too. He might not have carried it, or had morning sickness every day, but he'd been as much part of the pregnancy as she had. They hadn't planned the baby, but the second they'd seen the positive test, he'd started making plans. How he was going to decorate the nursery, what football team it was going to support, and he'd told her he was going to be the kind of father he wished he'd had. A present one. Not just a man who came and went and paid the bills in between.

Harrison had charted every precious day. A countdown until they became a family marked on the calendar with an *x*. They only made it a third of the way through the calendar before it had been torn down and thrown in the bin. Their dreams of a happy family over.

He'd shut down then. That was why she'd turned to her parents in search of emotional support. Travelling back to them rather than stay another moment in their home so full of reminders of everything they'd lost.

Harrison had stayed in contact at first. Always making excuses about why he couldn't follow her just yet. Phone calls soon became texts, until they'd dwindled away altogether. He'd even stopped answering her calls. It had been hard not to think she'd done something to make him realize he'd be happier on his own. How could she have known that had been a cry for help? She should have gone and seen him in person instead of wallowing in her own misery and feeling sorry for herself. Neither of them had fought hard enough to save their relationship, and failed at the first hurdle. Albeit a traumatic one.

When Harrison looked at her she could see the pain in his eyes as he relived it. They should have been there to hug and cry it all out together. Perhaps then they wouldn't still be holding on to all this pain fifteen years later.

'I just couldn't. You were already so broken and I didn't want to add to your burden. I thought I could just push on through. I was wrong.'

'So what happened?' Given the strength of his feelings, and the way he'd so desperately wanted to speak to her, Ruby suspected there was more to the story.

'I lost it for a while. Emotionally. A breakdown of sorts. It took me some time to get back on my feet. I knew you would have moved on by then and I thought a clean start was best for both of us.'

Ruby didn't know how to process what he was telling her. He was putting her through a range of emotions with every revelation. Sympathy for how alone he must have felt, anger for not including her in that decision-making process, but an overriding sense of sadness over their loss. Not only of the child they never got to meet, but of their relationship, past, present and future.

'It wasn't as easy as that for either of us.' By the sound of things, Harrison had taken his time grieving too before making some attempt at functioning. She knew how hard that was to let go and try and make a future again. One very different to the one they'd planned together.

'No, but I just wanted to explain. I'd probably do things differently now, but I was young and didn't know how to deal with all the emotions I had. It's not an excuse, but I owe it to you to tell you why I disappeared. I'm sorry.' He got up from his seat, grabbed his jacket, and moved towards the door as though the conversation was over.

It wasn't. Not by a long shot.

'Wait, Harrison. You can't go now.' Acting without thinking, she reached out and grabbed his arm. Circling her fingers around his thick, bare wrist. Skin-on-skin contact which felt as though she'd just grabbed hold of a live wire. An instant charge of electricity zapping through her body. As though one touch from Harrison had just reawakened her body from slumber. Her own Sleeping Beauty moment. Okay, so he hadn't kissed her, but that brief reconnection was enough to remind her of every kiss, every passionate, intimate moment they'd ever shared.

Ruby stared at her hand, his arm, and up at his face, to find him staring at her with equal intensity. It felt very much like she were having an out-of-body experience. On the outside looking in, trying to make sense of what was happening.

Now that he'd shared his pain with her, finally given her the answer to the question which had dogged her for fifteen years, she allowed herself to feel more than anger towards him. In hearing him out she'd given herself permission to still care, still be attracted to him and remember what they'd once had together. Except they were both very different people now, with different lives. Ones which didn't include one another.

She slowly withdrew her hand, still tingling from where she'd touched him.

'Sorry. I just wanted to say you've nothing to beat yourself up for. We can't change the past. We were young, and probably in over our heads. I wish things had been different…' It was hard not to think about how different her life would've turned out if they'd been brave and mature enough to deal with their problems the right way. They might have had a family together by now, living the life they thought they'd signed up for when they'd said their wedding vows.

'But then you wouldn't have Aimee, and I would never have denied you that.' His smile was equally as heartbreaking as his sad eyes. He was happy that she had gone on to have another child, even if it wasn't with him. Ruby wasn't sure that she would have been that understanding or generous if tables had been turned.

In fact, if he'd had a child with someone else and

she'd still been on her own, it likely would have devastated her all over again. She appreciated the fact that he'd said it so she didn't feel guilty, but it also proved his more mature attitude. It seemed they'd both done a lot of growing up since their marriage ended.

'No. I suppose there's no point in looking back.' Not anymore. Their baby would never be forgotten but the loss should no longer define who they were. At least now she had her answers, closure of sorts, it might not be quite as painful when she did find herself thinking about the past.

'Looking forward, I hope we can work together without letting our history affect us too much. I mean, I know it's something we can't deny that happened, nor would I ever want to. I just—'

'You don't want things to be awkward,' she offered for him, seeing how uncomfortable he looked. It was little wonder given how she'd 'welcomed' him to the department.

Harrison was going to be around for the foreseeable future. It was something she was simply going to have to accept. Even though it was going to take some getting used to. They already had one patient in common, and there were going to be others. They couldn't avoid one another if they wanted to. At least, not forever.

'Right. So, er, where do we go from here?'

Ruby noticed now that his demeanour had changed. They were back to being virtual strangers. Polite. Distant. She wondered if that was because he'd shared so much of himself that he now felt exposed, vulnerable somehow. Or, was there a chance that because she acted like a love-struck schoolgirl when she touched him, he couldn't wait to get away?

Either way, it was probably for the best that he left now. If they had anything more to say to one another it could be done at work. Where it might not feel so personal, intimate even.

'Tell me something, Harrison. What was it you wanted to achieve with this? Forgiveness? Clearing your conscience? Then I think we've managed that. Thank you for being man enough to share all of that with me. Not everyone would have been brave enough to confront those painful memories head-on in order to move forward. You've given me what I needed too. Closure. I don't see why we can't be civil to one another at work. From now on we're simply colleagues, and I look forward to seeing you again in the future.'

She managed to restrain from holding her hand out for a handshake, though that's exactly how formal she felt saying the words. Trying to keep all emotion out of it because right now they were all mixed up in her head.

Harrison gave a curt nod of the head and simply said, 'Thanks, Ruby.'

Then he turned and walked away.

She couldn't help but wonder if this marked the end of a chapter in her life, or the beginning of a new one. Perhaps both.

CHAPTER FOUR

'Hello, Eugene. My name's Dr Blake. I'm going to be performing your surgery today. I just wanted to come in and say hello.' Harrison didn't know if the child could hear him, or if he would remember the conversation. The extent of the boy's injuries were such that he had to remain sedated in ICU.

Nevertheless, Harrison liked to keep all of his patients informed of who he was and what he was going to be doing. It built up a rapport, or in this case, at least gave him a chance to see his patient before they went into the operating room. To remember Eugene was more than a name on a schedule.

He looked so small and vulnerable lying on the hospital bed hooked up to the machines monitoring his vital signs. His parents, who were still being treated for their injuries in the ICU at St Michael's Hospital in Boulder City, wouldn't be able to comfort him or walk him down to theatre. The least Harrison could do was give him five minutes of his time so he wasn't on his own.

His line of work meant he was always dealing with people at their most vulnerable, in pain, often with life-changing, or life-limiting injuries. The children were the hardest to deal with. He'd gone into the profession hoping to save lives when he hadn't been able to help his brother, or his baby. Unfortunately, that wasn't always the case. It had taken him some time to learn how to separate work from his personal feelings. At least to the extent where he didn't fall into another pit of grief.

He wondered how Ruby did it when she had a daughter she no doubt compared every young patient to. Putting herself in the parents' shoes. He supposed it was a mark of how good she was at her job that she didn't crumble either. The night of the gas explosion he'd seen for himself how motivated and efficient she was, despite upsetting circumstances.

It had been two days since he'd seen her and he'd been glad of a little space. Unburdening himself of the guilt and grief of that time fifteen years ago had come at a price. It had left a mark in sharing so much personal information with Ruby. Making him question if he'd done the right thing, and if she'd think badly of him.

Although she'd seemed to understand, there was still part of him that thought he should have been able to 'man up' at the time. That a stronger man would have been able to suck up those feelings of loss and simply get on with life instead of letting them overwhelm him. In opening up to Ruby, those questions had resurfaced again. Perhaps it would have been better to simply let things lie. Not to have interacted with Ruby in a personal manner at all.

Especially when they seemed to have fallen so easily into companionship, eating and chatting together as if they hadn't undergone the trauma of losing their baby and been separated all this time. Even though finding out about Aimee's existence had come as something of a shock, she had taken to him too. In their time at the diner they could have been viewed as any other family. Except Ruby was no longer his wife, and her daughter wasn't his.

Perhaps in a parallel universe another Harrison had coped better with his grief and he had that happy family, but not in this one. Not ever. Because he couldn't afford to open his heart again to anyone, much less a child. He'd had one chance to be a father and fate had decided otherwise. As far as he was concerned that was a sign. It wasn't meant to be, and he'd accepted that because, as he'd discovered, the alternative had the possibility of being too painful to even contemplate.

Harrison was about to leave to see his day patients when Ruby walked into the room. Despite knowing they were working in the same hospital, and there was always a possibility of running into her, his pulse picked up at the sight of her. He supposed it was due to years without a glimpse of the only woman he'd ever loved. Although that didn't explain why his body felt like it had been hit by lightning when she'd grabbed his arm in her kitchen. It seemed time and distance hadn't managed to tame that spark she set off inside him with a simple touch.

Their chemistry had always been off the charts. However, they weren't horny, loved-up teenagers anymore. They were divorced virtual strangers now, and he'd have to work reminding himself of that.

'I thought I'd check in on our patient,' she said, approaching Eugene's bedside.

'He's stable, at least. I'll be taking him to the OR later this afternoon to debride the burns. Then I'll be able to see if he's going to need further surgery.' Harrison was hoping Eugene wouldn't need skin grafts as it would be a long recovery process, but at least his young skin would hopefully stretch and lessen the chances of painful contracting as he grew.

'Bless him." She gestured for Harrison to step away from the bed obviously wanting to discuss something away from the boy. "I hear his parents are in a bad way too.' It was clear the family had been on Ruby's mind too. He should have known her interest in her patients wouldn't stop once they were moved from her department. She'd always been a nurturing figure. Even in school, whenever one of the younger children fell or hurt themselves, it was Ruby they went to for words of comfort before being patched up by the school nurse. She'd been born to be a nurse, and a mother. He was glad she'd achieved both. She'd done better for herself once he'd gone from her life.

'They are, but hopefully they will all recover. Even if it takes some time.' Not everyone's body reacted to burns the same way. There could be unforeseen complications that didn't immediately present, but that was where the burns specialists came in. Harrison knew the staff at St Michael's and they would perform whatever surgery was necessary in the future. For now, it was important to keep them stable in the intensive care unit.

It was difficult to see an entire family suffer in such

circumstances but he hoped they would help pull one another through. He hated to think that young Eugene could be orphaned, or that his parents might never see him grow up. From personal experience, he knew how traumatic that was, and they'd all been through enough already.

'Will you keep me updated?' Ruby asked, tucking the covers around Eugene's small form on the bed, her mothering instinct taking over. At least he would have someone to look over him even though his parents couldn't be here.

'I will. We haven't been able to track down any other family, so he'll be here on his own for some time.' Although there would be staff coming and going on the ward, it was a shame the boy wouldn't have anyone to come and sit with him, talk to him and make sure he wasn't on his own. Even though he wasn't conscious, there was always that chance that he'd be able to hear anything going on around him. He'd experienced major trauma and hospitals were frightening places at the best of times for children. A reassuring voice could make all the difference.

'I'll try and stop by when I can. I could bring some of Aimee's books to read to him.' It was clear the little boy had touched Ruby, as much as he had Harrison. Perhaps it was their shared experience of losing a child themselves which made them more empathetic with his plight, or they were simply two medical professionals who saw their positions as more than just a job. Either way, Harrison knew they weren't going to let this boy lie here without visitors for the duration of his stay.

'I'm sure his parents would appreciate that. How is Aimee doing by the way?' They'd both been on his mind since that day. More so than he would have hoped.

'She's good. Thinks she should have ice cream for breakfast every morning, but other than that she's recovering well.' Ruby narrowed her eyes at him so he knew he was responsible for that situation, but it wasn't long before she was smiling at him again. The quick change made his pulse flutter again.

Something about that look made him remember when they'd been together, and teasing had simply been part of their relationship dynamic. Keeping things fun between them. He was glad to see that she was still young at heart and not so changed despite the years and her important role in work and at home.

'Sorry, but I'm glad there are no long-lasting effects.' Harrison did his best to look sheepish so she would forgive him. Whilst he was used to being the fun doctor cheering up his young patients, he had no experience in parenting. Something he was reminded of when he'd seen Ruby and Aimee together. A sight which would forever cause a pang in his heart for what should have been.

'She keeps asking after you actually. You definitely made a fan.' Whilst Ruby didn't appear overly enthused by the development, Harrison was glad he'd made a good impression on one new acquaintance. And okay, it didn't hurt that she might put in a good word for him with her mother.

'And she has one in me. Aimee is a credit to you.' Now that they'd had a real heart-to-heart, he hoped

Ruby would thaw towards him too. Even though they would never have the same relationship they'd once had, she'd always been a big part of his life. Including those years apart. Just because she wasn't present in his everyday existence, it didn't mean he didn't think about her, or their baby. She was always there in the back of his mind, affecting his every decision.

He suspected that was what had even spurred him to finish his medical studies. Knowing that one day they might cross paths, and wanting her to be proud of him. Not always hating him, and believing that he was a poor excuse for a man. Hopefully now she understood that whilst he was probably too emotionally immature to deal with the tragedy at the time, their separation had been about more than she could ever have imagined.

Yet, he hadn't been able to find the words to tell her about his brother. Why the miscarriage had triggered such a catastrophic reaction in him. Therapy had helped him work through a lot of his issues, but talking about Joey was still painful. It was a subject which seemed a step too far to broach when they'd just met again after such a long time.

Perhaps he'd never have the opportunity, or motivation to share that most personal information. Certainly, it wasn't something he'd discussed with any other colleague, friend or lover. There was no reason to expect that Ruby would be anything more than a work acquaintance now. Only time would tell if they found it too difficult to be around one another, or if their bond was something they'd welcome back into their lives.

On his part, he'd missed Ruby. His reasons for not contacting her obvious in the circumstances. But now that they were on speaking terms again, he realized what he'd thrown away fifteen years ago.

Apart from being the love of his life, Ruby had been his best friend, his confidante and the only person who'd really made him feel loved since his brother had died.

And as far as she'd been aware at the time, he'd simply walked away from her as if none of it had meant anything to him. Never knowing it was thoughts of her which had kept him going in the darkest times. Telling himself that one day he would be well enough, free of his grief, to find her and tell her how sorry he was.

Except that had been a longer journey than he'd ever expected, and even when he was functioning again, he was too fragile, too afraid to make contact. Unable to take that step in case she rejected him. Instead, leaving the way open for her to move on even if he couldn't, by filing for divorce.

He was glad she had, and though she didn't owe him anything, he hoped he could have her in his life again in some capacity. But he wasn't going to push her too hard to make that happen when she'd been through so much, and had a lot to process after everything he'd shared with her so far.

He'd waited this long to see her again and he was sure it couldn't hurt any more to wait a little longer.

'I guess I should get back to work.' As much as he wanted to stay and spend time with Ruby, he was still new here, and he wanted to make a good impression on the rest of the medical staff as well as his patients.

'Me too.' Ruby moved away from Eugene's bedside as well, giving him one last lingering look as if trying to leave a part of her to comfort the boy.

'I'm sure I'll see you around.' Harrison found himself reluctant to make that final break away from her, not knowing when he would see her again, or if they would even get another chance to talk.

'I'm sure you will.' She gave him a little smile, offering some hope.

If they hadn't had a complicated, tragic history, and they were two single people who'd just met, he might have seen this as an opportunity to ask for a date. As it was, he was lucky she was even talking to him. Still, she was leaving the door open for a future meet and that was enough for now.

They were making their way towards the door when the alarms sounded from the patient's cubicle opposite Eugene's. Both Harrison and Ruby immediately turned back, knowing someone's life was in jeopardy. The monitors were already showing a sharp decline in the young woman's vital signs.

'Her blood pressure is dangerously low,' Harrison noted aloud.

'She came into the ER a few nights ago. Lucille, I think her name was. She'd had a miscarriage, but some of the placenta had remained. The last I'd seen of her was when she'd been wheeled down to theatre for surgery.' Thankfully Ruby was able to give him a quick patient history to save some time. This wasn't the area

Harrison specialized in, but he'd had some training in obstetrics during his placement.

Although the nurses would be on their way once they'd heard the monitors scream their warning, he hit the emergency button on the wall to call for extra help.

'It could be septic shock if infection has set in. Her skin is clammy and her heart rate and breathing is rapid.'

Except now the heart monitor was flatlining, indicating that the patient was in cardiac arrest. They needed to get her heart pumping blood around her body before they did anything else.

'Her lips are turning blue. I'm going to see where the resus team are.' Ruby rushed off, returning only moments later with the defibrillator and a team of nurses.

Between them, Harrison and Ruby attached the sticky pads to Lucille's chest, which would conduct the charge from the defibrillator to her heart, and hopefully restart it.

He let Ruby take over, figuring she would have more experience in this area since she worked in the emergency room.

'Stand clear,' she issued to the assembled staff once the defibrillator was charged, then delivered the first shock in the hope of restarting Lucille's heart.

Harrison checked the woman's vital signs. 'Nothing.'

'We go again. Charging. Stand clear.' A focused Ruby watched and waited before delivering another shock.

'Checking for shockable rhythm,' Harrison announced as per protocol, letting everyone know what was happening step by step.

Thankfully, the blip on the screen and the gradual colour returning to the woman's lips let them both breathe a momentary sigh of relief.

'We've got her,' he confirmed, then there was a flurry of activity whilst they did their best to stabilize the patient.

'Sorry if we stepped on anyone's shoes,' Ruby said tongue-in-cheek to the attending physicians now present. As aware as Harrison was that this wasn't their department. They just happened to be in the right place at the right time.

'No problem. We're glad you were here. Thanks.' The senior medic for the department came forward as they stood back.

Once Harrison gave them a rundown of what had happened, and what they suspected, he was happy to let them take over. He and Ruby had done their bit, and now it would be down to the surgical team to treat her.

As he made his exit with Ruby, the adrenaline rush wearing off, he was beginning to feel that familiar jittery energy which accompanied an unexpected medical emergency. The sort of post-trauma effect that needed to be processed before normality resumed. It said a lot about Ruby's strength of character when she did this every shift.

He stopped in the corridor just ahead of her, making her come to a standstill too. 'Are you okay?'

'Yes. Of course. I'm just glad we got her back.' Her eyes were too bright, her smile too broad, for him to believe. Although they'd been apart for years he still knew her, and this was Ruby putting on a brave face.

Apart from the near-death experience of the patient, there was the miscarriage aspect. A baby had died, along with whatever dreams of the future the young mother had harboured. Something too close to home to be ignored. It was playing on Harrison's mind, bringing back memories and emotions of when Ruby had lost their baby. A sharp stab to the heart with every recollection.

The baby books they'd read, marking the size of their little jelly bean with every passing week. Tiny bootees and cardigans Ruby had knitted in neutral colours for their son or daughter. Then there was the crib Harrison had been carefully building himself. A surprise for Ruby, which he'd smashed to pieces in the end without her ever seeing the labour of love he'd created. Too painful a reminder to have kept. Redundant along with everything else they'd been putting aside for their baby, except their love. That was one thing which had never been packed away in the hope of forgetting it had ever existed. He'd lived with that hole in his heart where his baby should have been, every day of his life since. Seeing someone else go through that pain and loss wasn't easy to watch. Yet he hadn't been the one carrying their baby. His body hadn't changed, nor had it struggled to adapt when the pregnancy ended much too soon. Ruby had gone through so much physically as well as emotionally, it seemed selfish that he'd been the one to run away and leave her to deal with everything on her own.

In his defence, he'd known her parents were looking after her better than he could, given the emotional state he'd been in too, but still, he hated that he'd left her side. Up until then, they'd done everything together, and he'd left her when she'd needed him most. When he'd needed her most. Who knew, if he'd been able to think clearer at the time, been able to express his feelings too, they might have been able to pull each other through the dark times. They might have saved their relationship, even gone on to have that family together. It was an even greater tragedy that he'd never know for sure.

'Are you okay?' Ruby was staring at him intently like she might have already asked the question and he hadn't heard her, so lost in thoughts of the past.

There was no way she'd come out of this scenario unscathed.

'I'm good. I was just thinking we should probably find the time to try and de-stress at the end of the day. In the circumstances, I don't think it's good that we keep everything in, and no one else would understand better than we do. I don't have anyone else to talk to.' Harrison realized as he was talking, as much as he was concerned about Ruby's well-being, that his mattered too.

He'd learned not to bottle things up, it wasn't good for anyone's mental health. As he was new in town, he had no one else to talk to. Despite not wanting to burden her with any more of his personal issues, it might be good for them to have one another's backs.

'What are you suggesting? A drink?' She watched him with suspicious eyes and he couldn't blame her. He'd already proved spectacularly that she couldn't trust him. But, on this occasion, he intended to be there for her.

'A drink sounds great. Point me to the nearest dive bar and we'll decompress once we're done.' He'd actually just intended a coffee or something, but since she'd brought up the idea, he wouldn't mind having a drink somewhere with Ruby. It would almost be like old times. Apart from the fact they were divorced, and they weren't likely to be ID'd these days.

'Hmm… I suppose we could probably both do with one. Give me your number. It's not like I have anyone else to talk to about work, or anything else to do. I should be finished by eight, but I'll nip home to sort Aimee out. I'm sure my parents won't mind babysitting if they think I'm going out for the night. On second thoughts, maybe I shouldn't tell them I'm meeting their ex-son-in-law. I'm not sure they've forgiven you yet.'

Harrison flinched, though it was a well-deserved blow. It was little wonder that they should still hold a grudge when he'd left Ruby's parents to pick up the pieces and stick her back together again. He didn't suppose any excuse would ever appease them when he'd hurt their precious daughter so badly.

'Hopefully in time…'

Ruby raised her eyebrows suggesting hell might well freeze over before that happened.

'You could put in a good word for me, and I know I've got Aimee onside.' He hoped he wouldn't be the devil incarnate forever.

'It'll take time, Harrison.'

Forgiveness wasn't something which could be rushed

and he understood that. He was just glad he and Ruby were on better terms than he probably deserved.

Harrison texted her so she had his number.

'I'm willing to wait.' He'd been on good terms with her parents until everything had become too much for him. They'd accepted him into their family and no doubt his disappearance had felt like a betrayal to them too. What no one knew, or could possibly understand, was how that separation had been devastating to him too. Losing everyone he'd ever been close to and suddenly finding himself alone, in despair, and not knowing where to turn. He'd spent some time with his mother, but they hadn't been close since Joey's death, and burdening her with his grief over the loss of his child had felt unfair. She'd almost seemed relieved when he'd moved on, seeking help from the medical profession instead of those he was supposed to be closest to.

'That makes a change,' she said, a mischievous twinkle in her eyes, letting him know that she hadn't completely forgiven and forgotten either. He still had a lot to make up to her, but he was willing to do it. His conscience demanded it, along with the new dynamic developing between them, which he was keen to explore a little more.

'Ouch.' He clutched his chest theatrically, making her smile. 'I guess I deserve that, but I promise I intend to do everything in my power to try and make amends.'

There was nothing he could do that would ever wipe out that mistake, but that just meant he'd be trying for a long time. Until Ruby got fed up with him, or got used to having him around.

'Drinks are on you, then, Dr Blake.'

'If you're lucky I might even treat you to some chips and dip.'

'Don't go spoiling me, I'm not used to it.' A laughing Ruby handed his phone back to him before walking away, looking and sounding lighter than she had since they'd become reacquainted.

This was the Ruby he remembered. Not the broken one he'd left, unable to bear seeing her in so much pain when he couldn't make things better for her—or for himself. Though he didn't know that if given that time over again he could do things any differently. To change the outcome of their relationship would have meant opening up to Ruby completely about the loss of his brother. A grief he still found too difficult to confront and he needed to avoid it, and Ruby, to ensure he didn't slip back into that darkness.

Although he had this deep need for her forgiveness, and their paths were inevitably going to cross at work, he had to keep himself protected. Just as he had all those years ago.

CHAPTER FIVE

'Where are you going, Mommy?' A sleepy Aimee curled up on Ruby's lap, burying her head in her mother's chest and making her feel guilty about leaving her again.

'I'm just meeting a friend. I won't be long, and Grandma is going to tuck you into bed.' Ruby gave her mother the nod to extract her clinging child and put her to bed. She still had to change before she joined Harrison for that much-needed drink. Though she had an inkling this was about more than winding down after a difficult day.

Harrison was likely wanting time to process what had happened with Lucille too. It was never easy dealing with the loss of someone else's baby at work. Trying to put personal feelings aside to concentrate on those of the patient, and treating her the way Ruby wished she had been treated. With sympathy and understanding.

Something which had been missing with some of the medical staff when she'd miscarried, because of her age. Many assuming 'it was better for her,' that she could always have more children when she was ready. Assuming that hers hadn't been a cherished, highly anticipated baby simply because it had been an unplanned pregnancy. It was still the loss of a precious child no matter what the circumstances, and nothing could ever hope to replace it. Even having Aimee hadn't filled that void inside her. It had given her renewed purpose, someone else to love, but as far as Ruby was concerned, she was a mother to two babies.

Perhaps the cavalier attitude from some towards her loss at the time had been what had spurred her on to finish her medical studies once she'd worked through her grief. So she could provide better treatment, more empathy, to young women just like her. She was glad she'd been able to do that for so many patients in the emergency room over the years, and it went some way to easing the hurt. Even if cases like Lucille's were difficult to deal with objectively.

Ruby brushed the hair from Aimee's face as her mother tucked her into her bed. 'Goodnight, sweet girl.'

She dropped a kiss on the forehead of her now sleeping daughter, before exiting the room with her mother.

'It's Harrison isn't it?' her mother said, arms folded, lips pursed, as soon as the door was closed behind them.

Ruby sighed. There was no point in denying it when she had nothing to hide. 'Yes. It's just a drink. We have a lot to talk over.'

Her mother didn't know they'd already had their heart-to-heart, or the very personal information he'd shared with her. It was private. Just like what had happened with them at work today. Some things they could only share with one another. She was telling herself that was the only reason she'd agreed to this drink.

A tut from her mother in response. 'I won't say anything to your father, because I don't want to send his blood pressure soaring but please be careful. I know you have a tendency to lose all common sense around this boy. Don't forget the state Harrison Blake left you in the last time you were together.'

Her mother's concern made her smile when it hadn't changed over the years. As far as she was concerned, Ruby was still her baby girl and she would go 'mama bear on the rampage' to protect her. Ruby suspected she would be equally as protective over her own cub.

'He's not a boy, Mom. He's a grown man, and I'm a grown woman. We're not together, but we do have a history I can't ignore. I'm well aware of how much he hurt me before, and you and Dad were the ones left to pick up the pieces, but this is just a drink between colleagues. Nothing more.' Ruby kissed her mother on the cheek, trying to convince her as much as herself that there was no need to read anything more into this.

Even though she proceeded to spread the contents of her closet all over her bed before settling on an outfit she thought looked good without conveying how much effort she'd gone to for simple drinks with a colleague.

Since Harrison was new in town, Ruby had decided to show him some of the tourist sights on the main strip. She met him by the fountains, just as they began their nightly light show, the water dancing in time to music and putting on quite the display.

He smiled when he spotted her walking towards him and she was powerless against the little flip her heart gave at the sight of him. One of the new attractions standing there in his well-worn dark denims and blue-and-white-checked shirt. He was leaning casually against a billboard, thumbs hooked in the waistband of his jeans as though he was waiting to be picked up. It gave Ruby a secret thrill that it was her he was waiting for, and seemed to be oblivious to the admiring glances from passers-by, when he was so focused on her approach.

Time and heartache apparently hadn't lessened the impact he still had on her. Her mother's words rang in her ears, reminding her that she had to keep her head. Not get caught up in romantic fantasies when their reality had been far from perfect.

'Hey,' she said when she was finally standing in front of him. Butterflies taking flight in her tummy when he kissed her on the cheek.

'Hey. You look lovely, Ruby.'

'Thanks.' It was ridiculous that she was feeling so nervous when they'd clarified that this wasn't a date. He was her ex-husband for a reason. Obviously, lack of physical attraction hadn't been part of that decision. As long as she kept hold of the emotionally closed-off part of him which had left her curled up in the foetal position, crying and alone, there shouldn't be a problem.

Apart from the fact he'd already opened up to her more over the course of these past few days than he had for the duration of their marriage…

'So, I'm at your mercy tonight. Where are we going for that drink? I don't see many dark quiet bars around here where we can hide away from the milling crowds.'

He glanced around at the throng of locals and tourists all out seeing the sights and sampling everything that Las Vegas had to offer, seeming almost overwhelmed.

It had that effect at first. The bright neon flashing lights, the loud music, and the smell from food vendors all conspired to overload the senses when first encountered. She didn't notice it anymore. Not that she ventured here at night very often. In fact, she couldn't even remember the last time she'd been out on a date. Meeting an actual man who wasn't a patient or a colleague, who simply wanted to take her out for the evening.

Relationships since Harrison hadn't exactly been successful, and she included Aimee's father in that group. Perhaps it was because she was already juggling work and motherhood, the most important things in her life, leaving no room for anyone else. There was also the possibility that she'd never loved anyone the way she'd loved Harrison, and since that hadn't worked out, she'd lost all hope of finding someone she would spend the rest of her life with. Still, it was nice to be out in any capacity, free from her usual responsibilities.

'You'd be surprised.' She pulled a bag of quarters from her purse and shook them at him.

'Gambling? Really? You've changed, Ruby Jones.'

'More than you will ever know,' she muttered, leading him to the dark side with her.

The intimidating security staff outside the casino nodded at them as they made their way up the steps to the entrance, flashing yellow lights directing them inside. Ruby strutted in through the marble hallway as though this were an everyday occurrence, when in reality she'd never set foot in this place. She'd heard a few of the nurses talking about this place with the sexy little bar in the back but never had the chance to check it out for herself.

'Wow. This place is a real assault on the senses, isn't it?' Harrison spun around, taking in the high ceilings and the armless statues, the noise of the whirring slot machines almost drowning him out.

'You ain't seen nothing yet.' Ruby grinned, taking him by the hand and leading him farther into the den of iniquity.

The main gaming floor was a hive of activity and sound. The buzz of the machines, clatter of coins and the happy cheers of winners gave it a carnival atmosphere. They walked the psychedelic carpet past the entranced zombie-like players feeding machines with their hard-earned cash, towards the dimly lit bar in the back. In stark contrast to the gamblers' paradise with its moody lighting and reserved clientele, it was an antidote to the madness outside.

'Well, this is a change of pace,' Harrison noted as they selected a booth to sit in.

'It's early. There's usually a show on later.' Ruby didn't anticipate they'd still be here at that time and had no idea if there would be a band playing, or a burlesque show provided as entertainment. It was hard to tell when the aged red leather seats and fringed table lamps alluded to either. For now, however, it provided the privacy and quiet Harrison might want to enable a conversation. As well as the alcohol he'd promised to get her through it.

'Very salubrious,' he said with a grin, pressing the brass button on the wall of the booth, which apparently provided table service.

A few minutes later, a broad-shouldered barman wearing a muscle-enhancing, too-tight black T-shirt appeared with a pad and pencil to take their order. It didn't seem the time or place to order cocktails, her usual go-to drink on the rare occasion she did go out, so she ordered a beer along with Harrison.

'I thought we could have our post-work analysis here, then we can use gambling to distract us from our emotional issues.' She was joking, though she would never have brought Harrison here if she thought there was any chance of him having a real problem with gambling.

He'd always been very careful with money. Saving every cent in order to give them both a better life. She doubted he'd changed that much over the years that he'd developed any sort of addiction. Harrison Blake had always been a very careful man and she'd loved that about him. Believing that he was safe, would always take care of her and never let her down. She'd been wrong then, but tonight was about trying to put that behind them and have a little fun.

'Dark. Very dark, Nurse Jones.' He shook his head, but the grin remained in place.

A dry sense of humour was needed in their profession to get them through difficult working days. They both knew gambling, like any other addiction, was a serious matter. She'd dealt with the aftermath of many huge losses in places like this. Depression often lead to more serious health problems when people lost jobs and relationships over their addiction. Las Vegas had more than its fair share of people for whom gambling was more than a bit of fun, and as a result, they'd seen those who'd hit rock bottom in the emergency room.

On this occasion, however, she was hoping a flutter in the casino would detract somewhat from the chat she knew they were about to have.

'So, today was a doozy, wasn't it?' She took a sip of beer from one of the bottles their waiter set down in front of them.

'You could say that. Is the hospital always this eventful?' Harrison asked, tracing the drops of condensation on his beer bottle with his thumb.

Ruby wondered if he was regretting his move already. The thought pained her more than it should. She was just getting used to having him around again. The idea that he wasn't happy, or worse, that he might move away again, would be hard to bear.

'I know Boulder City isn't too far away, but this is more of a tourist destination for people to enjoy all of life's excesses and we're probably busier than you're used to at St Michael's. In saying that, you've met with more challenges in a couple of days than I would usually experience in a week.' She offered him a smile, hoping she could persuade him it wasn't such a bad place to be.

Given their history, she should have been glad if he was having second thoughts about his new position. It would make life easier for her if he disappeared back out of her life. Not that it guaranteed that he would be gone from her thoughts. Fifteen years had proved that to her.

However, this time they were spending together was helping to heal some old wounds. Working through issues they should have discussed back then might just help them both finally move on from their tragedy.

'That's something, I guess.' He looked downcast, picking off the beer label with his thumbnail, clearly thinking about something that made him sad.

Ruby refrained from asking him what it was, waiting until he was ready to tell her.

'How do you help someone like Lucille without completely breaking down?' The question, combined with the anguish in his eyes when he glanced up at her, tugged unexpectedly on her heartstrings. It never occurred to her that dealing with the patient today would have triggered him, or that he might have been thinking about her during that frantic time.

Seeing his genuine pain stole away the bravado she would otherwise have tried to portray so he wouldn't see how affected she could still be. There didn't seem any point when he was clearly still hurting as much as she was over their loss.

Another swig of alcohol strengthened her resolve before she spoke on the matter.

'How do you know I don't?' She was only half teasing, there were times she did break down in the privacy of her own home after dealing with such cases, but she made it sound like a joke. Managing to tug his mouth into a half-smile.

'Because I saw you in action today. Calm, professional and compassionate. Knowing what you went through, and how you handled it, I'm in awe.'

'You did the same. We were both out of our comfort zone there today, but we did our bit to save Lucille all the same.' Ruby was uneasy accepting any praise for simply doing her job. As always, in putting the patient first, it was important that she did put her personal feelings aside. At least until she was no longer in the workplace.

'I'm aware of that. I have to say, though, my area of expertise means I'm not confronted too often with such stark memories of the past. It is something however, I feel you are faced with relatively frequently.'

Ruby shrugged. 'It's all part of the job. Yes, it hurts, Harrison. Is that what you want me to say? It will never not hurt. We lost our baby. It was traumatic and it's something I'll never get over, but I've had to learn to simply push through the grief. I can't let it affect me forever or else I couldn't do my job. I can see that you found it…challenging today, but I wouldn't have known if you hadn't told me. We worked together to save the patient, and that's what it's all about.'

It was heartening to know that Harrison wasn't the cold fish she'd taken him for when he left her, but she didn't want him to suffer forever either. And he was clearly hurting today.

He raised his bottle to her. 'Thanks for this.'

'The beer? I thought you were paying.' Ruby was deliberately obtuse, trying to keep things light. She understood why today had affected him so much. When Lucille had first come into the ER after her miscarriage, Ruby's heart had gone out to her, as it did with everyone who had gone through the same ordeal.

'The chat. I've learned not to keep everything bottled up inside, but that's not easy when you're the new guy in town. Or you've never told anyone else in your life that your child died.' After everything he'd told her, it didn't surprise Ruby that he'd never discussed his loss. She just felt sad for him that he'd never been able to confide in anyone.

'I guess no one except us understands.' Though she wasn't sure Harrison knew exactly what she'd gone through when he left, compounding her grief and loss. Just as she would never fully grasp what he'd felt at the time to think leaving her was the only option left.

'Well, thanks again for agreeing to this. I know it isn't easy for you either.'

'No, but you're right. It's better to talk things out.' She was as guilty as Harrison of not being able to open up about the past. When she'd discovered she was pregnant with Aimee there had been no discussion with the father, other than *I'm keeping the baby*. Without ever telling him about her previous pregnancy. It might not have changed the outcome, but if she'd been honest with her feelings, then perhaps they might have parted on better terms.

'Something I learned too late to save us.' Harrison gave her a look which sent the heat rising in her body.

Was it her imagination, or wishful thinking on her part, that there was more than a hint of regret in his words? Along with a flare of something in his eyes she was afraid to recognize. They'd always had great chemistry, it was communication which had let them down. Now that they were talking about their feelings, it was beginning to feel dangerous. As though the obstacles that had kept them apart were suddenly being eroded. Except she couldn't get over the fact he'd left her. Abandoned her with her grief and, though she was doing her best to forgive him, she would never forget. She couldn't, because letting him get close left her open to the same thing happening again.

And right here, right now, with Harrison looking at her so intensely, it would be easy to believe he would never hurt her. That there was a chance they could pick up where they'd left off. Especially when this was feeling more and more like a date. Something she needed to bust out of for her own sanity.

'If you're finished, why don't we go and try our luck outside?' She drained her bottle, keen to get away from the intimacy of the booth, the conversation and the company. A little distance to recompose herself.

'Sure.' Harrison sat back, that intimate connection broken, and finished his beer.

Ruby was already on her feet, waiting impatiently as he tossed a few dollars on the table, before he followed her out of the bar.

The blast of noise and light almost a relief, bringing her back down to earth and reminding her it wasn't just her and Harrison who existed.

'You'll have to take the lead. I'm a bit out of my depth on this one.' Bells ringing, and electronic screens presenting all matter of exciting opportunities to get rich quick surrounded them. A surreal experience on top of the moment he'd just had with Ruby.

Their connection, despite their years of separation, seemed as strong as ever. Which was exactly why they needed to be around other people. There was a danger of becoming too insular when they had shared experiences, and while he was open to talking these days, he wasn't ready to open up to anything more.

It was difficult. He wanted to be with Ruby because she was easy to be around. They knew each other, and had so much in common already that there was no awkwardness. At least now that they'd addressed the past and he'd acknowledged his own failings.

However, there was a danger of becoming too comfortable with her. Forgetting the reasons he'd had for walking out on their marriage in the first place. That overwhelming sense of loss he hadn't been able to properly cope with. Yes, he'd eventually been able to move on, but that hadn't removed the issue completely from his life. He'd simply taken steps to ensure he never found himself in that position again.

Safe sex, casual relationships and avoiding loving anyone the way he'd loved Ruby. That was what made his current situation so dangerous. Now that she was back in his life he had to find a different way to protect himself when they were already close. He had to find some way to keep some emotional distance, but he supposed quiet drinks and deeply personal conversations probably weren't the way to do that. Still, he'd needed to talk about what had happened today for his sake as well as Ruby's. Once they had their bit of fun in the casino they could go their separate ways again and he would try to keep their interactions limited to work.

'This isn't something I do regularly either. Maybe we should stick to the good ol' one-armed bandits.' Ruby handed him some quarters and they made their way over to a bank of brightly lit retro slot machines.

Harrison dropped a quarter in the slot, watched the wheels whir around with a sense of anticipation, before disappointment set in when he didn't win. He could see why the highs and lows of gambling became addictive. It wasn't long before he was one of those zombies going through the motions, hoping for a change in fortune. And when three red sevens lined up in the window, bells ringing, money pumping out into the tray, the euphoria was unexpected. It was barely enough to cover the cost of their two beers, yet he was pumping the air with his fist as though he'd won a million dollars.

Ruby was laughing next to him and caught up in the moment, he grabbed her into a hug and spun her around. Having her warm body back in his arms, seeing her smile, made him yearn for what they used to have. He reluctantly set her back down on her feet.

'Sorry. I got carried away,' he said, putting some distance between them again.

'That's okay,' she said, a little breathless. 'I'm just glad to see you cutting loose a little.'

'Excuse me? You think I'm not fun? Didn't we have ice cream for breakfast not so long ago?' It wounded him to think that Ruby thought he'd lost his fun side.

'Oh, yeah. You're such a rebel.' She rolled her eyes but he saw the twitch of her mouth as she teased him.

It made Harrison determined to prove to her that he was still young at heart.

He spotted a huge machine in the middle of the floor with 'Mystery Prize' spelled out in flashing LED red and amber lights atop. At a dollar per spin, it took him some time to load his previous winnings. He had no clue what he was doing but he did know that this was the first time he'd felt alive in a long time.

Having Ruby by his side, trying to impress her with his spontaneous side reminded him of when they'd been teenagers and he'd been showing off on the football field, trying to get her attention. Despite a spectacular fall, and the team's ultimate defeat, he'd had his wish granted. Ruby had spent the rest of the evening treating his cuts and bruises, giving him plenty of time to charm her. Although they were never going to be those love-struck teens again, that need to impress her was apparently alive and well.

He pulled the lever using two hands and watched the reels spin with bated breath. To no avail.

'Your turn,' he said, stepping back to let Ruby try her luck.

'Are you sure?'

'You might be luckier than I have been.' Whatever the outcome, at least he knew he'd taken a risk. Something he didn't do very often, and he had to ignore the warning bells going off in his head that Ruby should be the one making him break his own rules already.

'Fingers crossed.' She pulled the lever and stepped back, clinging onto Harrison's arm. The adrenaline rushing through his body on two counts.

Harrison held his breath, the buzz of anticipation crackling between him and Ruby.

The first reel came to a standstill, registering the 'Mystery Prize' symbol. Then the second spun around. Ruby's grasp on his arm became tighter as they fixated their gaze on that last reel. It seemed to take forever before it stopped, landing the much anticipated third 'Mystery Prize' icon. In the split second it took Harrison to realise they'd hit the jackpot, bells were ringing, sirens blaring and lights flashing. Announcing the win to everyone in the vicinity. A shower of gold confetti landed around them to confirm their win.

'Congratulations!' A smart-looking man in a black suit strode up to them with a gold envelope in hand. The badge on his lapel naming him as 'Gino,' the floor manager.

'Thanks.' Harrison was a little shell-shocked as he handed over the prize to him. 'What is it?'

'A VIP night in Las Vegas for two, courtesy of Jackpot Casino, redeemable for twenty-eight days,' Gino informed them, turning them to face a camera which had suddenly appeared in front of them. Capturing their open-mouthed shock forever.

Once Gino had delivered the news and posed for the photograph, he seemed as keen to disappear as quickly as he'd arrived.

'What do we do now?' Harrison asked, his big win suddenly feeling very anticlimactic. It certainly wasn't a life-changing prize. He suspected it was something for the tourist clientele rather than a Las Vegas resident.

'Give your details at the reception desk. Congratulations again.' With that, Gino disappeared into the crowd which had gathered around them.

He smiled awkwardly at the people who'd assembled to witness his win, until they gradually lost interest and returned to increase their own chances of a life-changing win.

'Can I see?' Ruby took the envelope from him and removed the contents.

'It says you have a limo for the evening, champagne dinner and a night in the penthouse. Sounds good to me.' She enthused about the details of the prize, perhaps sensing his mild disappointment.

'It's just as well because you'll be sharing it with me.'

Ruby's eyes widened. 'What? No. Why?'

'Apart from the fact you're the only person I know in town, you pulled the lever. This is your win as much as it is mine.' It seemed only fair to share the prize with her. He reckoned she could probably do with a treat when her time was taken up with work and motherhood.

'I don't know, Harrison—' Before Ruby could turn down the offer, there was a loud commotion behind them. A crash and a scream which couldn't be ignored.

When he turned towards the source of the noise, he saw a heavy-set woman lying on the ground, a stool overturned and a pool of blood gradually spreading across the garish carpet.

Harrison and Ruby rushed over to offer their assistance, just as a concerned-looking Gino appeared on the scene too. He radioed through for an ambulance and requested a first aid kit in the meantime.

'I'm a doctor and this is Ruby, a nurse. Can we help?'

Harrison offered their assistance until the paramedics arrived.

'Yes, please. I think she bumped her head on the way down.' Gino was hovering nervously as Harrison and Ruby knelt down beside the lady on the ground. She was beginning to come around and struggling to sit up.

'You've had a fall. It's better if you stay where you are until the paramedics get here to check you over. My name is Ruby. I'm a nurse. What's your name?' Ruby was holding the woman's hand and talking to her very calmly so as not to freak her out. She'd always been good in a crisis. Perhaps that was partly why he hadn't been able to cope with the aftermath of the miscarriage. It had been too hard to see her broken like that, knowing he was powerless to do anything about it.

'Moira,' the woman said, clearly a little disoriented.

'Do you know what happened, Moira?' Harrison wanted to find the root cause for the fall since it might give them a clue as to what was going on with the woman.

'I felt a little dizzy.' She put her hand up to her head and he could see the panic in her eyes as she discovered she was bleeding.

'I think you banged your head on the way down. When was the last time you had anything to eat or drink, Moira?' There could be all sorts of reasons behind a person fainting, but the most common cause was low blood sugar. He suspected in a place like this it was easy to lose track of time and forget to eat.

'I—I can't remember.'

'Okay. Could we get the lady some juice, please?'

he asked Gino, hoping to get her something sweet to give her an energy boost.

The floor manager radioed through the request just as another member of staff arrived with the first aid box. Ruby took it from him and set to work cleaning the wound on the side of the woman's head.

'This might sting a little but I'll be as gentle as I can. I just want to clean this up so we can see if you're going to need stitches.' Ruby carefully dabbed at the injury, showing the same kindness and understanding she did to everyone. It only made him feel more guilty about leaving her when she'd needed him most. That the one time she'd needed some care and attention she'd been denied it from the one person supposed to love her the most.

She caught him watching her and gave him a little smile. He'd never deserved her, hadn't realized how lucky he was until she was no longer in his life. Now that she was part of it again, he was being made acutely aware of how much she enhanced it simply by being her.

'Unless you have any other health issues we're not aware of, Moira, I think you're suffering from low blood sugar. It's caused you to faint and unfortunately you hit your head. I need you to take a sip of this juice to try and increase your blood sugar levels so you don't pass out again,' he told her. Gino handed him a juice box and Harrison held the straw to the woman's mouth so she could take a sip.

At that moment the paramedics came in and Ruby relayed the relevant information about what had transpired. She seemed to know the older paramedic and introduced him to Harrison as Wyatt Logan. He couldn't help but wonder what their history was, or if they had one.

A surge of irrational jealousy swelled inside him at the easy rapport the two appeared to have. Something she would not be happy about if she was aware. No doubt she would take great pains to point out he had left her, filed for divorce, and disappeared out of her life, so her private affairs were none of his business. It didn't make it any easier for Harrison being reminded of the fact that she would have been with other men in the intervening years, just as he had been with other women. However, he had been the one who'd ended their marriage and he had no right whatsoever to be privy to anything which went on in Ruby's life.

Harrison and Ruby moved back to let the paramedics take over, and in the end they decided to take Moira to the hospital to run some tests and keep her for observation. Leaving Gino thanking them profusely for their help.

'Let me get you some machine credits to thank you,' he said, clearly wanting to show his appreciation in some way.

'That's really not necessary, but thank you. I think we've had enough excitement for one evening.' Harrison shook his hand.

'Well, when you claim your prize we'll make sure to give you the VIP treatment.' With that promise, Gino's radio sparked to life with someone reporting a problem over at the video slots and he rushed off again.

'I think you're right, we should probably call it a night. I'll call a cab,' Ruby said with a yawn.

'I can drive you home. I've only had one beer.' The evening had been full of surprises. Mostly, the feelings towards Ruby which were beginning to re-emerge. It was best that they did call it a night before he got in any deeper.

'Are you sure it's not too much of an inconvenience?'

'Not at all. It will be quicker and safer. I promise. Just give me a minute to leave my details at the reception desk, then we can get out of here.' Harrison led the way back through to the lobby and registered for the prize he'd won. He had no idea if they'd ever claim it, but at least they had a night on the town to look forward to if they should ever want it.

'Well, that was a hell of an evening,' Ruby said on the drive back.

'Not quite what I had planned, but it wasn't dull at least.' The medical drama had provided some distraction from Ruby, even if he'd found himself watching her work and admiring the woman and nurse she'd become. Sad that he'd missed out on being part of her life all this time.

'It definitely wasn't that.' Another yawn and she closed her eyes, settling into the passenger seat, apparently comfortable with him driving.

It felt like the old days. Especially when she fell asleep, her head resting on his shoulder. He didn't even want to disturb her when they pulled up outside her house.

'Ruby? You're home,' he said gently.

'Hmm?' She took her time coming to, blinking awake to stare up at him.

'I said, you're home.' He leaned down closer and she took the opportunity to snuggle closer into him, shutting her eyes.

Harrison smiled. It was nice having her cuddled up to him again, feeling her warmth against him, her hair tickling his nose. He brushed a strand away from her face. She always looked so peaceful when she slept, and in the mornings he'd wakened her with a kiss. It seemed natural to do it again.

He pressed his lips gently to hers with no intention other than to wake her. Except suddenly Ruby was kissing him back, her hand caressing his cheek and completely undoing him. Since meeting her again it was all he'd wanted to do. To recapture what they'd had before their world had come crashing down around them. However, he knew they were different people and there was a reason he'd done his best to hold back. It hadn't occurred to him that Ruby would have had those same feelings.

Losing loved ones had made him back away from commitment, and getting involved with someone he'd spent the first years of his adult life with was only asking for more heartache. Ruby was absolutely the last person he should be kissing, but it felt so good, so right. Almost as if the last fifteen years hadn't happened. That's why it was so dangerous. He couldn't afford to forget what they'd both been through, or what could happen. Getting close and losing her again in any capacity would be devastating.

So he pulled away, breaking the connection, and ending the moment.

'You're home,' he said, his voice husky with the desire she'd awakened in him by kissing him back so passionately.

Ruby had retreated quickly to her own side of the car, eyes wide open now. 'Sorry. I was half asleep. I forgot where I was for a moment,' she said, the panic evident in her tone.

'Me too,' Harrison said with a half-smile. He should have been full of regret for lapsing, but he couldn't bring himself to be sorry for having one more taste of the woman he'd loved body and soul. At least they both seemed to know it had been a mistake. An accident that they could hopefully put behind them because nothing could come of it. There was too much painful history which had changed his outlook on life forever. During his recovery from that time he'd decided the only way to protect his heart was to keep it closed off. He couldn't afford to let Ruby sneak back in.

'Thanks for the drink. I guess I'll see you around at work.' Ruby was fumbling for the door handle, desperate to escape the close confines of the car. Along with the feelings Harrison had awakened inside her. Want being the one making itself known first and foremost.

Along with embarrassment. She couldn't believe she'd behaved so wantonly where anyone could have seen her. Worse, it had been with Harrison, who'd only come back into her life.

'Goodnight, Ruby,' he said as she slammed the

car door shut and hurried towards the apartment. As though putting some distance between them now was going to turn back the clock and somehow prevent that kiss from happening.

She knew he hadn't meant anything by it. It had become a custom of theirs back in the day for him to gently wake her with a kiss. Ruby expected Harrison had been driven by nothing more than a case of nostalgia. She'd been the one to try and turn it into something more.

Muscle memory seemed to have kicked into her entire body, including her libido, when Harrison's lips had met hers, and she'd wanted him. Despite all the pain and heartache he'd put her through, despite the years apart, in that moment they could have been teenagers again. Nothing else mattering except the chemistry between them and the urge to act on it. Thank goodness he'd come to his senses, because she'd seemed to have lost all of hers momentarily.

'Ruby? Is that you?' Her mother appeared and turned the light on, almost blinding her.

'Yes. I'm home.'

Her mother peered closely at her. 'What's wrong? You look upset. Did he do something? I told you to keep your distance from him.'

'What? No. I'm fine. He didn't do anything. We had to deal with a medical emergency, that's all.' It was mostly true. She was the one who'd passionately kissed her ex-husband in the front seat of his car, and currently dealing with a sense of mortification and confusion. Not knowing what had prompted that display, or why she was craving more even when she had come back down to earth.

Her mother narrowed her eyes at her. She had an uncanny knack of being able to see right into Ruby's soul and she didn't want to hang around for her to figure out what had happened. It was going to take a lot for her parents to forgive Harrison, if they ever would, so she definitely wasn't going to understand why Ruby had just been kissing him. Especially when she didn't know herself.

Ruby faked a yawn. 'If Aimee's okay, I think I'll just go on to bed. Thanks for looking after her.'

'Anytime. I'll go and wake your father. He'll be glad you're home safe too.' As Ruby headed towards her bedroom, she could feel her mother's eyes on her back.

She closed the door and collapsed onto the bed, hoping that by tomorrow morning it would all be forgotten. Though she had more than a sneaking suspicion her dreams were going to be dominated by memories of Harrison, old, new and imagined. All fuelled by the fire he'd lit inside her the second he'd touched her lips with his. Prince Charming awakening Sleeping Beauty with one kiss. She'd simply have to try and cling onto the fact that their fairy tale ending had become a living nightmare.

CHAPTER SIX

'Hey, Eugene. It's Dr Blake. I just thought I'd check in on you.' Harrison had stopped by to visit the boy at the end of his shift. Eugene had already been to theatre and had his burns debrided to remove all of the dead skin and clean out the wounds. Although he was looking better, he still had a long way to go to recovery and remained sedated for now. Eventually he would have to undergo skin grafts to start the healing process, but for now they were simply trying to keep him stable.

Harrison removed some of the dressings to check that there was no infection and, once satisfied, applied some new ones. It wasn't a complete surprise when he saw Ruby coming into the room, and he wondered if part of the reason he'd called here was the hope that their paths might cross. It had been several days since their night out and the kiss in the car and he hadn't seen her since. He wasn't sure if that was by design or accident.

No, he shouldn't have kissed her. That intimate gesture belonged in their past and that had been his mistake. However, he couldn't stop thinking about the way she'd kissed him back. Like no time had passed at all. Like he'd been forgiven for abandoning her and they'd picked up where their relationship had left off before the miscarriage. It was nothing but wishful thinking. They'd both simply been carried away in the moment after a dramatic night. It didn't mean they couldn't be in the same room together. He was sure he could rein his urges in now he'd had some time to think about the complications that getting involved with Ruby again would bring.

They were working together now. With him in a new job, having just moved here. She had Aimee. All things which they couldn't risk, even if she wanted anything more between them than an ill-thought-out kiss. The rate at which she'd fled the car made it pretty obvious she regretted it, so it was doubtful she intended to pursue anything further.

'Hey. How's he doing?' Ruby came straight over to check on Eugene without a hint of awkwardness, so perhaps she'd got over the kiss quicker than he had.

'As well as can be expected. I debrided the wounds, so it's just a matter of how quickly he'll heal. How are you doing? I haven't seen you around for a couple of days.' Without asking her outright if she was avoiding him, Harrison danced around the subject.

'I'm good. Just busy with work and Aimee.' There was no reason he should be a priority in her life, and she obviously had responsibilities, yet Harrison couldn't help but think she could take five minutes to see him if she really wanted to. Perhaps she was regretting having any contact with him at all. The idea that she would rather avoid him now was tough to swallow when he'd got used to having her in his life again already.

'That's good...' They fell into an awkward silence with only the blip of the monitors punctuating it.

'I just thought I'd check in on Eugene before my shift starts, so I suppose I should get moving.'

'Don't let me keep you. I'm on my way home. My clinic's finished for the day.' Harrison clung onto the fact that their shift patterns seemed to be different and that's why he hadn't seen much of her. Obviously she'd been working later.

'Lucky you.'

They both made their way to the door, just as Ruby's cell phone rang. 'Mom? What's wrong?'

It was clear something had happened to warrant a phone call at work, so Harrison hovered nearby in case she needed some help.

'Why didn't you say something before I left? I don't know how I can get away now. No, you need to go to bed. I'll see if I can get someone to cover, though it's late notice.' Ruby hung up with a sigh and a frown.

'Is everything all right?' It was obvious it wasn't but this was the time for her to share if she wanted help.

'Mom and Dad are both sick. They managed to drop Aimee off at school but they can't pick her up. I'm going to have to try and find someone to get her. I can't just leave.' Another heavy sigh as she rubbed her temples.

'I could collect her and take her to your place.' It was out of his mouth before he had time to consider what he was saying. This was the very opposite of keeping his distance from Ruby outside of the hospital, yet it was the obvious solution to her problem.

Ruby looked at him with uncertainty written all over her face. He wasn't sure if he should be offended. 'Are you sure that's not too much of an inconvenience?'

'I have nothing planned. I can swing by and collect her. As long as you trust me.' He was aware that Ruby wouldn't trust the safety of her daughter to just anyone, and he'd only reappeared in her life a matter of days ago.

She rolled her eyes. 'Of course I trust you, Harrison. And as you've pointed out, you have a fan in Aimee. However, I don't finish my shift until the early hours of the morning. It's a lot to ask of you to stay with her all night.'

He hadn't realized exactly what he was volunteering for but he wasn't going to let her down now when she was trusting him with the most precious thing in her life. 'It's fine. We'll order a pizza, pop a couple of beers, play a hand or two of poker...'

She slapped him on the arm. 'Seriously, though, I'll be forever indebted to you if you could look after Aimee until I get home. I'll try and get away as early as I can.'

'It's no problem. Just give me the address of the school and a key to your apartment and stop worrying.' Hopefully this would go some way to smoothing over what had happened and put them back on an even keel. They could be friends. Goodness knew when he might need a favour in return.

'Sure. Let me phone the school and make sure they know you're coming. Thanks for this, Harrison.' She flashed him a smile that more than made up for whatever a night babysitting a ten-year-old was going to throw at him.

'Yes, Dr Blake will be picking Aimee up today. Her grandparents are ill and he has my permission to collect my daughter from school. Yes, she knows him. Thank you.' Ruby hung up, glad she'd solved one problem, but hoping she wasn't causing herself more by letting Harrison further into her life. There was no greater responsibility than trusting him enough to look after her daughter and she didn't want to regret it.

She'd purposely tried to keep her distance after that kiss, trying to put it from her mind, expecting that the memory of it would fade away. One glimpse of him and it had all come flooding back. Though he hadn't managed to stay out of her dreams either these past nights. She almost blushed when she'd spotted him because of the X-rated thoughts her subconscious had conjured up during her sleep.

She couldn't be mad at her parents for falling ill, but the timing could have been better. Given her some time to find cover, or someone to babysit who wasn't her ex-husband.

'It's all sorted. The school knows you're coming to pick Aimee up. I can't thank you enough for doing this.' She handed the apartment key over to Harrison, feeling as though she'd just invited him to wreak some more havoc in her life. It was going to be difficult to carry on as normal knowing he'd crossed her threshold, and had become part of the fabric of her home. Where it had only been her and Aimee for as long as she could remember.

'It's no problem. Do I need a list of instructions, or shall I just get her a fake ID and we'll hit the town?' Harrison's insistent teasing wasn't helping calm her nerves.

'Stop! Just make sure she does her homework before dinner, and one hour of TV only. Bed is eight o'clock and don't let her sweet-talk you into anything later or else she'll be grumpy in the morning when I have to wake her for school.' It was likely going to be as odd for Aimee as it was for Ruby to have Harrison in the apartment. She never invited men back to her place, even on the rare occasion she had a date. There was no point disrupting her daughter's life when the relationship would likely never last, and she'd been proved right thus far.

This was different. Aimee had already met Harrison and knew he was Mommy's friend. She had no concept of the complicated dynamic of their past relationship and didn't need to. Harrison was simply doing them a favour, and there didn't have to be any more to it than that.

'No problem. Hey, stop worrying. It'll be fine.' Harrison did his best to reassure her, likely picking up on her anxiety. Ruby didn't have any qualms about him looking after her daughter, it was simply the implication of letting him cross that line into her personal life again which was causing her concern. Still, she didn't have any choice at present, and she'd be sure to point that out when her mother discovered what was happening.

'Thanks, Harrison. I appreciate this.' She knew he didn't have to do this, he was under no obligation whatsoever, and she was grateful. It was simply perturbing that he'd helped her out so much already within a few days of them getting to know one another again and the last thing she wanted was to come to rely on him. To think of him as part of her and Aimee's life. He'd already proved she couldn't pin her hopes on him because there was always a chance he would disappear again. This time she had Aimee to think of too. It wasn't just her heart on the line.

'Teeth brushed and bed for you, Aimes.' Harrison was looking forward to a rest once his charge was tucked up for the night.

As much as he'd enjoyed her company and been able to help Ruby, he was exhausted. He wasn't used to looking after children all day. Once he'd collected a happy, chatty Aimee from school, they'd been busy all day playing games and working on her art project. Goodness knew how Ruby managed to do this full time on top of her position at the hospital. Of course she had her parents' help, but even so, it was a lot for a person to do on their own.

'Mom always reads me a story.' Aimee emerged from the bathroom in her pyjamas, rubbing her eyes and clearly fighting her tiredness.

'Aren't you a little old for bedtime stories?' He suspected she was just trying to stay up a little later. A ten-year-old's power move that he couldn't deny her.

'It helps me sleep,' she pouted, sealing his fate.

'Okay, then. Into bed.' He stood at the door whilst she chose a book and clambered into bed. Then pulled up the covers around her and perched on the side of the bed.

'I had fun today,' she said, clutching her well-worn teddy bear.

'Me too.' As he said it, Harrison realized as tiring as it had been, he had enjoyed spending time with her. Of course it made him wonder what it would have been like if he had been a father. If he would always have been so patient and fun as he had been with Aimee today. Certainly he'd never intended to be as distant as his own parents had been with him, and from the day Ruby had discovered she was pregnant, he'd sworn to be present and involved with his child. Unfortunately, he'd never had the chance.

'Why do you look so sad?' Aimee was watching him, missing nothing, but it wasn't his place to tell her about his past with her mother.

'I'm just missing my family.' This moment was also bringing back memories of his brother, who'd read to him when he was younger too. Sneaking comics under the covers with a torch and making every bedtime feel like an adventure.

'You can be part of our family,' Aimee said with a smile. 'Then you don't have to be sad anymore.'

He wished it was as simple as that.

'Well, thank you very much. That's made me happier already.' He wasn't sure Ruby would be thrilled with that idea, but it was a nice gesture on Aimee's part to make him feel included. Her kindness and generosity clearly inherited from her mother.

'Will you be coming to get me from school tomorrow?' There was a hope in Aimee's eyes that he hated to extinguish, but he didn't want to promise something and not be able to deliver.

'I don't think so, but I'm sure I will still see you every now and then.' That seemed enough to appease her and she handed over her carefully chosen book before settling down into her bed.

There was a cartoon dog bookmark sticking out of the book and Harrison felt bad for doubting Aimee still had a bedtime story read to her at night. Perhaps it was her way of keeping that bond strong with her daughter when she was working full time. He could just imagine Ruby coming back from a late shift, cuddling up with Aimee on the bed and reading to her until she fell asleep. A heartening scene he almost had a yearning to be part of, because in an alternate reality they both would have been doing that for their own child.

He cleared his throat to try and move the ball of emotion suddenly blocking it. Thoughts of the past, of the future denied him and Ruby, had been uppermost in his mind recently. Likely because of seeing Ruby again and being reminded of it all. It had been easier to try and put those emotions aside when he was simply living the life of a bachelor, not a grieving man who'd lost his baby and left a wife behind.

He'd told himself over the years that he didn't need a family of his own anymore, that it would cost him his peace of mind worrying that it would all be taken away from him at any point. Being around Aimee and Ruby was showing him what he was missing. Ruby's life was all the richer for having her daughter in it. He couldn't help but think if he'd been stronger, if he'd opened up to his wife sooner, he might have been part of a happy family after all.

Ruby let herself into the apartment and closed the door quietly behind her so as not to disturb Aimee if she was sleeping. She'd half expected to find Harrison on the couch, watching TV, waiting for her to relieve him of his babysitting duties. Apart from the drawings scattered on her coffee table, there was no sign of anyone even being in here.

Then she heard the sound of Harrison's voice drifting from Aimee's room and she smiled, knowing her daughter had conned him into reading to her. She walked towards Aimee's room with every intention of taking over and getting her daughter to go to sleep, but, as she stood in the doorway watching the interaction, she was charmed by the scene.

'Elise took the potion and downed it. It tasted of burnt cabbage and dog food...' Harrison turned up his nose as he read the story.

'Yuck.' Aimee was reading the story over his shoulder but seemed engrossed as much by the reader as the book.

As unnerving as it was to see her ex-husband engaged in a bedtime story with her daughter, it was also quite sweet. Harrison had been robbed of his chance to be a father and she'd always thought it was a role he would have excelled at. Young at heart, patient and kind. All the qualities she'd loved about him were everything needed in a good parent. She should know when she'd been lucky enough to have a mother and father who embodied those very characteristics. It was a shame for her daughter that she hadn't been as fortunate in her own father.

It was little wonder Aimee was making the most of having Harrison around when she'd missed out on that male influence in her life. Ruby's father was always there, of course, when they needed him but it wasn't the same as having someone who'd let her daughter have ice cream for breakfast, or read her bedtime stories.

Afraid that she would get carried away with the sight before her, believing she could still have her happy-ever-after, she turned to leave. However, the movement must have caught Harrison's eye and he glanced up at her.

'Hey.' She walked into the room as though that had been her intention all along.

'Hey, yourself. I wasn't expecting to see you back so soon.' His smile, tired but happy, squeezed her heart like a vise.

'I managed to get some cover.'

'Hi, Mommy.' Aimee stretched out her arms, waiting for the hug she knew was coming.

Harrison got up from the bed and moved aside to give her access to her daughter.

'What are you still doing awake?' Ruby asked, tucking her daughter back under the covers.

'That's my fault, I'm afraid. I got too invested in Elise's adventures.' He waved the book at her, before inserting the bookmark and setting it on the dresser for Ruby to pick up again at another time.

'Easily done.' Ruby grinned back. This was always her favourite part of the day too, spending precious time with her daughter, the outside world locked away until morning.

''Night, Aimee.' Harrison took his leave, letting Ruby say goodnight in private.

'I like Harrison,' Aimee said as Ruby turned off the main light to leave a night light glowing in the corner.

'Me too. Now get some sleep. I'll see you in the morning.' She dropped a kiss on Aimee's forehead, glad she'd been able to get away from work in time to say goodnight.

'Will Harrison be here in the morning?' a little voice asked hopefully in the semidarkness.

'No, sweetheart. He'll be going back to his own house. Now get some sleep.' Ruby blew her another kiss and closed the door.

Aimee's innocent enquiry had taken her by surprise. Not only that she might expect Harrison to spend the night, but also that the thought didn't seem to bother her. It was obvious her daughter was very taken with him and was already seeing Harrison as a friend. The fact brought all manner of questions to mind. Did that mean her daughter was looking for a father figure? That she wouldn't mind if Ruby brought someone home? Or was it just Harrison she was comfortable with being part of their lives?

Up until now Ruby had been very careful about letting men into her daughter's life. Very few had made it, and none recently. She doubted Aimee remembered much of the relationships Ruby had been involved in when she was young, but none had worked out. As a result, Ruby kept that part of her life separate from her daughter. She didn't want to confuse her, or let her get close to people who weren't going to be in her life for very long.

Exactly the reason she should be wary about her

getting close to Harrison. Circumstances had already conspired to have him involved in their lives, but theirs was a complicated history she wasn't ready to share with Aimee. If she ever did.

She walked into the living area, her head full of thoughts about Harrison and wondering what harm she could be doing to her family by having him around. Only to find him in the kitchen dishing out a plate of food for her.

'I hope you don't mind. I know you're probably hungry after your shift so I saved you some leftovers. It's just some roast chicken and potatoes.'

'No pizza?' She was stunned that he'd gone to the trouble of actually cooking, never mind saving some for her.

'I'm trying to make a good impression, or at least make up for the whole ice-cream-for-breakfast thing.'

'And Aimee ate this? It's not a judgement on your cooking by the way, but she's a fussy eater. It's difficult to get her to eat anything that isn't shaped like a dinosaur or a smiley face. Please tell me the secret.' Mealtimes had become a battleground, and after a long day at work it was often the last thing she wanted to do, so frequently capitulated to Aimee's requests. It made her feel like a failure as a mother that she couldn't get her daughter to eat healthy, nutritious meals, which as a medical professional, she knew was important for her child's development. Yet, it was processed food which her daughter would eat without a protest. The fact that Harrison, a virtual stranger, had succeeded where Ruby had failed, wasn't helping.

Harrison helped himself to a carrot baton from her plate. 'I don't know what to tell you. We stopped at the store for supplies on the way home. I didn't want to take my eyes off her while I was cooking so I got her to help. She seemed to enjoy preparing a meal. Perhaps you have a budding chef on your hands.'

'Huh.' It gave Ruby some food for thought. She was so focused on sitting down to dinner with her daughter, she never thought about getting her to help cook with her.

'Hey, don't worry about it. I'm just a novelty to her. I'm sure she'd get sick of me and my cooking soon enough given the chance.' He was doing his best to make her feel better about it, yet the image of him here in her house on a regular basis was both exhilarating and terrifying. Ruby was afraid of what she'd already put in motion by letting him help her out to this extent. Showing her daughter that he was someone she could rely on, when Ruby knew from painful experience that wasn't necessarily true.

Yes, she knew now that he'd had his own demons and grief to deal with at the time, but that couldn't take away the pain his actions had caused her. There was nothing to say that in future something in his personal life wouldn't affect her or Aimee. The only way to avoid that was to push him back out of her life. Something which would be easier said than done now.

Especially when it was so nice coming home and having things done for her like this. It was a glimpse at the life they could have had. Were supposed to have had. Managing the childcare between them, having dinner waiting when she came home from work, this was the fairy tale. It was a shame none of it was real. Harrison was simply doing her a favour. Likely trying to make amends for the past, not because this was where he chose to be. He simply hadn't had anything better to do tonight and she'd needed help. There was no point in her reading more into it and hoping something could come of it, because she would only end up disappointed, or worst-case scenario, left heartbroken all over again when he was gone.

'Well, thank you for dinner, Harrison, and everything else.' She didn't know what she would have done without him tonight, and that was the problem.

'You're welcome. Now, if you want to go and have a shower, I can stay on for another half an hour and tidy up the kitchen.' He was already clearing away her plate and wiping down the kitchen surfaces. She wasn't used to anyone but her cleaning, and he hadn't been so domestic when they had lived together. Years of living as a bachelor had clearly had a positive effect on him.

'What are you smiling at?' Harrison caught her moment of reflection.

'I was just thinking about the difference in you since we lived together. It was always you making the mess and me tidying up around you.' The memory that made her smile was now making Harrison wince.

'Sorry about that. I guess I was too immature to be a decent partner to you, Ruby.' He looked genuinely upset and she was sorry she'd even brought up the memory when she knew he'd struggled with his later actions too.

'It's okay, Harrison I've forgiven you for everything. We were both too young to deal with everything that happened. Let's try and put it behind us. Now, if that offer of shower time is still on the table I would really like to take advantage of it. It's not often I get to do that without Aimee knocking on the door.'

She wasn't going to go along with the suggestion, keen to get him out of her apartment before he looked any more at home here, but she hadn't wanted to send him on his way under such a dark cloud. Although it had been difficult, she'd started her life over again after the miscarriage, and he shouldn't feel guilty forever over what had happened. Even if she hadn't realized it at the time, he'd been grieving too. Struggling to cope with the loss as much as she had been, only without the support of family around to get him through.

An extra thirty minutes wasn't going to make much difference to their current situation in the scheme of things.

Ruby took her time showering, enjoying the fact she didn't have to be on alert for Aimee, or have to spend the evening cleaning the kitchen. All she wanted to do after a long shift was veg out on the couch. Thanks to Harrison, it was possible tonight. These past few days he always seemed to be on hand to give her whatever she needed. She knew she couldn't afford to get too used to it. To let her guard down when he might disappear at any given moment, but it was nice to have someone to share the load with for a while at least.

Perhaps she'd be able to return the favour at some point, then she wouldn't feel so indebted to him.

She towel dried and moisturized her body before donning a pair of floral silk pyjamas. With anyone else it might seem a tad awkward, but Harrison had seen her in a lot less and she wanted to be comfortable. Hopefully he would take the hint that she was ready to say goodnight and head home himself.

'Thanks for that, Harrison. It's nice to have a shower without feeling as though I've got a time limit before Aimee gets herself into mischief.' Ruby walked into the living room expecting to see him either cleaning her kitchen or watching TV. He was doing neither.

The sight that greeted her was Harrison fully stretched out on her couch fast asleep. His shirt had ridden up so she could see his flat belly, the beginning of the dark trail of hair she knew intimately. Sudden erotic images of their past flashed behind her eyes. Harrison fully naked. The two of them showering together. Their honeymoon. All passionate encounters she'd tried not to think about these last years because no one and nothing had ever matched up to the times they'd shared.

She was tempted to wake him. To tell him to go home so she didn't have to look at him and be reminded of the good times they'd shared together, but he looked so peaceful she didn't want to disturb him. She reckoned he deserved a rest after a day playing house. As he gave a soft snore, she went and retrieved a blanket from the closet to cover him. Though she hoped he would do the decent thing and leave before Aimee awoke so she didn't get her hopes up that this would become a regular occurrence. The same could be said for Ruby tucking a blanket around him as if she had any right to be this close to him.

She leaned in to kiss his forehead. A simple goodnight kiss he never need know about. Except those full parted lips proved too much temptation. She pressed her lips softly to his for a brief moment, just long enough for her to have sweet dreams thinking about. Before she realized what was happening, Harrison had wrapped an arm around her waist and pulled her down on top of him. She let out a gasp of surprise but it was swallowed by Harrison's mouth on hers. His eyes were closed as he kissed her and she wondered if he was still half asleep. That was, until his hands moved to cup her backside and pull her flush against him, letting her feel every warm, hard inch of him. She sighed into the moment. A long, leisurely kiss that dreams were made of.

It was only when her daughter cried out from her room that Ruby came to her senses.

'Mommy. I don't feel well.'

'I'm coming, honey.' She scrambled off Harrison, embarrassed by her own behaviour, and rushed to take care of her child.

'Please be gone by the time I come back.' Ruby was aware she'd initiated the kiss, that she'd been enjoying it as much as he had, and that was exactly why she had to be so dismissive.

Aimee had to be her number one priority, and there was no way she was going to let her libido, or ancient history, ruin that special relationship.

CHAPTER SEVEN

'TRY AND KEEP the wound dry and covered to minimize the chance of any infection and make an appointment to replace the dressing.' Harrison saw off his last appointment at his day clinic. He was getting ready to finish his shift at the hospital when he got a message for a consultation down in the emergency room about a chemical burn.

He packed up his things and headed down as soon as he could. Time was always a vital factor when it came to treating burns of any description because it could mean the difference not only between full recovery or lifelong scars, but in some cases life or death. Despite the urgency on the patient's behalf hastening his attendance, there was also that possibility of seeing Ruby again which was spurring him on.

There had definitely been a distance between them since that night in her apartment a week ago. She'd made it clear after they'd kissed again that she didn't want things to go any farther. He didn't blame her. Despite all the reasons he knew he shouldn't be with her, every time she touched him he responded solely on a base level. So when she'd kissed him, those urges had flared back to life with a ferocity that had taken them both by surprise.

Neither of them wanted to rekindle the relationship, yet they couldn't seem to avoid the chemistry between them. The night hadn't ended how either of them had imagined and Harrison didn't want her to hate him for their moment of weakness. They still had to work together.

'I got a call about a chemical burn,' he informed the first nurse he encountered in ER.

'Oh, yes, that was Ruby. She thought we should get your opinion. She's through there.' The nurse pointed towards the first cubicle with the curtains pulled around.

At the mere mention of Ruby his stomach did a backflip. He hoped she wouldn't be as cold towards him as she had been when she'd ordered him out of her apartment. Then he realized she was the one who'd called him down here, and he steeled himself to be as professional as possible. Obviously she was willing to put aside personal feelings to consult him and he had to do the same for the sake of the patient.

He whipped the curtain back with the confidence of the expert he was in his field. However, his bravado faltered when he saw her standing next to the patient's bedside. She looked so pale, so thin, he was automatically concerned for her. Had he caused this by coming back into her life? Upsetting her to the point that she looked ill? The thought didn't sit well with him and it was clear he needed to talk to her to find out what had happened and what she wanted him to do. He might have to reconsider his position here if this was the effect his presence was having on her physically.

'This is Dr Blake. He's a burns specialist. I wanted

him to consult on your treatment, Mr McQueen, to make sure you have the best possible outcome.' She gave Harrison a half-smile, which went some way to reassuring him that she didn't despise the very sight of him at least.

'Hello, Mr McQueen. Can you tell me what happened?' It was an opportunity for the patient to bring the doctor up to speed on the events leading up to his admittance into the emergency room.

'I splashed some potassium hydroxide into my eyes at work. I tried to wash it out, but my vision is limited.' The fear in the young man's voice was evident and rightly so. Losing his sight permanently was a very real possibility.

'We've irrigated the eyes and applied antibiotic eye drops. I just wanted you to take a look at his eyelids as he's having trouble closing them,' Ruby added, clearly wanting the best outcome possible for her patient.

'May I take a look for myself?'

Ruby stepped aside to give him access to the patient's bedside and he carefully examined the affected eye and surrounding area. Turning the eyelid inside out to make sure there was no foreign object causing further irritation.

'Although the eyelid is swollen at present, I don't think it needs surgery. It should subside. However, I'd like to send him to ophthalmology for a thorough examination, Nurse Jones. Then I think if we can find him a private room somewhere we can keep the lights dimmed, it would help.' The bright fluorescent lights of ER were a help to the medical staff, but in this case it could exacerbate the patient's problem.

'I'll set that up now.' Ruby walked away to make the necessary phone calls but he didn't want to leave without checking on her welfare too. She did not look well.

'Am I going to lose my sight, Doc?' the patient asked, not knowing which way to direct his question.

'We will do everything in our power to try and prevent that. For now, just rest, and we'll get you some pain relief and dilating eye drops to help with your discomfort, Mr McQueen.'

'Thanks, Doctor.' The man settled back into the bed, though Harrison knew it would be hard for him to relax until he was able to see anything other than darkness.

Harrison caught up with Ruby at the nurses' station.

'Thanks for that. I just wanted to make sure we're giving him the best opportunity of recovery,' she said, leaning against the desk.

'Of course. That's what I'm here for. Are you okay, Ruby? You don't look so well yourself.' Up close he could see beads of sweat forming on her forehead.

'I feel a little hot.' She was swaying so much now he was forced to reach out and steady her.

'Can someone get me a chair for Nurse Jones, please?' A porter passing through immediately pushed a chair beneath her just as she collapsed into it.

'I got you some water, Ruby. You don't look so good. You should go home.' One of the nurses handed her a paper cup as it soon became apparent to everyone that she wasn't well.

'I can't. I'm on the late shift,' she protested.

'Ruby, if you've got any sort of stomach flu you can't be around the patients. You know that. Let me take you home. I'm finished for the day.' Harrison knew that she wouldn't go home for her own sake but there was no way she would put her patients at risk.

'Okay.' Her soft acceptance told him everything he needed to know about how ill she was, not fighting him over his offer.

It wasn't long before they managed to gather her things and make sure cover was in place before he helped her out to the car.

'I just feel so weak. It's probably the same virus my parents and Aimee had. I thought I would escape.' She gave him a weak smile as he pulled the seat belt around her before he got into the driver's seat beside her.

'No such luck. You need to rest up.'

They were only five minutes away from the hospital when Ruby grabbed his arm. 'You need to pull over, Harrison.'

'What's wrong?'

'I think I'm going to be sick.'

Ruby opened the car door the minute he pulled over to the side of the road, and retched. His heart went out to her, knowing this was the last thing she wanted. Never mind being sick, but being with him at her most vulnerable, fragile state would not have been her choice.

All he could do was rub her back and offer words of comfort as her shoulders heaved. When it subsided and she sank back into her seat he handed her a bottle of water to rinse her mouth out.

'Better?' he asked, his forehead knitted in concern.

She shook her head, her eyes watering. 'Not really.'

'We're not far from my house. Why don't we take you back there until you're feeling better?'

She nodded.

'What about Aimee? Is she being taken care of tonight?'

'Mom has her.'

'Okay, then, that's settled.' Harrison got the car moving again, his mind already made up that he was going to take care of her. There was no way he was going to let her go home on her own when she was so ill. He'd let her down before when she needed him and he wasn't going to do it a second time. He was going to be there for her.

Ruby was too ill, too weak, to argue with Harrison. He was her white knight, once again riding in with a lift home and an offer to help that she couldn't refuse. She hadn't felt one hundred percent when she'd started her shift but thought she was simply tired after running around after her parents and Aimee during their bout of sickness. It was only when she'd seen Harrison's look of concern in that cubicle that she realized she was in real trouble. Now there was absolutely no denying she was ill. All she wanted to do was collapse into bed. Right now, she didn't care whose.

That last night in her apartment when she'd kissed Harrison had been reason enough to stay away from him. Every time they were alone things got dangerously out of control where their libidos were concerned.

It was ridiculous she should have missed him these past days when he'd only been back in her life for such a short time, but he'd made his mark on her again. Aimee too, who hadn't stopped asking about him since. Ruby had almost been disappointed when she'd wakened the next morning to find the blanket neatly folded on the Harrison-free couch, regardless that she'd told him to leave.

Now that she was sick she was glad she had someone to lean on for the time being. There was no one at home and she wasn't sure how she would manage on her own when she was as weak as a kitten. As soon as she was feeling better she'd be out of here.

They pulled up outside Harrison's house, and though her head felt too heavy to lift she did take the time to view the surroundings. For all intents and purposes, it looked like a family home, not a bachelor pad. A charming two-story property with a garage and a garden in a family neighbourhood. Far too big for one man on his own. She couldn't help but wonder if he had aspirations of a family at some point in his life. Although she would be happy for him to move on from their painful past, the thought of him having that happy family they were denied caused a sharp stabbing pain in her heart.

'Let me get that for you.' Mistaking her hesitation as something to do with her illness perhaps, he reached across and undid her seat belt, before stretching farther across her to open the door.

That close personal contact still able to thrill her even when she felt at her worst.

'Thanks.' She followed him up onto the porch of the house and, while she waited for him to open the door, she looked down and saw the evidence of her spectacular display on the roadside down the front of her shirt.

'Oh, no. It's in my hair too,' she cried, horrified.

'Don't worry, we can get your clothes in the wash and I'll run you a bath.' Harrison's bright smile was in stark contrast to how dreadful she felt, and probably looked. As well as the nausea and the hot and cold sweats, she just felt dirty.

'Thanks, Harrison. I'm so sorry I'm imposing on you again.' If she had any girlfriends she would have called on them for help, but motherhood and a demanding job meant her social life suffered. She didn't see many colleagues outside of work except for the odd birthday meal or drink. There was no one close enough for her to lean on at times like this other than her parents and they were already babysitting across town for her.

If Harrison was someone she'd just met at work, she would never have dreamed of coming back to his place, much less strip out of her dirty clothes. It was that past relationship she kept trying to distance herself from that made her trust him. He'd always been good at taking care of her, even when she was sick, and that made her lean in to his offer.

During those early stages of her pregnancy when morning sickness and heartburn had been the bane of her life, Harrison had been there making her dry toast for breakfast. Making sure she had whatever pregnancy-safe remedies he could find to help ease her symptoms. He'd got her through the worst days when it all seemed too much and she was tired of feeling so sick all the time.

That was why his sudden disappearance after the miscarriage had hurt all the more. He was the one person she thought would be there to make her feel better, to tell her everything was going to be okay. But he wasn't.

'If you want to take off those dirty clothes, there's a robe in my bedroom you can use. I'll run you a bath, then we'll see if we can find you something to wear until your things are washed and dried.' He led her through the house where the white walls and tiled floor made it seem so modern and new compared to the homely exterior.

The white theme continued into his bedroom. 'I think I'm going to end up with snow-blindness,' she joked feebly.

'I know. I haven't had the chance to put my own stamp on things yet, or unpacked everything.' He moved a few boxes on the floor so she had a clear way through.

It was unsettling seeing a huge bed and nothing else except the two of them in the room.

'I'm sure you'll get things the way you want eventually. It's a nice place you've got.'

'Thanks.' He opened the closet where his shirts and pants were hanging, retrieved his robe and handed it to her. 'The bathroom's just across the hall. I'll run you a bath and leave you to it. If you need anything, just shout.'

With that, he made a hasty exit, closing the door behind him. Legs weak, she perched on the end of his bed to undress, noting the few personal items on his bedside dresser.

Some loose change, his watch, the same aftershave he'd worn when they were teenagers and, most notably, a ceramic cactus she'd painted for him on a craft evening they'd gone to on a date once. The sort of place that provided ready-made dishes and ornaments for you to decorate before glazing them for you. He'd painted a ceramic unicorn for her, which, at the height of her anger after he'd left, she'd thrown at the wall and watched shatter into smithereens.

Once she'd stripped and folded her clothes into a pile, she donned his robe and shifted her position on the bed so she could take a better look at the battle-weary cactus. The paint was chipped and it was missing a few spikes, but the fact that he'd kept it was touching. It wasn't a practical item, so he hadn't kept it for any other reason than nostalgia. Just as she couldn't resist spraying a little of his aftershave on the robe. The smell transported her back to their early dates, and the nerves she'd felt waiting for him after school. Even now the scent did something to her.

There was a knock on the bedroom door. 'The bath's ready when you are.'

'Thanks.' Ruby sprang to her feet, as though she'd been caught doing something she shouldn't. Like going through his personal belongings.

Before she was tempted to rummage through any more of his things, she crossed the hall to the bathroom and left her pile of clothes outside the door.

The steamy bathroom was filled with the scent of lavender. The tub full of bubbles. Just how she liked it. He knew everything she liked, and she'd forgotten how nice it was to have someone who anticipated what she needed. That was the good part of a relationship. She'd been so focused on the reasons she should avoid getting close to anyone, the pros of having a partner had been resigned to history. A small gesture like this had a way of transforming a bad day into a nice time.

As she stripped off and sank into the suds, she wondered if it was time to open her life back up to someone again. She closed her eyes and relaxed into the hot, soapy water. Despite the nausea, and that awful anticipation of when it might strike again, this was the most relaxed, most pampered she'd felt in a long time. It was all thanks to Harrison.

He used to do this for her in the old days when it was her time of the month, or if she'd had a particularly rotten day. A warm bath, some soothing music, and he'd wash her hair for her. Making her feel loved. The only person other than her parents or her daughter who'd managed that.

'Ruby? Are you okay in there?' Harrison called through the door, probably to make sure she hadn't passed out and drowned.

'I'm fine.'

'Do you need anything?'

'Could you…could you wash my hair?' She knew it was asking a lot, of both of them. Taking them somewhere they weren't supposed to go. An intimate act she would never ask of a stranger, but Harrison was much more than that no matter how hard they tried to fight it. Right now she was feeling sorry for herself and simply needed a little tender loving care.

It was a hot minute before he responded. 'Are you sure?'

'Please, Harrison.' She was tired, sick and emotional, and just wanted a little comfort.

As the handle on the door moved, she grabbed a hand towel and covered her chest, then scooped the bubbles around her to preserve her modesty. Regardless that Harrison was familiar with her naked body.

'Are you feeling any better?' he asked, seeming a little perturbed by her request. Ruby realised then what she was asking of him. She had no right to expect him to perform such an intimate act when they were no longer married, simply because she was feeling lonely and vulnerable.

'Just feeling sorry for myself. You don't have to do this. I shouldn't have asked.'

'No, it's okay. I know this used to make you feel better, I just want to make sure you're all right with me coming in here like this.'

'I asked you to, didn't I?' It was sweet of him to make sure she was in her right mind, that she wouldn't regret asking him to do this, but it was all she wanted at this moment.

'It's been a long time since I did this.' He rolled up his sleeves and kneeled at the side of the bath.

The admission warmed Ruby, knowing that this was something just between them. It wasn't part of any seduction routine he used with other women. Their secret love language that even now showed how much he still cared for her.

He scooped the water over her hair, slicking it back with his hands. That gentle touch soothing her to the point of near sleep. Eyes closed, she listened to the sound of a bottle opening, then the scent of raspberries filling the air before Harrison's hands were in her hair lathering the shampoo. He took his time massaging her scalp, his fingers firm but tender. Unknotting all the tension in her body with his touch. All too soon it seemed, it was over. He was rinsing out the suds with the same care, making sure none of the water splashed over her face.

'I've left some towels, and a T-shirt and some sweatpants for you. I'll go and make us something to eat and let you get dressed.' Harrison let her know her private head massage was over and left the bathroom.

Ruby sighed, so relaxed she could have melted into the bubbles. She hadn't realised how much she missed the touch of another person. Or was it Harrison's in particular that she missed? He'd been her safe place, her sanctuary for such a long time, it was easy to get comfortable with him again. Deep down she knew that was asking for trouble, but for tonight at least, she simply needed a little comfort.

She was almost asleep, the bath water cooled now, when Harrison called through to let her know dinner was ready. Although she was feeling better, she didn't have much of an appetite. Since he'd gone out of his way to take care of her tonight the least she could do was keep him company as he ate.

She dried off and slipped into the clothes he'd left her. The oversize casual wear was so comfortable it felt like slipping into a Harrison hug. As close as she was likely to get these days.

'I just made us some chicken soup. I thought that

might help settle your stomach a little. Sit down and I'll bring it over to you.' Harrison in the kitchen was becoming a common sight for her, along with having him looking after her. She knew she should fight against it before she got too used to it, but it was so nice she couldn't find the strength to protest.

'You're really spoiling me tonight.' Ruby took a seat at the dining table and waited for Harrison to join her.

'You deserve it. Plus, I don't really get a chance to have company for dinner. You're the first person I've had over.' He set down a bowl of delicious-smelling homemade soup and a plate of bread. She'd half expected him just to open a tin and heat it on the stove but he'd gone that extra mile. If he was trying to impress her, it was working.

'Surely you cook for other women.' Okay, it was a fishing exercise. She was curious about his personal life and his past relationships since her. It was only natural to wonder who else he'd done this for.

He screwed up his face. 'Not really. I tend to eat out if I have a dinner date. I like to keep things casual.'

'Oh. Okay.' Ruby contemplated that information as she ate her soup. A couple of things struck her. Firstly, that she was receiving special treatment, but also that he wasn't a fan of serious relationships. It hadn't seemed that way when they'd been together, when they'd been making plans for the future. The idea that he didn't want to be tied to anyone made her question if he'd decided that during their marriage or after it. Did it partially explain why he'd left, or, like her, had he been too burned to fully invest in another partner?

'What about you? Did you ever come close to marrying again?' The whole scene should have seemed absurd for her ex-husband to be asking about her love life while she was sitting having dinner with him wearing his clothes. Then again, she'd just had a bath in his house, with him washing her hair for her. The truth was, they'd always had such an easy relationship that even after their years apart they'd fallen into that same groove. Where everything felt natural.

Ruby shook her head. 'I was with Aimee's father for a while obviously, but he didn't stick around once I found out I was pregnant.'

'I'm sorry.'

She shrugged. 'There was no question of me keeping the baby. I wasn't going to lose another child, and he showed his true colours. It's just been me and Aimee since. I've dated on and off but I don't want to confuse her by bringing men home. Besides, I'm too busy with work to have room for a social life.'

'We're a sad pair, aren't we?' he said with a laugh.

'Speak for yourself. I'm very happy with my life.' Ruby bristled. Then she remembered how much advantage she was taking by being here. 'In saying that, it is nice to have someone run me a bath and cook me dinner.'

Tonight had opened her eyes to so many possibilities. Like perhaps dating again so she could have someone look out for her for a change. There was also the fact that she could still have Harrison in her life without the world falling apart. It was clear they had a bond which would take years to form with someone else. As long as they kept things platonic, perhaps she wouldn't have to distance herself from him completely.

Yes, she'd given in to temptation and kissed him, but she was hoping that was simply a hangover from their past. It was so easy being with him that sometimes she forgot they weren't still together. If she opened herself up to the possibility of being with someone else, perhaps Harrison would no longer have such a hold on her.

'My turn next,' he said with a grin.

Though he was only joking, the thought of him in her bath at home, with her washing his hair, was beginning to raise her temperature again. She moved her focus to her soup, doing her best to stop thinking of him in that way before she had to place a total ban on him being in her life. Tonight was proving how much she liked having him back in it. She would simply have to keep her pervy thoughts to a minimum.

'Thank you so much for that,' she said, pushing her empty bowl aside, feeling like a fraud now that her sickness seemed to have passed.

'You're very welcome. Now, your favourite film is on tonight if you want to watch it?' If Harrison had been planning a seduction, he couldn't have done it better, but Ruby knew he was just being kind. It was his way of trying to make it up to her over the past and she had to say, it was working. With every kind gesture, he was reminding her of the man she'd loved, who'd taken such good care of her. Not the one who'd left her heartbroken and grieving on her own.

Harrison didn't want to move. Ruby was asleep on his shoulder, curled up on the couch beside him. He'd never expected her to go along with any of this tonight, but it had proved how out of sorts she was to agree, and how much she'd needed some TLC.

It had felt good to do something nice for her, but he'd be lying if he said it wasn't a struggle for him to keep his feelings at bay. He was doing his best to be there as support, but with every minute they spent together, he was reminded of how it used to be between them. How he felt about her. And that wasn't what either of them needed right now. The bath, dinner and watching her favourite romcom were moments from the past, and as nostalgic as it was, there was no going back.

Here and now, Ruby was simply a sick friend and colleague who needed a good night's sleep. Preferably without him thinking about what the next step used to be after a bath and a cuddle on the couch.

'Ruby?' He gently tried to wake her.

'Hmm?' She began to stir.

'I think you'd be more comfortable in bed. Come on.' He scooped her up into his arms, feeling her slender frame through the baggy clothes she'd been forced to wear.

Strong, capable, confident Ruby wrapped her arms around his neck and nuzzled into him. The fragile woman he knew she could be sometimes beneath the surface. He wondered about the last time she'd been so vulnerable with anyone else, and silently thanked her for letting him offer her comfort this time. Knowing he'd let her down in the past. It took a great deal of trust for her to let her guard down like this and he was honoured. He just hope he deserved it.

Harrison carried her through to his bedroom and set

her down on the mattress. He pulled the covers over her and turned to leave.

'Where are you going?' Ruby mumbled sleepily.

'I'll make up a bed on the couch. You get some sleep and I'll see you in the morning.' With Aimee staying at her grandparents' place for the night anyway it made sense for Ruby to stay here in case she needed help.

'Stay.' She patted the bed.

'I don't think that's a good idea, Ruby...'

'Look, we've already proved we can be around one another without doing too much damage. You washed my hair for goodness' sake. For one night I just want to sleep with someone next to me.'

'You just want some company?' It was going to be a serious test of his restraint to sleep in the bed next to her without reaching for her, but all she was asking was a favour. The least he owed her.

'Be my big spoon,' she said with a pleading smile that made it hard for him to say no to.

It would have been odd for him to get into bed fully clothed, so Harrison did what he usually did going to bed, and stripped down to his boxers. Ruby turned away so he could cuddle up behind her. He slung an arm around her waist and she wriggled back against him so her curvy behind was pressed perilously close against him. Sleep was not going to come easy.

CHAPTER EIGHT

FOR A SPLIT second upon waking up, Ruby thought she'd been caught in a time-slip. She was in bed with her husband and living her happy-ever-after. It was crushing when reality came rushing back to remind her that they were divorced and he was only in bed because she'd begged him to get in beside her.

She cringed at the memory, blaming it on feeling so sick and vulnerable at the time. Simply wanting more of that familiar comfort he'd been providing for her all night. It had been nice falling asleep in his arms, even nicer opening her eyes to see him next to her. She missed this. Being part of a couple, having someone there for her, instead of being on her own. More than that, she missed having all of that with Harrison.

She watched him sleep. So peaceful. So handsome. He was bare-chested, displaying a more mature, muscular physique than the teen Harrison she'd married. It took everything in her not to reach out and touch him, yearning for the sort of closeness and intimacy they'd once had.

His eyes fluttered open and when he saw her watching him, a lazy grin spread across his face, making her pulse flutter.

'Morning,' she said, trying to control her impulse to kiss him.

'How are you feeling?' The fact that it was his first question, his concern for her uppermost in his thoughts, said a lot about him.

'Good. Thank you. I'm sorry if I put you in a difficult situation. I guess I was just feeling sorry for myself.' Although Harrison looked comfortable being in bed with her, she could see now it had been a big ask from his ex-wife. She hadn't really given him a chance to say no regardless of how uncomfortable he might have felt about it.

'It's fine. Best sleep I've had in ages.'

They were so relaxed together in that moment that Ruby voiced what was on her mind. 'Why couldn't we have saved us, Harrison?'

She saw the pain flicker across his face. The same thing she felt every time she thought about what they'd lost. Last night had helped her remember all the good times they'd had together. How great they'd been as a partnership, and how safe he'd made her feel. He still had that same ability, and it was becoming clear that now her anger towards him was dissipating, she still cared for him as much as she ever had.

He let out a heavy sigh before shifting his position so he was sitting upright, the covers falling down to his lap to give her a front-row view of his muscular torso. But now wasn't the time to be ogling her ex-husband, who appeared to be gearing up for a serious conversation. Ruby sat up beside him, their easy, lazy morning apparently over.

* * *

Harrison couldn't seem to block out the inner voice shouting, *Tell her*, in his ear. She'd put so much trust in him last night by letting him take care of her, he wanted to do the same in return. To open up and finally tell her about his brother, and why the miscarriage had devastated him to such an extent that he'd ended their marriage. She deserved a full explanation and he felt close enough to her right now for her to be the one person he felt comfortable confiding in.

'I wasn't completely honest with you about the reason I left, Ruby.'

He felt her bristle beside him and knew he had to expand before she got the wrong idea. 'I was crushed by losing the baby, and I did fall into a deep depression, that's all true. But I never told you the whole story.'

'I'm listening,' she said softly, her big blue eyes watching him, waiting for the truth.

It would be so much easier simply to kiss her again, because they had a habit of forgetting everything else when they were lost to the passion between them, but this felt like the right time to have that conversation he'd been avoiding for too long.

Last night, cuddled up next to her, feeling the soft curve of her behind pressed against him had been torturous, but also comforting. He'd forgotten what it was like to be so close to someone, physically…and emotionally. These past years he'd been so determined to protect himself, relationships had been casual, so when they ended it didn't hurt so much. That meant sleepovers were kept to a minimum, and he certainly didn't run baths, cook dinner and just cuddle with anyone else in his life. Ruby did, and probably always would, hold a special piece of his heart.

He wished he'd been able to share everything about the loss of his brother with her, but it had been too painful and he hadn't wanted to seem weak. Then, when everything had come crashing down, he hadn't wanted to burden her with that extra layer of grief he'd been struggling with. Now, however, he could see how much that had contributed to the breakdown of their marriage. That lack of communication, that inability to admit he needed help, let her think the worst of him. He didn't know what the future held for them but it was time to open up about the part of his life he'd kept to himself for too long.

'When we lost the baby it brought back a lot of unhappy memories for me. Something I never told you, never told anyone, was that I lost my big brother, Joey, when I was eleven years old.' Saying the words alone felt like a weight lifted from his shoulders, even if his voice still wobbled when he spoke about it.

'You had a brother? We've known each other for years. Been married for goodness' sake. Why couldn't you tell me?' The disbelief in Ruby's voice was to be expected. They'd shared so much with each other and been such a big part of one another's lives. It must feel like a betrayal of sorts that he'd kept that information from her.

His parents, divorced by then, hadn't really been an active part of his life. Harrison had spent most of his time at Ruby's family home when they were younger, so it had been easy to avoid the subject. He'd never outright lied, and like Ruby, most people assumed he was an only child. Something he'd never corrected when it would have meant pouring out the whole tragic story, which was too hard for him to do. It was easier for him to try and set aside that dark time of his life rather than talk about it. At least, until they lost the baby, then everything seemed to have hit him at once.

'I'm sorry. It was just too difficult for me to talk about him. I idolised Joey. He was more of a parent to me than Mom and Dad ever were. Always looking out for me.' Harrison couldn't help but smile. Telling her that brought back some of the happier memories he often forgot when all he could remember was how bereft he'd been left after his brother's death.

After a minute of silence, Ruby finally asked, 'What happened?'

That meant Harrison having to face the bad memories again. He closed his eyes, picturing that night. Sitting at the top of the stairs, seeing the coloured lights from the police car shining through the front door, listening to his parents' wails of anguish, and knowing life would never be the same.

'It was a hit and run driver. He was walking home from a party and killed instantly.'

'I'm so sorry, Harrison.' Ruby was such an empathetic person he could see his own pain reflected in her teary eyes. It gave him some comfort that she understood how hard it had been for him then, and now.

'Did they ever get who did it?'

He shook his head. That had been as difficult to accept as losing his brother. That someone had robbed him of his best friend and got away with it, never brought to justice and able to get on with the life Joey had been denied.

'Unfortunately not. It was likely another partygoer who'd been drinking. There were no witnesses, no evidence. Just my brother lying at the side of the road in the rain.' His voice broke as he was forced to imagine that scene again. His big brother cold and alone, not knowing how much his little brother wished he'd been there with him to hold his hand and tell him how loved he'd been.

'Then you never got closure.'

'I guess not. It destroyed my parents. They split up and I moved away with my mom. You know the rest.' He gave her as much of a smile as he could muster. Meeting Ruby had been his redemption. Given him something to live for again. Made him feel loved again.

'Why didn't you tell me?' she asked softly.

'I just couldn't. It was too painful. We didn't talk about him at home anymore and I just didn't know how to handle that overwhelming grief and sense of loss. It was easier to pretend that part of my life had never happened.' It almost felt like a betrayal to have wiped those early years hanging out with Joey and simply being a kid. After his death, Harrison was forced to grow up, the innocence of his childhood over.

'We were married, Harrison. Supposed to be a family. How could you keep that part of you closed off from me?'

He was ashamed of himself for being so weak that he felt he couldn't share that part of him. The sadness, the hole in his heart he didn't imagine that even Ruby could fix, so he didn't want to burden her with it.

'I—I thought I had to be the strong one in the relationship. I didn't want you to see that side of me. To think less of me. Then it went on for so long it never seemed right to tell you. I knew you'd be upset and it was easier just to keep that part of my life to myself. I'm sorry.' In hindsight, that was probably what had ultimately destroyed their relationship. His inability to open his heart fully to Ruby because it hurt too much to confront that part of his life. Something he'd only dealt with when it had been too late to save their marriage.

'I'm sorry you felt you couldn't share that with me.'

'I suppose I was acting the way my parents had by trying to just shut it out. Then when the miscarriage happened—'

'It all came flooding back.' Ruby understood. As she always would have if he'd been brave enough back then to let her in.

'I'm sorry I wasn't there for you. I know I've said it before, but I hope you understand why. I can't change what happened, or how I acted—'

'Ssh.' Ruby put her finger on his lips. 'I understand. I do. That grief of losing the baby was double for you because you hadn't fully dealt with losing your brother.'

'I just…yeah, I'm sorry.'

'I guess it helps knowing that. Not that you were suffering so much, but that it wasn't because you just wanted out of the relationship.'

'Definitely not. It killed me staying away, but in the end, I thought you'd be better off without me. I'd left it too long to go back, and just couldn't find the words to express what I was going through. It was never you.

You were the only good thing in my life.' Losing Ruby too, on top of everything else, had been what had tipped him over the edge, regardless that it had been his own doing. And now she was back in his life, in his bed, he knew he was treading a dangerous path.

Ruby leaned her head against his shoulder and took his hand in hers. 'I wish we'd been able to talk about this before now. I spent years being angry at you, and blaming myself that I hadn't been enough for you to stay.'

'That was never the case.'

Her sad smile up at him was heartbreaking. 'But I didn't know that, did I? I didn't know that neither of us were to blame, or that you were working through such difficult personal issues aside from our own loss.'

'Because I didn't tell you.' He nodded.

'Right, and we've wasted all this time bogged down in the past when all we needed was to talk.' The pain in her eyes was difficult to see when he knew he was responsible for putting it there. It was Harrison's fault he hadn't told her about Joey and how much his death had affected him. He didn't know what he hoped to gain from telling her now other than closure when it was too late for their relationship.

'I guess then you wouldn't have Aimee.' He could never have denied her the chance to be a mother, even if it meant that he wasn't part of that family. There was no way of telling how things would have panned out if they'd managed to save their relationship, and he couldn't punish himself forever over what had happened. He simply had to accept it.

'True. I just… I loved you, you know.' Ruby didn't have to tell him, he did know. That's what had broken his heart.

'I loved you too.' He didn't think he'd ever stopped.

Ruby looked up at him, her gaze full of regret, and what he thought was a longing to relive the good times they'd shared. It seemed right to bend down and kiss her. To lean into that bond they'd created all those years ago, but which hadn't seemed to dissipate. The soft touch of her lips felt like home. A time when everything had been good. When he was happy. Something he thought he'd never be again after Joey died. It was easy to imagine they were back there, carefree in their love nest. Especially when she was wrapping her arms around his neck, deepening the fantasy with him.

Before he knew it she was straddling his waist, making sure his whole body was wide awake.

'Are we really going to do this?' he mumbled against her lips, aware there would be consequences later of giving in to temptation now.

She put her finger on his lips again. 'Shh.'

An indication that she didn't want to think beyond this moment, and if Harrison was honest, neither did he. Because then he'd have to stop Ruby from kissing him the way she was right now. His face cupped in her hands, and her mouth latched onto his. Every flick of her tongue against his fuelling his desire and eroding any reason for putting a stop to this.

Ruby stripped off his sweatshirt, revealing her body to his lusting gaze. Motherhood had given her a fuller, womanly figure and he was here for it. Her full breasts pressed close to his chest as she continued to kiss him, desire overtaking every thought except the need for one another.

Harrison took possession of her breasts in the palms of his hands, kneading, massaging, hearing her gasp, seeing her close her eyes and give in to the sensation. He flicked his tongue over her nipple, teasing until it was puckered and standing to attention. Ready for him to take fully in his mouth, sucking, grazing to tip with his teeth, until she was bucking against him with want.

Harrison wasn't sure if this moment was something borne of nostalgia, or an exploration of potentially something new. What he did know was that he didn't want it to end. He'd never had a physical relationship with anyone like the one he'd had with Ruby. Likely because they had that emotional connection he did his best to avoid making these days. They'd loved one another. Deep down, he knew that love was still there. Mixed in with that passion which had been reawakened with their first touch, it made for an explosive time in the bedroom. Something it seemed they were both keen to revisit.

Harrison grabbed her by the hips and rolled her over so he was on top. Their bodies entwined, but that frustrating barrier of fabric prevented them from being completely as one.

He whipped down the loose sweatpants in one smooth action, with Ruby helping to kick them away. Her hands were on the waistband of his boxers pushing them out of the way, and releasing him fully to her exploration. That feeling of her first touch felt like letting out a too-long-held breath. As though he'd been waiting for it, needing it to survive.

Ruby took hold of his erection, claiming it with a possessive hand that made him gasp. And when she moved it up and down his shaft he thought he might explode. If this was the only time he got to be with her, he was going to make sure it would be one to remember for both of them. For all the right reasons.

He grabbed hold of her hand, then the other, before pinning them to the bed above her head. Ruby's eyes glittered as she watched him move his way down her body, pressing feather-light kisses across her skin. Teasing them both.

He felt her tense when he reached her belly, squirming as he released her hands from his grasp and dipped lower.

'Harrison...' It was a plea for him to relieve her frustration and he was only too willing to oblige.

Moving farther down the bed, positioned between her legs, he licked a path along her inner thigh. Her little groan of pleasure helping to steel his own arousal.

And when he lapped her core with the flat of his tongue, and dipped inside her, he was nearly undone himself. Her arousal was instant, as though she too had been waiting for this moment for too long.

In no time at all she was quivering beneath him, crying out as her climax came at his behest. Harrison couldn't wait any longer for his own satisfaction and once he'd donned a condom, he slid easily inside her with one thrust. Her tight heat encompassed him as he joined their bodies together. He felt uncharacteristically emotional about reconnecting this way with Ruby, but channelled that swell of emotion into a physical display to show her how much he still cared for her. Taking his time to make her feel as good as he did. Doing his best to erase those difficult memories and replace them with all new erotically charged ones.

With her limbs wrapped around him, clinging to him as though her life depended on it, Ruby climbed that peak of ecstasy with Harrison. And when he finally surrendered to that ultimate satisfaction, she came with him for a second time. Her body quivering and tensing, before finally turning liquid around him.

He wanted to stay here forever, pretending that they'd never parted. That they hadn't gone their separate ways, or led completely different lives. He'd never regretted what had happened more between them in the past than he did right now. Knowing he could have had this forever, sharing more than his bed and his body with someone. Being part of someone else's life, and having Ruby be part of his on a permanent basis. The reminder of what he'd been missing out on with her for all of these years cut deep.

Harrison lay down beside Ruby on the bed with a sigh.

'What's wrong?' she asked, pulling the bedsheet up to cover her nakedness, her brow knitted into a worried frown.

He was tempted to pretend he was fine, that he was the carefree happy bachelor he portrayed to everyone else, but he didn't want to lie to Ruby. Keeping his feelings from her had been what had caused their split in the first place. If he wanted her to be in his life again in any capacity, this time around he had to be open with her.

'I just… I don't know. Tonight's made me nostalgic I suppose for the life we used to have together.' He knew there was no point in looking back when they couldn't change the past, and he'd already told her that he didn't begrudge her going on to have her own family. It didn't mean he wasn't pining for that lost time.

Ruby shifted over and laid her head on his chest, her body pressed against his side. 'We can't live life with regret, Harrison. It's difficult enough.'

'I guess I'm just wondering what happens next. If this is it.' Now they'd rekindled that passionate fire, it would be hard to put it out and forget it had ever sparked to life. It would be impossible to see her at work and pretend this had never happened. That he didn't want her with every fibre of his being.

Harrison didn't want to sound needy, but this was a big deal to him. Being with Ruby was completely different to spending the night with anyone else. There was a lot more at stake, and he needed to know for his own peace of mind what he might be getting himself into. Either to prepare himself for disappointment if this thing between them didn't go anywhere beyond the here and now, or to completely reassess his attitude to relationships if Ruby wanted more from him than a place in his bed.

He never thought he'd be in this position again, but if there was one person that could persuade him to open his heart, to risk it on a relationship, it would be Ruby.

Regardless that she was the one woman who'd caused him to shut off that part of himself in the first place. When loving someone meant being afraid to lose them, and made him weak.

It was Ruby's turn to sigh. 'I don't know, Harrison. It seems too soon to be talking about the future when we've only just reconciled the past.'

'I guess I'm just asking if this is a one-time deal?'

With her fingers tracing circles across his chest she looked up at him coquettishly. 'I hope not.'

'So…'

'So, I'm not ready for anything serious but I'm enjoying this.' She reached up and kissed him full on the mouth. There was no arguing with her logic. By not putting a label on the nature of their relationship, it removed some of the fear of getting involved with her again. There was no pressure of commitment, of having to open up completely. Tentatively getting to know one another and being part of one another's lives again gave them permission to be together without promising forever. It was only natural that they should both be cautious this time around when the past had been so painful.

'Me too.' Harrison wrapped his arms around her, relishing the skin contact that reminded every part of him that Ruby was back in his life.

Ruby laid her head on Harrison's chest with a contented smile on her face, listening to the steady beat of his heart. A reassuring sound that always used to help her sleep, knowing he was there, making her feel safe.

She wanted to feel that way again after years of being too afraid to give herself completely to another man.

There was no promise that Harrison would be in her life forever, but perhaps that was preferable to believing he would be, only for him to let her down. This was enough for now. This feeling of connection, of passion with a man who already knew her so well, was more than she'd had in a long time. If nothing else, perhaps having this chance to be together would eventually give them closure on the past. Something they both desperately seemed to need.

The revelation about his brother, his depression and subsequent withdrawal from her life were things they'd never had the opportunity to work through together. Some time together now might help them move forward. Whether that would be together was yet to be determined. Caution was called for even though she was keen to share his bed again. She wasn't ready for anyone to be a permanent fixture in her—or her daughter's—life, but Harrison was managing to help remove some of those barriers she'd built. Letting her believe for the first time in years that perhaps she wouldn't be alone for the rest of her days. That eventually she might find someone who loved her enough to stick around.

If she was willing to risk letting Harrison back in her life, she might find it easier to let others close in the future. As long as she didn't let him break her heart all over again.

Only time would tell if she was making a huge mistake by listening to her heart instead of her head.

CHAPTER NINE

'How are you feeling?' Harrison asked Ruby as they passed one another in the hospital corridor.

The sight of him instantly made her smile, and want to crawl back into bed with him.

'Good. Tired.' Not that she was complaining. Her lack of sleep was a direct result of enjoying more of his sexual prowess between the sheets. Although it had meant for a frantic day at home trying to get everything done, and pick up Aimee from school to take to her mother's, all before she started another shift.

They'd been juggling their schedules for over a week now, trying to spend time together when they could. That had meant confiding in her mother too in order to get a babysitter when needed. Of course her mother wasn't happy that they'd rekindled their relationship, but Ruby had assured her it wasn't anything serious. Not that that detail had convinced her letting Harrison Blake back into their lives in any shape or form was a good idea.

Ruby was still a little wary herself. Although they were doing their best not to rush into anything serious, it felt as though they couldn't get enough of one another. Even now, just talking to him here she wanted to bundle him off into a private room and have her wicked way with him again. It was like being a teenager all over again. Heart beating quicker every time she thought of him, thoughts occupied by when she'd see him again. Dangerous territory she knew, but so intoxicating. That rush of blood in her veins, that excitement, was something she hadn't realised she needed in her life. She'd been so afraid of getting hurt, of messing things up at home for Aimee, Ruby had kept things safe. Predictable. Whilst she'd been comfortable with that routine, being with Harrison had reminded her there was more to life if she was willing to take a risk every now and then. She just hoped she didn't lose everything again because she'd put her faith and trust in those feelings. In the wrong man.

Harrison started to reach a hand out to her before snatching it away again. 'You know I really want to kiss you.'

'Me too,' she whispered. In line with keeping things casual, they didn't want any of their work colleagues to know there was anything going on between them. Plus, they still had to remain professional. It simply meant that desire kept bubbling away all day until they got to be alone. Making their quality time together all the more special.

'When am I going to have you to myself again?'

'I'm off tomorrow night if you are? I hear it's someone special's birthday…'

Harrison's eyes lit up as brightly as his smile. 'You remembered?'

'Of course.' She didn't tell him that she'd remembered every year since their split, and it had become a day of reflection and sadness for her. Hopefully this one would be different.

'I hadn't anything planned so maybe we could go out somewhere?' There was a hope in his eyes that she didn't want to dim, even though being seen out together was something they'd avoided so far.

Yes, they were being cautious. Overly, perhaps. With the fact they were sleeping together on a regular basis, going out shouldn't be such a big deal for them. Except perhaps that it was venturing out of the bedroom and into the real world. Which meant taking their relationship somewhere else. Deep down, Ruby knew that was what she wanted, she was simply too afraid to ask for it, or take that leap. For now, they'd have to take things one step at a time and hope things didn't blow up in their faces again.

'I'd like that. What about the prize you won at the casino? Maybe you could cash that in and we could make a proper night of it. Dinner, a night in a hotel…'

'Sold,' he said with a grin. 'I'll contact the casino and make arrangements, then we'll celebrate tomorrow.'

'Can't wait.' Ruby would be counting the hours until they could be together again, and praying the painful part of their history wouldn't repeat itself a second time.

Harrison couldn't remember the last time he felt this excited about a date, or his birthday. Neither were usually a particularly big deal to him, until tonight. This was different. He was getting to spend his birthday with Ruby, doing things that normal couples did. Of course, they hadn't put a name to their relationship status, but it seemed to be heading in that direction. Being a couple. He was beginning to realise that was what he wanted with her.

It was early days, but they had so much history already it was difficult not to get ahead of himself. There was still a lot for them to sort through, and he knew Ruby's life was complicated with Aimee. He couldn't just swan in and expect to be part of the family, even if he was ready for that, which he wasn't. Tonight was simply the first step out of their comfort zone. Testing the waters. Providing neither of them got too freaked out by going out as a couple, it could be the start of something new. A life he could share with someone.

The limo pulled up outside Ruby's apartment. He'd made the arrangements with the casino for their night and wanted to pick her up as though it were a proper date. Dressed to impress hopefully, he'd donned a suit and white dress shirt, and made his way to her front door carrying a bunch of red roses. Cliché, perhaps, but he owed her some tender loving care along with a smidge of romance.

When she opened the door he was almost lost for words at the sight. She was wearing a sleeveless silver sequinned minidress that showed off her fabulous legs, with a low-cut neck displaying her cleavage.

'Too much?' she asked, giving him a twirl.

'You look…amazing,' he managed to stutter eventually.

'These are for you.' He handed over the bouquet and she inhaled the scent.

'Thank you. I can't remember the last time anyone bought me flowers. I'll just put them in some water and grab my bag. Come on in.' She opened the door wider granting him access.

Harrison stepped into the hall to be greeted by Aimee, who threw herself at him. 'Hi, Harrison. Doesn't Mommy look pretty?'

'Yes, she does, Aimee. Very pretty.'

'Aimee, go back inside and finish your dinner.' Ruby's mother appeared wearing a cross expression, and Harrison suddenly felt like a nervous schoolboy.

'Hello again, Mrs Jones.'

'Don't you dare hurt her again.' It was all she said before turning and walking away, leaving Harrison calling after her.

'I won't. I swear.'

'What was all that about?' Ruby asked on her return, sensing the tense atmosphere between them.

'Me and your mother are just getting reacquainted. Now, are you all set for the night of your life?'

'That's a big promise,' she laughed as they made their way to the sleek black limousine provided for the evening.

'One I fully intend living up to,' Harrison whispered in her ear, feeling her tremble as he wrapped an arm around her waist.

They strapped themselves into the back seat and Harrison was able to show off all the extras which had been provided for them. At the push of a button music began to play, a disco ball began to spin and LED lights lit the interior of the vehicle.

'*Now* it's a party,' he said, pouring the bottle of champagne the casino had included and handing a glass to Ruby.

'Happy birthday.' She clinked her flute to his and he couldn't resist her for a second longer, leaning in for a kiss.

'I've been waiting to do that since yesterday,' he said, once they eventually broke apart.

Ruby leaned her forehead against his and he knew she'd been feeling the same way.

'So, where are we going?'

'I thought we could go to a drive-through chapel and get married.'

She narrowed her eyes at him. 'Not funny.'

'Sorry. I just thought we could do a tour of the strip. Be tourists for the night. Then we'll have dinner, a little wine and bed.' He kissed her neck, making his way slowly to the spot behind her ear he knew drove her insane.

'Sounds good.' Her breathy reply said they were both on the same page and their date was simply foreplay for the night they knew they were going to spend in bed together.

She leaned her head against his shoulder as they made their way along the strip. The bright lights and glitz of the world outside no competition for the feel-good factor of being here with Ruby.

They cruised along the main streets people-watching and enjoying the sights cuddled up together. Street performers entertaining them as well as the crowds with magic tricks and dance-offs. As much fun as it looked out there being part of the scene, he was happy being here in their little bubble. He didn't know how long this bliss could last. Experience had taught him not to get too lost in it, because when that bubble burst he ended up broken and alone. But it was hard not to wish this could be forever.

Suddenly, the car came to a sharp stop, almost sending them head first into the partition glass between them and the driver.

The chauffeur immediately lowered the glass to speak. 'Apologies, sir. There's an accident up ahead. We might have to sit here for some time.'

'Is anyone hurt?' he asked, but the driver couldn't see from his position exactly what had happened.

Harrison couldn't in good conscience sit here knowing someone could be hurt. 'I'm just going to take a look and see what's going on.'

He unclipped his seat belt only to find Ruby doing the same.

'What? You're not going without me. I'm the ER nurse, remember?'

She had a point and he wasn't going to start arguing when he knew she likely had more experience in this area than he ever would.

They stepped out onto the road where cars and crowds of people were creating obstacles to the scene of the accident. Harrison took Ruby's hand and guided her around the stationary vehicles until they reached the site where a man was lying prostate on the ground and a truck was half on the pavement, half on the road, the hood caved in. It didn't take a genius to work out it had hit a pedestrian.

'Are you okay to do this?' Ruby asked. Even though he'd only recently confided in her about his brother's death, she was already anticipating how triggering this scene could be for him. Thankfully, therapy and time had helped him to deal better with situations like this and he was able to compartmentalise to a certain degree so he could treat the patient in the moment. Of course, that didn't mean he wouldn't think of his brother at all, but at least he was able to function these days. It also helped having Ruby here with him, understanding how this could affect him and being there in a professional capacity to back him up too.

Harrison nodded. 'I'll check on the driver.'

'I'll take the pedestrian.'

They went their separate ways to check on both casualties while they waited for the paramedics to get here, in case anyone needed their immediate attention.

Harrison opened the cab door of the truck and the stench of alcohol filled his nostrils. He had to fight the rising swell of anger building inside to reach out to the driver.

'Sir, can you hear me? I'm a doctor. You've been in an accident. Can you tell me if you've been hurt?'

The man groaned and lifted his head from the steering wheel where it was resting.

'Sir? Can you hear me?' Harrison tried to look in the man's eyes as he had a head injury and he wanted to assess him for possible concussion, but the man batted him away.

'Leave me alone.' His words were slurred, his breath stinking of booze. In that situation it was difficult not to think about his brother, who'd been hit and left to die at the side of the road. It was likely by a drunk driver, though they'd never been identified to confirm that theory. This was another selfish man whose actions could have caused the death of another, but he still had to treat him the way he would any patient.

'Sir, you have a head injury. Possible concussion.' Harrison couldn't get close enough to examine the wound on the man's forehead, but at least he was conscious and talking, if belligerent.

'Get out of here.' The driver gave him a shove so he stumbled back.

At that point a police officer had arrived on scene so Harrison addressed him. 'I'm a doctor. I didn't see what happened but the driver appears to have a head injury. He's not being cooperative.'

'Thank you. I'll take it from here. The paramedics are on the way.' The officer would likely figure out for himself that he was dealing with a drunk driver and, reassured that his assistance was no longer required, Harrison went to help Ruby.

'Can I do anything to help?' he asked, kneeling down beside the injured pedestrian, where Ruby was hunched over the man.

'He's unconscious, unresponsive, breathing shallow, pulse weak.' As she relayed her assessment, the man suddenly began fitting.

Ruby worked quickly to undo the zipper of his hoodie to provide him some breathing room. Harrison stripped off his jacket and bundled it around the man's head. It was possible the fit was a direct result of his head hitting the pavement, and all they could do was wait until it subsided. Making sure that he wasn't in danger of swallowing his tongue or injuring himself further.

'Can you help me move him into the recovery position?' Ruby asked, once the man began to still again.

Between them they managed to roll him onto his side so he didn't choke if he vomited. Another police officer arrived bringing a first aid kit and a foil blanket to cover him with.

'Thanks,' Harrison said, accepting the offered items. 'We don't want to move him until the paramedics get here. They will stabilise him with a neck brace and back-board to prevent any further injury.'

'How bad are his injuries?'

'We won't know until he's had a CT scan but I think he's sustained a serious head injury.' Ruby was calm and clear as she conversed with the officer and in that moment Harrison was unbelievably proud of the woman she'd become.

More than that, he knew he was still in love with her. That was why he'd carried on seeing her, sleeping with her, and he couldn't fool himself any longer that this was merely some sort of casual fling. The question now was whether or not he was brave enough to act on his feelings this time. To be honest and put himself out there, regardless of the consequences.

* * *

'Hey, Wyatt.' Ruby greeted the paramedic, glad to be handing over responsibility of the scene.

His eyes widened at the sight of her. 'Wow. You scrub up well, Rubes.'

'Thank you.' Ruby blushed, and felt Harrison bristle beside her. There was no need for him to feel jealous but the fact that he did gave her a little thrill. Perhaps he wasn't as relaxed about their relationship as he suggested. She knew she wasn't. Although the night wasn't going as planned, it had proved to her that her feelings for her ex-husband weren't completely resigned to the past. He was back to being her safe place. The man she could cuddle up to, or who would back her up in a medical emergency. A risky turn of events when it was still so important that she protected herself from getting hurt again.

Once she and Harrison had given all relevant information and observations on the casualties, they made their way back to the limousine where the driver was clapping them for their assistance. Ruby was glad to get back into the anonymity of the blacked out car, away from the crowds and the pressure to be strong.

When Harrison closed the car door, she immediately curled up beside him on the back seat. 'I'm sorry your birthday didn't work out as planned.'

'It's not over yet.' He lifted the remainder of the bottle of champagne from the ice bucket and poured out another two glasses.

She grimaced as she looked down at her ruined dress covered in dirt and blood. 'I'm not sure I'm really dressed for dinner anymore.'

'Nor me. Maybe we can get room service instead.' Harrison sounded as weary as she felt. The adrenaline rush from the drama now leaving her body, so all that Ruby wanted to do now was crash out. Thank goodness they appeared to be on the same page. They always had been which was what had made them such a good team in the past.

'Sounds good.' She sipped at her champagne, though it was making her sleepy rather than fuelling her for a night on the town.

Once the ambulance had left the scene and the traffic began to move again, Harrison directed the driver to take them to the hotel where they had a suite waiting for them. He'd already checked in, so they were able to go on up to the penthouse in the elevator, bypassing too much public scrutiny of their bloodstained clothes.

The room was like nothing she'd ever seen before except on television. Marble floors, gold embossed wallpaper, and crystal chandeliers hanging from the high ceiling. Full-length windows all around gave a full view of the city lights below, with enough couches dotted around the vast space to accommodate an entourage.

'We could have a real party in here if you wanted.' She walked over to the bar area which was fully stocked with every drink imaginable. It seemed overkill for just the two of them.

Harrison grabbed hold of her and pulled her hard against his body. 'I prefer it being just us.'

He kissed her slowly and thoroughly until she was sure her legs were about to give way beneath her. Then

Ruby took him by the hand and led him towards the master bedroom. A vast room dominated by the bed in the middle. Dark panelled walls, modern monochrome geometric patterned carpet and angular lamps made it into a sleek space. Not least because of the floor-to-ceiling windows.

'I wanted to let you unwrap your birthday present,' she said, stripping off her dress to reveal the sexy lingerie she'd bought specially for the occasion.

'Happy birthday to me,' Harrison growled before lunging towards her.

Ruby let out a squeal as she backed up onto the high bed. He kissed her and pushed her gently back onto the mattress, with his body fully covering hers. She heard his shoes drop to the floor as he kicked them off, and the rustle of his shirt as he pulled it out of his pants and over his head without unbuttoning it. The urgency he was showing to get naked with her was such a turn-on.

He kissed her all over, every touch a distraction from the thoughts in her head telling her she needed to know if he was going to commit to her. When Harrison was peeling away her underwear, tasting every part of her with his tongue, she didn't care about anything else.

There was a feverish need for one another she suspected had been ramped up by their restraint at work, and the adrenaline rush from the accident scene. So much so, neither of them seemed to want to take things slowly for once.

Harrison stripped away the rest of his clothes and only stopped to put on a condom before thrusting into her in one fluid movement to bring her instant satisfaction. She felt complete, content and happy. Then he began to move and elevated her into that now familiar state of bliss.

Life with Harrison had never been boring, always passionate and exciting, and that hadn't changed at least. Ruby knew she didn't want to be without him, or those feelings he elicited within her, for another day, never mind another fifteen years. They didn't have to move in together or remarry to cement their relationship status. All they had to do was take another chance on one another and try to get it right this time.

Harrison's climax came just as Ruby let go too, both giving themselves over to that overwhelming pleasure. He was able to lose himself with Ruby so easy it should have terrified him after spending years holding back from any sort of emotional attachment. Except he knew this was everything. Being with the woman who'd always had his heart.

'We didn't even close the window blinds,' she giggled as he lay down beside her.

'I think we were both too preoccupied to care, though I don't think anyone can see what we're getting up to here.' Despite potentially exposing themselves to the outside world, neither made a move to cover themselves. Apart from being on the top floor of the building, the room was dimly lit, and people were more likely paying attention to the fireworks going off outside rather than the ones inside the hotel room.

'Look, they've put on a show just for us.' Ruby spooned against his naked body in their increasingly familiar post-coital position. She wasn't always able to stay for the night because of Aimee and work obligations, so tonight made a pleasant change. Especially since his bed seemed so empty the moment she left.

'It's only fair since we put one on for everyone else,' he teased, earning himself a playful slap on the backside.

'I'm sorry we didn't get to celebrate your birthday the way we'd planned, Harrison.'

'I'm not complaining. Although I think I've worked up an appetite, along with a thirst. I'll call for room service once I've recovered the use of my limbs.' He didn't want to move at all, content to lie here with Ruby in his arms, but he would need sustenance when he planned to spend the night showing her just how he felt about her.

'Harrison?'

'Mmm?' He was doing his best not to drift off to sleep, though he was so comfortable and content it was a tough call.

Ruby twisted around so she was facing him, her breasts pressed tightly against his chest and helping to keep him awake.

'Do you think perhaps we should introduce you to Aimee as my partner, instead of just a friend?' She was worrying her bottom lip with her teeth, clearly anxious about raising the matter with him.

Harrison knew she wouldn't suggest it if she wasn't serious about being with him, and that meant moving their relationship into more permanent territory. Something they'd both said they didn't want, but he'd come to the conclusion it was all he wanted. He was glad

Ruby had been seeing their time together as something special enough to move to the next stage. A huge deal for both of them, but given how well things had been going for them, not a huge surprise. It was a relief to know that he was more than a casual fling to her when being with her was the highlight of his day.

'Is that what you want?' That in itself was a big step. It meant a commitment to Aimee too, and a promise not to hurt either of them. Ruby knew that and she would never suggest such a thing if she wasn't putting her trust in him. After how their marriage had ended Harrison knew it was a leap of faith for her and he didn't want to let her, or Aimee, down. He just hoped he lived up to expectation.

'Only if you do. I don't want to pressure you into a commitment you're not ready for.'

'We can take it slowly. We don't want to cause Aimee a big upheaval. Why don't I just tag along on days out, or come over for dinner until she gets used to me?' A gentle introduction for all of them for a new dynamic. Having a family wasn't something he'd considered since they'd lost their baby, and being invited to join Ruby's felt like a huge responsibility. As much as he would like the fairy tale ending, he wanted some time to accept the new nature of their relationship too.

A challenge he was ready to meet if it meant having Ruby in his life permanently.

CHAPTER TEN

'HARRISON IS GOING to take us out for burger and fries, Aimee. Is that okay with you?' Ruby had waited until Harrison had arrived at the front door before sharing that information with her daughter. It was such a huge thing for her to introduce a man into Aimee's life, even if Harrison was already known to them both.

Since their night on the town a few weeks ago when they'd both voiced a desire to take their relationship to the next level Harrison had dropped by to watch a movie with them, or to have dinner. Just so Aimee got used to having him around before Ruby was upfront about the nature of their relationship.

She knew her mother didn't approve and that was only natural after she'd watched Ruby's suffering the first time she'd been with Harrison. Still, her parents were always there to babysit when she wanted to spend time with Harrison and didn't try to interfere, and she respected them for that.

'Sure. Can we get milkshakes too?' Her daughter was more easily persuaded onboard. Ruby had always worried it would be too big of an upheaval introducing a male figure into their lives, or perhaps it had simply been a convenient excuse to keep everyone else at arm's length. Harrison was slotting into the family nicely. As though he was always meant to be part of it. That's what scared her. If something happened now, if he were to disappear out of their lives the way he had out of hers before, she'd be devastated all over again. An even greater loss now that they were becoming the family they were always supposed to have been, and she didn't want Aimee to go through the same heartbreak if he walked out on her too.

'If your mom says it's okay.' Harrison checked with her before agreeing to anything. He was learning. Setting boundaries in place so that Aimee didn't think she could wrap him around her little finger to get her own way. Since Harrison seemed equally as besotted with her as she was with him, there was a very good chance of that happening.

"Okay."

'Yay,' her daughter exclaimed at the answering nod. Aimee grabbed Ruby's hand, and Harrison's, swinging between them as they made their way to the car.

It was hard not to get carried away with this comfortable feeling of the three of them together, because it was perfect. Too perfect. Harrison had become such an integral part of her work life, family life and her love life, she couldn't imagine living without him again. She hoped she would never have to.

Once Aimee was strapped into the back seat, Ruby got into the passenger seat, with Harrison driving. This marked their first trip out as a trio. To anyone on the outside they would have looked like any other happy family and she hoped this was only the start. That there would be plenty more trips like this until they were all comfortable with that label. Safe in the knowledge that nothing was going to ruin it.

They drove to an old-fashioned diner on the outskirts of the neighbourhood. She wasn't sure who was more excited about lunch, Harrison or Aimee, by the way the two bounded in, chattering about what they were going to order. Ruby loved the casual, relaxed atmosphere of the family-friendly place, which was all red leather booths and chrome bar-stools. A proper '50s-style hang-out complete with black-and-white-chequered floor and waitresses wearing cute pink sweaters and poodle skirts.

'What can I get you folks?' The gum-chewing pony-tailed waitress asked once they'd had a chance to view the laminated menus.

'Can I have a cheeseburger, please?' Aimee asked, proud of herself for being able to order her own dinner. Tonight made all the more special because Ruby usually kept fast food to a minimum, preferring to cook fresh, wholesome food when she was home. It would be nice for the three of them to have dinner every night. Coming home to Harrison and even having someone to help her. Real teamwork.

'And Dad?' The question directed at Harrison seemed to throw him, colour infusing his cheeks. He glanced at Ruby, then Aimee, as though expecting them to get upset by the misunderstanding.

'I, er—'

'You said you were getting a cheeseburger and fries too,' Aimee prompted him without a hint of confusion or upset. She'd accepted Harrison so readily as part of her life that Ruby wondered if she'd been waiting, ready for her mother to find someone again. Or, just like her mother, perhaps Harrison made her feel safe and loved enough to let him into her life too.

'That's right, and strawberry milkshakes.' Harrison flashed Aimee a smile and in that second Ruby wished he were her real father. They already had a connection and she knew he'd protect Aimee with his life. More than her ex had managed.

'Mom?' the waitress asked, unaware of the significance of her mistake. Not one of them had taken umbrage or thought to correct her. The three of them knew Harrison wasn't Aimee's father but he was slowly fitting into that role so it hadn't seemed to matter that a stranger would assume it as fact.

'Make that three of everything.' Ruby handed over the menus and sat back, watching her daughter and her ex-husband chatting as though they'd known one another their whole lives.

When Harrison looked up and caught her watching him, the contented smile he gave her made Ruby's heart flip. She just hoped this picture-perfect life wasn't too good to be true.

'Do you have any plans for later this afternoon?' Harrison asked once they'd cleared their plates and filled their bellies.

'I'm all yours,' Ruby said with a grin, causing his body to stir with interest which he was forced to quell for now. Hopefully later, once Aimee was in bed, they'd be able to act on it. He was aware they needed to take things slowly in front of her and as hard as it was, he was exercising serious control. Not touching Ruby at all so they didn't draw the child's attention. So far Aimee had been going with the flow and hadn't raised any objection to him being more involved in their routine. However, that might change if she had any suspicion they were more than just work colleagues. He wasn't Aimee's father and couldn't expect to simply become part of the family overnight. Therefore any kissing, or even hugging, had to remain in private for the foreseeable future.

He wanted to get this right for everyone's sake, and that meant making sure Aimee was as comfortable with him being around as he was being with them.

'I thought we might go to the beach. Once our food gets down of course.' His surprise brought a gasp of delight from Aimee and a puzzled expression from Ruby.

'The beach? Isn't it going to be a little late to drive all the way to the beach?' she asked, understandably confused when they essentially lived out in the desert.

'When is a beach not a beach? When it's an artificial one created at a hotel. I've got passes for us to go and enjoy the afternoon there. There's a pool, a waterslide, sand, a beach bar...' This was all new to him. This feeling of having to prove himself extended not only to Ruby, but to Aimee as well. He wanted to be accepted, to be fun and someone they both looked forward to seeing.

His chance to be a father had been taken from him. Even his time as a brother and husband had been cut short, making relationships a difficult thing for him to navigate. Though he was willing to try. Regardless that planning happy family-oriented days out were beyond his comfort zone.

'I'm sold.' Now that he'd explained they wouldn't have to travel as far as expected Ruby looked as thrilled as Aimee, who was literally bouncing in her seat.

'Can I go home and get my swimsuit, Mom? Can I wear the blue one with the seahorses on it?'

'Of course. I'll have to go and get mine too. What about you, Harrison? Do you have anything suitable?' Ruby's eyes were glittering with mischief and he wondered if she was imagining him in his swimwear just as he was picturing her.

'I was going to wear my blue swimsuit with seahorses but I guess I'll have to pick something different now.' He gave an exaggerated sigh making Aimee laugh.

'You're so silly, Harrison. Can we go now?' Keen to start her adventure, Aimee was now out of her seat.

'I guess so.' As soon as he paid the cheque Aimee was out the door and waiting to get back into the car.

'You really do know how to keep a girl happy.' Ruby gave him a quick kiss on the cheek out of Aimee's sight before they joined her outside.

'I do my best,' he whispered in her ear, feeling triumphant when he felt her shiver.

Today was all about family time. Something he thought he'd never have and he was working hard to deserve, but tonight was going to be adult alone time, proving to Ruby how much he loved her.

* * *

'This is the life.' Ruby relaxed back into the sun lounger with a cocktail in hand. She looked beautiful in her black one-piece. Modest, but form-fitting enough to attract Harrison's attention. Aimee was in her element building sandcastles on the manmade beach nearby where they could keep an eye on her. So far, everyone seemed to be enjoying their day.

He was doing his best to get into the spirit of things, though fun family time had ceased in his life when his brother died. No one had the heart to even be together after that, never mind pretend they were enjoying life without him. There hadn't been much call for Harrison to be part of anything like this since. It was heartbreaking in a way, reminding him of when he was younger and he and Joey played on the beach together. However, it was also heartwarming knowing he was able to provide Aimee and Ruby with a nice day out and hopefully some good memories to hold on to. Like the ones he had with his family before their world fell apart.

'I could get used to this too,' he said, meaning being part of this with Ruby and Aimee, not necessarily just lounging around. It wouldn't matter if they were on a beach, or at home watching television on the couch, this was the happiest he'd been since his marriage had ended.

Ruby had always been his happy place. The person who'd moved him on from the grief of losing his brother without ever knowing it. They would never be able to replace the child they lost but Aimee was giving him so much joy she felt like family. He should have been terrified by the prospect of also becoming part of the little girl's life. The sort of responsibility he usually shied away from, but this all felt so right. As though it was always meant to be. He'd spent years wondering what kind of father he would have made and perhaps he'd finally be able to find out.

'Have you got sunscreen on?' Ruby asked, lowering her sunglasses to address him.

He shook his head feeling chastised as she tutted before reaching for the bottle of lotion in her bag. The magic bag which appeared to have everything anyone ever needed for a day at the beach. Towels, snacks, Band-Aids, all the essentials for a prepared mom. He'd always known Ruby would make a good mother, but he'd worried he wouldn't be up to the parenting job himself when his own hadn't been the greatest role models. There was a lot to learn but he hoped if he was going to become a father figure for Aimee he would be able to provide the sort of love and support his big brother had shown him.

Joey had been the substitute parent in his life and he would try and emulate him best he could, though Aimee and Ruby made it easy for him to love them. There was no doubt in his mind that was what he felt for them, otherwise he wouldn't be playing happy families like this, and revelling in every second of it.

Even now as he turned around so Ruby could apply the sunscreen, he was appreciating having someone who cared about him in his life. It had been such a long time, he'd forgotten how it felt. How even such a small gesture meant that someone was thinking about his welfare. He considered himself extremely lucky to have been given a second chance not only as Ruby's partner, but perhaps as a father as well.

'Mom, can I go down the water slide?' Aimee appeared beside their sun loungers when the pool apparently became more attractive to her than the mounds of sand.

'Just be careful. And no running,' Ruby called after her as she hurried towards the covered flume which twisted and turned from a great height to drop the riders into the pool. They'd made sure to cover her burn and make it waterproof so she could fully enjoy the day out.

'Will she be all right?' Harrison couldn't help but worry. He didn't know how Ruby ever let her daughter out of her sight when he seemed to fret about her every move. He'd seen enough injuries in children, and seen their distraught parents, to know how easily accidents happened. Ruby was the parent, the expert, and he would have to follow her lead, but he doubted he'd ever stop worrying.

Ruby smiled. 'Relax. We can see her from here and she's a great swimmer. She's been taking lessons since she was a baby.'

That went some way to reassuring him. Along with the wave Aimee gave them as she ascended the steps. Both he and Ruby watched her, waving back, even though his heart was in his mouth once she climbed into the chute. When she plunged into the pool with a mighty splash he could hear her shriek of delight, and saw the big smile when she resurfaced, pushing the wet hair from her face.

He breathed a sigh of relief. Until she shouted over, 'I'm going again.'

Although he lay back again, he still watched her climb the steps and disappear into the chute. This time however, she seemed to be hurtling down faster than the last time and as she shot out the bottom, he heard a thunk as she hit her head on the slide before disappearing under the water.

When she didn't immediately reappear, Harrison leapt to his feet and ran towards the pool. He was vaguely aware of Ruby running behind him, and the sound of the lifeguard's whistle before he jumped in. He grabbed Aimee's seemingly lifeless body and swam over to the side of the pool where Ruby and the lifeguard managed to haul her out. By the time he climbed out Ruby had Aimee lying on her back and was making sure her airways were clear. She put her ear to her daughter's mouth and checked for her pulse.

'She's not breathing. Someone call the paramedics.'

Harrison could hear the fear quivering in her voice and he took over to give Aimee rescue breaths. Delivering much-needed oxygen to her lungs. Tilting her head back to open her airway, pinching her nose shut and making a seal with his mouth over hers. He blew in gently, enough to make her chest rise, and repeated five times. Ruby checked her pulse again and shook her head, dislodging a torrent of tears, so Harrison began the chest compressions.

With one hand over the other, he pushed down on Aimee's chest hard and fast, alternating the compressions with rescue breaths. Eventually, she coughed up some water and Ruby cried out her relief as Harrison rolled her daughter into the recovery position in case she vomited.

'She's okay,' he told a sobbing Ruby before folding her into his arms.

They covered Aimee with towels provided by other swimmers and spectators and waited for the paramedics to arrive. Even though she seemed fine now it was important Aimee was checked over at the hospital in case of secondary drowning where the lungs could still fill with fluid. Someone handed him a blanket and regardless of the fact he was cold and wet, he wrapped it around Ruby's shaking shoulders.

'Hey, Rubes, how is she doing?' The paramedic she seemed to know arrived on scene with his medical bag.

'I think she's all right now but Harrison had to give her CPR,' she managed to get out through sobs.

'Okay, I'm just going to give her a quick check over here but we'll take her to the hospital just to be safe. I'm afraid I can only take one of you in the ambulance.' Both the paramedic and Ruby looked at him.

'Go. I'll pack up and follow you in the car.' Even though he wanted to accompany them, he wasn't Aimee's parent and had no rights. All he could do was watch helplessly as Aimee was stretchered off with Ruby walking alongside holding her daughter's hand.

It was only once they were out of sight he allowed himself to feel all the emotions which had been coursing through his body as he collapsed onto the sun lounger. That overwhelming panic he'd felt when she disappeared under the water wasn't just for her safety, but brought a lot of feelings he'd been trying to avoid for years. If they hadn't got her back, if they'd lost her the way they'd lost their baby, the way he'd lost Joey, it would have destroyed him all over again.

He was beginning to realise that fear as a parent, even a substitute one, was never going to leave him. Being part of a family meant being responsible for their safety, and unless he was watching Aimee twenty-four hours a day, he couldn't always ensure it. This was a prime example, and everything he'd feared.

It had been his choice for fifteen years not to be in this position. Feeling weak and helpless. Not getting close to anyone because of this very reason: the possibility of losing anyone else in his life. He'd chosen not to be a father, yet he was on the verge of making the decision to be part of Ruby and Aimee's family.

It was clear he couldn't be the partner, or father, they needed. Not at the cost of his own peace of mind. He hated to walk away again when they were on the verge of something good, but it was better he did it now than later when they were planning a future together again. Aimee had one fantastic mother in Ruby and he simply wasn't going to measure up to the parent role when his fear of losing them was preventing him from committing completely. Ruby and Aimee both deserved better than he could give them.

CHAPTER ELEVEN

'Hey. How's the patient?' The moment Harrison walked into her apartment Ruby just wanted to run and hug him. Not only had he saved her daughter's life, but his very presence made her feel safe. She didn't know when she'd stopped being the independent, bulletproof parent, but Ruby needed his comforting embrace to remind her that everything was all right. Even though Aimee had been home safe for several days.

'Good,' Aimee croaked from her makeshift bed on the sofa, her throat still sore from coughing. She'd been kept in hospital overnight for observation after the incident at the pool, while Ruby slept next to her in a chair, checking her breathing every few minutes. Thankfully she hadn't suffered any lasting damage.

It had been one of the most harrowing days of Ruby's life when she'd nearly lost another child. It was no wonder Harrison looked pale when he was probably still as shaken by the events as she was.

'I brought you some groceries and a few comics and candy for Aimee. I'm sure you haven't had a moment to get food in.' He handed over the grocery bag, a thoughtful gesture in keeping with the man Ruby knew, but there was something awkward in the interaction, as though he couldn't wait to get out of the place.

'Thanks. Is everything okay, Harrison?' He'd been a little distant these past couple of days. Although he'd remained in contact, he'd been quiet on the phone and there was just something about his antsy demeanour that immediately put her on high alert.

'Can I talk to you for a moment, Ruby?' He gestured that he wanted to speak to her in private, out of Aimee's earshot, and that fear that something was wrong took a greater hold.

She followed him out into the hall and closed the door behind her, a growing sense of dread curling up from her stomach. 'What's up?'

'Look, there's no easy way of saying this…' He was squirming, trying to find the words she had a feeling were coming, but she wasn't going to make it easy for him. If he was going to break her heart again, this time she wanted him to face her as he said the words.

'I just don't think this is going to work.'

'Why not?' She couldn't believe he was doing this after he'd convinced her he was always going to be there for her and Aimee. Literally saving her daughter's life and making her believe that he was committed to both of them.

'I'm just not cut out to be a parent. I know we're not there yet in our relationship, and perhaps that's a good thing so we can end this now, but you and Aimee need someone strong and fearless. That's not me.'

'What are you talking about? You jumped in to save

Aimee without a second thought. You brought her back to life before my eyes. I don't understand why you think that you're not up to the job.'

He scrubbed his hands through his hair. 'Okay, to be more precise, I'm not ready for this level of commitment. Yes, I want to be with you, Ruby, but I can't do this. I thought perhaps given time after the accident I might feel a little differently, but I don't. Having some space has only confirmed to me that I'm not the man you need in your life. You deserve someone who won't spend every day worrying that something is going to happen to you or Aimee and wonder how he'll get through it. It's not good for any of us. I'm sorry but I can't lose anyone else.'

'Except me, apparently.' Ruby was almost doubled over in pain as he twisted the knife. She'd thought it would be better to have an explanation but this didn't make her feel any better knowing there was nothing she could do. Aimee was her daughter and would always come first, but she'd let Harrison into her life because she'd believed him when he said he wanted to be part of it. That included being there for her daughter.

'Trust me, I don't want to walk away from you again, but I think it's the best thing for everyone for me to go now rather than in the future. At least Aimee won't know any different.'

It was a blessing that they hadn't declared their relationship status but Ruby knew her daughter would feel the loss just as she did, if not the anger along with it. He was taking the coward's way out. Instead of facing his fears, believing that being with them was more important than his illogical reason for leaving.

Ruby did know better. She knew what it was to go to bed at night with him, wake up in the morning and know he was going to be there for her no matter what. At least that was what she'd believed until this very moment.

'This is really what you want, Harrison? To give up on us because something might happen? Children get sick, they get hurt, just as we all do. It's a fact of life. As parents all we can do is our best to keep them safe, and as the accident at the pool proved, with two of us being medical professionals we can do that job better than most.'

Worrying about her daughter was simply part of her life. Unlike Harrison, she couldn't just decide she didn't want to do that anymore. It was how she showed she cared. Harrison was proving the opposite.

'But I'm not her father, am I?' And there it was in a nutshell. He didn't want the responsibility, and that left no room for compromise. She wasn't going to let him, or anyone else, into her life who couldn't make room for her daughter.

'No. You're not.'

'I'm never going to be and she deserves someone who can be strong for her no matter what. As you do.'

'You don't need to make excuses. As you've pointed out, you have no responsibility towards either of us so you're free to leave anytime you like, Harrison.' If getting her permission to go this time would make him feel better, that was on his conscience, not hers.

She shouldn't have to persuade someone to love her enough to try and make things work. It was her fault for thinking he'd changed. At the first sign of trouble he was gone, again.

'I'm sorry, Ruby. I really am.' It didn't matter that he looked as upset as she felt when he was the one causing the pain. He might have saved her daughter's life but he was killing her.

She'd bought into the idea of the family he'd sold her, and he'd let her down for a second time. He was overreacting to something he had no power over. Ruby would never have sacrificed the chance to be a parent, to have a family, simply because she was scared.

Of course she understood to some extent why he didn't want to fully invest in a relationship with her and Aimee after all the loss he'd suffered, but he couldn't feel strongly enough for her if he wasn't even going to try and work through his issues. That wasn't someone she or Aimee needed in their lives. From now on it would be back to just being the two of them again because they couldn't rely on anyone else.

'Just go, Harrison. I wish you'd never come back into my life.' It wasn't true of course. These past weeks had been the happiest time of her life in years, but now it was coming at the ultimate price. A broken heart. The pain so immense she couldn't help but lash out. Harrison's wounded look as he walked away giving her some sense of justice that he might feel as dreadful in this moment as she did.

Ruby wanted to cry and rage at the injustice of it all,

just as she had the last time he'd given up on them, but she had a daughter to take care of this time. Aimee's welfare took priority over everything. Even her mother's breaking heart.

'Breakfast is ready, Harrison.' The wake-up call from his mother rang from downstairs and for a brief moment he was transported back to his childhood. The smell of bacon and pancakes filling the house and rousing him and Joey from their beds. Except his brother wasn't here and he wasn't a kid anymore. He was a grown man hiding from his problems. A pattern he hadn't quite grown out of.

After leaving Ruby and Aimee he'd taken some time off work and with nowhere else to go, no one else to turn to, he'd contacted his mother. She'd been surprisingly happy to hear from him and had told him he could stay as long as he wanted to. Taking a couple of weeks off hadn't been a problem as holidays weren't something he took regularly. It had made him realise that until Ruby and Aimee had come into his life he hadn't spent a lot of time with anyone outside of work, and likely wouldn't again.

Although his mom had provided him with refuge she still had to work, so when they weren't out for a coffee together or making dinner, he was often left alone with his thoughts. It wasn't helping his mood. He had hoped coming here, dealing with a different difficult relationship would distract him from thoughts of Ruby, but in that respect, his trip had been a failure. In other areas, however, this visit home had been a success. His relationship with his mother recovering more with every day they spent together.

He got out of bed and pulled on a pair of pants before joining her in the kitchen. 'Morning.'

'Morning, sleepy-head. I thought you were never going to get out of bed. It's like having a teenager in the house all over again.' His mother joined him at the table she had laden with food. It was nice having someone to fuss over him when he thought he would never have that again after walking out on Ruby.

'We didn't always get to have breakfast together though. This is nice.' He reached for the maple syrup to pour on the stack of pancakes his mother had lovingly cooked for him before tucking in.

His mother set down her knife and fork, a sudden look of sadness on her face. 'I'm sorry your father and I weren't always there for you, Harrison.'

His fork stopped midway to his mouth with shock. 'It's okay. I know you were both working hard to provide for the family.'

'I mean after your brother died. We weren't there emotionally for you then, or when you lost your own baby. I'm so sorry. It brought back a lot of the emotions for me about losing Joey and it was easier for me to back away completely than to face my grief as well as yours.' Something he knew about. It seemed perhaps he'd taken his lead from his parents' way of dealing— or not—with emotions.

'I understand that, Mom. I haven't found it easy myself.'

Her face eased into a smile. 'Don't you think I've noticed that? Why do you think I'm telling you this now. I don't want you to make the same mistakes I did. Perhaps if your father and I had talked more about what we were going through after Joey died, or been there for you, we could have saved our family.'

Harrison nodded. He appreciated that she was recognising how difficult that time had been for him too. Even more that she was trying to make amends. He put down his cutlery and reached across the table to take her hand. 'We still can.'

Although his father wasn't in the picture anymore they could still have a family with just the two of them. Infinitely better than a future alone.

His mother took his other hand and drew them towards her, forcing him to look at her. 'I'm not talking about just us, Harrison. We should have had this talk the first time your relationship broke down with Ruby but I wasn't in the right headspace then. I let you walk away from that marriage to lick your wounds whilst I dealt with mine. Now we're both older, with more life experience, I hope you'll listen to what I have to say. Does she make you happy?'

'She does.' At least until he'd ended things and every time he thought about her now he was overcome with sadness.

Until now he and his mother had avoided talking about why he'd come here. All he had told her was that he and Ruby had briefly reunited but had ultimately ended things for good. Perhaps now that he and his mother were making roads in their own relationship she thought it was safe to talk about the other one he'd let disintegrate.

'Then why did you leave her?' It was a simple enough question but not one he could answer easily.

He let go of her hands and sat back in his seat, suddenly feeling defensive. 'Because I love her too much.'

His mother gave a half-smile. 'I'm not trying to tell you what to do, Harrison, but don't make the same mistakes I did. Talk to her. Whatever is wrong I'm sure you can fix it. If you want to be with her don't let fear get in the way.'

'It's not that easy, Mom. I can't seem to get past the fact that I might lose her, or Aimee. I struggled so much after Joey died, then when we lost the baby, I know I couldn't go through that again.'

'There's nobody who understands that better than I do, Harrison, but look where it's got me. Alone, and until this week, estranged from everyone I love. I don't want you to end up like me.' She looked so sad Harrison just wanted to hug her. He wondered if he would be doomed to wear that same forlorn expression for the rest of his days too.

The whole point of walking away from Ruby and Aimee was to prevent further pain, from being depressed and miserable and unable to function. Yet, that was exactly what he was now. He wasn't any happier now having ended things and no longer having to worry about anyone's safety other than his own.

'You can't hide away here forever, Harrison. One day you're going to have to decide what it is you really want and fight for it.'

His mother's words struck a chord. Hiding was exactly what he was doing. Just as he had back then.

Avoiding the reality of his feelings, afraid to deal with them. He'd spent these past years trying to forget Ruby, living a life of solitude and pretending it made him happy. When, in reality, he knew the only thing that could do that was being with her. He didn't want to spend another fifteen years regretting his actions. At least if he took the chance of being with her there was a possibility he might be happy again.

Except he'd already had his second chance with Ruby and he'd blown it. He doubted she'd let him back into her life for a third time.

'What if Ruby doesn't want me back?' Harrison knew his mother couldn't predict what would happen any more than he could, but at least he was voicing his fears. Even considering returning, speaking to her, wanting to try again was a step forward. Hopefully, that meant there was a chance he had the potential to be the man Ruby and Aimee deserved in their lives.

'That's a risk you have to take, otherwise you're going to lose her forever. Is that something you're prepared for?'

His mother's words made him stop and consider a world without Ruby. Something which seemed incomprehensible. Even a week without seeing or talking to her, she'd been constantly on his mind. How would he survive the rest of his life like that? Especially when he'd had a glimpse of the life available to him with her and Aimee, as a family?

Yes, he was always going to worry, be afraid of losing them, but perhaps that was simply part of loving someone. A symptom he could learn to live with if it meant having Ruby in his life.

* * *

With Aimee in bed and work over for the day, Ruby settled down onto the couch in her pyjamas with a glass of wine in her hand. It had been a tough week for all manner of reasons. Not only were they both haunted by what had happened at the pool that day, but losing Harrison had been difficult for them both. Aimee was missing him, asking where he'd gone, and why he was no longer coming around for dinner. Believing it was her fault for getting into trouble in the water and upsetting him, Ruby had to tell her that Harrison had gone away. He wouldn't be coming around anymore.

Unsurprisingly Aimee had been just as confused and upset as her mother by his sudden disappearance from their lives, but Ruby knew they had no choice but to move on. It would take time but she'd done it before and she had to do it again for her daughter's sake. Even if it hurt like hell.

There was a knock on the door, but she was hesitant to answer it at this hour of the night. She knew her parents would have phoned before turning up and she wasn't about to open the door in her nightwear, so she ignored it.

The second knock was followed by the sound of Harrison's voice. 'Ruby, can we talk?'

She sat up so quickly she almost knocked her wine all over herself. He was the last person she expected to call at her door and she was curious as to what had brought him here.

Ruby set down her glass and went to answer the

door, opening it just a fraction. 'What are you doing here, Harrison?'

'I want to talk to you.'

'I thought we'd said everything that needed saying.' She hadn't. She hadn't told him how much she'd loved him, how much he was breaking her heart by leaving again, but it was the last bit of control she'd had by refusing to admit any of that.

'I've had some time to think.' He looked tired, not his usual groomed self, with stubble lining his jaw and his hair unkempt. Although, nonetheless sexy.

'And what?' Ruby folded her arms across her chest as if it was somehow going to prevent him from hurting her again even though she knew it was futile.

'Please, can I come in? Just let me say what I need to and if you want me to leave and never come back I will.' There was a plea in his eyes as well as his voice for her to hear him out and it touched her deep inside. Clearly he had something on his conscience and regardless of what had gone on, she didn't want to see him in pain, or be the cause of it.

She opened the door and walked back into the apartment, letting him follow behind.

'I heard you'd taken some leave.'

'I went to see my Mom for a few days.'

She was surprised to hear that when they'd never seemed especially close. Although Mrs Blake had been her mother-in-law, they'd only met on a couple of occasions, including on their wedding day.

'How did that go?'

'Good.' He gave a half-smile. 'Really good. We

talked for the first time ever about the important stuff. About Joey, and the fact that none of us ever properly dealt with our grief. I'm hoping we can get our relationship back on track.'

She was genuinely pleased for him. He deserved to have family around him. Ruby didn't know how she would cope without Aimee or her parents. Especially now in the wake of their break-up. It was always good to know she had emotional support when she needed it. People she loved, and who loved her in return. He deserved to have someone like that in his life even if it wasn't her.

'I'm pleased for you. Is that all you came here to tell me?' If so, it was unbelievably cruel to turn up on her doorstep looking all rugged and sexy just to tell her he was happy when she was miserable without him.

'No. It made me think about us. About what I'd let slip through my fingers.'

Ruby hated that her heart quickened at that one glimmer of hope that all might not be lost. Even after all the hurt, Harrison Blake still made her love him and believe that he was the road to happiness.

She didn't speak, preferring to let him say what he'd come to say before she made any admission about how much she'd missed him.

'I'm sorry for leaving. *Again.* I was just so overwhelmed by my feelings for you, and Aimee, that it terrified me. I thought it would be easier to not have you in my life at all rather than love you and run the risk of losing either of you. I was wrong.'

'What do you want from me, Harrison?' It was a

plaintive cry straight from her heart. A need to know where she stood once and for all, because having and losing him time and again was killing her.

'Another chance. I know I don't deserve it. You already gave me another chance and I failed you, but I couldn't do it this time. I couldn't just walk away and never see you again. I want to be with you, Ruby. I'm sorry. Please forgive me.' It was a big ask, and as much as she wanted Harrison, and what they had together, she had to protect Aimee as well as herself.

'How do I know you're not going to leave again?' She'd gone against every instinct and let him into her life before only to regret it. To do it a third time would be welcoming more pain with open arms. As much as she loved him, at some point she had to love herself more.

He gave a heavy sigh. 'I don't know how to convince you. I can only tell you how much I love you. How you and Aimee mean the world to me, and I promise to do everything I can to make this work. To make you believe in us.'

'I always believed in us. It was you who never did.' She saw him flinch but it was true. Harrison hadn't stayed to fight for their relationship. At least this time he'd come back. He was doing what she'd wanted him to do then and opened up to her. Showed he still wanted her by turning up here tonight and exposing his heart instead of taking the easy way out.

Now it was down to her whether or not she was brave enough to do the same. She thought of the days and nights they'd spent together. The family picture they'd made together with Aimee, and how happy they'd been. How happy they could be. Ruby owed it to herself to grab hold of the possibilities instead of the painful past.

'It wasn't that I didn't believe in us, it was that I didn't believe in happy-ever-afters, but I know now that's something that isn't promised to anyone. All we can do is our best to make one another happy and I'm committed to doing that for you and Aimee. If you'll let me?' She saw the hope written in his face for a future together as a family. Something he'd been too afraid to show before, and it helped persuade her that he was worth another chance.

'Show me.'

'Pardon?' He frowned, clearly not understanding what she was asking of him.

'Show me how you're going to make me happy. How much you love me.' She smiled, letting him see that she was committed to giving him another chance to prove himself.

Harrison grinned and closed the space between them to take her in his arms. He kissed her full on the lips, taking his time to seduce her mouth with his firm but tender touch until arousal robbed her of coherent thought.

'Convinced yet?' he asked when they finally broke apart.

'Yes, but keep going.' Ruby wrapped her arms around his neck and submitted to her desire, her passion and her love for the only man who'd ever had a claim on her heart.

EPILOGUE

'YOU MAY NOW kiss your bride.' The registrar gave Harrison permission to kiss Ruby. Something he would never grow tired of doing.

He swept her into his arms and kissed her fully, almost forgetting they had a small audience. Along with their bridesmaid, Aimee, Ruby's parents and his mother were in attendance to see them tie the knot for a second time.

He'd proposed only a month after she'd given him another chance to prove his love to her. It seemed pointless to wait when they already knew one another so well and he'd wanted to start their life together as soon as possible. Thankfully Aimee had been over the moon when she found out about their relationship, even if Ruby's parents had been a little harder to win over. He appreciated the fact they were here giving their support and making the day complete.

It was only when their guests began to clap that he remembered they weren't alone.

'Well, Mrs Blake, I guess we've done it again,' he said, taking her hand in his.

'This time it's forever.' It wasn't a question, it was

a statement Ruby made, confirming her trust in him and he was grateful for it.

'I have one last gift for you.' He reached across and took Aimee's hand, bringing her over to join them at the front of the small gathering. She looked as pretty as her mom, dressed in a matching ivory silk shift dress but with a baby-pink sash tied around her waist which complemented his grey suit and pink pocket square.

'But you've already given us both so much.' Ruby touched the silver locket he'd gifted to her this morning, which carried a family photograph of the three of them together. He'd bought Aimee one too since it felt as though he was marrying both of them today. Even though they were already living together in his house, today marked their official commitment. There was just one more thing he wanted to do to prove he was devoted to their family.

'With Aimee's and your permission, I would like to officially adopt Aimee. If that's what you want of course?' At the last second his confidence wavered that he might be overstepping again. That they might not want him to claim any rights as her father even though that was definitely the role he wanted. It had come easier than he'd expected and he cherished every moment of having her in his life.

He shouldn't have worried. The second he said it, he found himself swamped in hugs with Ruby's arms around his neck, and Aimee's around his waist.

'Of course that's what we want, isn't it Aimee?' A teary Ruby looked to her daughter, who was nodding enthusiastically and bringing a lump to Harrison's throat.

'In that case, I think we should let the celebrations begin!' He took the hands of the two most important women in his life and led them down the aisle to another round of applause and tears. Ready to begin their new life together.

The family he hadn't realised he needed until Ruby and Aimee had crashed into his life. Lifting him out of the darkness and making his world so much brighter.

* * * * *

*Look out for the next story in
the Sin City Nurses duet*

Coming soon!

*And if you enjoyed this story, check out these other
great reads from Karin Baine*

A Nurse, a Pup, a Second Chance
Winter Nights with the Midwife
Spanish Doc to Heal Her

All available now!

ONBOARD AND OFF LIMITS

LOUISA HEATON

MILLS & BOON

Remembering Sheila Hodgson. Sorely missed x

CHAPTER ONE

'OH MY GOD. It's huge!' Dr Madeline Finch had just escaped the confines of the dock terminal at Southampton, where she'd spent a good hour going through her final bits of paperwork with the cruise line. She emerged in sunshine to stare at *Serendipity*, the brand-new ship sailing out to take its maiden voyage around the Mediterranean. This vessel, her home for the next six months, was a whole lot bigger than she thought it'd be. Her only experience of sailing had been on a canal boat many years ago, and one or two rowing boats when she'd studied at Cambridge, but this…behemoth…was still nothing like she'd ever imagined! She'd known that the ship was capable of carrying over four thousand passengers and nearly two thousand crew, of course, but to actually see it up close was like looking at a sailing city. Brilliant white, its name emblazoned in azure-blue, it towered above her so high, she had to shade her eyes to see right to the top.

'Wow.'

She let out a soft sigh. The nerves that had been held at bay whilst she'd dealt with some particularly headache-inducing paperwork a moment ago were now beginning to build again. What she was about to do was a spectacular pivot from her normal life. She'd always worked in busy, oftentimes dangerous, Accident and Emergency departments, but that part of her life was over, and now she was taking a new direction. She'd still be a doctor, but in an environment where it didn't need security guys standing ten feet away decked out in stab vests, ready and willing to protect the staff against patients. She'd been informed that life on board a cruise ship as a doctor, though still busy, would be much less dangerous than she had allowed herself to get used to—with the added benefit of good weather and beautiful destinations.

She could travel the world this way: live life, relax on beaches, explore cities. Have experiences that didn't result in her being attacked: a patient had lashed out when she'd refused them drugs. She'd taken time to recover from her surgery, and she had been given counselling, but the PTSD from the event had caused her to feel that she could not return to her old post at London Saint Hospital. Attempting to walk through those doors had caused such a significant panic attack, she'd ended up in her own department, surrounded by staff treating her as a patient as she'd breathed into a paper bag.

Her therapist had suggested a break and that she broaden her horizons—maybe take a busman's holiday, in which business could be mixed with pleasure. And, *serendipitously*, as she'd switched on her computer that day there'd been an email from Jenna, a friend with whom she'd gone to university. She'd extolled her new adventures on board a cruise ship that sailed around the Caribbean: how delightful it was; how relaxing and less *pressured*. She couldn't imagine working in an actual hospital ever again.

Maddy had looked up the cruise line's website, checked for vacancies and seen a posting for a doctor on the Venture Cruise Line's new flagship, *Serendipity*. In a moment of madness, she'd sent off an email, and now here she stood, about to board her new home and sail around the Mediterranean, stopping in ports such as Vigo, Port of Rome, Naples and Cagliari.

She'd never been to any of those places. She had only ever left the country once, going by train to Paris to enjoy a hen weekend with friends, and she'd never been able to remember much about it. This was going to be different—a whole new world. And a bright, wonderful new start to her professional and personal life.

This job was meant to help her recover from her trauma and ease her back into the world of work; it was meant to heal her wounds. Hopefully this ship, its people and its ports of call, would be just the ticket.

And maybe, just maybe, there might be a holiday romance: a Greek god with rippling abs; an Italian poet, perhaps? Or a Spanish *señor* who would whisk her onto a dance floor and then into his bed. Didn't she deserve something crazy like that, something carefree? Someone who would treasure her and treat her like a queen; who would blow her kisses and wave her goodbye as she sailed away with happy memories of their time together?

She'd told her therapist she was fed up being fearful, that life had to start getting better and she was going to make sweeping changes. So she'd left her old job, rented out her flat and decided to see the world. First, the Mediterranean for six months on this contract and, if it went well, then maybe she could message Jenna and see if she could get a posting on her ship on the other side of the Atlantic. She'd not seen her friend for so long.

Pulling her wheeled cases behind her, Maddy began to make her way across the crew gangway. She gazed down at the water as she crossed, then up again at the boat, her anxiety making way for excitement, and was met on the other side by a crew member stood behind a small podium.

His name tag said he was Michele, and he was very handsome—olive-skinned and with a strong Italian accent. 'Welcome on board *Serendipity*; do you have your crew card?'

'Hi. Yes.' She pulled the ID card from her pocket and passed it over for him to scan.

'Dr Finch! Welcome to the family.'

'Thank you.'

He tapped away at his screen and then passed her some more paperwork she would read later. 'Your cabin is on deck three. Your ID card should open the door. Inside, you should find the itinerary and your onboarding schedule. *Bon voyage*!'

'Thank you.' She accepted back her ID and pulled her cases further into the ship, meeting with what seemed like an endless white corridor that turned this way and that, until she came to a set of stairs and a crew lift. She learned that she was on deck five and needed to go down two floors to find her cabin. She pressed the button for the lift and turned to smile at another crew member who'd arrived with her bags. 'Hi.'

'Hi. My name's Angie. I'm a singer in entertainment. You?'

'Maddy. Ship's doctor.' She shook Angie's hand.

'Oh, wow! Which deck are you heading to?'
'Three. Yourself?'
'I'm on deck two.'

The lift door slid open and they wheeled their bags and cases in and Maddy pressed the buttons for both floors. They arrived in a moment at deck three and the door pinged before it opened. 'Well, I'll see you around, I guess?' Maddy said.

'Mess deck hopefully, rather than in the medical bay!' Angie laughed as the door slid shut between them, giving her a quick wave before disappearing from sight.

Maddy turned. There were a couple of small signs indicating cabin numbers on the deck. Her cabin was 302 which, according to the sign, meant she should go left. She gave a nod of acknowledgement to people she met, smiled or said a hello back when one was offered, until she arrived at her cabin, stomach rolling with nerves. The ID card slid through the reader, the light changed from red to green, her door beeped and pushed open.

The cabin was larger than she'd expected. She'd looked at crew cabins online to see what she should expect and was happy to see that she had a single occupancy cabin. The living space had a bed as well as a sofa, a large desk with computer and monitor and some overhead shelving filled with a variety of medical textbooks. There was a fitted wardrobe that contained a small fridge at the bottom of it and a small chest of drawers upon which sat a tray with a kettle, two cups and an assortment of goodies with which she could make tea or coffee. A large porthole currently gave her a view of Southampton dock. There was also a door that led to a nice-sized bathroom and shower cabinet.

On the desk she noticed a small welcome basket: chocolate-chip muffins, some fruit and a card that read: *Welcome onboard! Nate x*

Weird. She'd known a Nate once, years ago as a junior doctor. It couldn't be him, though. There was more than one Nate in the world! Perhaps he was the cruise director or something and doctors just got a special welcome basket. Because, if it was the *other Nate*, well... It hadn't ended very well for her. In fact, he'd broken her heart when he'd left her without a word of explanation. Maybe this one here on *Serendipity* would be more reliable.

'Home sweet home!' She placed her cases off to one side and slid the messenger bag off her shoulders and onto the bed. There was a wad of papers—all the promised documents, a welcome pack and an onboarding schedule which would take place before they started letting on passengers tomorrow afternoon for setting sail at four-thirty p.m.

She almost couldn't believe she was here! There'd been an element of fantasy to the whole thing. She'd interviewed via video connection with Venture Cruise Line, the head office of which was in London. She'd filled in endless rounds of compliance paperwork, and ensured she had the relevant maritime medical training. There'd been a second in-person interview. It had all seemed so far away from the reality of the fact that she'd be soon living and working on board a huge, new cruise liner. A ship! She had no idea if she'd even get sea sick!

I guess I'll find out.

And now here she was, actually on board. Tomorrow they would set sail and her job would begin. She knew no-one here, and maybe that was a good thing. She could be whoever she wanted to be. She could be what she wanted others to see: a good, talented doctor. One who had quickly risen to become head of her Accident and Emergency department in London. One who was relaxed, friendly, confident. She would not let them see the doctor who was attacked and had PTSD. Or the doctor who had her heart broken after being abandoned by a guy she'd begun to fall in love with. Or the little girl she'd once been, hauled through the foster-care system. They wouldn't get to see any of that, or know that *Serendipity* was her chance to regain her confidence and put her past behind her.

She took some time to unpack, making her cabin a home, storing her cases under the bed. Then she sat at her desk for some time to familiarise herself with the onboarding schedule. She was due at the medical bay, which was equipped with its own laboratory and radiography equipment, tomorrow morning at nine for a tour of the medical bay and a meet-and-greet with her new colleagues. And then they would go through the submitted medical information of the crew and passengers. At two o'clock, there would be a crew clinic and then the day schedule would change once the passengers arrived and shift work would begin.

She was excited about it; ready to get back to work and to get her teeth back into the whole reason she'd got into medicine in the first place: to help people; to heal people…including herself.

Dr Nathaniel Blake wasn't used to feeling nervous. It was a strange state to find himself in. During a job interview once, someone had asked him to use three words to describe himself and he'd answered confident, decisive and passionate. Confident and decisive, because he moved through the world assuredly. He wasn't a man who dithered. He wasn't a man who questioned his own decisions. He thought through problems, made a decision and then executed it without doubt. He'd chosen passionate because he was passionate about his job. Passionate about his work, about being a good doctor and making choices for patients that were right for them.

So, the fact that he'd woken that morning feeling incredibly edgy and nervous was not a comfortable feeling for him to experience, and it was all because Dr Madeline Finch—dear Maddy—was on board.

Serendipity was a new ship for him to be on, but this was not his first contract as a cruise-ship doctor with Venture Cruise Lines. He'd worked on their ships *Decadence* and *Pacific*, the last of which had been with his brother, Lucas. His brother was on *Serendipity*, too, as an ice dancer. They walked through this world together again. There'd been a time when it had not been like this and he valued every minute they got to be together.

But Maddy... Maddy was from his past, from when he'd worked in a busy, fast and frenetic London Accident and Emergency department. Both of them had been brand-new junior doctors at the time and there'd been so much going on, so much to learn, so much to understand, so much responsibility and so many patients; he'd been overwhelmed and it had caused him to turn to Maddy for comfort. Friends with benefits, they'd agreed, and she had been amazing—just the release he'd needed at the end of a long day of pressure and worry. Maddy had been the welcoming arms when he turned up at her door, and later the hot vixen between the sheets, allowing him to forget the pressures of their jobs and their lives for an hour or two.

Just thinking about those nights... *Wow.* They had been intense! She had needed the release just as much as he had, and he had many fond memories of sex in all kinds of places! They'd done it up against a wall—worth a try at least once, but only if they didn't mind having terrible leg ache the next day when they had a long twelve-hour shift to get through. They'd had sex in his car—not enough room, but fun—and, once, sex in an empty patient room in the hospital, with no locks on the door and extremely risky every time they heard footsteps getting closer. But they'd had fun. Lots and lots of no-strings, adult fun.

But then he'd received the telephone call that had changed everything and he'd had to leave—immediately. First, taking holiday that had been owed to him, then getting in touch with the hospital and letting them know that he would not be coming back. He'd been needed elsewhere, a family matter. And, though it had pained him to know that he didn't have a chance to say goodbye to Maddy, he'd hoped that she would understand. After all, it wasn't as if they'd been involved or anything. No strings, friends with benefits—that had been all. He'd owed her nothing.

And yet...he'd felt bad, leaving without a word, not even a telephone call or an email. It wasn't the honourable thing to do, but he'd not been thinking straight at the time. His family matter had consumed him to begin with, but then, as time had become more his own, he'd thought how upset she'd be with him for just going like that. But too much time had passed to contact her and he'd just thought it would be easier somehow to maintain no contact. What would he have been able to offer her anyway except for sex? It would only have dragged up again any hurt she might have felt at him leaving. And so he kept it no contact—decision made.

You're no good anyway—just what Bill used to tell him.

And then he'd arrived on board and received a list of his new medical crew, his new colleagues. Some he knew from previous ships, but among the new doctors coming on board was a name that had stood out straight away: Dr Madeline Finch. And he'd known, in an instant, that *this* maiden voyage was going to be crazy with her here.

Hopefully, she would be fine about it. Hopefully, there would be peace between them—friendship, acceptance. They were both adults, more mature than they'd been eight years ago when he'd left.

He'd not wanted her to be surprised by his being there, by being her boss, so he'd sent a welcome basket. A little heads up. It had seemed the decent thing to do. He'd faltered on communication before; he would start off right here.

Because there'd be no real reason for her to hold a grudge, right?

It had just been sex—hot and heavy sex. They owed each other nothing.

CHAPTER TWO

Maddy woke refreshed the next morning, after an early night. Yesterday, she'd gone for a walk around the ship, trying to familiarise herself with the layout, what was on each deck and how to access all the crew corridors, stairs and lifts. The ship was like two cities: the one above, where the passengers existed, lived and enjoyed whatever the ship had to offer; and the one below, where the crew lived and ate and had their own entertainment areas.

She'd found one of the two crew mess areas, grabbed a bite to eat and chatted with a few new friends. She'd met Laila, who had travelled over from France and was a singer; Maribel, from Finland, who was a chef; and Bogdan from Poland, who was there as a cruise director. Everyone had seemed nice and Maddy had done her best to project positivity, confidence and welcome, with no sign of the woman who just a year ago had been almost too afraid to leave her house in case she had a panic attack.

Thankfully, there'd been no sign of anyone from her past. That welcome basket, signed '*from Nate x*,' had niggled at the back of her brain and she'd almost not gone to the crew mess at all, in fear that somehow the man who years ago had unwittingly claimed her heart might be onboard this very ship. But then she'd given herself a very stern talking to in the mirror. The likelihood of him being here was miniscule! And was she really going to hide away in her cabin because he might be there? Ridiculous! She was a grown woman, and besides he wouldn't be on this ship; there had to be thousands of people around the world called Nate and it was simply a coincidence, that was all.

Today, she dressed in dark trousers and a fitted white blouse, and hung her ID lanyard around her neck. Standing in front of the mirror, she took some time to twist and pin up her long red hair and she applied a little make-up, but not too much, smiling at her reflection, proud of how far she had come.

You can do this.

She knew the nerves would go soon enough. Once she was busy, everything would be fine; it was just this bit, hanging around, waiting, anticipating, imagining. There was no reason for her to be nervous. She was an experienced doctor. There would be no drug addicts on board looking to score meds from her. She just had butterflies because it had been a long, long time since she'd had to experience a first day on a job.

Maddy thought back to her first day at London Saint Hospital. She'd been so excited, so nervous! Her legs had felt like jelly and she'd been so keen to get down to working with patients. Of course, it hadn't turned out to be like anything she'd imagined. There'd been almost a whole week of induction, sitting in lecture rooms listening to their bosses and educators talk them through hospital policies that she'd already studied at home. She'd found herself turning to the guy sat next to her when he'd yawned at the same time as her and they'd smiled at one another. He'd had a spark in his eyes and he'd been cute!

Nathaniel, but everyone calls me Nate.
Madeline, but everyone calls me Maddy.

They'd stuck to each other's sides like glue at the beginning. If there'd been something one of them wasn't sure about, they'd turned to the other in hope of an answer before going to a superior, if need be. That closeness had become a friendship, that spark in their eyes an attraction. It had been exciting, thrilling, and, after that first time together in the folly, Maddy had laughed, resting her head against his chest, sweat coating her body in a delightful way. She'd imagined that this could really be something, when he'd said, *We don't need the pressures of a relationship, what with everything else going on, so we should just do the friends with benefits thing—what do you think?*

His words had been a bucket of cold water on her hopes. But she'd *liked* him, really liked him. And she'd figured, if she just agreed, then she'd keep getting to hang around him, be close and experience the physicality that they shared. And she'd so wanted to seem cool with it. So wanted to seem as if she could just roll with anything and not feel that she might not be enough to be anything more. So she'd agreed, hoping that maybe one day he would change his mind. She'd simply nodded, smiled and straightened her clothes before they'd returned to the party.

It was only later she realised what a mistake it had been because, whilst it had been 'no strings' for him, she'd very much felt that there *were* strings. She'd begun to have feelings for him—strong feelings. Ones that she'd secretly kept inside, hoping that one day he would turn to her in bed and tell her that he was actually falling in love with her, the way she was with him. She'd put him on a pedestal, but she should have known she'd never be able to reach him up there.

But, then again, she'd always had an active imagination.

Maddy checked her watch. It was nearly time. Probably best to get there early, make a good first impression and seem keen, eager. And she was! Even though her nervousness at being back in a medical setting niggled at her with all the 'what if?'s—*what if a passenger had too much to drink and got aggravated?*—she left her cabin and pushed through. She'd spent enough hours in therapy to know that it was just anxiety, her PTSD.

I need to face my fears. See some patients, prove to myself that I'm safe.

The thin corridors were busy in the bowels of the ship with crew members wearing uniforms and in casual clothes, going this way and that. There was an energy to everyone this morning. Today passengers would come onboard, and tonight they would set sail from Southampton and head towards their first port—Vigo, in north-west Spain.

She saw Bogdan and gave him a wave as he headed up some stairs dressed in a very posh suit, his hair slicked back. She took the stairs down to deck two, where the medical bay was located. She wasn't sure what to expect. Would it be tiny, quiet?

She saw a woman in a nurse's uniform head in and she turned to hold the door for Maddy. 'Thanks.'

The nurse gave her a nod. 'Hi. Genevieve. Nice to meet you.'

'Maddy. Nice to meet you too.'

There was a reception area, staffed by a woman whose hair was so tightly pulled back into a dark bun, her face looked taut. 'Good morning,' she said, standing to reach out with her hand to say hello. 'I'm Sylvia.'

'Genevieve—nurse.'

'Madeline—doctor.'

Sylvia cross-checked their names against a clipboard. 'Ah, yes! Excellent. Everyone else has arrived. Come with me and I'll take you to the staff room for induction.'

A cloud of sweet-smelling, floral perfume seemed to follow in Sylvia's wake as she led them down a small corridor towards a room at the end, swinging the door wide and holding it open for them. Genevieve went through first and dipped right to head for a spare chair. Maddy assumed she would just follow her, but as she stepped into the room, her gaze went to a guy standing at the front of the room and she felt her steps falter.

She was unable to tear her gaze away from the man standing there. Her mouth was dry, her heart pounding.

No. It can't be!

His eyes met hers and he smiled at her and that smile was *everything*. For so long, she'd told herself that he'd never been as handsome as she remembered. That his smile was *not* as she kept imagining, but something she'd invented. She saw his dark, wolfish hair, his eyes twinkling in the medical bay lights. He wore a trimmed beard now, that if anything only served to make him more distinguished. It was as if he'd grown into himself and become the man he was always going to be, rather than the young twenty-something he'd been before. And that smile…those lips… How many times had she kissed those lips? How many times had that mouth trailed over her expectant body, dropping hot kisses onto tender skin?

He had sent that welcome basket. It was *her* Nate. He was here, on this ship.

'Maddy, come over here, there's a seat.' Genevieve called to get her attention.

Somehow, she tore her gaze away, tried to control her beating heart and, blushing, made her way over to the nurse at the back of the room and sat down.

It felt as if her cheeks were on fire. Her whole body tingled with adrenaline and she realised her legs were trembling, and she wanted to run.

This was meant to be her fresh start. This was meant to be a place where she could be the new and improved Dr Madeline Finch—a doctor not haunted by what had happened to her in the past.

But her past was *here*.

The man who'd unknowingly broken her heart was her new boss!

CHAPTER THREE

THE FIRST DAY onboarding new crew and getting to know his new team was always an exciting day for Nate and this was the first time he'd be the team lead on board. He felt the weight of the responsibility for all the crew and passengers, and wanted to show Venture Line Cruises that he was capable and would do a fine job as Chief Medical Officer. But all the excitement he'd been feeling, all that apprehension, went right out of the porthole the second Maddy appeared in the doorway and saw him for the first time since he'd left London Saint.

She looked *amazing*, as she always had. Her rich, auburn hair contrasted with the beautiful creaminess of her skin, still delightfully freckled. Her eyes were blue and sky-bright. The gloss on her lips drew his attention to her mouth, and the way her lips had parted in surprise at seeing him. Was it surprise? He'd sent that welcome basket. Hadn't she realised it was from him? Because she'd looked shocked and then her cheeks had coloured. Genevieve, with whom he'd worked with on *Pacific*, called her over and Maddy edged her way through a row of people to go and sit with her, almost hiding at the back.

So...not a pleasant surprise for her. That was a little disconcerting. He'd hoped that they'd both be able to put the past exactly where it belonged and move forward. They'd got on brilliantly last time, and he'd enjoyed the many occasions when they'd found each other on short breaks to talk through what has been happening with their patients. If her mentor had been just as bad as his, she'd had a sympathetic ear. She'd been someone with whom he could share a joke or take some space if a patient hadn't made it—someone who'd told him that everything was okay.

Maddy had been by his side since the beginning of his journey as a doctor. He hoped that she would stand by his side just as steadfastly now and help him lead this department so that they got through this voyage, and all the ones to follow, with the support he knew she could give him.

'Good morning, everyone. To those I haven't worked with before, my name is Nathaniel Blake and I will be the Chief Medical Officer on board the *Serendipity*. We have three other new doctors joining us for the next six months, Dr Muhammed Bedi, Dr Theo Galanis and Dr Madeline Finch—if you'd all like to stand and make yourselves known?'

They all stood and smiled, or raised a hand in greeting to their new crewmates, but his gaze couldn't help but go to Maddy. She looked uncomfortable, blushing, but she'd never been one to enjoy the spotlight.

After they sat down, he explained rotas and shift patterns, responsibilities and duties, pairing one new doctor with an experienced one. Behind him on a screen was a floor layout, like a blueprint for the medical bay, and he went through it briefly, detailing where everything was, giving everyone the codes for doors and utility rooms, explaining what sort of equipment they had and what levels of treatment they could provide on board *Serendipity*. He went through some safety procedures and fire-drill procedures and explained where their muster stations were, in case the ship had to be evacuated.

Once he was done, he announced the shifts. 'Dr Finch? You'll be working with me on day shifts to begin with.'

Once the briefing was completed and everyone dismissed, he waited for everyone to filter out so he could speak to the only member of staff left behind. If he were being honest, he'd thought she might try and escape with the others.

Nate was left looking at a rather uncomfortable Maddy in the staff room. 'Hey.'

'Hey.'

'It's good to see you, after all this time.'

She stood, straightening her clothes and forcing a smile. 'I guess we ought to get started? The briefing mentioned that we should be checking the medical histories the crew and passengers have provided.'

All business, then. 'Of course. We'll head to my office. After you.' He stepped back so she could go past him towards the door.

But she didn't come to the front to go past him. She stayed in the back row and edged past the chairs and towards the door. When she got there, she turned to face him. 'Did you pick me to be on the same shift as you because of what we had?'

As the images of their nights together flooded his

memory at her prompting, he felt his pulse increase and felt a surge of awareness for her: their bodies writhing in the dark; the way she bit her lower lip and arched her back, her hands scrunching the bedsheets. He smiled. 'No. Venture Line Cruises picked you for the day shift because that was what you told them you'd prefer.'

He saw her think about it, realising the truth of his words, and then she blushed again. 'Right.'

Did she wish now that she'd asked for a night shift, or to be one of the part-timers who covered weekends and illnesses in the senior medical staff? Because, if so, that was disappointing. He'd hoped they could put what had happened between them, in the past where it belonged. He was keen to see what kind of doctor she was now. Before, they'd both been juniors, uncertain and not yet confident in every decision. He'd grown a lot in the intervening years since he'd last seen her; he'd had to. Had she?

Nate stepped up close to her in the doorway, inhaled the soft perfume she was wearing and felt his senses go dizzy. She still had a certain physical effect on him, that was for sure.

'This way…'

His office was the size of Maddy's cabin and she found herself looking around it with a careful eye as she stood just inside the doorway and Nate went to his desk. He dragged another chair over from its position against the wall and stood behind it, his hands on its back.

'Take a seat.' He smiled at her, that beautiful smile of his, that she'd seen so many times in her dreams. A smile that had once haunted her, which she'd thought she'd never get to see again. And yet here she was, in an office with him. He was so different, and yet the same and she had to fight with every fibre of her being not to gush, run into his arms and tell him how happy she was to see him.

She was happy in one way: he wasn't dead, at least! She'd had no idea about what had happened when he'd left without a word. There'd been gossip after he'd gone; of course there had. People had speculated—mostly the other juniors, but then the senior team had sat them all down and told them that there'd been a family matter and that was the end of it.

'A family matter' could have been anything. And, as she'd sat there in that small room at London Saint, Maddy had realised that she knew absolutely nothing about his family, because he'd never spoken about them. They'd not spoken about personal matters at all. It had all been work. And sex—lots and lots of sex.

But she'd also been angry, angry at him leaving without a word. Could he not have sent her an explanatory text or an email? Couldn't he have called her? Hadn't she deserved that? Or had he thought so little of her, when she'd thought so much of him?

And she was angry at herself now, for asking for day shifts.

She gave him a look that suggested she would not sit down until he had stepped away from the chair, which he did with a small smile, settling into his own chair and waiting for her to join him.

'It's good to see you, Maddy.'

'Only friends get to call me Maddy,' she said, still standing by the doorway.

He nodded. 'You're upset?'

'Of course I am!'

'Well, I understand, of course, but that was a long time ago, and it's in the past now. We are here to do a job, and time is ticking, so shall we move forward and go through these medical histories, so we're both familiar?'

So, no apology, then; still no explanation. Did she not deserve either? How could she have got their relationship so wrong? 'Fine, let's just get on with it.' She settled herself down into her chair, adjusting its position so that it wasn't as close to him as he'd initially placed it, and gazed at the screen.

Nate began going through the more notable medical histories of the crew that were onboard *Serendipity*—nothing too major, but just conditions to be aware of. Generally most of the crew were young and in good health. Some of the passengers embarking the ship had a few more serious things to be aware of, and Nate ran through them with her as best he could, whilst she sat and nodded, choosing not to say much—because why should she, if he wasn't going to say much to her either?

'We become a family on board, Maddy. Sorry... Madeline. It doesn't work unless we do. We're confined together on board for six months and we have to have each other's backs.'

She stood, then turned to face him. 'How can I have the back of someone who abandoned me?'

'I was in an impossible situation. If it helps, it wasn't about you.'

No. It didn't help. 'Did you not think to call me? Not even once?'

'I did.'

'And?'

Nate sucked in a deep breath, then let it out. 'Too much time had passed. I thought it might be too little, too late, so I just...let it go. I never thought I'd see you again. I thought you'd just move on, and that was probably for the best anyway. I mean, look at you! You look amazing; you must be doing well?'

If only he knew about all that she had been through! If only he had been by her side, she might have got through her trauma easier! Would he have sat by her bed and held her hand? Made her laugh with his bawdy jokes as she recovered? Would he have stopped her from being attacked in the first place? They'd always seemed to have some sort of extra-sensory perception when the other needed support.

Maddy felt barely restrained tears prick the backs of her eyes and hated herself for getting emotional. It simply wouldn't do! She sniffed and checked her watch. He didn't deserve to see her cry. He didn't deserve to hear about her life, not any more. From now on, she was going to keep it purely professional between them, even if her body did still stir at being close to him. Even if it did yearn to push aside all the unresolved anger she had from his disappearance years ago and just rush into his arms.

She pushed down her desire to touch him, to hold him. She focused on how she'd bristled when he'd mentioned that they were *family* here. Anger would get her through this. It always had. 'Staff clinic starts at two?'

He nodded.

'I'll see you then.'

* * *

Ysabel Demetriou came limping into the crew clinic that afternoon, wincing and favouring her left leg. But she was smiling as she came into Nate's consultation room and lowered herself slowly into a chair.

'How can I help you today?'

'I've hurt my ankle and I need you to look at it for me. Hopefully, it's just a sprain.'

'Okay; what were you doing that caused you to hurt it?'

'I'm an ice-dancer, and I was doing a warm-up on the ice just before lunch and took a fall doing a triple lutz. Stupid, really. I always nail them, but I think I landed funny.'

'Did you use the correct edge of your skate?'

She smiled at him. 'You know skating?'

'My brother is an ice-dancer here on board. I've watched him practise often enough and heard him speak about it. You pick up on things,' he said, shrugging.

'What's his name?'

'Lucas.'

'Oh, Lucas! Yes, I met him last night.'

'Okay. Otherwise, fit and well? You didn't bang your head during the fall?'

'All good and no, no head injury. I got straight back up and carried on. It's only since then that the ankle is really hurting and I've got a show tomorrow night that I need to be in. I've got a solo skate and so I need to be on point.'

'No dizziness beforehand?'

Ysabel shook her head.

'Alright. Let's take a look at this ankle, then, shall

we?' Nate got up from behind his desk and indicated she should get up onto the examination bed.

She was wearing joggers, socks and trainers, so he was able to see both ankles easily side by side. Her right ankle did look a little puffier than the left, but not by much. He palpated the ankle, foot and lower leg and then began to rotate and test the ankle joint to gauge the range of movement and the patient's pain level.

The ankle itself moved how he expected it to move, though clearly it was sore for Ysabel. 'Does it hurt all the time, or only when you bear weight on it?'

'All the time. A bit worse when I step on it, but not much.'

'Okay. I think you've got a mild sprain. I definitely don't think you've broken anything. So what I'm going to recommend is that you follow the usual procedures for an injury like this. You're going to do five things. Protect your ankle, so wear your boots. I want you to rest the ankle as much as possible and apply an ice pack for up to twenty minutes at a time. Wear a compression bandage around the ankle during the day and try to keep the ankle elevated as much as possible ahead of tomorrow's show. Do you have a stand-in?'

'Yes,' Ysabel said, grudgingly. 'But this is my first solo dance in a lead role. It's important. I can't let someone else take what I've worked so hard for.'

'I understand, but your health comes first. No point in pushing through and ruining your ankle so that you can't skate again. I want you to rest and take it easy. Take painkillers if you need to. Do you have any?'

'Of course. Is paracetamol okay?'

'Absolutely. Promise me you'll rest until tomorrow and maybe try a skate in the afternoon; see how you go and make a decision then?'

'Fine. Maybe you could come and watch the show? Hopefully I won't need you, but it'd be nice to know you were ringside.'

Nate sighed and smiled. 'Okay. I'll try, but only if you promise me that if it feels worse, you will let your stand-in do the show.' He held out his hand.

Ysabel eyed it and then shook his hand. 'Deal.'

The nurses triaged the patients first as they arrived to clinic. It was a similar system to how it worked in an Accident and Emergency department and Maddy liked that, because she knew then that there wasn't anyone sitting in a waiting room who really ought to be seen straight away. Thankfully, it being the embarkation day and with everyone new to the ship, there weren't actually that many patients at all. She'd noted that Nate was seeing a query sprained ankle and she'd been called to one of the bays because one of the ship's chefs had got a nasty burn to his hand.

It was her first patient since the attack. It was the only reason her mouth was so dry, her palms sweaty and her stomach rolling as if they were already at sea.

Paolo Conti sat on the examination bed in the bay when she entered, with his hand resting in a bowl of water, and a huge frown on his face. The nurse had written that the burn wasn't serious, and that Paolo had not even wanted to come to the medical bay, but Venture Cruise Lines had a very strict policy on injuries received whilst on board, no matter how minor. They all got reported and each injury had to be seen by a medic.

Before she pulled open the curtain, Maddy centred herself by taking a huge breath.

I can do this.

She painted on a smile of greeting and pulled open the curtain.

'I am fine,' he said, his voice filled with irritation before she'd even walked in. 'Honestly, look.' He lifted his hand from the water, moving it, twisting it this way and that, scrunching his hand to show a full range of movement. His mood, however, was unhappy. 'It does not hurt all that much any more. Can I go back to the kitchens?'

Maddy hesitated, sensing his antagonism straight away, her blood pounding through her system in an instant alert. This was not what she'd expected from her first patient. The desire to flee reared up, but she'd been preparing for this. It wasn't going to happen again, but she kept her distance by the curtain. 'I need to assess the injury, Mr Conti. How did it happen?'

'How you think? In the kitchen! I tell the nurse this already!' he said, voice raised.

Maddy put up both hands in a placatory way, trying to calm him, her heart pounding, sensing the potential danger, backing away to her exits. 'I understand, but I'm going to need you to calm down.' Adrenaline was coursing through her. She wanted to run. She'd faced an angry patient before and it had not ended well for her.

'I am calm!'

'Sir, I need you to—'

'What's going on in here?' Suddenly Nate was there, behind her, looking at Mr Conti and then stepping between him and Maddy.

She felt relief flood her system that someone else was there to help her deal with the patient, but why did it have to be Nate? Now he was going to think her incompetent in handling a difficult patient. She touched Nate's arm and instantly regretted it. A frisson of electricity shot up her arm. She had to take back control! 'It's fine. Mr Conti is impatient to get back to work, that's all.'

Nate turned to look at her, then back at Paolo. 'You will lower your tone when you speak to my staff, is that understood?'

For a moment, there was a standoff. The much bigger, angrier chef, staring at the cooler, calmer, collected Nate. There must have been something in Nate's gaze that had the chef nodding and backing down, holding his other hand up in surrender. 'My apologies. Onboarding day is a busy day for the buffet and I am needed in the kitchen.'

Nate turned to her. 'Are you alright?'

'Yes.' It was difficult to meet his gaze. Earlier she had been so angry with him and now... Well, she was still angry, but he had just come to her rescue, and she was embarrassed by it, yet grateful. It was a weird set of emotions to feel all at once. 'Thank you.'

'I'll be in my office. I'll leave the door and this curtain open,' he said, directing the last part at Paolo as Nate walked away.

Maddy watched him go, feeling a little disconcerted. 'Accidents in the kitchen are easily done, but you did the right thing by putting your hand in water.' She gave him a hesitant smile as she put on some gloves to examine his hand. 'May I?' There was redness to the skin, but no blisters, no swelling. 'Can you feel me touching you here? And here?'

Paolo nodded.

'Does it feel tight?'

'No.'

'Pain?'

'Little. I've had worse.'

'Alright. Well, you should be fine, but if you get blisters you must come back and see me, alright? We'll cover the burn so you can return to work, but any sign of infection, or difficulty moving the hand and fingers, you come back for that as well. Take painkillers if you need to.'

'Thank you. I can go now?'

'In a minute.' Maddy helped him pat dry his hand and then covered it in cling film, knowing he would be returning to the kitchen and handling food. 'Okay. Be careful, alright?'

'Thank you. And…my apologies. For earlier.'

She gave him a quick nod, letting out a big breath once the fiery chef had gone. He was a big guy, much bigger than her. She stood five foot seven; Paolo had to have been at least six feet or more, easily—solidly built, too.

She headed to a computer terminal to write up his notes, swiping her card to access the system and then noting the way her fingers trembled as they hovered over the keys.

This was not the start she'd hoped for by coming to work on a cruise ship. They'd not even left Southampton dock yet and already she'd been quaking in her boots! If it hadn't been for Nate, then… No, it would have been fine. Paolo was just frustrated, that was all.

Why am I making excuses for him? Because I always do.

Even when she'd been attacked before, she'd tried to excuse the guy. It hadn't been his fault, because he'd been an addict. It hadn't been his fault, because he'd been in pain. It hadn't been his fault, because he'd been in withdrawal. If she hadn't have got in his way…

Maddy made fists with her hands, then relaxed them, imagining all the stress leaving her body, the way her therapist had suggested. She looked up over the console and down the corridor towards the end, where Nate's office was. He'd not hesitated. He'd come straight to her assistance, as she imagined he'd do for any of his team. She put everything into the notes, including Nate's intervention, just in case. Then she got up and walked towards his office, hesitating by the door before rapping her knuckles on the wood to get his attention.

Nate looked up.

'I just wanted to thank you. For just now.'

'No problem. Are you alright, Madeline?'

Looking at him right now was so hard to do! She just wanted to run into his arms and have him hold her. Feel him in her embrace once again. Breathe him in. But it had been so long. She had no idea whether he was still single, or married, or involved with someone. They could even be on this boat! It could be one of the nurses! Who knew! Not that she could ever get involved with a man like Nate ever again. He'd broken her heart once, she'd be a fool to give him the opportunity to do so again. She would have to keep her distance.

She nodded. 'Yes. I just needed to say thanks, that's all.'

'You're very welcome.' He smiled. A smile that clutched at her heart, just like it had all those years ago. A smile that left her helpless. Vulnerable. He could have asked her anything with that smile back in the day and she would have done it. Run away with him? Yes. A hundred times yes. Did he know the power his smile had on her?

'I guess you can call me Maddy.' It was an olive branch.

He nodded.

Because he was right. They *had* to work together on this cruise for at least six months. That was how long her contract was and she wasn't entirely sure how long she could be mad at him. Not now that he was here. Back in her life. Just as charmingly irresistible as he'd been before, being all heroic and coming to her rescue and protecting her, like she was a damsel in distress.

He could never know how much that meant to her.

'Do you have a moment?' Nate had gone looking for Maddy and found her at the reception desk, talking to Sylvia, their receptionist.

Delightfully, her cheeks flushed with colour at seeing him, but he knew she had nothing to do and at that moment, and neither did he. Crew consultations were over and an important moment was coming up.

'Sure. What's up?'

He smiled. 'Come with me.' He wished they had the

old easy association in which he could have just taken her hand, but they weren't who they used to be any more.

Nate led her away from the medical bay, down the corridor and over to a crew lift that would take them up to the promenade deck. 'The *Serendipity* is about to leave Southampton. You don't want to miss the sail-away party,' he said as they emerged into the sunshine and they saw all the people who had gathered. Music was being played, and crew members were dancing, trying to get passengers to join in. He walked her over to the railing and they looked down at Southampton dock. He knew no-one there—his only family was on board—but still he waved.

'Who are you waving to?' Maddy asked.

'Anybody.'

She looked at him as if he was crazy. 'Are all your goodbyes this weird? Or just the ones I get not to witness?'

He laughed. He wasn't going to get pulled into an argument about how he hadn't said goodbye to her. That was in the past—a very painful past. 'It's called living in the moment. You should try it!'

The ship's horn sounded, long and loud, and slowly the ship began to move away from the quay.

'We're off!' He beamed at her. 'Go on! Wave!'

'I have no-one to wave to.'

'Do you think all these people do? Those are dock workers down there, sailors. It's not their family members, but they wave anyway; it's what you do on board. It's all part of the fun. Come on—wave. Smile. Enjoy!'

Maddy sighed, but lifted her hand and began to wave,

rather half-heartedly at first, as if she was embarrassed, but then as the ship pulled further and further away she really seemed to get into it.

He stole glances at her when she wasn't looking, his heart aching for all that he had lost with her. Could they have been something more than a hot fling? It was a real possibility. He could have fallen hard for this woman and, though something horrible had pulled him from her orbit, he was also grateful for the family crisis that had got him out of a tight spot. Because he'd not been ready for her. He'd not deserved her good, kind heart and there'd been moments between them when he'd felt that she was beginning to develop feelings for him, and that had scared the living crap out of him. He'd been so isolated for so long then along had come Maddy, swimming out to his island in the middle of an ocean and encouraging him to swim back with her to land.

But there'd been a reason he'd been isolated, a reason he'd been stranded, and the truth was, he'd stranded himself—because relationships with people he'd cared for had all been destroyed. He wasn't going to destroy Maddy, so he'd kept her at arm's length and told her they could only be friends with benefits, because that was all he'd been able to give.

He was in a different place now, but he had no idea where she was. Maybe she was settled. Maybe she had a love waiting for her somewhere. Maybe she wasn't as alone as she had been before. That had been part of the attraction back then—they'd been two lonely, hurt people, salving each other's wounds with sex, sex and more sex. Hot, passionate sex—almost as if they'd been starved of affection all their lives and were hungry for touch and connection.

They'd had a lustful thing going on and so it was understandable why his body reacted to her presence once again. It knew what she was capable of making him feel. It craved her, like a drug. But, until he knew her situation, he would be the perfect gentleman.

Behind them, the holiday music blaring out from the speakers on board filled their ears, and when a song came on that he absolutely adored he touched her arm and indicated she should follow him. He led her down some steps and out onto the deck where the entertainment crew was dancing near the swimming pools and hot tubs. He waded into the group and began to dance, crooking his finger at her to join him, laughing and calling her name.

Maddy stood there, blushing and shaking her head. 'No way! I can't do that!'

'Come on! Let yourself go for a moment!' She'd always been highly strung. The only time he'd ever seen her let go of her inhibitions was when they'd been intimate. She'd become a different person when she'd got dressed. It was as if she'd been putting on a mask and costume to be someone else. Who had been the real Madeline Finch? Was she still all buttoned up?

Nate rolled his hips, swaying this way and that. A passenger joined him, a young woman in a short sun dress, and he took her hand and twirled her round. He really wanted Maddy to join in, but the next time he looked for her she had gone, disappearing into the crowd, and he felt his heart sink, even if outwardly he maintained his smile for everyone else and carried on dancing.

Lying on the bed in her cabin, Maddy pressed the heels of her hands into her eyes and groaned out loud in frustration. How could one man still hold such sway over her emotions, even after all this time?

He seemed full of abundant joy, confident and sure of himself—whereas she still felt as if she were that young junior doctor, afraid, uncertain, still finding her way in a world that seemed keen to keep beating her down and holding her prisoner with all her fears and doubts.

Watching Nate smile and wave to the dock workers had been one thing, but then to see him joyfully join the dancers, moving his hips in that provocative way, feeding off of the energy and happiness of others... Maddy had felt so jealous of that woman he'd danced with, the way she'd twirled in his arms and then had drawn close to salsa, pressing her body against his, her skirt swishing around her perfectly tanned thighs and elegant legs, so sure of her body, oozing confidence. *Why can't I be like that? Why can't I just let loose?*

They'd looked good together, Nate and the passenger. How was she going to keep their relationship totally professional if he was going to do things like that? *I cannot fall for him again!*

He made it so easy, though. He was the type of guy who opened his arms wide for her and welcomed her in. He was easy on the eye, too. He could have gone for lots of women at that hospital. Plenty had made it clear that they were up for some fun with him, if he so desired, but he had never looked beyond her. Despite the fact that they'd been only friends with benefits and had no claim on each other, he'd only ever slept with her, and she with him.

And he'd been perfect! She remembered one night when he'd driven them out to Surrey and they'd gone to this perfect little village pub and sat outside in the pub garden. There was a small river that ran along the bottom of it, dotted with ducks and two resident swans. She and Nate had sat with their backs against a wooden bench, staring out over the water, his arm casually resting around her shoulders. She'd leaned in and rested her head on his shoulders in this perfect moment, and she had felt him turn to kiss the top of her head. It had been a warm summer's evening. The air had been thick with the scent of honeysuckle and jasmine, and in that moment she had felt wanted and adored. After a lifetime of never quite being enough for anybody, he'd captured her heart with that one small gesture.

A simple moment. There'd been no need for flashy restaurants, diamonds, or trying to impress her with money or status. Just a quiet moment, by a river, with his arm around her, giving her a kiss.

Maddy groaned again at the memory and tried to force it back down into the recesses of her mind. *I cannot keep thinking of him in this way!* He was no longer that boy. She was no longer that girl. Time had moved on, and so had he, and it was time for her to do the same. Hadn't she come here for that very reason—a fresh start, sailing the Mediterranean, exploring the world? Pushing her own boundaries and seeking a new and different life? If she was going to do that, then she needed to find a way to deal with Nate.

If he was going to continue to be delicious and sexually attractive to her, then she needed to define new ways of dealing with him. Because she was even more broken now and he had no idea. And, if she was going to put herself back together again here, then she needed time and space to heal. She did not need to think about diving into a new relationship. What she needed to do here was focus on being confident again, being a good doctor again.

So she needed to harden her heart against Dr Nathaniel Blake. She got up and decided to go and get something to eat. Passenger clinic would be in less than an hour and she wanted to be fully fuelled before that started. And then afterwards she would come back to her cabin, maybe read some more of that self-help book she'd bought, and then get some sleep. Keeping her life simple meant keeping away from the distractions.

And Nate was the biggest distraction of them all.

'Good morning.' Nate handed some paperwork to Sylvia as Maddy arrived at the medical centre. 'Sleep well?' He wanted to extend the hand of friendship after her disappearance yesterday, show her that he didn't mind her having absconded from the sail-away party, because hey, he could hardly have a go at her for that, could he? He'd disappeared on her once, without a word. Comparatively, they were hardly the same thing, but...he didn't want there to be any hard feelings.

'No, not really. I always find it difficult to sleep in a brand-new place.'

Of course. He'd forgotten that. The first time she'd ever stayed over at his digs, he'd woken in the morning to see her just lying there, staring at the ceiling, having waited for him to wake up so they could go into work together. It was a hangover from her childhood. She'd been an orphan, raised in the care system and sent to so many different child-care centres and foster homes.

'Well, I hope you're okay to work, because we've actually got a call-out—a passenger whose family are concerned about her. I thought we could go together and you could take point; what do you think?'

She seemed to brighten and then nodded. 'Perfect. Who's the patient?'

'Seventy-nine-year-old female, travelling with her son and daughter-in-law. She's been unable to get out of bed this morning.'

'Right. Okay. Do we take anything with us if we go to a patient's cabin?'

'We have a go bag with basics. I should have shown it to you yesterday; apologies.'

She nodded. 'Which deck?'

'Deck ten. Room 1035.'

'Let's go.'

As they headed for the lifts, Nate fell into step beside her. 'I'm sorry about yesterday, if I made you feel uncomfortable, asking you to dance.'

The lift pinged open and they stepped inside, Maddy jabbing at the button for deck ten. 'I don't dance.'

'Oh, I don't know. I think I remember you dancing with me once. New Year's Eve?'

He'd known her about a year and they'd gone to a New Year's Eve rooftop party in the heart of London. It had been freezing cold! The wind had whipped around them that high up in the city as they'd partied hard. He remembered her wearing this shimmering silver dress that skimmed the tops of her thighs, revealing her delicious legs. And all he'd been able to think about all night was how he wanted to trail his fingers up and down her thighs, find the swell of her bottom and pull her against him. But she'd been determined to dance, champagne glass in one hand, her long red hair free about her pale creamy shoulders. She'd laughed so much that night that she'd been like a wild thing, letting loose after a long and difficult day.

Maddy had wanted to stay in and not go out, but he'd persuaded her that, if they were to survive their job, then they needed to be able to disconnect from the trauma and not take it home. That New Year's Eve had been a time for fresh starts and celebration. She'd looked up at him, nodded, pulled him into her arms and whispered, 'Thank you,' into his ear. She'd felt so good in his arms that he'd taken her in that moment, in a frantic, passionate moment to celebrate life. Celebrate that they were alive.

Afterwards, they'd showered and dressed for the party and, though there'd been many beautiful women at it, his eyes had only been for her and the way that she'd danced: free, as if no-one was watching.

Only, he had been.

'That was a long time ago and under different circumstances,' she answered sharply.

'Yes, but you do, in fact, dance.' He kept his own tone light.

They emerged on deck ten and followed the numbered signs to find cabin 1035, and Maddy rapped her knuckles against the door.

It was opened by a woman in her late forties, maybe early fifties.

'You called for a medical consultation?'

'Oh, yes! Do come on in, she's over here, still in bed.'

'Thanks. I'm Dr Finch and this is Dr Blake.'

The woman nodded, then turned to the older woman in the bed. 'Peggy? The doctors are here.'

Nate stood at the end of Peggy's bed, as Maddy took point, as he'd suggested earlier.

'Hi, Peggy. I hear you're not feeling very well; can you tell me what's been happening with you?'

Peggy looked pale and weak. When she didn't speak, her son, standing next to Nate, spoke up. 'She's been a little confused lately, but we just put that down to her age, you know? She hasn't been sleeping well, and she's been slowing down a bit, but we thought it was tiredness and figured this cruise would do her some good—rest, relaxation, a bit of sea air. But she took to her bed last night, saying she felt a little nauseous, and we just assumed it was a bit of sea sickness. She's never sailed before, but when she couldn't get out of bed this morning, we got worried.'

Maddy nodded and opened her bag to get out a few things. She turned to the patient. 'Peggy, I'm going to take some basic observations, if that's okay? I'm going to check your temperature and blood pressure; is that alright?'

Peggy nodded and Maddy placed the oxygen saturations monitor on Peggy's finger, whilst she used the aural thermometer to take her temperature. 'Slight fever. Heart rate ninety-four. Let's take your BP.' The cuff took a moment to inflate and then it deflated and the machine beeped its result. 'Ninety-six over fifty-five. Can I do a brief examination, Peggy?'

Peggy nodded again.

Nate watched carefully as Maddy performed a primary survey of the older woman, examining her head to toe and palpating her abdomen. Peggy seemed tender there.

'Right then, Peggy, your respiratory rate is twenty-three and you're showing signs of dehydration and, with your slight fever, the confusion, the weakness and the tenderness you're showing in your abdomen, I'm thinking that this is most probably a urinary tract infection. Are you eating and drinking normally?' Maddy asked.

'Not really, no.'

Maddy turned to face Nate. 'I think we should perform a urinalysis, give IV fluids to counteract her dehydration and prescribe antibiotics.' She seemed happy with her diagnosis and smiled at him, as if expecting him to agree. He could tell that she was trying to show him that she was capable.

However, there were some things that she had missed in her eagerness to impress. Normally, he would say if it sounds like hoofbeats, think horses, not zebras, and confusion and weakness in an elderly female was very often a UTI, but one couldn't assume. The urinalysis was a good test to perform, but there were one or two questions she'd left out. 'Peggy are you on any other medications?'

'I take some tablets but I don't know what they are.'

He saw Maddy realise that she'd not asked the question and knew she'd be beating herself up inside.

'She's on digoxin for her atrial fibrillation,' the younger woman said. Atrial fibrillation was a condition with which the heart's upper chambers, the atria, could beat rapidly or irregularly. Digoxin helped stabilize the heartbeat and make it stronger.

'Anything else?'

'Erm... Eric, what was she given for the swelling in her legs?'

Eric rummaged in his mother's toiletries bag and pulled out medication, turning it to read it. 'Furosemide.'

Furosemide was a diuretic. He looked towards Maddy. 'Peggy, we'd like to do a tracing of your heart. Would that be okay?'

The older woman shrugged. She was tired.

Maddy blushed as she set up the machine. He knew she was kicking herself for not asking about the recent meds, but he would salve her conscience later. Right now, they had a patient to care for. With the leads attached, the machine ran a trace and it was clear that Peggy's heart was beating slower and there was some PR elongation, revealing that it was taking longer than normal for the electrical impulses to travel from her atria to the lower chambers of her heart, the ventricles.

It was now time for Nate to take charge of this case. 'Okay, I think it's best that we take your mum into our medical bay for monitoring, IV fluids and urinalysis, as Dr Finch suggested, and blood tests. I'm hoping that this is a simple UTI, as my colleague suspected, but because of the digoxin I also just want to check to make sure her levels aren't elevated. I'll send some nurses up with a chair to bring your mother to sick bay. Is that alright?'

Eric and his wife nodded. 'Of course. Whatever you think is right.'

'Someone should be up within half an hour. You're welcome to come down with Peggy, if you wish; there's a seating area where you can wait whilst we get her settled.'

'Thank you.'

Out in the corridor on their way to the lifts, Maddy swore. 'I can't believe I missed asking about recent meds!'

'Maddy—'

'I'm so embarrassed! Patient history is key! I can't believe I did that; I'm so sorry. Honestly, I'm a much better doctor than that, it's just that I…'

He stopped her and placed his hand on her arm. 'Maddy, considering her symptoms, it was easy to assume that she has a UTI. She may very well have one! But we must make sure we ask the right questions on a cruise ship. We're *isolated* at sea, and we don't have the support of an entire hospital to back us up, so we must absolutely pinpoint our diagnoses.'

She nodded. 'Understood. I'm sorry. I promise you, I'm a much better doctor that that. I was just…nervous.'

'Why?' He didn't understand why she was nervous. She'd been a doctor for years.

Maddy looked at him uncertainly, as if she had something to say, but didn't know whether to say it. 'I had some time away recently. Took some time for myself. Coming here, returning to the job after a break, I… What with yesterday's patient that you needed to help me with, and then you saying we'd come to see this patient together, I thought you were *judging* me and I wanted to impress. And we were in that room, with everyone looking on... I thought it was an easy diagnosis and I jumped on it, without being thorough.'

She sounded so dejected, so disappointed in herself. He didn't want her to feel that way. And it was his job to support her here and help her find her confidence again after a break from medicine. 'When Peggy gets to the medical bay, what tests do you think you should run?'

She sighed. 'Check for elevated digoxin levels, urinalysis, give IV fluids for rehydration, but also check her potassium levels and renal function.'

He smiled. 'You see? You do know what to do. You just needed the breathing space. When Peggy gets to the medical bay, you're in charge of her case. You can update me as and when you get results.'

'You're putting *me* in charge? After that display?'

'Yes. Because I know you can do it and you had a blip.'

'Doctors shouldn't have blips.'

He looked down at her. 'But they do. Because they're human. Come on, let's get back. We can discuss semantics another time. We've lots to do and other patients to see.'

Peggy was diagnosed with digoxin toxicity, aggravated by dehydration from her diuretic. But, as she was now stable, the digoxin and furosemide had been stopped and she was being supported, there was no need to airlift her from the ship. Maddy had ordered continuous cardiac monitoring, IV fluids and repeat bloods in the morning to recheck digoxin levels, but there were no signs of heart arrhythmias or any further confusion and, with the fluids on board, Peggy was beginning to seem brighter.

Maddy was happy that things were looking good, but she still felt bad for having missed an obvious question in her patient history, and even more embarrassed at having done so in front of Nate.

He could have called her out. He could have berated her or written her up, but he hadn't. He'd been kind, empathetic. And he'd used it as a teaching moment. But twice now he had come to her rescue, and that was really annoying, because she'd wanted to come here and stand on her own two feet. To go and make a silly mistake like that, after years of practice, when she'd wanted to show him what she could do... *Stupid.* Luckily, it wasn't a mistake that had proved fatal. But it had been in front of Nate and God only knew what he thought of her privately.

Even though Peggy was getting better, she could feel her anxiety rising. As she sat at a terminal updating Peggy's notes, a young guy walked in. He was handsome. dark-haired like Nate, but this guy wore his hair a little longer and was clean-shaven.

'Hi. Nate around?'

'He's with a patient. Can I help? I'm a doctor, if you need medical assistance.'

'I'm good. Healthy as a horse, as far as I know. I just wanted a quick word with Nate.'

'I can take a message.'

'Okay. Can you tell him we're going to be dining in the Orchard tonight? We've got a table booked for eight p.m.'

'Okay. And your name?'

'Lucas.' The man smiled, seeming to expect her to know who he was, but she didn't. She had no idea. Was he crew? A passenger? An old friend? A new one? Maddy must have looked blank enough for him to fill the silence and explain.

'I'm his younger brother.'

Maddy blinked in surprise. 'I didn't know Nate had a brother.'

'Well, here I am, and he does. And you tell him he'd better be there, if he wants Carlos and us to celebrate properly.'

'Who's Carlos?' she asked, confused.

'My fiancé.' Lucas presented his left hand to reveal an engagement ring, a solid-gold band inset with a diamond. 'This is the only night of the cruise in which we've both got the same night off.'

'You're crew? What do you do?'

'I'm an ice-dancer. Carlos is an acrobat in the circus show.'

Maddy had a vague idea of what Lucas was talking about. She'd browsed the ship's itinerary in her cabin last night before bed. 'Oh. Okay. Well, I'll let him know.'

'You know, it's typical of him not to mention he has family. But I suppose I can excuse him, because there were all those family issues, but…we're good now, so… Anyway, listen to me, talking like there's no tomorrow! Good to meet you, Dr…er…?'

'Finch. Madeline Finch.' She shook his hand, still surprised at this development. Nate was clearly a dark horse. Why hadn't he mentioned his brother before when they'd been junior doctors? She'd asked him once if he had any siblings—she knew she had! But he'd mumbled something about not having any, and she'd wondered if he'd been in care too, but he had said no. But now it turned out he had a brother. Why would he have kept his brother secret?

'Nice to meet you, Madeline Finch.' Lucas looked her up and down and smiled. 'You know, if he doesn't have someone to bring and he wants to bring a plus one, you'd be more than welcome.'

'Oh! You're very kind, but we're not that close,' she said, blushing, thinking about just how close she had been with Nate. There wasn't a single inch of skin on his body with which she hadn't been intimately familiar. She knew he had a birthmark on the sole of his foot. She knew he had a small circular scar on his right butt cheek from when he'd had chicken pox as a child. And she knew all about the tattoo just below his right pectoral muscle. The staff of Asclepius: a serpent-entwined rod, wielded by the Greek god Asclepius, which symbolised healing and medicine. Maybe he had more now.

But why had Nate never introduced her to his brother?

Because I wasn't important. Or a real girlfriend. I was just a warm body he needed when he wanted to rid himself of the difficulties of our days.

Had she made it too easy for him before? Had she been so willing for any form of affection, she had taken whatever he'd chosen to dole out?

'Plus this sounds like a family thing, and I'm not family,' she said.

Lucas raised a solitary eyebrow. 'Oh, puh-lease! I've sat around listening to my brother give the whole "we're a family" speech when he talks about every new team on board.'

'Does he?' Maddy smiled, amused.

'Of course! He really gets into character. Sometimes I play the role of naughty nurse just to try and derail him, but I'll give my brother credit where it's due: he can maintain focus like nobody can. I mean, you must have noticed that, right?'

She nodded. She liked Lucas. He seemed fun, easy to talk to.

'You single?' Lucas asked.

Maddy laughed. 'I'm not prepared to answer that.'

'Hah! That means you are—you just don't want to admit it. So, you're single, he's single, you're both adults and you seem like you'd be his type—gorgeous, intelligent, redhead...' Lucas leaned in and whispered, 'I shouldn't tell you this, because if he ever found out he'd be mortified, but he once told me he knew a redhead *very well indeed*, if you catch my drift?' Lucas raised both eyebrows and waggled them suggestively.

She could feel herself blushing. Lucas obviously had no idea that she was probably the redhead in question!

'Anyhoo... Do pop along this evening. If you're free, of course.'

'I'm on call,' she lied. 'But I'll pass on your message.'

'You're a star. Mwah!' He blew her a kiss and sashayed away.

She watched him go and disappear round a corner, just as the patient Nate had been with came out of his consulting room. Nate and the passenger shook hands and then he came over to stand by Maddy at the console. 'Everything okay?'

'Yes. Absolutely. I have a message for you.'
'Oh. Who from?'
She smiled. 'Your brother. Lucas.'
Now it was his turn to blush.

CHAPTER FOUR

'CARLOS! CONGRATULATIONS! So you're finally going to make an honest man of my brother?' Nate gave him a big hug. Carlos was Spanish, with thick dark hair and twinkling eyes.

Carlos glanced at Lucas and laughed. 'As honest as I can, though to be truthful with you, I'm not sure it's doable.'

Nate smiled. 'You know him well.'

Carlos reached for Lucas's hand and squeezed it in his own. 'Well enough to put a ring on his finger. He makes me happy. Happier than I've ever been.'

Nate was pleased. It was amazing to see Lucas happy and settled with someone who loved him. He was pleased that he had found someone to be in his life. If it went well, then maybe Nate could go off and do his own thing. Not that he hadn't loved being there for his brother, and getting to know him again after all those years apart, but he'd seen him at rock bottom. Nate had vowed not to leave his side, until he saw Lucas at the peak of happiness. It was a sacrifice he'd been willing to make, and sitting here now, seeing his little brother in love, engaged to be married, well…it made his own heart sing.

Not that he could say his brother was completely out of the woods yet. Relationships were tricky things and they could go wrong any time. No, he would stay until he'd seen Lucas walk down the aisle and say 'I do'. And God forbid Carlos ever broke his heart... 'Have you named the day?'

Lucas glanced at Carlos and smiled. 'We're going to get married on board! We've asked the captain to officiate, and he's said yes, and then we'll have a second official ceremony in Spain so Carlos's family can be there.'

'Wow. So soon?'

Nate listened as Carlos expounded on his vast network of siblings, cousins, aunts, uncles, nephews and nieces. It was confusing at times, trying to remember all their names, but it was nice just to sit there and hear Carlos tell funny stories about them all, hear about how stable an upbringing Carlos had had and how close they all were, how supportive. And how this huge Spanish family was about to become his brother's.

It was what Lucas needed—stability, love, warmth. He would be welcomed into Carlos's family with a warm embrace and it would make Nate feel easier about branching away to follow his own dreams that he'd put on hold for his brother.

'Are you happy for me, Nate?' asked Lucas.

'Of course I am! You've found the love of your life.' He smiled and sipped his drink.

'Now we just need you to find yours and we'll both be happy.'

'I am happy.'

Lucas leaned in. 'You think I don't realise that you

pressed pause on your own life so that I could find my feet in mine?'

'I've not pressed pause.'

'No? Why have you not come to dinner tonight with someone? A ship full of beauties and you sit here alone!'

'A ship full of potential patients, Lucas! I can't date them.'

'You could date that pretty doctor in your clinic—the redhead, Dr Finch! She's gorgeous! And I know you have a thing for redheads!'

Nate sipped his wine. He'd made the mistake of once telling Lucas about Madeline. But not by name, so his brother had no idea that the much-missed redhead he'd left behind in London was the very same person he was suggesting should have joined them for dinner.

They'd been sitting together one night in Nate's flat. It had been Lucas's first night out of rehab. He'd been clean, sober for the first time in years, and they'd been telling each other about the missed chances in their life. The missed chances when they both could have had something big.

Lucas had mentioned the day he had come out to their parents, so sure that they would be happy for him, so certain that there would be happy tears and hugs, and that they would embrace him and tell him that they loved him. They'd always adored him—he'd had no reason to suspect any other reaction. But it hadn't happened that way. His dad had kicked off, their mother had gone silent in shock and, in the middle of a raging row with his father, Lucas had run out of the house, heartbroken, his dreams in tatters, his very identity, who he was, dragged through the mud.

His father had accused him of causing them shame and embarrassment, saying that he would not have *someone like that* in the house, when *someone like that* had made them so proud with his GCSE results. The *someone like that* who had impressed them so much when he'd starred in his school's production of *Frankenstein*. The *someone like that* who had captained his cricket team and took them to victory for the first time in the school's history.

'They liked me enough when I followed their path, but couldn't love me enough when I found my own,' he'd said.

Lucas had begun to live on the streets and got in with the wrong people, turned to drugs.

'A different reaction from them and my future might have been different. They might still be alive.'

They'd both sat in silence that night, no words needed. Nate had learned that his parents' drinking had got much worse after he'd left. They'd gone out in their car and his father Bill had caused a car accident that killed them both instantly.

And Lucas had wrongly carried the guilt of their deaths into rehab, until Nate had come back into his life and put him right. He'd told him he wasn't to blame. That it wasn't his fault. That their parents had been flawed, that they were all flawed. That everyone made mistakes. And then he'd then listed his—including walking away from a redhead...

Lucas could never know she was on this ship. Because if he knew he would not stop until he tried to get them back together. Which was a terrible idea.

'I can't date a colleague,' he said, trying to derail that line of conversation.

'Why on earth not? She's your type! Are you telling me you're going to be celibate for the entire contract?'

'Can we talk about something else?' he asked, feeling uncomfortable.

'Leave your brother alone,' Carlos said, placing his hand on Lucas's.

'Thank you, Carlos. See? He's on my side.' Nate smiled and they clinked glasses.

'Hmm,' Lucas said, trying to sound annoyed and failing.

The rest of the evening went very well and Nate discovered a lot about Carlos that he liked. He was the right man for Lucas. He knew about his brother's struggles with drugs and accepted him for who he was, which was all that Lucas had ever looked for.

Nate often felt guilty about not having been there during those turbulent years after Lucas had come out. If he had not abandoned his brother to save himself, then maybe everything would have turned out differently. But he'd had to leave. He couldn't wait to escape.

His stepdad, Lucas's father, had made it clear that he'd never liked Nate, being the son of his wife's first husband, who'd passed. They'd never warmed to one another and, though Nate had initially been thrilled at the idea of having a younger brother, it had quickly become clear that Nate was second best. Even his own mum, to keep the peace, had often sided with her new husband and, feeling unloved and unwanted, feeling a burden, Nate had left, tearing apart the two brothers.

He'd hated leaving Lucas behind. He loved him and,

when Lucas had fallen off the radar, he'd just assumed that his stepfather had poisoned Lucas against him, not realising that Lucas had already turned to drugs and was lost in a world of pain.

So much hurt and destruction, all because one man—his stepfather—had come into their lives like a grenade, blowing them apart in all directions, broken, bleeding and forever maimed.

'Let me raise a glass…to Lucas and Carlos. Congratulations on your engagement and may you have a happy lifetime ahead of you both.'

Maddy had come up to look at the stars. There was an observation deck at the top of the ship, with a room that had star charts decorating the walls and ceilings and a selection of telescopes bolted to the floor.

She'd never been to sea before. She'd never really been out of urban areas, really, and she'd heard someone say once that, the further away from light pollution, the clearer the stars. Tonight was such a clear night and the skies were inky black. As she wanted to explore the ship, as well as open herself up to new experiences, stargazing had seemed the perfect choice.

I might like it!

It would be looking at something bigger than herself. She imagined each star as a sun, millions of miles away in a vast galaxy; imagined looking at constellations, maybe other planets! She'd perused the beginner guides in the room and, as the ship cruised through the darkness of the mouth of the Bay of Biscay, Maddy gazed up at the skies and allowed herself to imagine other worlds, other galaxies.

It made her own situation, her own difficulties, seem insignificant. What did it matter that she was sharing a ship and a medical bay with Nate? She ought to be grateful she'd become reacquainted with an old friend! What did it matter that he'd left without a word? That wasn't *her* fault! That was *his*.

The stars were beautiful. Life was beautiful. Here she was, forging a new path, finding new possibilities. She was going to travel the world as a cruise-ship doctor and she'd told herself that, if this contract went well, then would travel the entire world before she stopped and returned to England. Why not? She had no-one waiting for her at home. Why not lead a different life, full of exploration?

The stars seemed to twinkle acknowledgement at her. *Good idea*, they seemed to say. Peaceful, soothed, she headed back down into the ship and towards the lift that would take her down to her deck. She passed a row of restaurants and saw couples through the window, smiling at one another, in love, one couple holding hands. She was happy for them and did not envy them their happiness. She would find joy in other things. Someone was being surprised with a birthday cake adorned with a firework fizzing and sparking away as their family launched into a rendition of *Happy Birthday*.

She briefly thought of her own past birthdays, in care homes. The other kids would gather around and it had been okay. She'd made peace with her childhood. Lately, her birthdays had been spent with colleagues and friends, but no-one important in her life. Afterwards, she'd always bought a beautiful cupcake for herself, put a candle on it, blown it out and made a wish. She missed her old colleagues—Jordan, Imran and Kelly.

She saw groups chatting and laughing, everyone having a good time in each other's company, and felt alone. She hoped that Nate was enjoying his evening with his brother and new fiancé. That he was happy, raising a glass to celebrate the engagement. As she turned the corner that would take her down to the crew area, she bumped into someone coming in the other direction.

'Oh! I'm sorry, I...'

It was as if thinking about him had conjured him, like magic.

Nate. Looking devastatingly handsome in a dinner jacket and open-necked white shirt, a hint of tanned skin below.

'Sorry, I didn't mean to bump into you. I must pay more attention where I'm going,' he said, cheeks flushed, eyes sparkling as his gaze raked over her.

She'd not put on anything special. She'd just wanted to be comfortable, even though it was formal night on the ship and most people were dressed up to the nines. Maddy reckoned she probably stuck out like a sore thumb in her grey jogging bottoms, trainers and oversized top but, after a day of being dressed smartly and attending crew and passengers, it had felt good just to kick back and wear something comfortable. 'No, no, *I* wasn't looking where I was going,' she apologised, stepping back from him, taking herself out of the danger zone.

Because, the second she'd bumped into him, her body had fizzed into life. First of all, he smelt *good*. And not the kind of good that was something simply having a pleasing aroma, such as recently cut grass or freshly brewed coffee, but the kind of good that drove her senses wild. That made her want to step into his personal space and breathe him in some more. The kind of good that urged her to rip open his shirt, sending buttons flying, place a hand upon his flesh and her cheek to his pecs and just *enjoy*. To trail her finger down his chest and over his smooth skin and slip that shirt from his broad shoulders and trail kisses over his body...

Secondly, he *looked* amazing, casually cool, as if the suit had been made just for him. It draped his body just so, hugging it perfectly, emphasising his neat waist and fit body, as if he was born to model this suit in particular. The dark jacket brought out the honeyed hazel in his eyes, the white shirt giving him a healthy glow.

And thirdly, in the moment she'd bumped into him, her hand had gone to his chest and she'd felt the solidity of him, the hardness of him. All together, her mind had gone into overload and had provided her with many flashbacks of many nights spent with this man and what he could do to her. What he had done to her and how he had made her feel. And that had been years ago! What could he do now? The possibilities were endless and, though she yearned to find out, she knew she had to hold herself back from him and protect herself, because this man could so easily take her heart again and crush it beneath his perfectly polished shoes, like he had done once before.

The memory that he had abandoned her, without explanation and without apology, was like a bucket of ice water dashed over her head: stark, bewildering and utterly sobering.

'Have you been out to dinner?' she asked, her brain

reaching for something safe to ask, even though she knew the answer, having delivered his brother's invitation herself.

'Yes, at the Orchard,' he replied, nodding, seemingly happy to stick with safe topics too.

Had he had as much of a visceral reaction to her as she had had to him?

Probably not.

She was only in a jogging outfit that hid her body. Her hair was up in a messy topknot, and she'd no make-up on, and no perfume. *He probably thinks I look like a slob. Probably thinks he had a lucky escape!*

A twinge of annoyance washed over her. Why couldn't she have looked amazing? Why hadn't she put on her best party outfit and gone dancing down in the crew entertainment area with her hair done, her make-up completed to perfection, wearing a dress that pulled her in, in all the right places, hugging her body and emphasising her curves, showing legs up to there and a cleavage that drew the eye?

Actually, I don't think I've ever dressed like that in my entire life.

'With your brother. Lucas, right?'

He nodded. 'And his fiancé.'

'Carlos, if I remember. Did it go well?'

'Absolutely! Lucas has found himself a great guy… someone who balances him perfectly. Provides the sense to his crazy…'

He was looking her up and down, taking in her grey jogging outfit.

She felt herself blush. 'Sounds like he's found the right one. He's lucky. Not many people get that.'

'No.'

Was he getting closer? It felt as though he was.

She could feel her heart pounding in her chest. 'Those sorts of people are hard to find...' she said, her words faltering as Nate stepped even closer.

Was he drunk? Or were his eyes glazed because of something else...such as lust?

She'd succumbed to that look so many times before, unable and completely unwilling to protest, because she'd wanted him so much too. And it had felt good to be wanted, even if it had just been for her body and nothing else. Just to be seen, noticed, wanted... It had been enough for someone starved of affection and attention.

It felt for a moment as if they were back at London Saint and Nate had found them a corner to be in, to share a moment: a touch, a brush of lips, something to sate them both.

She was up against a wall now and he was so close. As she gazed at his face, she tried to not let herself be hypnotised by the beauty of it: the soft swell and fullness of his lips, the sharp slice of his jaw, the delicate curve to his cheekbones. Those eyes that she'd so often stared into as they'd had sex, watching the ways his pupils dilated and grew darker, larger; the way his hair fell about his face... 'Nate, we...'

She didn't get to say anything else, for suddenly he was kissing her. Those lips melted against hers, his body squashing her against the wall, his hard body grinding into her. A low moan came to her throat as she whimpered in surrender and felt utter unfettered joy at being kissed by him again.

How long had she spent mourning the loss of his

touch? How long had she grieved, thinking she would never see him again? Those first few weeks of him being gone had been awful. She'd felt as if she'd lost everything: her colleague, her best friend...her lover. He'd been the one person who saw her, who got her, who understood her. She had loved him so much, but had been so afraid to tell him, and he'd had no idea what it had done to her when he had just upped and left. And still she *did not know why*.

Maddy knew she ought to do the sensible thing and pull away, not allow herself to be dragged back into his web, to be swept away by his kiss, but it was Nate! He was kissing her again; how many times had she lain in her bed after he'd left, praying to a god she wasn't sure that she believed in that, if she could have just one more kiss, just one more moment with him, then she would be satisfied. That it would be enough.

And so selfishly, not knowing if she would get this chance again, she pushed aside her anger, her pain, her grief and her *questions* and simply kissed him back with everything that she had.

It was like time travel, like going at hyper-speed, like going in slow motion. It was fireworks and electricity. It was her oxygen, her light and dark. She could feel herself being pulled in all directions as his kiss deepened. And the *heat* of it...she couldn't breathe, she couldn't think. She just knew that she *wanted*: wanted more.

His body was against hers, his arousal pressed up against her. She knew without a shadow of a doubt that, if they'd been back in her cabin and not in a public corridor, she would have been ripping his clothes off him by now and dragging him into her bed, where she'd be able to consume every single inch of him.

Sod the past, sod the pain, sod being abandoned! 'Nate...' she breathed as his lips trailed down her neck and then back up, reclaiming her mouth, his hands in her hair, as if he couldn't touch enough of her. She soaked up every sensation, trying to commit them to memory so she could enjoy them again later. His thumb ran over her bottom lip and she grabbed at his hand with her own and licked it.

Nate groaned and his eyes met hers and suddenly, somehow, the spell was broken. He stepped back, away from her, dishevelled from their contact, his gaze glassy, and he was frowning.

She stepped forward, still needing more, not sure why he'd ended it, why he'd stepped away. She was stunned, her body in a state of fission.

'I'm sorry, Mads, that was a...mistake. We should never have...' He blinked, shook his head. '*I* should never have... I've had too much to drink, I... I'm sorry.' He looked down and away, and headed away from her without another word, leaving her breathless and confused.

She watched him depart, mouth agape, left wanting, left by him *yet again*!

How many times am I going to let him do this to me?

Disgusted with herself, ashamed, she wiped her mouth on her sleeve, pulled up her hood and headed in the opposite direction.

Nate woke with a stinking hangover and groaned. How had this happened? Dinner with Lucas and Carlos. His brother stuck to mocktails during dinner, and Nate had joined him to support him. But then, as the night had worn on, someone had encouraged them to have something stronger. *We should celebrate properly.* Champagne had been ordered. Corks had popped to toast the happy couple. They'd ordered a bottle and, judging by his headache, the way his body felt and the taste in his mouth, Nate feared he had drunk the entire thing!

Ugh.

Standing, he made his way to the *en suite* and switched on the light, wincing at its brightness and his stark reflection in the mirror. He needed a shower; he needed to freshen up to look less like a zombie and feel more like a human being.

Turning on the water, he stripped himself of his clothes, feeling that he was missing something important, but he couldn't think what it might be. He soaped himself down and washed his hair, and was rinsing out the shampoo when a stark and vivid image came into his mind: kissing Maddy.

Wait...

He forced the recall into full Technicolor vision. He'd bumped into her. They'd collided in the corridor. Carlos and Lucas had already left and gone to their cabin, as their room was in a different direction from his. Nate had just been to the bathroom and come round the corner, and then there she was, looking beautiful and effortlessly gorgeous in jogging bottoms and an over-sized top with a hood. She'd looked so warm and cosy...inviting!

His gaze had fallen to her mouth as she'd said something...what had she said? He wasn't sure about that part, but what he did remember was watching her lips move: full, soft, pink lips. Lips that he remembered had once trailed down his body, bringing with them delight and ecstasy, and he wasn't sure what had happened in his brain then. He'd spent the entire evening watching Carlos and Lucas so happy and in love and he'd envied his brother having someone. Of course Lucas deserved happiness after all he had been through, and Nate craved the same, but everyone on this boat was a potential patient. He could hardly go dancing, end up kissing someone in a darkened corner and have a one-night stand, not when that wasn't what he was looking for.

I wanted what Lucas has. Someone I knew. Someone I had a long history with. Someone I felt comfortable with. Someone who I had deep feelings for.

And there she was, in all her natural, beautiful glory—like a gift! And he'd succumbed to his desires in that moment without thinking it through. For a moment there, he'd been utterly lost in how she'd made him feel that he'd forgotten to think with his brain...though, to be fair, that part of his body hadn't had possession of the blood flow right there and then.

Suddenly he'd been right where he was meant to be.

Kissing Maddy had felt so right, feeding his soul and his senses in a way they'd long forgotten. For too long he had felt like a neglected and unloved plant in the middle of an arid desert, and Maddy had been the rain, dropping refreshing water onto thirsty leaves and into his roots. All he'd wanted to do was drink her up, drink every drop she had to give; take everything.

And then...reality and logic had crept into his brain, reminding him that he wasn't good for her, and he'd stepped back, suddenly aware that he had stepped over a line. Stepped over a boundary that he should never have crossed. Maddy was his past, and he'd made a promise to himself that he would never go back there. Besides, he wasn't sure she deserved to get involved with him again. He'd abandoned her, left just as things had been starting to get complicated in his mind, and she deserved more than he could give. He was selfish. He left when things got tough, and she'd been deserted enough in life without him adding to it even more.

Besides, she probably wasn't even single any more... even if she had kissed him back.

And now he would have to face her at work.

I'll apologise again—clear the air—then everything will be fine.

By the time he reached the medical bay that morning, the two painkillers he'd taken were just starting to tackle the champagne headache, and the water he'd chugged was sloshing around unpleasantly in his stomach, but he forced a smile for the staff. He asked Sylvia to send Maddy through to his office when she arrived.

There was a knock on his door five minutes later and he looked up to see her standing there, a vision in blue scrubs. He felt his body respond at seeing her again and he had to fight down the urge to rush over to her, close his office door, let down her hair from its clip and kiss her until his lips got sore and he needed to breathe.

'Ah, yes, Maddy. Come in, close the door.'

She raised an eyebrow. 'I think it's best that we leave the door open, don't you?'

Of course. He nodded. 'Then at least take a seat.' The words 'I won't bite,' were on the tip of his tongue and he had to count to ten until the urge to say them was gone. Unfortunately, the image of him *actually* biting her was very distracting.

Maddy settled herself into the chair furthest from him.

'I would like to formally apologise for my behaviour last night towards you. It was inappropriate and you caught me in a low moment.' He sighed. 'Sorry, I don't mean to try to excuse my behaviour. You are welcome to file a formal complaint, if you wish.'

Maddy frowned and shook her head. 'I don't think that's necessary. We all make mistakes.'

He let out a breath, relief flooding him. That she might have taken this further was not out of the question; he'd have hated, yet accepted, the black mark against his name. Clearly their friendship and previous relationship had saved him from that. 'So, you're happy for us to continue on as colleagues?'

She met his gaze sharply at his last word. 'Yes. That's all we ever can be.'

The feel of her pressed up against the wall, her soft body melting into his, flashed back into his mind like a torment. 'Of course.'

Emily Simons came into the medical bay with her mother. It turned out the cruise was a kind of celebratory holiday they were sharing together, as Emily had finished her exams. Unfortunately for the sixteen-year-old, she'd been up all night with gastrointestinal pain and now she was feeling sick and couldn't stomach the idea of food.

'What time did this start?' Maddy asked the young girl.

'About ten o' clock last night. We'd had a celebratory

meal at the Sakura Japanese restaurant, and then gone on to the circus show, but we went back to our cabin early because I didn't feel great.'

'Eat anything new or strange at the restaurant?'

'I tried oysters for the first time.'

Maddy smiled. 'What did you think?'

'Yucky on the way down *and* on the way back up.'

'You've been vomiting?'

'No, but the burps I've had feel like I might.'

'Okay. Any episodes of diarrhoea?'

'No, just pain.'

'Since ten o' clock last night?'

Emily nodded.

Maddy was writing everything down on a piece of paper, gathering her thoughts. 'And do you have any medical issues I ought to know about?'

'No.'

Maddy looked to Emily's mum for confirmation, but she seemed to agree. 'Any medications that you usually take or have had recently prescribed?' There was no way she was going to forget *that* question again. She couldn't afford to mess up, not after all that had happened with Nate. That mess up with Peggy—who was already feeling much better, thankfully—and then the kiss…

That kiss…she felt so stupid for letting it happen! To allow him to get inside her walls once more. So much for fresh starts. All she'd managed to do was repeat the past mistakes. She would not embarrass herself again and they would remain strictly professional.

'No, nothing.'

'Alright. Well, I'm going to need to check you over— perform some obs such as your temperature, your blood pressure, that kind of thing—and have a little feel of your tummy, would that be alright?'

Emily nodded.

She smiled. 'Don't worry. We'll help get you sorted.'

The young girl's blood pressure was slightly elevated, but nothing to worry about. Probably as a result of her worry about being in the medical bay and having been up all night in tummy pain. There was no temperature, so that was good. Blood sugars were normal and, when she palpated Emily's abdomen, she found no signs of tenderness over McBurney's Point which might have indicated an appendicitis, though her patient did report tenderness directly over her stomach.

Once her patient was sitting back with her mother, Maddy gave her assessment. 'Well, I think what we have here is a mild case of gastritis. That means your stomach is inflamed, possibly aggravated by the new foods you're trying or the stress of having finished exams, maybe both. I'm going to suggest you rest, get lots of fluids, even if you don't want to eat, and I'll also prescribe you some antacids to help deal with that. If you do eat, I suggest soft, plain foods, nothing exotic, alright?' She smiled.

Emily smiled back. 'So, I'll be okay?'

'Yes. But if you start being sick, or get diarrhoea, or if you feel like it's getting worse, you come straight back and see me, okay?'

'Thank you, Dr Finch.'

'You're most welcome.'

When her patient was gone, Maddy tapped her clinical notes into the computer, noting all her observations, her reasonings, conclusion and recommendations. The more she wrote, the more confident she was in her assessment, and she pressed *save*.

She had no patients waiting, so she carried out some admin, but her mind was on last night and this morning: the kiss; Nate asking if she wanted to file a complaint. That would have been a fine start to her career on cruise ships, wouldn't it, filing a charge of sexual harassment against her boss? No, she couldn't do it. If it had been someone she hadn't known, then maybe, but she and Nate had a history and it was different. She could complain if she wanted, and she felt any woman would be well within their rights to do so if a boss had overstepped the mark like that, but she didn't want to.

She felt that she and Nate could get through it. Their friendship had always got them through anything and it had been there first, before any sexy shenanigans had ever happened between them, and she didn't want to lose that, even if he had just upped and left for years without explanation.

Speaking of which, he still hasn't told me why, or said sorry for that.

She figured she would never get an explanation. Not now. Too much water had gone under the bridge. *Too much sea under the* Serendipity, she thought, with a wry smile.

What had last night's kiss proved, anyway? That he still felt something for her? No. He'd had too much to drink, he'd said. He'd spent the evening watching a loved up couple and had felt...what?

Maybe he'd felt a little of what she'd felt for years, seeing everyone else finding someone, creating their own families. And Maddy...she was on her own, had always been on her own. And no-one had ever made her feel for them the way she'd felt for Nate. They'd not even come close and she hated the fact that she still had Nate on a pedestal, despite the fact that he had hurt her.

What did that say about her? That she was misguided? Used to being treated badly that she'd accepted it from him too? That she was so used to being overlooked that his behaviour had not been abhorrent, but just what she was used to?

You sad, sad woman. And you always get maudlin when you're hungry.

Maddy headed off to the crew's mess, grabbed herself a jacket potato and chicken salad with dressing, sat down at a table and opened up on her phone a book she was reading. It was a non-fiction title about a woman stranded on a desert island and how she'd survived. She'd just got to the part where the woman used her bra to make a pair of slippers for her bare feet when she felt someone arrive at her table. She looked up. 'Hey.'

'May I join you?' It was Nate, holding his own tray.

By rights, she ought to tell him to go away, to keep his distance. How did he expect her to sit there and eat her food, when being this close to him kept reminding her of that kiss last night? But she'd told him that there wasn't a problem and that they could work together, and what did colleagues do but have lunch together? 'Take a seat.'

He slid into the chair opposite her. 'How are you enjoying ship food?'

'It's good.' She looked down at his plate of chilli. 'You never used to like spicy food.'

He smiled wryly. 'No, I know. But when you start

travelling the globe, you begin trying other cuisines, don't you?'

'I'll tell you at the end of the contract.'

He took a moment to stir his drink.

Maddy gazed at him. Just last night he'd pressed her against a wall and kissed her, and now they sat opposite one another, distanced, propriety ruling once more. 'How's your head?'

He laughed. 'It was bad first thing, but I'm feeling better now.'

She nodded. 'I should have shouted more. Maybe slammed a cupboard or two—most definitely the door on my way out.' She winked at him to show she was joking, then flushed. *What the hell am I doing?*

'I appreciate you not doing *any* of those things. I don't think my skull would have taken it. I saw your notes this morning on that teenage girl, Emily.'

'Oh yes?'

'I thought they were great. Very thorough. A solid work-up of the patient; clear differential and notes. You documented everything and your diagnosis and prognosis were exactly what I would have thought too.'

She was relieved. After her initial embarrassment at forgetting to ask Peggy about recent medications, she'd been keen to redeem herself in Nate's eyes. 'I was worried that it could be food poisoning after she mentioned she'd had oysters, but without the sickness and diarrhoea I leaned towards gastritis and didn't want to second-guess myself.'

'And that's what I need from the doctors in my team: confidence. And you handled it well. It's smart medicine.'

She smiled at his praise. It meant a lot to her. She'd once had so much confidence leading the A&E department, confidence that had been broken and shattered into a million pieces after her attack. When she'd screwed up in front of him, she'd been appalled, so this felt good...very good. And she sensed that he was keen to give her some good feedback after his behaviour. 'Thank you.'

'You're welcome.' He smiled back at her.

She very quickly realised that she was staring into his kind eyes and losing herself a little in them. She looked away, breaking the contact. It wouldn't do to think that he had any other intention towards her other than that of being her boss, her mentor. Losing herself in his eyes could only lead to more heartache. She pushed her plate away. 'I, er, ought to go. There's a crew clinic coming up.'

'You haven't eaten your lunch.'

'No, um...' She was about to say everything was fine—she would grab something later—but there came a huge bang from the crew galley, voices shouting, plates and trays tumbling to the floor, and smoke—lots and lots of smoke.

And then the shrill sound of a fire alarm began to sound.

Nate got to the crew galley first, stepping back as some of the kitchen staff made their escape from the kitchen that was quickly filling with smoke. The air seemed thick with a smell. *Oil?* A crew member caught Nate's arms as he stumbled out, face sweating. 'I think one of the fryers went! Tried to put it out, but...' He shook his head and coughed, struggling to breathe. 'I think Manuel is still trying!'

He watched as Maddy assessed the man for any visible burns. 'Get to the medical bay! Tell them to send help!' she said.

The man nodded, coughing, and staggered away into the arms of some other crew who helped him walk away.

Nate knew that if someone was still in the kitchen, still trying to breathe in these thick fumes and smoke, then they were in real danger, not only from the fire, but from damage to their lungs and throat. He saw a towel hanging on a rack by the door and grabbed it, then rushed over to the drinks station in the mess and poured water over it, then he looked to Maddy. 'Stay here. I'm going in for Manuel.'

'Not on your own, you're not! It's dangerous. We go together!'

'I can't risk having you injured too!' he yelled, trying to be heard over the alarm. Hopefully, the maintenance and fire crew would arrive soon to assist.

'We go in together or not at all!' she insisted.

He could sense that he was not going to win this one, so he ripped the towel in two and gave her half. 'Put it over your mouth, it should help against the fumes. Stay low!'

She nodded and clutched the cloth to her face.

He could see in her eyes that she was scared, but by god, the girl had some steel balls! She was determined to go in with him, and he was most grateful for that, but also terrified that she would get hurt. If something happened to her...

His heart was hammering in his chest from fear,

from worrying about her, the thick smoke, the crackle of flames he could hear in the kitchen. He could hear someone trying to use a fire extinguisher, then the sound of a clunk, as if it had been dropped to the floor. 'Manuel?' he yelled.

No answer. Overhead the sprinklers sprang into action, raining down on them and soaking everything.

'Over there!' Maddy pointed through the smoke and water. He followed her finger.

Just barely visible, they saw a shape on the floor: a cook, an extinguisher by his side.

He could feel the heat of the flames as they got closer, scurrying low across the floor, blinking back the burning smoke in their watering eyes.

They reached Manuel and Nate pressed his fingers to the man's pulse. It was there, but thready. 'We need to get him out!' he tried to yell, coughing his way through the words. Now he was glad she was there. It would take both of them to get the cook out of there. If he'd been alone, he'd have had to try and drag the man himself, and in this thick smoke, with oil on the floor. It could have been impossible. With her to help, they had some luck on their side. Thankfully, there weren't many flames, it was mostly smoke.

Shielding Manuel, they began to drag him back the way they'd come, hoping they were going in the right direction. There was another bang, another flare of light, and Nate threw himself over Manuel and Maddy, knocking her to the floor as flames flared from a pan or grill.

Maddy yelped. For a very brief moment, a millisecond maybe, time stood still. The fire alarm still blared loudly all around them, sprinklers soaked them, the smoke still billowed, the stench of oil continued to coat his nasal passages and his throat and he was very concerned as to why Manuel was out cold. Nate lay over Maddy, his body covering hers like a shield, her scared eyes looking up at him above the cloth that covered her lower face and his heart pounding like it had never pounded before.

'Are you alright?' he asked.

She stared back at him, shocked, uncertain, confused. 'Define alright.'

He felt himself smile, despite it all. Sarcasm; she was okay.

At that moment, extra crew came in to fight the blaze and oil fire dressed in fire-resistant clothes. Manuel got handed over to the other doctors who had attended after receiving the emergency call, and Nate and Maddy got to their feet and exited the galley kitchen back into the mess, where the air was most definitely cleaner, though not great.

Genevieve fussed over them, sat them both down together and began examining them.

He saw a tear in Maddy's top and a red line of blood on her shoulder. 'You're bleeding.'

Maddy looked at it blankly, then over at him. 'So are you.'

She was staring at his chin and he reached up to touch it and found warm wetness. His fingers were red. 'It's nothing.'

'You did amazing in there,' she said softly.

'So did you. I couldn't have done it without you,' he replied, meaning every word. She'd been so brave, going into the kitchen with him to rescue Manuel.

The crew's mess was filling with people—medics, other crew—and then the captain of the ship appeared. He was tall and looked pristine in his perfectly white shirt as he hurried over to them. 'Are you both alright?'

'Minor abrasions, captain. Nothing serious,' Genevieve said.

'Was anyone seriously hurt?'

'Maybe Manuel. He tried to put out the fire,' Nate said, coughing slightly.

'I'll find out. You two get to medical.'

'Aye aye, captain.' He gave a mock salute. Captain Thomas laid a reassuring and thankful hand on Nate's shoulder, smiled at Maddy and then headed over to get information from the fire teams.

'Think he'll turn the ship around?' Maddy asked.

'Depends on how bad it is.'

Genevieve applied gauze to Maddy's shoulder. 'Come on, you two. Medical bay… And no offence, Dr Blake, but I'm in charge right now, okay?'

Nate smiled. That was just fine.

CHAPTER FIVE

SHE AND NATE had got away with very minor abrasions. The kitchen staff had luckily not been close when the fryer had gone, and one man had suffered a small burn that was easily dealt with. Manuel had slipped on oil and had simply been stunned when they'd dragged him out. The fire crew had got control of the fire and thankfully, with their quick response and the sprinkler system working effectively, there'd actually been minimal damage to the galley kitchen. It had all just simply seemed a lot worse than it was due to the smoke caused by the oil in the fryer.

The passengers on board had not noticed a thing, and there was a secondary crew mess, so the captain decided to continue with the cruise and the maintenance team was busy repairing the crew galley as they sailed into Vigo. The captain had given Nate, Maddy, Manuel and the kitchen crew strict instructions to disembark and enjoy the port for the day. So that was why Maddy had Nate knocking on her cabin door that morning to escort her into town, dressed casually in a white polo shirt and navy shorts that showed off his gorgeously tanned and toned legs, to escort her into town.

'Wow. Look at you!' she said, not used to seeing Nate like this. Normally he was dressed in trousers or scrubs. Or was naked. She'd never seen him in holiday mode.

'I was about to say the same about you. That dress is beautiful!'

She'd chosen a summer dress that skimmed just above her knee. It had spaghetti straps and was white with a dark-blue pattern printed on it. Somehow they'd matched colours. She'd left her long hair loose, but it was held back with large sunglasses and, of course, she'd smothered herself with the obligatory suncream. The scratch on her shoulder from the fire was a dark line and slightly bruised, but she barely noticed it.

Somehow, strangely, she was looking forward to spending a day in Spain with Nate. The fire, and being in a dangerous situation like that, had made her feel that maybe her long-held grudge seemed petty on the face of things. Nate hadn't known the extent of her feelings. They weren't committed, so maybe she ought just to forget it.

Last night, she'd read up a little on Vigo, the 'olive city'. It was famed for its seafood, had a historic port and was a gateway to the beautiful Cies Island—a national park that boasted stunning beaches, rich birdlife and beautiful scenery, which sounded right up her alley.

Since her attack, Maddy had often sought solace in nature when she could. It was in parks, mostly, as she'd not really left the city, and she'd used a lot of meditation apps that synthesised the sounds of nature and birdsong. And, since she and Nate had just been through something traumatic, the island of Cies sounded perfect.

Nate had offered to book them a place on the ferry that would take them there.

'Thank you. Ready to go?'

'As I'll ever be.' She was excited. Right now, it seemed hard to believe that she'd never travelled like this before. In the care system, there'd been a trip to the seaside booked once and Maddy had looked forward to it hugely. But on the day in question she'd not been very well, having woken with an upset stomach, and the decision had been made to leave her behind—which basically seemed to be the story of her life.

But now she was here, in the port of Vigo, and hugely excited about exploring all that it had to offer.

'As it's high season, I had to arrange official authorisation for us to go to Cies.'

'Really?'

'Yes. It's a protected area and the beach there, the Praia das Rodas, is apparently one of the most beautiful beaches in the world.'

'I can't wait!' She felt like a little girl, going on holiday for the first time. And after the stress of yesterday she needed a little relaxation. The repairs in the crew mess were coming along nicely and Manuel and the cook with a minor burn, were both doing well. 'I never, ever thought that I'd be abroad for the first time with you.'

'And I never thought that I would get to see that smile again, but…here we are.'

She glanced at him as they walked towards disembarkation. So he had thought of her after leaving, then; that was interesting—good, even! He hadn't just walked away with no regrets. He hadn't just walked away from her and forgotten her. He'd *missed* her.

Or he's just saying that to make me feel better.

She didn't want to doubt him. She didn't want anything to spoil this moment. They might not be together, but they were friends, and they'd just been through something traumatic together, so it was only right that they got to have some fun. Maddy didn't mind there being a ceasefire where her feelings were concerned so they could just forget the past and enjoy *the present*.

The sun shone down on them as they stepped off the ship and, feeling the warm rays soothe her flesh, she felt herself relax in an instant. Maddy could see palm trees, and she laughed. Palm trees were one of those things that existed in her mind as being *elsewhere*; somewhere exotic and abroad. She was used to oak, silver birch, or horse chestnut trees. Palm trees meant *holidays*, and already she could feel her happiness increasing.

Nate guided them to the ferry that would take them the forty-five-minute journey over to Cies Island. She sat nervously on her seat in the open deck and snapped pictures with her phone as they sailed across the sea towards the island.

She saw green hills and craggy cliffs, the air above the islands dotted with white gulls, and pretty soon they were sailing into a shell-shaped harbour that had beautiful white sands and clear blue waters. 'Oh my gosh...this place is *beautiful*!' She could already feel the stress leaving her and could already feel the desire to explore and enjoy this place! And, with Nate at her side, this was...well, unbelievable. If this had been before, then she would have taken his hand in hers without thinking twice.

But it wasn't before, this was *now*, and they were both different people. And she'd told him—colleagues only.

Nate hauled his backpack onto his shoulders. 'I took the liberty of bringing a little food for us to enjoy later. Maybe a beach picnic? But first, do you want to take a walk with me up to the viewing point?'

'Sounds great.'

There seemed to be a group of new arrivals doing the same thing. A lot had gone straight down to the beach, but some were walking ahead of Maddy and Nate. She began to take a lot of pictures. 'I want to remember everything,' she said, laughing.

'Here. Let me take a picture of you over there. We'll get the beach and the cliffs as a backdrop.'

She blushed standing in front of him, tucking her hair behind her ears when a soft breeze blew it in front of her face.

He showed it to her and she couldn't stop smiling. She wasn't usually a fan of herself in pictures, and luckily there'd never been anyone around her who'd wanted to take them. But in the one Nate took, he seemed to capture something about her.

'Let's do a selfie. Join me,' she suggested, not really thinking it through when Nate pressed up close against her so they could both be within the frame capture. She felt his arm snake around her and rest on a post as he moved in close and they both smiled and laughed nervously. When she pressed the button, the picture showed a very happy couple. *Anyone who didn't know us might think we were in love.*

Maddy put her phone away for a while as they continued the walk. It had boardwalk in places, but was mostly a stone, uphill path that weaved its way through rocks and trees until they finally reached the viewing point over an hour later. She was hot and tired, yet exhilarated when she saw the view of the rolling green cliffs, the crystal-blue waters, the curved slice of white sandy beach. And beyond the sea, the port of Vigo and *Serendipity* moored within it. Spain lay beyond it, all rippling in the heat of the day. 'I don't think I've ever seen anything so beautiful in all of my life!' she said.

'I know what you mean.'

She thought he was agreeing with her about the view, but when she turned to look at him he was staring at her. She flushed with heat and turned away. 'You shouldn't say things like that.'

'I'm simply admiring the view.'

'It's that way,' she said, pointing away from herself and turning away from him so that she could pull her phone out once more and take more photos of this stunning place. 'And you said you wouldn't do this.'

She knew what he was doing. He was trying to pull her back in. Maybe not all the way, but a little. Because it was familiar, that was all. And they both knew how much fun they could have between them. Out here, away from the medical bay in the glorious sunshine and the beautiful views, relaxing, chilling, it was too easy to forget all the stuff that made them impossible. And hadn't he kissed her recently and known it was a mistake? So flirting with her was wrong, too. It was downright cruel.

He had walked away. He had kissed her and called it

a mistake. It was as if in kissing her like that—getting what he wanted in that moment and then apologising—he had got what *he* wanted and *he* needed, but her wants and desires had been completely ignored.

She had loved this man once. She had thought she had found her soul mate. But clearly he had never felt the same and she needed to remember that pain every single time she was tempted by him.

'You're right. I'm sorry,' he said.

It wasn't enough. Despite her thoughts earlier, she couldn't help but ask. 'Nate, why did you leave, without a word?'

'Maddy—'

'Did I not deserve an explanation?'

Nate sighed and looked down at the ground. 'I didn't think. I wasn't thinking clearly back then. There was a family emergency and I had to go. By the time my brain wasn't so muddled, so many months had passed and it just seemed easier to stay away. I mean, we were only casual, weren't we?'

She nodded, but internally she was screaming. She wanted to let him know that for her their relationship had been something far more serious than casual. That she had fallen in love with him. That the sex had been great, of course, but that that wasn't all that had drawn her to him. He was funny, kind and, she'd thought, loyal. He'd been intelligent and caring and he'd had her back at work. He'd been her best friend. 'Tell me what happened.'

He shrugged. 'It's complicated.'

'We have all day together. I'm happy to listen. Maybe if I understood then it wouldn't bother me as to why you walked away without telling me. Did you not think I deserved a second thought? Some consideration?'

He laid his hand on hers. 'Of course I did. But things moved so fast, and I barely had time to sort things out with the hospital. Every second mattered and I had to make choices. Prioritise.'

'And I wasn't one?' She pulled her hand out from under his.

'I'm not saying that.'

'Then what are you saying?'

Nate sighed. 'Like I said, it's complicated. You'd have to know my family to understand.'

'How could I have known about your family? You told me nothing. I didn't even know you had a brother until I met him the other day.'

'I told you that me and my family didn't speak. Lucas and I were estranged, so no, I chose not to tell the colleague I was having casual sex with about my very personal past!'

Maddy flushed and looked around them. Anyone could hear! Thankfully, it seemed no-one was listening, or if they were they were doing a very good job of hiding it. 'Fine. Don't tell me if I was just a colleague to you.' She walked away from him and over to the other side of the viewing point, trying to let go of her hurt and instead absorb the raw beauty of nature that she could see from up here, allow it to soothe her. They were in a magical place. She should be in awe. But instead she was hurting.

She busied herself taking photos. She got a couple to take a picture of her by the railing, then thanked them and returned the favour. When she checked her phone and compared the photo the couple had taken to the photo Nate had taken, she could see a huge difference.

She looked happy in Nate's photo, stilted in the second one.

Why do I let him have such power over me?

Maddy stalked over to him. 'Look, this is ridiculous! We're in this beautiful place. Let's not make it ugly by raking over the past. What's happened has happened and neither of us can change it, no matter how much we want to. The captain told us to rest and enjoy ourselves, so can we agree to just get on with that?'

Nate nodded. 'Of course. Shall we head back down—find a place on the beach or the sand dunes to have our picnic?'

Maddy agreed and forced a smile. 'That sounds wonderful. Let's do that.'

Nate had asked the kitchen to put together a few things for their little picnic and as he pulled out the sandwiches Maddy smiled.

'Egg and cress? You hate it!'

He winked at her. 'I've grown to love it.'

She remembered their first day in the emergency department together at London Saint Hospital. It had been their first shift and they'd been shadowing the same doctor, who'd been rushed off his feet. It was the middle of the afternoon before he'd even thought to tell them to go and have thirty minutes for their lunch break.

Their heads had been swimming with information. It was one thing to sit in a lecture room and learn about the human body, but quite another actually to be in the action of a real Accident and Emergency department and be responsible for people's lives. It had been overwhelming, but they'd both been buzzing as they'd made it up to the cafeteria in the hospital to grab a quick snack and the only sandwiches left in the fridge had been egg and cress.

'Ooh, lovely!' Maddy had said, grabbing them, along with a packet of crisps from the selection offered and a bottle of water.

'You like egg and cress?' he'd asked.

'I love it! You don't?'

He'd ended up having to grab cold chicken pasta in a plastic container, as it had been the only thing left, along with a badly bruised apple and a plain vanilla yoghurt. It hadn't exactly been dining like kings, but it'd had to do. He'd figured they were lucky to get a break at all, with the department having been so busy with patients. His chicken pasta had been tasteless, bland, and he'd pushed it to one side and eyed the yoghurt with apprehension.

'Here…have one of mine.' Maddy had offered him one of her sandwiches.

'No, no. That's yours. One of us should eat.'

She'd leaned forward then and made him make eye contact. 'No, we both should eat, or we're going to drop like flies. And those people sitting in that A&E waiting room are depending upon people like us to be at the top of our game. We can't be that if we don't eat properly.'

'Okay.' Reluctantly, he'd taken the sandwich and had had to admit that it wasn't half bad. She'd shared her crisps with him and they'd sat there discussing their morning, laughing about the moment when he'd struggled to get a cannula in because his hands had been shaking. And about the female patient who had come in with a fever and low belly pain and how Maddy suspected a urinary tract infection. She'd asked her patient for a water sample and left her to it, returning moments later to find a sample filled with beautifully clear water. Maddy had thought the woman extremely well hydrated, until the female patient had held up the water bottle she'd been drinking from and said, 'I hope this brand is okay. It's not the one I normally drink.'

Realisation had dawned rather quickly!

'Oh God, do you remember those days? We were so enthusiastic! So young!' Maddy said as she helped him lay out the picnic now.

'So naïve.'

She laughed. 'We had no idea what was ahead of us, did we?'

'Nope.' Now he smiled. 'It was a steep learning curve, that's for sure. I remember going home each day and flopping onto the sofa, absolutely shattered.'

Maddy nodded. 'I remember one day, I had a day shift. Seven in the morning until five. Five minutes before the end of my shift and I'm called into Resus to assist with the incoming patients from a large road-traffic accident—five patients, all in various states of injury, all serious. I finally left the hospital a few minutes to midnight and I got into my car and thought I'd just close my eyes for a few minutes before I drove home. Next thing I knew, you were rapping your knuckles against the driver window and it was minutes before our next day shift.'

He laughed, remembering, shaking his head. 'You'd been there all night!'

'You gave me your banana and the rest of your

mocha.' She smiled. 'If only you'd had a toothbrush and toothpaste on you.'

'Sadly, I didn't carry that as standard.' He laughed.

'You looked out for me from that day onwards.'

'You had my back too,' he said, smiling at her.

Those early days had been hectic. Foundation year doctors had to learn so many things that they just didn't get taught in a university lecture room. They'd had one lecture on how to deliver bad news to a patient and, whilst theory had been good in hypothetical situations, when it came to actually telling someone in real life that their family member had cancer or had died, people didn't always react the way they'd been told in books or lecture notes.

He'd always struggled with how long he ought to sit with someone after delivering bad news. He'd felt he should stay, answer questions and be there for them if needed. But in a busy A&E department he'd been needed elsewhere. Someone might just have lost a father, a mother, a wife, husband or child, but all the other patients had needed him too, so he'd not been able to stay with grieving family members or patients for as long as he would have liked.

There'd been one couple who'd come in with their daughter, a type-one diabetic who had gone into a diabetic coma at home. They had tried their best to revive her, but it had been too late and there'd been nothing they could do. The little girl had been ten years old, an only child. An IVF baby: precious, wanted and adored. Their reason for being had gone and they'd both collapsed in grief in the family room as he'd delivered the news. He'd taken them to her and stood with them, head bowed, as they had told her how much she was loved. And all the time his beeper had been going off, demanding his attention, calling him to other things deemed urgent.

There'd never been a lecture about *that*. The shame he'd felt, standing there as that beeper had interrupted those grieving parents over and over again… The embarrassment he'd felt to have had to make his excuses and leave them to it…

Maddy had covered for him as much as she could. She'd known where he was and had instructed the nurses to beep her for his patients and his patients' results, so that he'd be able to spend time with that couple, but even she hadn't been able to do everything. And, when he'd finally left them to return to his work and paste on a smile for others, he'd noticed the vast array of work that Maddy had got through—along with that for her own patients—just so that he could give his time to the grieving parents.

'Your colleagues become family. You can't help it,' she said.

'Sometimes they become something more,' Nate said, thinking of how his feelings towards fellow medic Maddy had changed. 'Sometimes they see them at a party in a beautiful red dress and realise the most gorgeous woman in the world has been by their side all the time.'

She blushed, even now. 'And they take you by the hand and lead you down a garden path…'

The party had been for a colleague having a thirtieth birthday party. His parents had offered to let him throw it at their place, which had turned out to be some large house in Surrey.

Somehow, miraculously, the party had fallen on a rare weekend on which neither Maddy nor Nate had been working and so they'd been able to go. Sick to death of scrubs and having her hair twisted up onto the top of her head, Maddy had taken the opportunity to go all out, to feel like a woman again. She'd worn a red dress that had emphasised her bust and hips and a hemline that had revealed her long legs. She'd worn her hair down and tamed into luscious waves, with smoky eye make-up and a black choker at her neck. She'd wanted to walk into the party and have all eyes turn to her, for the men that she worked with to realise that there was more to her than bags under her eyes, hair that hadn't been washed for a while and a strong pair of arms capable of popping a dislocated shoulder back into its socket. She'd wanted to feel feminine, she'd wanted to feel attractive, and, yes, she'd wanted to capture Nate's eye most of all. They'd been spending so much time together and she liked him—liked him a lot. But all they'd ever seemed to do when they'd had spare moments together was complain about how tired they were and how much they just needed a quick catnap, or the ability to go to the toilet whenever they wanted.

'It's so hypocritical!' she'd said. 'We sit there lecturing patients on staying hydrated and making sure they eat properly and I'm sat there having not eaten or drunk anything for over twelve hours straight!

Maddy had planned to drink whatever she wanted at the party, eat whatever she wanted and dance the night away. She'd wanted to have fun, to kick back, to relax—

and why shouldn't she? she'd thought. She'd been putting in so much overtime at work that very often she'd barely made it home. That weekend, that party, had been for her to remember who she used to be.

The Surrey house had ben amazing. At the end of a large, sweeping driveway, the house had seemed more of a manor than anything else. There'd been butlers handing out drinks when she'd arrived—butlers!—and she'd taken a flute of champagne and entered. She'd realised that birthday boy Rupert really hadn't been lying about Mummy's and Daddy's pad in the country.

Music had blared and she'd followed the noise towards a room that had been packed, not only with medics, but people she hadn't known—Rupert's friends and family, presumably. A radiologist she knew had noticed her and waved, mouthing that Maddy looked gorgeous. She'd smiled and moved on, looking for Nate, and then she'd seen him, dressed in a dinner suit, laughing and joking with the birthday boy himself.

Rupert had noticed her first and then Nate had turned to see what had drawn his friend's eye. Maddy had felt thrilled inside when she'd seen Nate's eyes widen in shock and admiration as she drew closer.

'What vision do I see before me?' asked Rupert, laughing, clearly already drunk, dropping an air kiss either side of her face.

'Happy birthday, Rupe.' She passed him a small gift-wrapped box, tied with a bow.

'You look amazing,' Nate said, drawing in to drop a real kiss onto her cheek. She'd blushed.

'I'm going to take this over to the present pile!' Rupert said, holding the gift in the air and making his way through the throng of guests.

'There's a pile?' she asked with a raised eyebrow.

'Looks like it. He's a popular guy.'

'More popular now everyone knows he's rich.' She laughed.

'Lot of surprises tonight. Rupert is practically an earl and you…you are bloody stunning! Come dance with me!'

'Alright.' She smiled, hoping it was demurely, and allowed him to take her hand and lead her out onto the dance floor. She dropped her now empty champagne flute onto a passing tray and, facing Nate, began to move to the music. He was a great dancer, in tune with his body. He threw some shapes, making her laugh, and then all of a sudden the music changed and became slower and Nate smiled at her, took her hand and drew her into his embrace.

She laid her head against his shoulder and began to realise that something was changing between them. To be fair, she'd felt her feelings towards him change quite a lot just recently. They were still the friends and colleagues they had always been, but she'd begun to notice things lately: how his smile made her feel; how his laughter lifted her mood; how just being around him soothed her soul. He had a cute smile. He was easy on the eye, and she'd noticed how the nurses and other people looked at him. He was effortlessly good-looking, even with bedhead, which was how he often rolled into work.

And now, with her body up close to his, her awareness of him increased. Her heart thumped wildly in her chest and she kept trying to calm it down. Her pulse pounded in her ears as much as the music did. She was aware of the way he had his hand wrapped around hers, and how his other hand lay on the small of her back, very close to the top curve of her bottom.

She kept wondering what it might feel like to kiss him.

And then the moment was lost as the music changed again, someone bumped into them and dragged Nate away to see something and Maddy was left in the centre of the dance floor feeling bereft and alone.

She ended up chatting with other people, but she found herself constantly looking for him and, when she couldn't stand not seeing him again for another moment longer, she went looking for him, searching the crowd and the thronging dance floor. And, just when she thought that maybe he'd left without saying goodbye, a hand enclosed her own and turned her around…and there he was, smiling, eyes sparkling as he dragged her out of the room and down a corridor, through a doorway and out onto a patio lit by the stars in an inky sky above.

She could still hear the music, but out here in the gardens it was muted and cooler. Nate led her down some steps, across the grass and over to a stone folly that stood in the centre of the garden. 'Our own dance-floor. Less crowded,' he said, still holding her hand as he pulled her close once again.

Maddy smiled back at him. 'You want to show me some more moves?'

'I've got plenty.'

'Oh yeah?'

'Yeah. Want to see them?'

He was teasing her and she liked it. 'Of course.'

Nate laughed and stood back to admire her in her dress. 'I have never seen a woman look so beautiful as you do tonight.'

'Just tonight?' she teased. 'Wow, thanks. You're going to have to do better than that, you know.'

But then he stared into her eyes, mirth in his gaze that slowly turned serious as they stood in the dark folly. Shadows encompassed his face as they moved slowly to the muted music, occasionally the moonlight gifting her light to see the look of desire in his eyes.

Her mouth went dry as her gaze dropped to his lips. She had thought about kissing Nate; of course she had! Many times. She'd wondered what it might be like. He was a handsome man; clever; kind. He was her best friend at the hospital and she'd always been wary of overstepping that boundary.

But tonight it was as if there was magic in the air, anticipation. Electricity sparked as they gazed into each other's souls. She was aware of every touch: how his hand held hers as they danced; where their bodies met; the heat of him; the feel of him. And, for just a moment, they weren't friends, colleagues or doctors but two adults dancing in the dark, softly swaying in the moonlight, gazing into each other's eyes and thinking incredibly naughty things they could do to one another.

Nate made a little groan as he looked at her.

'What?' she asked. 'Tell me what you're thinking.'

'I'm thinking that I want to have you, but I'm wary of ruining our friendship and…now I'm aware that, just by saying it, I may have changed something between us. Have I?'

Of course he had. But by telling her that he wanted her too he had made her heart explode with joy. They both felt the same thing! 'If I said I wanted you too… what would that mean?' she whispered.

He smiled. 'Everything.'

She could feel his arousal pressed up against her as they softly moved, swaying from side to side.

'I don't want to make it awkward at work,' he said.

Maddy smiled. 'Neither do I.' She'd had enough people let her down. She didn't need to lose him. Apart from work, he was the most important thing in her life. He was her everything.

'Then if we do this there should probably be some rules,' he said, nuzzling at her neck, as if he couldn't bear not to touch her. As if he needed to sample her, taste her.

She could feel his breath upon her neck, and the brush of his lips was electrifying. Every nerve ending tingled delightfully.

'Okay,' she breathed, tilting her head to the side to reveal her neck more, to submit.

'Friends first but…with benefits.'

She felt his tongue lick her skin.

Maddy murmured assent, unable to think, not really processing what she had agreed to. Even afterwards she reckoned it would change, because what they had was so great, but in that moment she would have agreed to anything.

And then his hands were exploring her, his lips met hers and, before she knew what was happening, he moved aside her underwear and they were having sex up against the wall of the folly.

It was hot, fast and furious and she couldn't get enough of him as he thrust inside her. She gasped, gripping him to her, looking up at the sky and the moon high above, hearing the hoot of an owl as she wrapped her legs around his body and tried to ignore the feel of the stone on her back, which was uncomfortable, but she didn't care in the moment.

Afterwards, panting heavily, they both laughed at each other, realising how crazy they'd been; anyone could have seen them! They adjusted their clothes and tried to look less rumpled as they returned to Rupert's party just in time for his speech, before he cut the massive cake that no doubt had been baked for him by some celebrity chef or something.

Maddy kept catching Nate's gaze and they smiled at one another.

And she believed it was the beginning of something exciting, something special.

And she hoped, naively as it turned out, that he felt the same way…

Cies Island was amazingly beautiful. The kind of place that took a person's breath away. That took all their cares and worries and made them forget them as they took in the views, breathed the clean air and gazed at the blue skies and along the white, sandy beaches, realising that all those concerns didn't really matter in that moment. They could return to them later, but right then they should enjoy, relax, sunbathe or paddle barefoot in the sea, jump the gentle waves. Let the warm rays of the sun caress the skin and just chill.

Maddy tried to do that. She tried to forget the fire in the kitchen, the fire in Nate's recent kiss and the fire in her soul that fuelled her confusion about him. Would she ever be clear in her thoughts about him? Would she ever douse the flames of her attraction to him? Could she get the furnace currently burning down to a spark, a small, tiny, glowing ember, and then stamp it out somehow?

She felt that, if she could, then this, right here, right now, would be so much easier. They'd just be two old friends who knew each other and had reunited for a work contract. She'd feel glad to see him and to be back with him, but that was all it would be, and she could explore the ports and make new friends and regain her confidence in her job and find her footing once again. She was getting there. She could feel it. There was less apprehension now, seeing her patients, and she could feel her old self coming back. But her old self had let him kiss her and call it a mistake. In the past, this man had slept with her on multiple occasions and then had left without a word. How could she feel safe with him? He'd not earned her trust.

'Do you regret what we had?' he asked, looking at her from across the small blanket he'd brought.

She shook her head. 'No, I don't. Being with you like that, even for a short time, made me very happy indeed. You made me feel wanted and I'd not felt that before, so…no, no regrets for that part. But I do regret allowing my feelings to become something more than our original rules stated for our relationship.' She blushed.

He sat forward and gazed at her. 'What?'

He'd not known? She'd thought he knew! Or at least suspected… 'You didn't know?'

'No! I mean, I knew we got on really well, and we were great friends and you really liked spending time with me, but I never dreamed for one moment that…' He trailed off, his gaze focused out to sea, as if regretting a life decision.

Did he regret it? 'So I felt very upset when you left without a word. In fact…' She swallowed her pride and decided to hit him with the truth. Maybe then he'd understand why she kept bringing the subject up, despite her request for them to forget it, because that was impossible. 'In fact, your leaving…it broke me a little. Hurt me *a lot*. It took me a long time to get over you going.'

Nate kept shaking his head as if in disbelief, then he turned to her. 'I'm sorry.'

'For leaving?'

He nodded. 'I'm sorry for leaving you and I'm sorry for not realising that I'd hurt you. I honestly believed that you'd just move on, that you'd be fine. You never said a word about…how you felt.'

Maddy smiled. 'How could I? Every time in my life that I'd hoped for more from someone, hoped for commitment, I was disappointed. I thought I might scare you off; you were so determined to stand alone and not have feelings for anyone. You just wanted the fun, without the scary part, so I gave you that.'

'I feel terrible. I'm sorry.'

'It was a long time ago,' she said, trying to cut him some slack, even though the pain of it still felt raw. But at least he'd apologised now. At least he'd finally admitted that what he'd done was wrong and that he'd never meant to hurt her. And honestly, if he truly hadn't known about her more romantic feelings for him, why would he have suspected that his leaving would hurt her? He'd have just assumed she'd say *adiós* and move on.

'Have you met anyone since?' he asked.

She shook her head. 'Our jobs don't leave us much time for romance. I've dated, but the relationships never really become anything. Not a lot of people are happy to know that they come second to our jobs, or that we'll miss special occasions really often, arrive late or not at all, and generally let them down all the time. How about you?'

'Same. I've dated, but it's hard to prove to someone that they're important, when patient care and the demands of a hospital take precedence every single time. Maybe that's why a lot of medics turn to other medics—because they know that that person will understand.'

Maddy nodded.

Nate laughed. 'I can't believe it. What a pair we've both turned out to be. We both leave London Saint and we both end up working on the same cruise ship. It's a small world.'

'And I want to see every corner of it,' she told him.

'You will. Listen, I accept that I made a lot of mistakes in the past, and I wouldn't blame you if you hated me for ever because of them, but...can we agree to live for the present and just enjoy what we have now?'

'And what do we have now?'

'I would like to think respect and admiration for one another. I would like to hope for friendship. But, if that's too much, then I'll understand.'

She couldn't hate him. That could never happen. 'Friends. I can do that,' she said.

Nate smiled and held out his hand for her to shake.

She shook it, trying to ignore how it felt to touch him once again. Maybe *friends* might still be a little bit of a stretch…

CHAPTER SIX

THINGS WERE GREAT for the next week. Maddy and Nate were on their best behaviour with one another: perfect colleagues, bright, happy; working well together. They'd moved on from Vigo to Lisbon, then Gibraltar and, most recently, Palma. Maddy had left the ship each time to explore the ports and always brought a little something back with her to remind herself of the place.

In Lisbon she'd bought a little *azulejo* tile to use as a coaster in her cabin. In Gibraltar, she'd bought a little keyring with a Barbary macaque on it. And in Palma a beautiful leather belt to go with a white *broderie anglaise* dress that she owned. She wanted to own a little piece of every place to which she went, to claim it and remember the happy memories she had of wandering their streets. She'd felt for a long time that she didn't actually have very many happy memories and it was time she made some. She was fed up with just reacting to life. She wanted to be proactive, make her own happiness and stop waiting for happiness to happen *to her*. So she explored, she made new friends, she worked hard and she went and checked on Manuel and the other chefs who were now back in the ship's cleaned and re-fitted crew mess.

So she was in a good mood when a passenger came limping into the medical bay, looking for help. He was an older gentleman with hair greying at his temples and, because he was wearing shorts, she could easily see what his problem was straight away. He had quite the swollen knee, and she helped him to a bed in one of the bays.

His name was Michael Stanton. 'It felt a little achy yesterday, but I woke up this morning with it looking like this.'

'Have you had an injury recently—slipped, fallen, banged it?'

He shook his head. 'No. Nothing like that.'

'And the swelling appeared overnight?'

'Yes.'

'And the pain, how would you describe that? Is it an ache? Is it burning, or sharp?'

'It was very sudden…severe. It woke me up.'

'And have you had any problems with this knee before, with issues like this or otherwise?'

'I damaged it once playing cricket—a ball smacked into it—but that was when I was a teenager. It's always been a little achy since then.'

'And would you say the pain is localised to this joint only? What about your hips or ankles?'

'Maybe in my big toe. That hurts like a…' He flushed a little. 'Like hell. Swelled up too once before.'

Maddy examined both of his legs, comparing them. The left knee had less movement and caused Mr Stanton considerable pain. Plus it looked quite red and felt warm. 'Any fever or chills?'

'A bit tired, and I always run warm anyway.'

She took his temperature. It was slightly raised, indicating a low fever.

'What's your diet like generally?'

He chortled. 'I eat well!' He slapped his belly, which hung slightly over his belt. 'Must admit I have a taste for fine things.'

She smiled. 'And I bet you've been indulging on board!'

'It's what holidays are for, enjoying yourself! Last night I had the finest surf and turf I have ever eaten in my life: medium-rare T-bone steak, langoustines, washed down with the wonderful rioja.'

'Sounds amazing. Now what about medications? Do you take anything?'

'Just aspirin every day. My doctor recommended it.'

'And any medical conditions I should know about?'

'Type-two diabetes. I'm working on it, trying to eat right, but… I'm on holiday! I'm allowed a little time off the diet, right?' He gave her a nudge with his elbow.

She smiled and said nothing. A lot of patients thought that they could abandon their diets on holiday and found that it led to a bit of a deterioration in their wellbeing. Examining him, she confirmed the swelling and redness was confined to the knee. The skin looked shiny, as if stretched, and it felt hot to the touch. There was bulging either side of the patella and Mr Stanton had reduced movement and pain. And, when she removed his shoes, she found he did indeed have the same affliction on his left big toe and she could feel crystals beneath the skin: tophi.

'Well, it looks, Mr Stanton, like you have gout in the knee joint and your large toe on this side. I'd like to confirm it with a needle aspiration to obtain some of the synovial fluid. This will confirm diagnosis and rule out any infection, and may even reduce some of your pain by relieving the pressure in the joint.'

'*Gout?* But my dad had that. Isn't it an old man's disease?'

'No, it can affect anyone, but now I know that you have a family history that makes the diagnosis even more likely. But I'd like to aspirate just to make sure we don't have any septic arthritis happening.'

'Oh. Okay. Will it hurt?'

'No, I can do it under a local anaesthetic.'

'Oh…right…well, I guess you better do that, then.'

'It'll just take me a moment to gather everything. Stay here and I'll be straight back.' She smiled and left him in his cubicle to gather the antiseptic solution, sterile equipment, anaesthetic, needle, syringe and the containers she'd need to place the sample in. She arranged it all onto a trolley and then pushed it back into Mr Stanton's bay. He seemed to be staring past her shoulder, looking slightly aggrieved, a change from his previous happy-go-lucky attitude.

Maddy glanced to look behind her and saw Nate talking to one of their nurses. 'Everything okay, Mr Stanton?'

'You know him?' He indicated with his head towards Nate.

'Dr Blake? Yes, of course.'

'Nathaniel. Hmm. You need to keep an eye on him. I wouldn't trust him as far as I could throw him.'

Maddy turned to look at Nate, then back at her patient. 'Why?' Afterwards, she would berate herself for having asked, but in the moment, she was surprised and curious.

'Took me a moment to recognise his face, but… I knew his family back in the day. Always causing trouble for his parents, and when his brother needed him by his side he never came home. Abandoned him. He just didn't care! Thought he was above them…and him a doctor, too. You'd expect him to care more about the ones he's meant to love.' Mr Stanton leaned in. 'If you want my advice, I'd keep your distance, because that man only cares about himself.'

Maddy frowned. Was that true? Had Nate abandoned his brother in a time of need? Abandoned his parents? She knew he'd abandoned her once, so maybe this was what Nate was like. Maybe she ought to be more careful and less naïve in believing his promises…but she'd seen for herself that Nate and Lucas were great. So was what Mr Stanton said lies? Or had Nate and Lucas made amends? Maybe the reason Nate had left her all those years ago was to sort out his relationship with his brother. Because they were here together on this ship and they were close…or at least, seemed to be.

The idea that there was still so much she didn't know about Nate niggled at her. He had always been a closed book and kept her at an arm's length when it came to anything about his past or his family. Maybe this was why. Was he ashamed at how he'd treated them, and thought that she might judge him if she knew? He'd still only given her the bare minimum of an explanation about what had happened.

Should I go and talk to Lucas? No. That would be going behind Nate's back. I have to talk to Nate.

But, as she performed the needle aspiration on Mr Stanton's knee, her own doubts began to surface, her mind muddied by her patient's comments about Nate's past. Was she repeating patterns of getting involved with someone unavailable to her? All her life, even as a kid growing up in care, she'd pinned her hopes on other people making her happy. She'd hoped that she would get fostered. She'd hoped that she would one day get adopted. She'd hoped that she would one day be loved and cherished and put first.

But it had never happened. She'd always been let down by others, and here she was, hoping that this time with Nate they might be happy if only she put to one side her doubts, her fears and the fact that he had already shown her how he was going to treat her. He'd abandoned her once. He'd kissed her here on the ship and made her think for one brief moment that there was still something there between them, then had backed away, telling her it was a mistake. The man blew hot and cold. How much longer would she let him do that to her?

I need to grow a spine. Nate looks after himself and I need to do the same!

Cagliari was a beautiful port with gorgeous blue skies and calm, clear waters. Nate asked Maddy if he could accompany her when she disembarked.

'I was going to look at the citadel on the top of the hill—the Castello district,' she said.

'Sounds great.' He was keen to make sure that the two of them were okay. She'd seemed a little distant yesterday afternoon and evening and, if he had done something, he wanted to show her how important she still was to him, even though the two of them were just friends.

The citadel was made of pale stone that helped reflect the soaring heat of the day and had ramparts, battlements, domes and towers. The ground was cobbled and uneven, so he offered Maddy his arm as they walked, but she said she was fine.

She looked beautiful today. She looked beautiful every day, but today she looked even more so, in a long, flowing white dress, brown leather belt and sandals. Her hair was loose and flowing down her back, sometimes held off her face by the sunglasses she wore. The more time he spent with her, the more he regretted having walked away from her all those years ago, especially now he knew how she had felt about him, but he knew that if the same thing happened again, he would do the same thing. A fact that reminded him that he and Maddy were never meant to have been together and that somehow fate or the world was showing him this lesson even now.

They joined an organized tour of Il Castello, the citadel, exploring the cathedral and the ramparts, and gazing out at the views from the top of one of the towers of all Cagliari and the green trees of Sardinia. He could sense the history in a place such as this. It was dripping with it. He could imagine guards walking the corridors, prisoners down in the cramped, dark cells without the chance of freedom; armies trying to attack the walls.

Once the tour was done, they made their way to a small café and sat outside under a large purple umbrella, the tables covered in white PVC decorated with bright-red chilli peppers.

They ordered two aromatic coffees and a mandarin croissant each. Maddy had bought herself a trinket in a nearby gift shop—a beautiful filigree pendant with tiny blue stones.

'It's so beautiful here,' she said, leaning back in her chair and sighing. 'I wonder why I didn't take a cruise ship contract years ago. Would have saved me a lot of trouble and angst.'

'Well, first off, you need the experience in hospitals first, before you can be a cruise doctor.'

'Yeah, well, no-one tells you just how sometimes your dream of helping people can turn into a nightmare. But, if they told you from the get-go that you can help people and see the world and relax on a cruise ship?' She laughed. 'Maybe there'd be a lot more happier doctors.'

'You weren't a happy doctor?' he asked.

'I was, generally. But then you meet certain people and they pivot your life and change how you feel about something. How you feel about your job.'

Was she talking about him? Because back in the day they'd both seemed to love their job. He had so many memories of he and Maddy sharing smiles and laughter at work. Had she really lost her joy for the job after he'd left?

'Who did you meet?' he asked, curious to see if the reason she'd been cool since yesterday afternoon was because she'd been thinking about all the times he'd seemingly messed her around. 'Not me, I hope.' He laughed and sipped his coffee. It was dark, strong and bitter.

'There was a time when I wondered how I'd carry on without you. Especially as you'd been there with me since day one. But, no, I wasn't talking about you, but about someone else I met. Years after you—a patient, actually.'

'Oh?' He was curious. Some patients could really stay with a doctor. There could be a tragic story: cancers, brain tumours, children coming in with terminal diseases that they could do nothing for. It made him question being a doctor. Made him question if he was actually helping by prolonging their life with drugs, when he could see, as a doctor, that they were tired of it all. Of fighting every day in pain.

Maddy sucked in a breath and looked out over Cagliari. 'A guy in his twenties came in with abdominal pains. He was nauseous. Shaky. Dehydrated. We struggled to get fluids into him because his veins had collapsed and that was when we learned he was a drug addict in withdrawal. He was after pain meds and…' she paused to take a breath '…because I didn't give him what he wanted, as quickly as he wanted them, he became aggressive and cornered me. He pinned me to a wall, his arm against my throat, and then proceeded to physically attack me.'

'Maddy!' He couldn't believe it….well, unfortunately, he could. She'd been working in a central London emergency department; of course they were going to get drug-addicted patients in. It was par for the course, unfortunately, as was the risk of assault on staff. 'Were you okay?'

She shook her head. 'He fractured my orbital bone. My nose. Knocked out a tooth.' She tapped one of her front teeth and gave a wry smile. 'Security arrived a little too late and I was unconscious on the floor. I had to have surgery, and in recovery I started to have panic attacks. After that, I struggled with the idea of returning to work. I'd been in therapy for six months when I got the job on board *Serendipity*. My therapist had told me to find a way back and this is it—my way back to being a doctor. I love what I do, Nate, but I needed to feel safe, and I needed to have a life, and so this is what I chose. And in order to feel safe I have to have confidence in the people that I work with…and that includes you.

'But… I still don't know what happened with you. And yesterday I met a patient who knew your family. He told me some things and it's made me wonder if I can trust you. I want to. But I've already been hurt and damaged so much, and I don't want that to happen here, because this is my way back to reclaiming my power over my own life. And you? You're a threat. Do you understand?'

He nodded, shocked, appalled by what she had been through! If he had known…

What would I have done—abandoned Lucas and gone running back?

No. He would have felt torn. Lucas had needed him and he'd promised him that he would stay by his side until he was stronger. If he'd run out on him because Maddy had needed him he'd have hated himself, because he'd made his brother a promise never to do so again. 'I never knew you got hurt,' he said. 'I'm so sorry.' And who the hell was the patient who had known his family? And what had they said to her?

'Can you tell me the truth, Nate? You've never given me a full answer and I think…no, I *deserve*…the truth from you.'

He wanted to give it, but how could he tell her everything? He'd made a promise to his brother. But maybe he could give her fragments of the truth and leave certain parts out to protect Lucas. To protect *Maddy*.

'When I was really young, it was just me and my mum. My real dad passed when I was a baby. My mum was great, but she was lonely, and then she met this other guy who became my stepdad—Bill. Mum adored him. Was completely in love, even though Bill tried to hide the fact that he wasn't best pleased to be raising another guy's kid.'

'What happened?'

'Mum got pregnant and had Lucas.'

'He's your *half*-brother, then?'

He nodded. 'I loved having a baby brother, but Bill made it clear that I was second best in his eyes. I could do no right. I was often punished by him, and my mum began to take his side in the arguments. We used to be *so close* and suddenly with Bill and Lucas around I lost her. Me and Lucas, though, we were great, until he started to get older. With Bill's favouritism and Mum's enabling of Bill's behaviour, me and Lucas got pitted against one another. There were arguments, rows. I would stay out as often as I could, because home was a terrible place to be. Mum and Bill were drinkers by this time, and that made everything worse, so I left home when I could. Went to university and never looked back. Lucas stopped talking to me and I just assumed he'd had his head turned by Mum and Bill.'

'I'm so sorry. I never had any idea. Why didn't you tell me before?'

'It was a part of my past I didn't want to remember.

I felt like I'd lost everyone I'd ever cared for. Even my home. You, my job, working at London Saint—that was all that mattered.'

'But then something pulled you back. What?'

Nate sighed. He hated that he had to bring up such ugliness in a place that was so beautiful. 'Lucas was struggling privately. I didn't know at the time, because we weren't speaking, but I found out that he'd been struggling with his sexuality, and when he came out to Mum and Bill they didn't accept him and threw him out. They were out in their car one day, and they'd been drinking, and got into an accident that killed them both.'

This was the part from which he'd have to divert some of the truth and use omission. 'Lucas couldn't deal with it and he called me and I left London Saint to help him.'

Maddy gazed at him with such sorrow and softness. 'I'm so sorry that you lost your mum and Bill that way. So that's why you left!'

He nodded. 'I needed that time to reconnect with my brother. We were all we had left.'

She reached forward then and laid her hand on his, squeezing his fingers. 'I'm so sorry.'

He liked the feel of her hand upon his, her reassuring touch, but he felt bad because he was still keeping some of the truth from her. 'Thank you. It took some time but…here we are! Lucas and I are close again; we've got each other's backs. And whoever that patient was who told you they recognised me and that you weren't to trust me or whatever, they didn't know the full story, and they most certainly did not understand what went on behind the closed doors of my childhood home.'

'No-one ever can. We're all fighting battles that no-one can see, aren't we?'

'I'm sorry I never contacted you. I was just overwhelmed with everything I had to process. The loss of Mum. Lucas.' That was the truth. He had been overwhelmed by coping with the loss of his mother, learning that Bill had caused the accident from drink driving and essentially killed her. And discovering his little brother had actually not been able to handle any of it, had taken a drug overdose and was an addict with a history of hospital and rehab admissions.

It had been so much to take in, so much to deal with! And Lucas had fought so hard so get clean this time and return to a passion he'd had as a child—ice-skating. It was something he'd done in secret, because Bill had hated that his son was into that and not something Bill considered more manly. Ice-skating had begun to replace the drugs Lucas was addicted to, and with his brother's support he'd got a job on a cruise ship as an ice-dancer and Nate had gone along for the ride—not just to be with his brother, but to keep an eye on him. To be close, to give him support and rebuild what they'd once had all those years ago.

Too much had been taken from them and Nate had wanted to reclaim their lives. And he had—they had. And now Lucas was engaged to Carlos and it was time for Nate to let someone else take the reins in his brother's life. He would always be there for Lucas, but he had to let the guy stand alone too and have space. He was so happy that his brother had found someone to love after all that he had been through, and Carlos was amazing, perfect for his little brother. And now it was time for

Nate to start thinking again about his own happiness, having put his own life on pause for so long.

So sue me if I kissed this beautiful woman after I'd had one too many to drink! He never drank, not really; just socially, and only one or two, but Lucas and Carlos had got engaged and that had been worthy of a celebration, as well as the fact that fate had brought Maddy back into his life and he'd like to think it was for a reason.

'Thank you for telling me, but now I know and the past is in the past, so shall we just move on? Take a moment to appreciate where we are? All of this?' She swept her arm wide, indicating the town of Cagliari far below, the beautiful dark green of the trees in the distance against an azure sky, the brilliant white of the cruise ship docked in the port against the clear blue waters; the happy people all around them; the good food on the table.

The company they kept.

Nate lifted his coffee cup in the air. 'To now and all its infinite possibilities.'

Maddy met his cup with her own, clinking it softly. 'The now.'

Her smile, when it came, warmed his heart immensely.

Nate's revelations in Cagliari were shocking, and she hated all that he had been through, but there'd been something in his delivery that had told her that he was still keeping something back, in the way he kept looking at her to see if she believed him. But what? And why didn't he feel he could trust her with it? It was why she had suggested they move on. That they stop dwelling in a past filled with secrets he wouldn't share and just accept where they were: in a beautiful place, in the here and now. Maddy was inwardly annoyed that she was being told half-truths, not trusted, and if he couldn't fully trust her how could she trust him?

You and I will always be together. Nate had said that to her once, when they'd been together at London Saint for about a year. *Fighting one accident and emergency at a time!*

She thought about that a lot as she returned to the medical bay the next day. They'd set sail from Cagliari about five the previous evening and woken up docked at Civitavecchia. Lots of passengers had disembarked and she was making her way through a crew clinic. She'd seen three patients so far, one for recurring migraine, one for a dislocated finger and her last patient for a follow-up after a previous accident, and she'd given them permission to go from light duties to full. She would call their supervisor later to confirm, but right now she had another ice-dancer in her clinic.

'The receptionist said I had to see *you* and not my brother.' Lucas looked over her shoulder towards his brother, who was leaning against a wall observing the consultation.

'The receptionist was right. What happened?' Nate asked.

Maddy turned to give him a stare. This was *her* consultation. 'Tell *me* what happened, please.'

'Good for you, Madeline. Put him in his place!' Lucas smirked. 'It was stupid, really. I was doing a warm-up on the ice, slipped when I came off my edge and fell against a barrier. I've hurt my shoulder and I need you to tell me I have my shows, and a wedding!' He smiled at her and she saw Nate's features in his face. They had the same smile, cute and attractive, the kind that could charm birds from trees.

'Okay, let me take a look.' She examined him thoroughly, knowing that Nate was watching and would want a thorough assessment of his brother to make sure nothing was missed. Clearly he was protective. Lucas was developing swelling on his shoulder and had difficulty moving his arm and seemed to be in a lot of pain, despite his desire to drop quips and jokes into every bit of conversation they had. 'I think we need an x-ray,' she concluded. 'I can't feel a break, and there's no dislocation, but the x-ray will tell us for sure.'

'Will I be radioactive and get special powers?' he asked with a grin.

'Unfortunately not, but it will give *me* special powers to see inside your body, and I may even refer you to a clinic in Civitavecchia to get a CAT scan of the soft tissues.'

'Double radioactivity? Hmm. All I need is to get bitten by a spider and I'll turn into a super-hero.'

Maddy laughed. 'No such luck, I'm afraid.'

'Damn, there's always a catch.'

Maddy performed the x-ray and Nate scanned it intensely. 'No break. He's been lucky.'

'Maybe a tear in his pectoralis major muscle?' she suggested.

'Possibly. What are you going to do?'

She frowned, amused by the way he was hovering, being overly concerned. She'd heard of helicopter parenting, but not with siblings. But maybe this was what family was like. They only had each other. 'Offer a sling and painkillers.'

'No. No painkillers.'

'Why?'

Nate shrugged. 'He won't take them. I know him.'

'Okay. He can tough it out then, but I'm still going to advise them.'

Back in the cubicle, she gave Lucas the results. 'I'm going to get you a sling for your arm to support it. I want you to rest it for a few days.'

'A sling? What colours do they come in?'

She smiled. 'Well, there's black, or you could choose…black.'

'Nothing with a bit of bling?'

'No, but I guess you could add that yourself if you wanted.'

'Honestly, Nate. You need to look at different stockists.'

'Not my choice,' Nate said with a smile.

Maddy began to put the sling on Nate's brother. 'So… you and Nate have a good evening the other night?'

'Oh, the best!' Lucas said. 'You missed a great night. You should have come! Why *didn't* you bring this wonderful woman, brother dear?'

'Lucas.'

'What?' Lucas asked innocently. 'Do you know, Maddy, that I asked him to be my maid of honour at the wedding and wear a nice dress, but he said the best he could do was wear a suit and be my best man. Honestly, what does a girl have to do to get a pretty bridesmaid?'

Maddy laughed as she tightened the straps, making

sure the sling supported the arm perfectly. 'Maybe look elsewhere. Have you seen his legs? Not sure they're right for heels,' she joked.

Lucas looked at her weirdly then, his head tilted to one side. 'What about you?'

'I'm sorry?'

'You could be a bridesmaid! I know I've only met you twice, but Nate speaks very highly of you, and with that red hair of yours you'd look wonderful in pale green silk!'

'Oh, I don't know about—'

'Come on! Please?' he wheedled, then leaned in conspiratorially. 'You know I've heard that best men often get off with bridesmaids…'

Maddy flushed, aware that Nate was right there behind her and stepped away, laughing. 'I have no desire to get off with your brother!'

She could feel Nate's gaze upon her. She could feel his eyes boring into the back of her head. She was almost afraid to turn round. Had she hurt his feelings?

'Even so…what do you say?'

'I hardly know you. Don't you want to ask someone else?'

Lucas shook his head. 'I've got all my friends coming already. I want Nate to have someone there that he likes. Come on! Do it as a favour to me. Please?'

Her cheeks felt hotter than the sun, her mind whizzing with excuses and reasons not to do it. But what if she did? She'd never been part of a wedding before, never a bridesmaid. It might be fun to get dressed up and she liked Lucas a lot.

She nodded. 'Okay. I will.'

* * *

'He's asked the ship's captain to marry them, did you know?' Nate said, sliding into a booth opposite her in the crew mess.

'Really? That's nice. Is Captain Thomas going to do it?'

'Apparently he's happy to be part of it, though it will be more of a performance and symbolic. Lucas and Carlos want the excitement of being married on board and then getting the legal and official part done in Spain.'

'Am I going to have to be a bridesmaid at both?'

'I don't think so, but you'd better ask him.'

'If he really wants me, then I don't see why not. I came on board for new experiences and this would most certainly be one.'

Nate smiled. 'Then I'll see you at the other end of the aisle!' He got up and walked away and, whilst she was grateful that he'd not mentioned Lucas's 'getting off with the best man' comment, she couldn't help but imagine what it might be like to walk up an aisle with Nate at the other end...

Hadn't she once dreamed of it? Imagined it so perfectly in her head that she knew every detail? She knew what her dress would be like. How he would turn to look at her and openly cry as she walked towards him. She knew the flowers she'd hold. The way everyone would gaze at them—the perfect couple—and weep at the sight of such love.

She'd not allowed herself to remember that for such a long time: foolish, silly dreams of someone who often let her mind fly away on flights of fancy. She'd lived in her imagination as a child. What was so wrong in that?

It was how she'd survived the disappointments of real life, imagining herself so loved, so cherished, about to embark on a journey of creating her own perfect family. That was why it had hurt so much when he'd walked away without a word of explanation or apology, as if she didn't matter. As if she wasn't important.

Only now she knew why he'd left, and realised how it had been nothing to do with her, but with a tragedy in his family and now she was being pulled into *their* family, *his* family. Nate's—as if her life was maybe destined to be forever entwined with his. Just not in the way she'd expected.

But, if Lucas wanted her as a bridesmaid, she'd do it to feel as though she belonged. To share in his day. To see that true happiness did happen to other people and that maybe, if she stayed in its orbit, then some of that happiness, well…might just rub a little of its magic onto her too.

As they sailed away from Civitavecchia, they received the report from the clinic on land: Lucas's CAT scan showed soft tissue damage, as suspected. He was told to rest for two days and then come back in for a check-up, to see if he could go on light duties.

He was not happy to miss out on shows, and Carlos had declared that Lucas was being insufferable because he was bored and couldn't work out. So Nate checked in with his brother each day and, when the swelling had gone down and the shoulder was feeling much better, Lucas returned to the ice show.

'You and Maddy ought to come and watch it!' Lucas enthused. 'You'll love it! It's a story of two lovers who can't be together and if the end dance—in which yours truly performs—does not leave you with tears in your eyes, then I won't have done my job!'

And so Nate asked Maddy to the ice show. When he went to meet her at her cabin, he tried not to be overwhelmed by how beautiful she looked. By her wonderful scent, the way her eyes sparkled as she took in his suit and open-necked shirt. How great it felt to walk down the corridor with her on his arm.

In the ice studio, they discovered that Lucas had reserved the two best seats in the house for them and they sat ringside, waiting for the lights to go down.

'This is exciting,' she said. 'Have you seen him skate before?'

'Many times. I took him to many training sessions and sat ringside. I remember being cold a lot.'

'But impressed too, I bet?'

He nodded. 'He comes alive on the ice. You can see it in his eyes. He's so *present*. He looks the same way when he's with Carlos. That's how I know they're perfect for one another.'

She smiled at him, and when he met her gaze he wondered...*is that the same look I see in her eyes right now? Is she thinking I might be perfect for her?*

It sent a ripple of yearning through him of want, of possibility. His mind had been all over the place since he'd kissed her again and being by her side in the medical bay, working with her, spending time with her in ports and seeing her laugh and smile made him want to hold her all over again. The way the wind played with her loose hair, the way she made him feel about himself, made him want to feel her in his arms once more.

There was something about the way the sun gleamed on her skin, that made him want to reach out and touch her, just to make sure that she was still as soft as he remembered.

And he remembered so much about her. The way she challenged him. The way they might meet each other's gaze in a serious staff meeting and try not to laugh. The way she sought him out to tell him something ridiculous, and the joy and fun in her eyes would sparkle with such a life of its own, it enthused her words with delight.

He remembered the way she felt beneath him; her soft gasps and moans of pleasure. The way she seemed to need him. How he could do so much with just the stroke of one finger...

He missed her. Even when he was with her, he missed her, because he couldn't have her the way that he wanted. Being with her in consultations was torture. His feelings for her had never truly gone away, but he didn't feel deserving of her. He'd failed his family. He'd failed his brother and he'd already failed her once too. He'd put her through so much; he'd hurt her and he didn't want to do that again. She didn't deserve that, so he was trying to keep his distance. Trying to honour the promise just to be friends, colleagues, nothing more.

But sitting with her like this, by her side in the dark, close enough to smell her delightful perfume, her leaning in to say something about the set on the ice, meant all he wanted to do was stare into her eyes, place his hand on the back of her neck and draw her face into his for a kiss.

The lights came up then went down again three times, signalling the start of the show, and music began to fill the room, haunting violin music, as a lone female skater emerged onto the ice.

He couldn't help but keep glancing at Maddy, watching Maddy's face as the ice show continued. He watched her delight, her rapt attention; the way she sometimes caught her bottom lip. He watched her smile, her joy, how she gasped when Lucas emerged onto the ice dressed as a monster, all fierce and cruel. She glanced back at him as if to say *it's your brother* and he smiled back and gripped the arms of the chair to stop himself from taking her hand in his. From grabbing her hand and leading her away from the ice studio, out into the bright corridors, down into the depths of the ship and to his cabin, then doing all the things his body was screaming at him to do.

But he didn't. He simply smiled back and maintained an image of calm on the outside, whilst internally he screamed. It was torture to sit next to the woman he yearned for and not be able to do anything.

Above everything, he respected her, admired her. She'd been attacked by a drug addict. His own brother had been one, and he'd made a promise to Lucas never to tell anyone about it. He'd made a promise to his brother that he would forever put him first, and he'd made a promise to *himself* that he would never hurt anyone the way he had hurt people before, and that meant not getting close to Madeline.

She would be hurt if she got involved with him again because he wasn't sure that he was good enough for her. Sure, there was a physical connection—they'd proved that before—but was there anything beyond it? Would she cheer his brother and clap for him the way she did now if she learned that Lucas had also once been addicted and had stolen to get money for drugs?

He'd accepted his brother had been a different person then. Life had forced him into a corner and the addiction had made him into someone he wasn't. *That* Lucas didn't exist any more, but would *she* accept that? Would she still be Lucas's bridesmaid if she knew that?

He tried to imagine Maddy in a bridesmaid dress. He saw her walking down an aisle in a beautiful dress and somehow his mind morphed her from being a bridesmaid into a bride, wearing a white dress and long veil, walking towards him.

His heart skipped a beat. He grew hot and he had to take a sip of his ice-cold drink to cool himself down.

As the finale of the show began and the music increased in power and volume, his gaze returned to the ice to honour his brother in the finale. Lucas skated with heart and passion and he could see how he emoted his feelings so clearly, now that he was no longer a monster but human, and how it felt to grieve a lost love that he could now no longer have.

Nate felt tears come to his eyes as, Lucas died from a broken heart on the ice. The lights changed, the music became ethereal and his lost love came to claim his soul so that they skated into the ever after together.

The idea that he could not be with the one he loved until after death… How heartbreaking.

The ice studio erupted in applause as everyone got to their feet, entertained and moved by the show, and the skaters all came onto the ice to accept the applause. Lucas even skated forward to have a hug with them both, and Nate noticed Maddy wipe her eyes.

'That was so moving!' Maddy said, crying and dabbing at her eyes with a tissue as they walked out. 'I've never felt that way before. Lucas was amazing! They all were amazing!' She half-laughed, slightly embarrassed at being so emotional.

'I guess he warned us.'

'Yes. Oh my goodness, should we go and get some fresh air? I think I need it.'

He led her up to the open deck. It was a beautifully warm night. The skies were clear and lit with stars as they cruised through the sea towards Malta.

'Lucas is so talented. You can see he adores what he does.'

'He really does,' Nate agreed.

'I want to feel that way about my work.'

'Don't you?'

She smiled. 'I enjoy what I do, but am I passionate about it? I think I'm still getting used to being back in work, though it has been nice for things to be less hectic than an A&E. I just wonder if there's more.'

'More what?'

'Ways to help people. Sometimes I feel like… Well, like I'd like to know how their story ends. It's great being on board, but it's so transient, isn't it? Passengers come and then they disappear.'

'I suppose.'

'Have you ever thought about putting down roots? Because I think about that all the time. As a child, I wanted a family more than anything, but I was never in the same place for more than a few months. Being at London Saint was the longest I'd stayed anywhere!

And that would probably be where I would still be, if I hadn't been attacked.'

He nodded, listening carefully.

'Sometimes I have this dream about putting down proper roots. Setting up a clinic for women, maybe. But settling down and staying somewhere and making a difference to their lives and seeing that difference in the community.'

'And what about for you?'

She frowned. 'How do you mean?'

'Do you see yourself settled down with someone? Like, in a relationship?'

She smiled. 'It would be nice, if I was ever able to trust someone enough for that.'

'Would you ever trust me?'

She blinked and looked away out to sea. 'We said we'd just be friends, Nate.'

He nodded, disappointed, but supposed she was making the right decision. He had proved to this woman that he would only fail her and let her down. It was no wonder she couldn't contemplate anything like that with him. He needed to atone for his mistakes, and that meant not to keep pressing her into an uncomfortable corner.

But the vision she'd presented of settling down, a clinic in a small community so that it got that continuity of care, called to him. He'd felt so adrift for so long now, helping Lucas chase his dreams, supporting him, getting him back on his feet... It felt good to see his brother improve and make his life, but wasn't it now time for Nate to do the same? 'You should do that, if it's what you want. Settle somewhere. Start a family. I know that's always been your dream.'

She talked about it once, all those years ago, before they'd got intimate. About how growing up without a family, without any blood relatives, had made her crave her own, and how she dreamed that one day she'd find true love, settle down and have lots of little kids. And the best thing was he could envision her as a mother. She'd be amazing at it—she had such a big heart.

She nodded. 'It has. When I lay in that hospital bed after surgery, it made me realise how short life is. There was a moment during the attack when I thought I might die, that he might kill me. And how I was too young, and that my life hadn't really begun. How I'd experienced nothing! And I promised myself that if I made it through I would make changes. I would see the world. I would travel and I would seek out joy.'

'And so you came to the *Serendipity*.'

'Yes. And, though I love my job, for a long time now I've felt like there's something missing. I'm there for other people, but there's no-one there for me. An empty flat. An empty cabin. It makes you wonder just what you're doing and who you're doing it for.'

'You're not fulfilled?'

'Sometimes I feel so alone here, in the middle of the sea.'

'I'm here for you.'

She smiled. 'But you're just a friend, Nate. My boss. My colleague. I can't afford you to be anything else, because you broke my heart, and I'm not sure I can stand the risk of giving it to you again.'

She gave me her heart? 'We were just meant to be friends with benefits. No strings, we both said.'

Maddy gazed at him softly as a gentle breeze played

with her hair. 'And I meant to keep it that way, only things changed for me. I fell for you, you fool! And then you just upped and left.'

He stared hard at her. He'd not known! If he had…

No, I can't think about that, because I know I would have gone to Lucas, but…

But he might have found a way to have both. Somehow, he might have found a way! The pain tore through him at the thought that he'd left her hurting, knowing now that her feelings for him had run a lot deeper than he'd ever imagined. The fact was that he'd begun to feel the same way about her, he'd been developing feelings, but his had terrified him!

I was a coward and Lucas's troubles gave me a way out.

Nate turned to her, reached for her hands and held them in his. 'I am *so sorry* that I left the way that I did. If I could go back and change it…'

'It's fine. Your brother needed you; I understand.'

'No! It's not fine! I…' He searched for the right words to say to her. To let her know just how much she had meant to him. How her friendship had meant everything. How being in her arms had soothed his soul. How much he used to look forward to being with her and having her all to himself. How he'd thought he couldn't tell her about his growing feelings because he'd definitely not been good enough for her back then.

He'd only given her the best of himself: fun Nate. The man behind the mask he'd worn to make himself feel good. The mask that had presented him to the world as a cool, confident doctor, fun and amiable, clever and dedicated, passionate and popular. When inside he'd felt as if he was crumbling. As if he was barely getting through each day, sometimes making mistakes. Fighting to prove to himself that he was more than Bill had told him he was—a nobody, not worthy of anyone's time or attention. Useless, a waste of space who no-one could ever love.

He'd grown up hearing nothing but negativity, and sometimes it was all he could believe. And his mother had died without him having got the chance to put things right between them; Lucas had almost overdosed... He'd vowed to atone for the abandonment of his brother and he thought he'd been doing a good job until he'd run into Madeline again and realised just how much he'd hurt her too.

'I wish I'd never hurt you, because you were so much more than a friend to me,' he said, finally, realising the words themselves were inadequate. They didn't feel enough, but he'd never been good at expressing himself because he'd never been allowed to.

'It's okay, Nate! I understand. You lost your parents... you had to be there for Lucas. I get it!' she said, cradling his face with her soft, gentle hand.

He leaned into it and closed his eyes at her touch and, when he opened them again, he realised that she was looking at him with such love and such yearning that he couldn't help what happened next.

Nate gazed at her for a moment and then he pulled her close, her body to his, feeling everything come alive at the feel of her against him, at the look in her eyes, knowing he would find the strength to let her go if she stopped this.

But she didn't stop him. She kissed him! And he let go of all the torment and allowed her kiss to whisk him away to another world.

Maddy wasn't sure how they made it back to her cabin. It was all a bit of a blur up on deck, a frenzy of need, when the kissing had made them both hungry for more. They'd both realised that out on the open deck, beneath the stars, was not the perfect place for them to sate the desires they both felt, however romantic. For that, they needed privacy. There was a brief memory of walking through the crew corridor as if everything was normal, a blurry image of her fumbling for her key card and then...

And then *everything*.

Clothes were pulled at and removed. Hands went on skin, desperate, hot, fevered. She was kissing him, fumbling with his belt buckle, falling backwards onto her bed. There was laughter, then the feel of his hot lips, his tongue upon her. She kicked off her shoes, struggling with a zip—'Just rip it, I don't care!'—and then... came the heat of him. Bare flesh pressed against her, solid muscle, hardness. She gasped for breath in between every lick, every bite, every kiss. She felt him sliding into her and arched her back, hands grasping, pulling him closer, urging him on, needing, needing, needing *more*...

'Faster. Harder. Like that. *Oh, yes...*'

She felt his lips on her neck. Heat grew within her

chest and she wanted just to lie there and absorb everything he could give, but she didn't want it over just yet. It was too soon, so she rolled him over onto his back and then straddled him, her long hair swaying forward over her bare flesh, tickling at his nipples; she rode him, controlling the movement, slowing it down, rolling her hips as he reached for her breasts and told her she was beautiful.

She felt beautiful then. Felt *strong*. Felt all her feminine power as she smiled deliciously at him, and teasingly rocked her hips from back to front as he lay there, breathless, admiring her. Then before she knew it he'd rolled her onto her back and pinned her, arms above her head, slowly controlling the rhythm, grinning, kissing her neck and trailing his lips up its length to find her mouth, before he began to thrust hard again, grinding down against her, long and so deep, it almost hurt.

Almost.

As he thrust, she could feel her orgasm building. 'Keep doing that…yes,' she breathed, arching to meet every grind, every delightful movement that brought that orgasm closer and closer.

Had it been like that before? She couldn't remember. Did it even matter? She didn't care. Not in that moment; not in that heavenly moment as her breathing increased, they both got louder and then…her very soul seemed to explode as she came, Nate coming seconds later, riding the wave of her orgasm with his own.

And then everything slowed and time returned, reality coming back. The real world reinvited itself back into their lives.

Someone banged on the wall from the cabin next

door and said, 'Nice finish! Well done! Can I get some bloody sleep now?'

Maddy looked up at Nate and they both laughed, before he collapsed into the bed next to her and held her close. And she knew that this time it was different, and this time she would never let him go.

CHAPTER SEVEN

HE SHOULD HAVE slept well but didn't, and the more he lay there with Maddy softly sleeping in his arms, the more guilty he felt. Had he used her for sexual gratification, knowing that he should never have let this get this far?

He didn't want to use her. Didn't want her to think that once he'd got what he wanted, what he needed, then he would walk away from her again. Because he didn't want to do that. If anything, he wanted to stay! And he would, but…what if he wasn't enough for her? What if he hurt her again? They worked together on a boat, for crying out loud. If this went wrong there would be nowhere for either of them to hide, and then she would leave. She would be the one walking away and he would never see her again.

He needed to be able to tell her the truth, to establish the parameters of this, the way they had before, but once he did she would look at him with disappointment and he couldn't do that. So, as he lay there with her in his arms, he told himself he would just pretend that everything was perfect, so that she wouldn't run for the hills when she found out the truth about Lucas. She wouldn't ruin his brother's big day and she wouldn't be mad at *him*.

He still doubted that he was good enough for her, so

if he just kept it in the forefront of his mind that this was as before—friends with benefits—then he could hold back his heart from getting hurt, if it all went wrong. Because, if he was honest with himself, it had been easy to put Lucas's happiness and wellbeing first in everything because then he hadn't had to examine his own self-worth for too long.

Maddy stirred slightly and he nuzzled into her hair, inhaling her scent. He couldn't get enough of it. He couldn't get enough of her and he told himself that, if he soaked her all in, then if it did all go wrong, this time he would remember these sorts of moments, because before he'd thought nothing would come along to ruin it. It was simple. It was no-strings. They could do what they did guilt-free, because she wouldn't want anything from him, like a commitment. But this time he knew the risk of it going wrong, of losing her again. And that terrified him, because he knew his feelings for her were strong and getting stronger with every day.

'Morning,' she said, sleepy and happy.

'Morning.'

She turned in his arms to face him, tantalising him as she pressed her body even closer to his. He felt himself stir, and couldn't resist putting his fingers into her hair and pulling her close for an early-morning kiss.

'Sleep well?' he asked.

'Like a baby. You?'

'Same,' he said, lying, but knowing that he couldn't tell her that he'd lain there all night worrying about this going wrong again. But how could he not worry? Every relationship he had ever had with anyone had gone wrong. Life had been great with his mum until

Bill had come along and then they'd become estranged. He'd loved his baby brother, until that relationship had become strained. Any time he'd been with a woman during his university years, it had been a one-off, and he'd quickly earned a reputation among the female students that he was not someone to go with if they wanted someone who would be there for them.

And with Maddy, the first time round, he'd screwed that up, too. Bill was right: he wasn't good enough. He didn't have what it took to keep someone.

'What time is it?'

He sighed. 'Time for work—we've a crew clinic in about an hour. I ought to go back to my cabin and have a shower before then.'

'You could shower here with me,' she said.

He could picture that, standing in the hot spray with her, their wet, soapy bodies entwined in the steam, hot kisses and slick flesh... 'Mmm, sounds wonderful, but if we do that I'd never leave the shower cubicle and neither would you. Best I leave now and see you later.'

She mock-pouted. 'Okay. One last kiss before you go?'

He pressed his lips to hers and, though his body had fully responded in desire, he knew he had to pull away. He did so with an agonised groan and turned away from her, pulling on his clothes and standing, buttoning up his shirt and watching her as she lay, half-naked except for a sheet on the bed, her red hair haphazardly spread across the pillow.

Once he thought he had everything, he smiled at her. 'I'll see you in an hour.'

'Yes, boss.' She smiled.

He smiled back and then he was gone, closing her door and hoping that he hadn't made the biggest mistake in the world.

It had been inevitable really, she thought as she headed into work, that she and Nate would end up back in each other's arms. She'd felt it from the first moment she had seen him again—a tension in the air, electricity, the kind felt before a big storm. She'd felt it instantly and they'd both been pulled towards that meeting between the sheets, like moths drawn to lanterns burning brightly, unable to help themselves, destined to turn towards that which attracted them. She'd tried to fight it, tried to turn away, but there was no fighting the inevitable. There was no fighting fate, or whatever she wanted to call it.

And now she was glad that they hadn't. Being with him again had reawakened her dormant body in ways that other men had never been able to do, because there had been one or two others after he'd left. There'd been a couple of one night stands, just to scratch an itch, to let out frustrations from the day when things had gone wrong and she'd searched for something for herself. Something to make herself feel better, but of course it never had. If anything, she'd always felt worse, so she'd stopped doing that. She'd practically been celibate for the last two years.

But with Nate, the world seemed brighter. The very air seemed fresher.

The boat was moored off the coast of Corsica and, as was usual on a port day, they held a longer crew clinic as most passengers would disembark to see the sights and explore.

Maddy walked into the clinic feeling all bright and breezy and picked up her first patient file. 'Marco Giordano?'

A young man wearing engineering overalls stood up.

'Come with me.' She led him to a cubicle and got him to sit down on one of the examination beds. 'How can I help you today?'

'Is my hand.' He held it out, palm upwards, towards the ceiling, flexing and unflexing his fingers. 'I'm getting the…how you say…needles and pins? I drop things. Drop my tools.'

She nodded. 'Okay and how long has this been happening?'

'A couple of weeks.'

Weeks? That wasn't good. 'Anything make it better?'

Marco shrugged. 'Sometimes rest, but when you engineer, you don't get much.'

'I guess not. Are you alright for me to touch and examine you?'

He nodded.

'Okay.' Maddy performed an examination of not just his hand, but his wrist and shoulder, checking for impingement, any pain or numbness. She got him to grip her fingers, to pull, to push and tested his strength and grip against his other hand to see if there were any anomalies. 'Well, that all seems normal. Can you press the backs of your hands together, wrists bent, and hold it for about a minute?'

He did so.

'Any tingling?'

'Yes.'

Maddy nodded. 'I think you have something called

carpal tunnel. It's caused by pressure on a nerve in your wrist. It makes you feel pain or numbness in your fingers and hand, and it can cause weakness and the problems that you've been having. I'm going to suggest you wear a wrist splint for a while, see how you get on with that, and then we'll have you back in a week to see how you're getting on.'

'And if it worse?'

'There are lots of options. We could do steroid injections, pain medication, or some people have to have surgery, though your doctors would need to do an ultrasound first. Let's do the splint and see how you get on. How does that sound?'

'Good. I don't want surgery—I need to work.'

'Of course. I'll let your supervisor know what I've suggested as well, so that they are aware.'

'Thank you.'

'No problem. I'll just get you that splint.'

Maddy was really enjoying her work now on *Serendipity*. It had eased her back into medicine nicely and it felt good to feel confident about being with patients again. And everything was turning out great with Nate, too! Life was certainly looking up, at last.

There was a bounce to her step as she thought about how her life had changed. She'd been so scared to accept this job, wondering if it would be too much being away from her home, away from everything and everyone she knew, sailing the seas, seeing the world and seeing patients again after her attack… She had never been at sea and had no idea if she got seasick. And, if she didn't like it then she'd be stuck doing so for half a year!

But, fortunately, she loved it and Nate was here and

everything was finally working out for them… Maybe she would get a happy ending in her life. She felt that she'd certainly earned it!

After she'd fixed the splint to Marco's wrist, she sent him on his way and typed her notes into the system. She'd just finished her call with her patient's supervisor when Nate appeared, carrying two mugs. 'Tea break?' he said, smiling.

She nodded, smiling back. 'Sounds perfect.'

Nate was feeling terribly conflicted—fearful, full of doubt. Yet also hopeful that maybe all his fears were not founded and that he and Maddy could be fine, even if he was still keeping his fears about himself and Lucas from her. 'How's your morning going?'

She smiled at him, her eyes full of mischief and sexual allure. 'Well, it started great.'

Yes, it had. Waking up with her in his arms had felt like coming home. That he was back in the place he was always meant to have been. He'd missed her so much over the years! But he couldn't trust what he was feeling. He wasn't sure of anything any more. He wasn't used to thinking about himself and what he wanted or needed.

'After crew clinic, we've a couple of hours before the ship sets sail again. I wondered if you'd like to come and explore Corsica with me? Grab a bite to eat somewhere?' He suggested it so that they didn't end up back in one of their cabin's. He didn't want this to get too deep. Who knew what she was feeling? And he didn't dare ask, because what if she thought this was something more and he had to tell her otherwise?

'Sounds amazing! I'd love to.'

'Perfect. I've one patient I need to see in their cabin and then I'll be free. Dr Galanis and Dr Hicks will be on call whilst we're away from the ship in case anything crops up in the meantime, so…pick you up at twelve?'

'I'll be waiting.' She reached for his hand as he stood and pulled him in for a long, hot kiss that stirred his loins and dizzied his senses as he inhaled her perfume and flashed back to last night.

How could he be so hungry for her and yet, at the same time, feel so cautious?

I just don't want to hurt her but I might.

No-one knew about Lucas's past here—that he'd been a drug addict. No-one knew about Nate's uncertainties. He'd never dated anyone on board, even though he'd received plenty of offers. If anything, he had a reputation for being standoffish. He wasn't even sure he knew how to be in a relationship any more.

Could he give Maddy what she needed, what she *deserved*? Because she deserved happiness. A guy that could give her everything: commitment and a family. She wanted to settle down. And she deserved truth and honesty from the man she was with and he couldn't be honest with her. He yearned to be. But, if he told her his fears, then she would pull away from him and he didn't want that either. He just needed to keep up the charade until after Lucas's big day. Because he wouldn't risk disrupting his brother's big day—not when he was so close to happiness and setting himself free to work on himself.

Because he knew he loved Maddy. Maybe he always had. And the idea that he might be letting down the woman he loved pained him terribly. He wanted to give her his all, to be able to talk to her about anything, to tell her the truth of why he'd left all those years ago—and not just the sanitised version he'd given her.

But if he got it wrong, he could lose her...and he was terrified of that.

Because only love could cause the level of pain he anticipated, if it all went wrong and *she* walked away from *him*.

When clinic was over, they signed out and headed dockside in Ajaccio, the capital of Corsica. They were only a few minutes' walk from the old town and it felt good to have her walk by his side. He wanted to show her all the beauty of this place and give her good memories, so that if it did all go wrong she might look back and remember that once, they'd been great.

She slipped her hand into his, surprising him. She looked happy, carefree. Sunglasses held her hair back from her face on this beautifully warm day with clear blue skies.

Plane trees in rich greens juxtaposed beautifully against the daffodil-yellow houses as they walked the alleys and boulevards towards the market, and once there they soon lost themselves, tasting cheeses, delicatessen meats and locally made honey on soft, warm bread. It was a veritable delight to the tastebuds and he smiled when she spotted a stall selling sweet, anise-flavoured biscuits and bought a box, alongside a slim bottle of myrtle oil. Touristy gift acquired, they headed for a local restaurant with a patio to eat *al fresco*.

They were seated beneath a canopy of grape vines and ordered wild boar stew served with fries and green beans and gâteau à la Farine de Châtaigne, sweet chestnut cake that would be served with a vanilla-bean ice-cream. The food was delicious, of course delicious. But he enjoyed the company more.

Maddy leaned back in her chair, full and satisfied, smiling, eyes crinkling behind her sunglasses. 'I'm so glad I came on board. You know… I had reservations when I realised you were here. Things ended so abruptly before, but now, I'm so, so happy.' She leaned forward then and took hold of his hand. '*You* make me happy.'

He smiled, thrilled with the compliment. 'You make me happy, too.' He couldn't say anything else. He most definitely couldn't say *I love you* because that would pull her deeper into his life and then, when the truth came out, she'd be even more hurt that he'd kept things from her. He told himself he was protecting her by not saying it, when in reality he was really protecting himself. He reckoned that, by holding back, by not giving his all, he would stop her from falling in love with him, because if he knew she loved him and then walked away that would be the most terrible thing of all.

She glanced at her watch. 'Ship sails in an hour, we should get back soon. Even if right now I feel like I don't want to leave this beautiful place. I think it's my favourite port so far.'

'And there's still so much we didn't see—the cathedral, the citadel, the Parata peninsular…'

'We can do that next time the ship docks here.'

Her fingers were still entwined with his and he glanced down at them. They were long, elegant, a faint pink blush on them. He could imagine a ring on her left hand on her ring finger, shining with a large diamond, and then he pushed the thought from his mind. What was he doing, torturing himself; thinking of weddings simply because Lucas was getting married? 'Lucas will be married by then. Has he been in touch with you about a dress for the ceremony? It's soon.'

'There might have been one or two emails.' She smiled. 'There's a dress I'm going to be picking up when we dock in Nice. Lucas showed it to me.'

'Really? What's it like?'

'It's a surprise. I want you to see me in it for the first time on the day Lucas marries. Your brother is very excited.'

'Who wouldn't be, to marry the love of their life?'

She smiled. 'I envy him his certainty.'

Nate frowned. 'You do?'

'Of course! To *know*, the way he does, that Carlos is the man he wants to spend the *rest of his life* with!' She shook her head in disbelief. 'I think that's amazing. I don't think I've ever felt so sure about someone the way he does.'

'How do you mean?'

She shrugged. 'I've always second-guessed everybody. They say the right things, give you all the great soundbites, but when it comes to it? People let you down. But Lucas doesn't think that. He knows that Carlos has his back and won't ever let him down, and that's a gift, a certainty, I wish I had.'

Was she fishing? Nate felt guilty because he knew he'd let her down, proving her point. She could probably never, ever truly trust him, even if she did say that he made her happy. Because, if she couldn't trust him fully, she could never love him.

He hated that his thoughts and worries about this kept going round and round his head. 'We should get back to the ship.' He paid the bill and then stood and, when they left the restaurant and headed back to *Serendipity,* they no longer held hands. Simply because he'd been reminded that, no matter how much he wanted to love her the way he did, she could never be his. She would never trust him, because she couldn't trust anyone, and when she discovered the truth he would reinforce the fact that he could never be trusted.

Maddy was confused as they headed back to the ship. They'd walked into Ajaccio hand in hand and she'd felt amazing—like everything was working out. They'd had a great time at the market, and walking around the old town, and then at dinner something had changed and she wasn't sure what. Suddenly Nate seemed to hold part of himself back. But what they had was all so new; she didn't want to ruin it by asking him what was wrong.

Being with him last night had been amazing. To sleep in his arms had been wonderful, and she'd woken this morning wondering if this could possibly be her future. That, despite him leaving in the past, she knew what had happened now and understood him leaving. But the pain she'd felt upon losing him was not something she wanted to experience again. So, rather than ask him if anything was wrong, she decided to ignore the warning in her gut that he might already be pulling away again and told herself to keep quiet. It was probably just anxiety because of what had gone before. *He wasn't really going to leave!* Not after the perfect night they'd shared.

'Got anything planned this evening?' she asked him, knowing they were both off-duty until tomorrow now.

'I've a meeting and then I'm going to see Lucas. Help him plan his stag do on board.'

'Of course. It's not long now, is it?'

'Couple of days.'

'Well if the stag is the night before, don't let him get too hungover. He's going to want to enjoy his day.'

'Oh, he won't be drinking.'

'No? Why?'

Nate paused, then laughed, as if caught out by something. 'He just...doesn't really like the taste of it. I think he wants a sort of sports night—do the climbing wall, the on-board surfing, that kind of thing. Can't do those if you're paralytic!'

'I guess not.' It made sense.

They signed back on board, swiping their ID cards, and then Nate planted a kiss upon her cheek and excused himself. 'Gotta prep for my meeting. I'll see you tomorrow morning at work?'

'Of course.' But as she watched him go that strange feeling she'd felt earlier came back. She felt like he was holding something of himself back—that she wasn't being told everything.

And he did that before, remember? said the insidious, tiny voice in her head that was slowly getting louder.

Madeline bit her lower lip and headed in the other direction towards her own cabin.

Maybe everything would seem brighter in the morning.

Halfway through her morning passenger clinic, a young woman arrived, supported by her best friend as she hobbled in, clearly unable to bear weight on one of her feet. She was wearing a white bikini and patterned sarong and her friend wore a red swimsuit with a towel wrapped around her midriff. Both had wet hair.

'I slipped on some water poolside.' The hobbling woman, whose name was Sarah, cried as she hopped onto an examination bed.

Madeline frowned, looking concerned. The ankle did look malformed, and to have got here from the pools with just the help of her friend was very impressive indeed. 'Let's get you some painkillers first, before I examine you. It's a clear dislocation and I need to give you an intra-muscular opioid injection of morphine.'

'Dislocated?' Sarah looked upset, wiping at tears on her face. 'This all just gets worse and worse! Am I going to have to leave the boat?'

'We need to get this x-rayed to ensure there aren't any fractures and, if there aren't, then we should be able to perform a reduction on board and keep you here, if there aren't any complications.'

Maddy checked and double-checked the dosage, before injecting the painkiller, then gave it a moment to take effect before putting on examination gloves and eyeing the injury. There was no skin break, thankfully, which would have made this more complicated, and no vascular compromise. Hopefully the x-ray would confirm she could do a simple reduction. 'You just slipped? You weren't dizzy beforehand?'

'No.' Sarah's friend, Anna, passed her a tissue as she continued to cry.

Maddy looked up at her friend to see if she would explain why Sarah was so upset. Maybe it was just the pain, or feeling that her holiday was ruined... 'You might be off your feet for a bit, but don't worry, you've not ruined your holiday.'

'It's not my holiday!' Sarah cried. 'It's my honeymoon.'

'Failed honeymoon,' Anna added.

As Maddy arranged the x-ray, manoeuvring the portable machine over Sarah's foot to get a good angle, she frowned. '*Failed* honeymoon?' she asked.

Sarah put down her tissue and looked at Maddy with panda eyes. 'I was supposed to be married now to the man of my dreams and enjoying this honeymoon cruise with him! But the jerk let me down and never showed and, because I didn't want to lose my money, I came on my honeymoon with Anna!'

'Chief bridesmaid and best friend,' Anna added.

'Oh. I see. I'm sorry to hear that.' She carefully and gently placed the x-ray plate beneath Sarah's ankle and made final adjustments with the machine. 'Did he say why he didn't show?'

'Said he wasn't ready. That he couldn't give me what I needed. You'd think he'd have worked that out before the morning of the wedding!'

'Jerk,' agreed Anna, clearly no stranger to helping Sarah vent.

The x-rays confirmed no break and Maddy gave the good news to a rather resigned patient. 'I can do the reduction here. You won't have to leave the ship. But afterwards, I will have to immobilise the joint with a splint and take a final x-ray just to ensure everything is where it's meant to be, okay? And we'll book you in for a follow-up at a clinic in Nice.'

'Will it hurt?'

'I'll sedate you so you shouldn't remember it.'

'The ankle or my idiot of an ex-fiancé? I'm telling you, doc, don't ever fall in love. The cost is much too high to pay.'

Sarah was probably right. Look at how much her own feelings were being bounced around already with Nate and they weren't planning a wedding, she thought. Well, not their own, anyway. Love certainly didn't have a smooth path.

Was it meant to? Was love *meant* to be easy? Was that how she'd know for sure she was in love, because there weren't any problems? Because, if that was the case, then what did it say about Nate and her?

'Okay, I'm going to go and get someone to help me with this, and when I come back I'm going to sedate you, okay?'

Sarah nodded and dabbed at her eyes. 'Fine.'

Nate helped Maddy provide traction on an ankle reduction for a patient who had slipped by a pool. After examining the x-rays together afterwards, ensuring the joint was realigned, they placed the patient, Sarah, into a special supportive boot, gave her a set of crutches and told her to be careful.

'This was meant to be her honeymoon,' Maddy said to him after their patient limped away, aided and abetted by her friend, Anna.

'Meant to be?'

'The groom was a no-show, so she's here on the cruise with her chief bridesmaid instead.'

'She got jilted at the altar? Poor girl. I can't even imagine.'

Maddy looked at him. 'I can. Imagine being so totally in love with someone and discovering the other person didn't feel the same way. Sarah must be in hell.'

Did she know? Or was she talking about before? She couldn't know his true feelings...

'Do you think you could ever imagine being in such a situation that you wouldn't show up to your own wedding?' she asked.

He thought about it for a moment. If the bride were Maddy, he couldn't imagine it. 'No. I mean I'd like to think that, if there were doubts or cold feet, I'd have the wherewithal to discuss those with the bride before it even got to that stage. In fact, if there were doubts, I don't think I'd have even proposed, never mind have got to the altar.' But it was easier said than done, wasn't it? Hypotheticals were all well and good, but when it came down to it no-one wanted to hurt another person intentionally. Not like that.

'So...logically then...if you had worries about us, reservations, you'd talk to me about them?'

'Of course.' He smiled, feeling his cheeks colour. Did she suspect he had reservations? He desperately wanted to be fully committed. He wanted just to take her by the hand and tell her that he loved her! He was holding back the truth about Lucas, because he had sworn him to secrecy. And because, if Maddy found out afterwards that she had been a bridesmaid for an addict, he didn't want her hating him.

No. It's easy to blame my reservations on that. It's me. I don't think I'm good enough for her. What if I'm not? 'But it's not like we're in something serious, right? We're just having fun.'

'Fun?' Her smile faltered and she distracted herself by putting things away, tidying up after herself in the small cubicle. 'Of course. It's not like we're committed; we've made no promises to one another.'

'Exactly.' He nodded, watching her busy herself, wishing with all his might that he could take hold of her, pull her close and say, 'I was lying just then. I want us to be more. I want us to be official.'

But he didn't. Fear kept the words and the desire to say them choked up in his throat. He cleared it and pushed the curtains of the cubicle open. 'Well, I'd better let you get on. Has Lucas told you yet about the wedding rehearsal?'

'No.'

'Tomorrow, in the Captain's lounge. Just so we all know where we'll be standing and what he needs us to do, is that okay? About three?'

Maddy nodded and gave him a bright smile. 'Fine!'

She was okay with it. *Cool*. 'Great. I'll see you later.'

CHAPTER EIGHT

IT WAS LOVELY to see Lucas again. He was one of those people that just made Maddy smile to be with him. He was fun and outrageous and clearly the star of his own life, and right now he was the romantic lead. His love for Carlos and his eagerness to get married, on board in front of all of his friends, was beautiful and Maddy felt that she needed beauty right now with her heart being broken yet again by Nate.

They'd arrived in Nice that morning and Maddy had collected the bridesmaid dress that Lucas had approved. It was hanging in her cabin and she would not let anyone see it until the big day. It was an asymmetrical, off the shoulder, pale-green, floor-length, silky delight that showed off Maddy's red hair beautifully and she felt wonderful wearing it. Lucas had let her know that there would be a small floral hairpin for her to wear, as well as a small bouquet to hold. He had spent an hour with her in her cabin, discussing which shoes would go well with the dress and, as she didn't have anything suitable, they'd gone to the very expensive shop on *Serendipity*'s promenade and Lucas had paid for a beautiful heel, with a diamanté flourish on the side.

He wanted everything to be perfect. During the time

she'd spent with him, she really felt she'd got to know him. Lucas was amazing and she couldn't wait to see him marry the love of his life.

'So you and Nate will go up the aisle first, starting here, okay?' Lucas drew an imaginary line. 'And where those chairs are, imagine the arch and where the captain will be waiting to perform the service.'

'The captain isn't part of the rehearsal?'

'He's done this before and, between you and me, he probably doesn't need an ice-dancer from his ship tell him what to do!' Lucas winked, positioning Maddy closer to Nate. 'You'll want to slip your arm into his or something. What's the matter with you two?'

'Nothing.' Maddy turned to face Nate and smiled, before sliding her arm into his and facing forward.

'And play the music.'

The Captain's lounge filled with a piece of soft, classical music, a known love ballad.

'And walk.'

Lucas stood in front of them, backing away, smiling broadly as she and Nate began their slow walk up the aisle.

Maddy reminded herself quite strongly as she did so that she and Nate were just bridesmaid and best man and would never be the bride and groom. But she couldn't help herself. It was almost impossible not to think about it!

Ever since she'd been a little girl, alone in her communal room, she had imagined the day she might get married. She'd pulled a pillowcase from her pillow and draped it over her head for a veil. She's scrunched up a floral print top and pretended it was her bouquet, and imagined walking up an aisle, knowing that all eyes were on her. The eyes of loved ones, of friends who loved her: co-workers, besties. They would all gaze upon her and think her the most beautiful bride in the world! And then she would get to the end of the aisle and there would be the man of her dreams.

When she'd been a child, the groom's face had always been a blur, but she'd known that he loved her more than he loved life itself. That she would forever be his princess, his queen, his bride and best friend... and he would *love* her.

As a child, she'd not really known what love felt like and it had been something she had chased for a long time. And then, when she'd got it, she'd not realised just how much pain it would cause her when the man she loved disappeared without a word. The man who now held her arm in his as they reached the end of the aisle.

'Bellissima!' Lucas clapped, beaming, placing a head on Carlos's shoulder before turning to his husband-to-be, holding his hands and gazing into his eyes.

They went through the whole imagined ceremony, practising it a couple of times over, Lucas explaining in great detail what would be happening to ensure that not a single thing went wrong. When it was over, Maddy and Nate headed back to the medical clinic.

'It's going to be a lovely wedding,' Maddy said conversationally.

'Yes. I can officially sign off care of my brother to someone else.'

'And then what will you do with all that free time?'

Nate laughed. 'Oh, I don't know...take off somewhere? Go explore the Sahara or trek across the Arctic?'

Was that a joke answer because he didn't know what he was going to do? Or was it a real one, to let her know that, in all likelihood, he was going to take off again? The idea that he might disappear on her *again* sullied the day. 'Well, I'll miss you, if you do,' she said. 'But you must do what's right for you. After all, you did go running the second he needed you, so I guess your life will become your own to do with how you please.'

She would miss him, terribly, but she would not let it show. Would not let him see that he had made a fool of her again. He did not deserve that power. If he did think they were just friends with benefits, then friends with benefits they would be!

'Just let me know before you go this time,' she said, pushing open the door to the bathroom and disappearing inside just as the pain of her tears hit her eyes. She would not cry over this man again!

'Damn it!' she swore softly to herself as she stood in front of the mirror, dabbing at her eyes with a blue paper-towel from the dispenser. Why had she let herself hope that, because they'd slept with each other again, they were something more? That they were *involved*, in a *relationship*. He'd made no such declaration and nor had she asked him. *I should have set out the intentions from the start!* Only she'd not, because she'd been busy tearing off his clothes, seeking out his skin and giving in to the lust that had been building.

When will I ever learn when it comes to him?

Well I'll miss you, if you do.

He'd made some off-hand comment about exploring some far-off remote places once Lucas was married, but only because each time he'd walked her down that pretend aisle in the Captain's lounge, he'd thought about how it might feel to see Maddy in a beautiful white dress, walking up the aisle *to him*.

He could imagine himself marrying Madeline, and that terrified him, because that meant his feelings for her ran so deep he was imagining for ever with her and that meant he was getting hopeful. That he was making plans. But he was so terrified of not being good enough for her; having broken her heart once already, he was terrified of doing so again. What if he got this part wrong, or the next part? It could all fall apart so quickly and he didn't want to lose her. And she would clearly miss him if he did decide to take off and get some space for himself, because when was the last time he'd actually been by himself?

In his first job at London Saint, he'd had Maddy, and then he'd come rushing home at the news of their parents' death and Lucas's overdose and he'd been with his brother. He'd been with him intensively these last few years, watching him get sober, helping him recover, encouraging him to build the life for himself that had always been denied him. And then, when Lucas had got the job on board the cruise ship and had been nervous about what would happen if he lost his brother, his support system by his side, Nate had got a job on board too. To be there. Backup. Just in case. They had been on many different ships together.

Now Lucas was going to marry Carlos and it would set Nate free—but he wasn't sure *how* to be free. Who would he be without his brother to need him? Nate had never been by himself and maybe he needed that space to know what he wanted for sure, whether he wanted a full-on relationship with Maddy or not. So, yes, he'd suggested he explore the Sahara or the Arctic, be by himself and sort out his feelings, because being this close to her was scrambling his brain, and sometimes he didn't know which way was up. One inner voice told him just to be with her and another told him that he would just hurt her again.

I don't want to hurt her.

Could he really walk away and take some time for himself? Maddy said she'd miss him, but he knew for sure that, if he did, when he came back the door to them being a thing would be closed—permanently. No, he had to decide before then if he was good enough.

Maybe I should ask Lucas if I can tell her about his addiction. That way, he'd be telling her the whole truth about why he'd left, but then he'd hurt Lucas by bringing up a past he had worked so hard to put behind him. His brother would always be an addict, but he'd been sober for years and, with the exception of Carlos and him, no-one knew about it. His brother would not want to be thought of differently, lose friends or have someone think they could tempt him back with something.

He felt stuck between a rock and a hard place.

Nate picked up a patient admission file. A woman, aged thirty-six, had come to the medical bay with intense back and hip pain. The file said she was struggling to walk. At least he could help his patients, even if he couldn't find the right path to help himself and free himself of all the turmoil he felt.

'Marissa?' A woman in the waiting area, sitting with

a man holding her hand, stood with difficulty, wincing slightly as they made their way over to him.

'Let's get you to a cubicle,' he said, guiding her and slowing his pace as she ambled along behind him. 'I'm Dr Blake and you are...?'

'Mason. I'm her husband.'

'Nice to meet you both. Okay, Marissa, what's the most comfortable position for you? Sitting? Standing? Lying down?'

'Can I just lie down for a moment please?' She sounded a little breathless.

'Sure thing.' Her husband helped her up, and she winced and groaned as she settled herself with some relief onto the examination bed. 'So, tell me what's been happening.'

Marissa shook her head as if she couldn't quite explain, or understand what was happening. 'I don't know. Everything's been fine. I'm usually in good health and I don't usually suffer with my back or anything like that.'

'She does yoga, pilates. She's always been fit,' her husband added.

'Have you done anything recently that might contribute to this back pain?'

'We did the climbing wall yesterday and I was in a harness. Could I have stretched funny, do you think?'

'Possibly. On holiday people try a lot of new things they don't normally do and using different sets of muscles can trigger a problem. If you had to rate the pain from zero to ten, with zero being no pain and ten being the worst pain you've ever felt in your life, how would you rate it?'

'It's hard to say...it seems to come in waves and,

when it does, I'd put it at maybe a six or a seven. Oh, it's coming now...' Marissa groaned and scrunched up her face as she dealt with the pain.

Nate grabbed a blood-pressure cuff, which he placed around her upper arm, and a SAT monitor, which he placed on her finger. Her blood pressure was slightly elevated, which was no doubt from the pain, and her pulse was slightly high too, but her oxygen SATs were normal. 'Does the pain come and go like this all the time? When did it start?'

When she could breathe again, she nodded. 'Yes. It started this morning. I woke at about four. I figured it was muscular, took a painkiller and went back to sleep, but the tablet did nothing and it kept waking me up.'

'I'll just take your temperature.' He placed the electronic thermometer in her ear, but her temperature was normal. 'Eating and drinking okay?'

'I felt a little nauseous earlier, but I had my breakfast.'

'Toileting okay? No diarrhoea?'

'I did have some cramps and had a bowel movement, but no diarrhoea.'

'And when was your last menstrual period?'

'Two weeks ago.'

'And they've been normal lately?'

Marissa nodded. 'Yes.'

'What do you think it is, doc?' Mason asked.

'Could be any number of things. Can you roll onto your side so I can examine your back? I'll feel down your spine and you tell me when and where it hurts, okay?'

'Okay.'

He palpated her vertebrae, starting at her neck and moving down to her lower sacrum, where Marissa indicated it was sore. 'And, when the pain comes, what does it feel like? Is it burning? Sharp? Dull?'

'I don't know how to describe it, except to say it's powerful and comes in waves.'

'Any pattern to these waves?'

Marissa and Mason both shrugged. 'We weren't timing them, so don't have a clue.'

'Could I examine your abdomen, would that be alright?'

'Fine.' Marissa manoeuvred herself into place and lifted her top.

Her stomach looked unremarkable, but when he palpated he could feel a mass...a mass that felt remarkably ominous. But he kept his expression blank and told her she could lower her top. 'I'd like to do an ultrasound and maybe bring in a colleague. I won't be a moment.'

'What's wrong? Did you feel something?' Mason asked.

'I'll be back in a moment.' Nate pulled the cubicle curtain across and let out a breath, then he went looking for Maddy. He reckoned he would need her for what he suspected was coming next. He found her in one of the utility rooms. 'Got a sec?'

She nodded. 'Sure. What's up?'

'I need your help with a patient, who I strongly suspect may be in labour with a cryptic pregnancy.' A cryptic pregnancy was a pregnancy which passed by the full nine months completely undetected by medical professionals or the mother herself.

'You're joking!'

'No. She's having what I think are contractions, even though her belly is flat. She's been having periods, but when I palpated her abdomen I could feel what felt like a term baby. I'm going to ultrasound her, but if we've got a labouring mother on board she might prefer a female doctor, so thought I'd get you to co-consult and then, if she wants you to take over her delivery, you'll know each other.'

'Wow. Okay. I've never seen one of these before. You?'

'No. Never. And I've not told them of my suspicions yet. I thought I'd do the ultrasound first to confirm and then tell them.'

'Okay. You're the boss.'

He nodded. Yes, he was, and he had that to think of too. There were thousands of people on this ship who depended on having a good team there for them any hour of any day of their cruise. He wanted Maddy to feel wanted, needed, even if he couldn't give her everything he wanted to.

When they got back to the cubicle, he pushed the ultrasound machine in and began to set it up, whilst introducing Maddy.

Marissa experienced another wave of pain and, timing it surreptitiously, Nate noted that it was almost a minute long. If he was right, her pains were going to get a lot more frequent and a lot more powerful.

'Now, Marissa, I'm just going to squirt this gel onto your abdomen; it can feel cold, okay?' Her belly was so flat! It was hard to believe that there was a baby tucked away in there.

'Okay,' she breathed, coming down from the pain.

Mason reached for her hand and held it with both of his.

Nate was glad that Marissa had her husband as support, because he suspected they were both about to have the surprise of their lives. He placed the transducer wand onto Marissa's belly, smearing the gel widely, and then began to focus his attention on what could be seen on the screen. He had it angled towards himself and Maddy, who stood behind him, watching closely.

And he'd guessed correctly. Marissa was pregnant to term! The baby measured at thirty-nine weeks and six days.

Nate turned to glance at Maddy and they both nodded to one another.

'What is it? What do you see?' Marissa asked.

'This isn't easy to say and it's going to be a shock.' Nate reached for the screen and turned it round. 'The pains you are having are contractions and you are about to give birth to a full-term baby.'

There was a moment of thick, stunned silence as Marissa and Mason stared hard at the screen. There was their baby, clear as day.

'Pregnant?' Mason said.

Marissa shook her head in denial. 'But...I've been having periods! It's got to be wrong!'

'It's not wrong. The measurements indicate a nearly forty-week baby. Your periods were probably breakthrough bleeds—it happens sometimes in what we call cryptic pregnancies.'

'I can't be pregnant! Not full term!' Marissa cried, then winced as another contraction hit.

It did not escape Nate's notice that Mason had pulled his hand free from his wife's. A moment ago, they had been united by her pain, and he had seemed supportive and loving. Now, Mason looked shocked and—if Nate had to guess—angry.

'We've only been back together for four months, so… whose is it?' Mason asked his wife.

Nate did not expect that. He wiped the gel from Marissa's belly and when her contraction was over and said, 'We'll give you a moment alone, but Marissa, you're in labour and we'll need to get you on some foetal monitoring. I'm assuming you've had no pre-natal care.'

Marissa began to cry.

Mason stood staring at her, as if he didn't recognise her.

Nate and Maddy left the cubicle.

'We need to get her in a private room,' Maddy said.

'We will, but let's just give them a minute. They've had a shock.' Nate and Maddy walked over to the reception desk.

From where they stood, they could hear the argument.

'You lied to me!'

'You never told me the truth, ever!'

'How will I ever trust you?'

Mason was shouting…a lot.

'We should go back,' Nate said. 'She doesn't need this right now.'

'Maybe not, but he's asked a valid question. Trust is everything and if you feel like someone is lying to you, or you know that they are, it can ruin everything.'

The way she's looking at me… 'Maddy, I really don't think that now is the time.'

'It never is with you.'

But there was no time for them to discuss it, or for him to ask what she meant. *'Dr Finch…'* He reined in his anger. He'd tried, he'd tried so hard, but this was what he did! This was what he was trying to protect her from! Could she not see that he was protecting her? 'Let's go tend to our patient. Mason can get his answers after we make sure mum and baby are okay. Can we get the captain notified of the imminent delivery in case we need to get them both airlifted out of here?' He gave instructions.

Maddy blanched and picked up the phone as he headed back to the cubicle with a wheelchair, so that he could wheel Marissa to a private room for the delivery.

They had all they needed to deliver a baby, but if the baby needed support afterwards, or there were complications with the delivery and it became an emergency situation, Nate would prefer Marissa and her baby to be in a facility fully equipped to deal with such a situation.

Mason followed forlornly as Nate wheeled his patient to a private room and got her onto a bed.

Maddy followed a moment or so after. 'The captain is going to divert to the closest port just in case, and an obstetrician is going to be on standby to receive them. Dr Ottilie is available to virtually assist, if we need it.' Her tone was curt.

'Thank you.' She was pulling away. He'd hurt her again. He knew it. But there was no time for him to address it. Marissa and her baby were the priority here. 'Marissa, as you're in labour, we're going to need to examine you internally, see how you're progressing. Either myself or Dr Finch could do it. Do you have a preference?'

'Dr Finch.'

'Maddy?' He turned to her. She was already washing her hands and preparing to put on gloves. 'I'll get the CTG machine so we can keep an eye on baby and your contractions as you progress.'

He'd only ever had to use the machine once before on a cruise. Venture Line Cruises had a ruling that no one was allowed to sail after the twenty-third week of pregnancy, and anyone sailing before that had to have a letter from their doctor confirming that they were low risk and healthy to board. But there'd been one poor lady who started contracting in her twenty-first week and the ship had been so far from a port that she'd been airlifted off. Thankfully, the hospital she'd ended up at had managed to stop her contractions. He'd never had to use it on a woman at term before.

'Okay, try to relax,' Maddy said as she performed the internal examination. 'You're at seven centimetres, you're moving fast!' She sounded impressed.

Marissa let out a moan of fear and grasped for her husband's hand.

Nate could see by the look on the man's face that he was torn. Clearly they'd had a tumultuous relationship, from what he could tell a break-up and then a reconnection, and in that time his wife had slept with someone else and not told him. Now he was having to deal with the fact that the woman he loved was about to give birth to someone else's baby.

He couldn't imagine how that felt. The idea that Maddy might find a haven in another man's arms… Would he have been able to do it? Would he have been able to forgive her?

'Oh God, here comes another one!'

'Marissa, would you like some gas and air? We have Entonox on board,' Maddy said.

Marissa nodded frantically, her hands gripping the mattress as she contorted and tried to breathe through the strengthening contractions.

We're going to deliver this baby. It's coming fast. His mind went into automatic mode. All other thoughts, all other concerns about himself, Lucas and Maddy, went out of the window.

Her waters suddenly broke and thankfully they were clear. Even though he knew this was happening, knew that he'd seen a term baby on the ultrasound, there was still an element of disbelief about the whole thing, because Marissa didn't look pregnant. She looked three or four months' pregnant, nothing more. Her belly was gently rounded like any woman's, but nothing that screamed advanced pregnancy.

'Oh God, I want to push!' Marissa screamed.

'Try to breathe through it. I need to check you,' Maddy said.

He and Maddy moved perfectly as a team. Just like the good old days when they used to surround a new incoming patient to A&E, assessing, checking and working together to ensure the safety and health priorities of their patient. It was like a dance. Perfectly coordinated, they began to coach Marissa through pushing as, unbelievably, she was fully dilated.

Marissa sucked in breaths and began to push.

By Nate's estimate from the ultrasound, the baby was nearly seven pounds—a good weight, a healthy weight. He could only pray that, when it was born, the baby would be able to breathe on its own and not need any assistance. He'd not seen anything of concern on the scan, which was good news, but he could never know for sure.

'And push again, Marissa! Just like that! Perfect!' Maddy coached.

The head was beginning to crown. The baby had thick, black hair, just like its mother.

'I don't think I can do this! We don't have anything! We're not prepared! You hate me!' Marissa cried.

'I don't hate you,' Mason said. 'I love you. We can work this out, but not if you don't push!'

Nate looked at him, surprised, but glad that he was choosing to support his wife, despite all he'd had to take in during the last hour: that his wife's back pain wasn't from rock-climbing; that she was pregnant; that she was full term. That she was in labour and that the baby she was delivering was not his. But he was there for her. It gave him hope that maybe things would turn out just as well for Maddy and him.

'Okay, on the next contraction, the baby's head will crown and I'll tell you when to stop pushing and when to just breathe it out and let it come nicely so you don't tear, okay?'

Marissa nodded, then sucked in another breath and began to push with all her might.

The head slowly emerged and, just as it got to the widest part, Maddy instructed Marissa to stop pushing and let the head crown by itself. 'Just breathe…that's it…you're doing great. Okay, head's out! Do you want to touch your baby?'

Marissa reached down. 'Oh!' She smiled and laughed, her head flopping back onto the pillow.

'Next contraction is the shoulders and your baby will be here in no time.'

Nate gathered the towels and blankets that he'd taken

from the cupboards, ready to wrap the baby. He also had scissors for the cord, and a clamp that he'd thought he'd never have to use, but which they had in stock just in case of emergencies such as this one.

Marissa pushed and Maddy caught the baby as it slithered out and instantly began to cry as she placed the baby on Marissa's chest and into her waiting hands.

Marissa and Mason were crying.

Nate placed the towels around the baby, drying it, keeping it warm, whilst Maddy dealt with the afterbirth and checked Marissa for tears.

'Just a first-degree tear there, Marissa, but that should heal on its own. You did good!' Maddy said.

Nate knew the sex of the baby. He'd seen it during the delivery and on the scan. 'Know what you've got yet?'

Marissa looked, then gasped with delight. 'It's a boy!'

Once everybody was cleaned up, Nate and Maddy left Marissa and Mason to bond as a family. Nate informed the captain that the baby had been born and everything was well. The ship would still sail into Cannes and offload mum and baby for a proper check-up by Dr Ottilie, an obstetrician.

'Never thought I'd do that,' Nate said as Maddy brought him a cup of tea afterwards.

'Nor me. But life always likes to throw you little surprises.'

'It certainly does,' he said, thinking back to how he'd felt when he'd learned that Maddy would be joining his ship as a doctor—a woman he'd never thought he would see again.

'Do you think they'll be alright?' Maddy asked.

'Marissa and Mason?'

She nodded.

'I hope so. If they can get through that, they can get through anything.'

Maddy went silent for a moment, staring at her cup in her hands, then she lifted her head and looked directly at him. 'I know what it feels like to realise that the person you love is withholding something from you.'

His heart began to pound. She *loved* him!

'I know that you're keeping yourself held back but I don't know why. I don't understand why you aren't able to commit to me, when clearly there's something powerfully strong between us.'

'Maddy—'

'Do you not love me? Is that it? Am I not worthy of you loving me? Because that's how it feels, and I don't want to continue this contract on this ship knowing that I want to give you all of my love, but you can't do the same.'

He felt lost for words. He wanted to explain, but was not sure that he was able. She was asking him perfectly reasonable questions! So why did his throat feel as if it had seized up?

'Have I read too much into what we have? Is that it? Have I fallen back into old behaviours and hopes and given my heart to the *idea of us*, when there is no *us*?'

Maddy stared at him, waiting for an answer. Why couldn't he just put her out of her misery? Tell her straight? He looked uncomfortable at her questions, at her declaration of loving him. *Oh God, why did I tell him that I love him?*

She felt embarrassed, humiliated, especially if it wasn't reciprocated.

He kept opening his mouth, as if he was about to speak, but no words emerged for a moment, then he said, 'You deserve someone who can give you *all* of their heart. All of their love.'

'And?' She stared at him. 'You can't?'

'I could, but...you deserve someone better than me. Someone who hasn't hurt you. Someone who hasn't let you down.'

'You let me down when you don't communicate. When you hold something back of yourself. What are you holding back? What aren't you telling me? You should trust me. Don't you trust me?'

'Of course I do!'

'So why won't you tell me what's wrong?'

He didn't answer. And that in itself was an answer.

She stood, unable to be in the small room with him a moment longer. 'I'm going to check on the baby.'

Upset, disappointment and hurt filled her heart as she walked away, unable to believe why he couldn't give her an answer. Why he couldn't even explain to her why he held back part of himself. If anyone should hold themselves back it ought to be her! She was the one who had been hurt by him before. She was the one who had been let down!

Maddy had never let *him* down. So why did he not give her all of himself?

It's always been complicated with him! I should know this.

She rapped her knuckles softly against Marissa's door and entered, forcing a smile. 'How are we all doing?'

'We're good,' Marissa said, smiling, her arms filled with her son, still wrapped in a blanket.

'We'll arrive in port soon. We'll get you seen by specialists and maybe give you the opportunity to get some baby things.'

'My family are going to be so surprised. You expect to come back from a holiday with a tan, not a baby.'

'Have you thought of a name yet?'

'I like Elliot. Or Jacob. I haven't decided.'

'How about you, Mason?' Maddy asked.

'It should be Marissa's decision. It's her baby.'

His wife turned to him. 'It's our decision. I'd like your input. I'd like to know what you're thinking.'

'My opinion is important?'

'Yes! I didn't plan this, Mason! It happened to me too, but we both need to be grown-up about it and talk to one another if we're going to get through this. This should be a happy day for us. We always said we wanted to try for a family and, like it or not, we've now got one, so what are you going to do about it?'

'I'll leave you to it. Would you like a cup of tea? Something to eat? I could get the kitchen to bring you both something down,' Maddy suggested.

Marissa nodded. 'Thank you.'

Maddy closed the door and sighed. It looked as if they were having communication issues too. But Marissa was right, they would have to communicate to get through it, just as she and Nate ought to. She knew she'd need to talk to him before the wedding, but right now she needed space from him because it would be no good talking to him whilst she was still angry.

Nate would have to wait for her for a change.

CHAPTER NINE

THE CAPTAIN'S LOUNGE had been transformed for the wedding ceremony. Chairs for the guests sat in neat lines, each one adorned with a small posy of flowers in the heart of a pale-green ribbon. An arch of fresh flowers sat at the end of the aisle and flower petals covered the floor. Captain Thomas stood beneath the arch, resplendent in his finest uniform, waiting for the two grooms.

Maddy had felt apprehensive dressing in her bridesmaid's dress. She'd meant to find Nate and talk to him about their argument yesterday, to clear the air, at least for the wedding. But she'd gone to her cabin and fallen asleep almost instantly, exhausted by the day and her emotions, and now it was too late. But for the sake of Lucas and Carlos, who deserved nothing but happiness on their special day, she would not give them any reason to think that there were hostilities between Nate and her. It would be difficult, but she would do it.

A beautician from the ship's spa had done her hair and make-up. Maddy had sat in the chair, looked at her pale face and watched as the beautician had created a miracle of healthy glow upon her skin. She'd put soft curls into Maddy's hair and pinned them with flowers and now she was ready.

She saw Lucas and Carlos separately before the service, gave each of them a kiss and wished them both the best. Then, before she knew it, the music began and Nate was there. He looked stunning in a dinner suit and he held out his arm for her to take to walk up the aisle together in time to the music, as they'd practised.

She gave Nate a polite smile, wishing so much that things were different, and began her way up the aisle with him.

Everyone was looking at them: all of Lucas's and Carlos's friends and colleagues who had been invited and the captain. She could feel her heart pounding in her chest, and it felt as if it would burst out of her ribcage at any moment. Nate's reassuring arm held her upright and she felt him look at her as they glided up the aisle to their positions.

Strange to think that she'd once imagined walking up the aisle with Nate. But not like this.

Looks like I never will either.

The thought saddened her so powerfully in that moment that she felt herself gulp and force back tears, but it was fine, because she knew everyone would just think that she was trying to hold back her joy for the happy couple about to come up the aisle themselves.

Maddy pulled her arm free to take her place but, unexpectedly, Nate took her hand, brought it up to his lips and kissed it, his gaze never leaving hers. Breathless, she stared at him, wondering what it meant, but unable to ask, because at that moment the music changed and Carlos walked up the aisle.

Maddy turned away from Nate, bewildered, confused, forcing a wide smile back onto her face as Carlos came to stand in front of the captain. Carlos wore a pale-cream suit, with a tie the same colour as her dress, and a buttonhole of a white rose and pale-green eucalyptus. Carlos met her gaze and beamed at her before turning to look back down the aisle as Lucas appeared.

With no parent to walk him up the aisle, all he had was his brother. Nate now walked back down the aisle and offered his arm to his brother, surprising him.

Lucas pressed his hand to his heart, looking incredibly touched, and together they walked up the aisle, Lucas looking resplendent in his own off-white suit. At the end of the aisle, Nate and his brother embraced, then he took his brother's hand and placed it in Carlos's, before stepping back.

Maddy could not take her eyes off Nate during the service. She could see that his eyes were full of love for his brother and she knew that he would give his life for his brother. That he would do nothing that would make him turn away from him. That they knew absolutely everything about one another and still loved each other fiercely. That patient, Mr Stanton, had been wrong about Nate. There'd been problems, but he'd never abandoned his brother, and he could be trusted.

If only he could feel that way about me.

The tears in her eyes were as much for her as they were for the happy couple and she wasn't too aware of the words being exchanged, or the vows said. Her own heart was breaking as theirs were joining in matrimony. She managed to pull herself together for the rings, though, the captain announcing them as husband and husband and the kiss they shared. Then, before she knew it, Nate was there again, offering her his arm as they followed the happy couple back down the aisle and off to the reception.

There was a whirlwind of greeting people as they entered. and the meal was a blur of courses that she picked at, unable to eat, then there were speeches to listen to, dances to watch and then finally...*finally*...she could slip away, stand under the stars on the top deck and simply *breathe*.

She felt as if she could hear her own heart beating. That her own heart was trying bravely to carry on, despite having broken, but then she became aware of someone standing behind her and knew who it was.

'Maddy...are you alright?' It was Nate.

She turned to face him, appalled that she still found him handsome. She still found him incredibly attractive, especially now that he'd pulled off the bow-tie, which hung undone around the collar of his opened shirt. 'I will be.'

'It was a good service.'

She nodded. 'It was.' What she could remember of it. 'You disappeared after the meal. I thought maybe you didn't want to see me.'

'I wanted to see you very much. I wanted to put everything right between us, but there was someone I needed to speak to first before I could.'

Maddy frowned. What was he talking about? 'Who?'

'Lucas.'

Now she was even more confused. 'Why?'

Nate came to stand by her side, reaching to take her hand. 'You asked me before about why I was holding a part of myself back and I couldn't tell you—partly, because I'd made a promise to my brother long ago, but also because I didn't feel worthy of you.'

How did a long-ago promise to his brother have anything to do with them? 'I don't understand.'

'I told you about our parents.'

She nodded.

'We did not have the best relationship. My stepfather, Bill, hated me. Made me feel all my life like I was nothing, not worthy enough of his time or attention or love. He put me down at every opportunity and favoured Lucas. It soured everything and I left as quickly as I could. I figured Lucas would be fine. Bill was his real father and Bill loved his son. At least, until Lucas came out as gay, then that changed too.'

Maddy stared at him, wrapped up in the pain of his story.

'I hadn't spoken to my family, or my brother, for years when you knew me, when we first got together. I kept you at a distance because I honestly believed I wasn't good enough for anything else. That I didn't know how to commit, or what love truly was, and that I was probably bad. So I held you at arm's length, not realising the depth of your feelings. At the same time, Lucas had...well...he had come out and been rejected and he...he succumbed to the temptations of drugs to block out the pain he felt.'

'Drugs? He was a drug addict?' Now she began to see. To *understand*.

He doesn't take painkillers.

He doesn't drink.

Flashbacks to being attacked by the drug addict flooded her mind and she grew hot and uncomfortable. Struggling to reconcile her feelings for the event that had given her PTSD, but also the man she knew as Lucas, the happy, funny guy she'd just been a bridesmaid for. The wonderfully warm human being whom she had come to like and love.

'Yes. And when our parents had their car accident and died, because Bill had been drinking heavily, Lucas turned to the only comfort he had left, because I'd not been there to help him. He took too much and overdosed and was rushed into A&E in Manchester. They found my details in his wallet and called me at London Saint.'

'That's why you disappeared so quickly.'

'Yes. I did look for you. I wanted to tell you, but you weren't in the department. You'd escorted a patient up to a ward and, though I wanted to wait and see you and explain, every second counted and I knew my brother needed me, so I just left. Without a word. Because he might have died and I wouldn't have been there.'

Maddy couldn't quite believe it. All this time she'd thought he'd left without a word because she wasn't important enough to him to have been considered. She'd been wrong the whole time!

'Lucas was barely alive when I got to Manchester and, once I was there, he was the only thing in my mind. Our parents were dead and I was grieving them and spending every minute by my brother's bedside, waiting for him to gain consciousness. And when he did, he was distraught and grieving, just like me. And more than anything he just wanted another hit to take the pain away. I watched him go through withdrawal and got him into rehab and I visited him every day, vowing never to let him down or leave his side ever again, in case he relapsed. I felt guilty that my leaving had contributed to his drug habit and I saw it as my job to get him off them.'

'It must have been terrifying for you.'

He nodded. 'It was. But slowly, week by week, Lucas started to get better. We went to counselling together to work our way through everything that had happened to us. We did a lot of work on ourselves and, by the time I felt strong enough to even think about what I had lost with you, so much time had passed I just felt it was probably better to just wipe the slate clean and leave you alone. I had no idea how much my going had affected you.'

'I was broken.'

'I know that now, but I didn't then. I thought staying away from you was for the best. That you'd find someone to settle down with, someone worthy. You'd always told me how you'd hoped to find someone special one day. Someone who would love you the way you'd never felt before. Someone who would choose you.'

She'd thought she had found that someone. She'd thought it was him. 'What happened with you and Lucas next?'

'I encouraged him to pursue his dreams. He'd always loved ice-skating and so I went with him to the rink so he could practise. I even paid for him to have a private coach and he finally started to have dreams and aspirations for his life. He applied for a job as an ice-dancer on a cruise ship and he got it, but he was terrified of doing it alone. I was only working as a locum in Manchester, so I offered to join the ship as medical crew to be with him.'

'That's amazing.'

'He made me make a promise, though.'

'Which was?'

'He wanted a fresh start. He wanted to be rid of his past and the only way he knew how to do that was to not tell a single soul about his addiction or past problems. He made me vow that I also would not tell a soul, ever.'

Now she began to understand. She'd told Nate about being attacked by a drug addict and he hadn't been able to tell her that his brother, the man for whom she was going to be a bridesmaid, was one. 'That's why you went to see him just now.'

'Yes. To ask for his permission to tell you. So I could explain to you why you never got all of me, why I held myself back. At first it was because I did not feel worthy of you. When you've spent your childhood being told you're worthless with nothing to offer, you start to believe it. And then I had the promise I'd made to my brother. I thought, if you knew, you'd be triggered by the revelation and refuse to be Lucas's bridesmaid, when I knew how much my brother liked you.'

She had tears in her eyes now. So much hidden pain, for both of them! 'You are worthy of love, Nate. You do have something to offer. I hope you know that.'

'Your love has made me see it and I hope that, now I've been given permission to tell you everything, you will see that I stand here with my heart wide open to you and that I never meant to hurt you by holding back, but that I was afraid to give my all, in case it got rejected.'

'Oh, Nate!' She cradled his face with her hands and pressed her lips to his, hungry for his touch, hungry to be in his arms once again. She had felt bereft for so long!

'I thought *I* wasn't good enough,' she breathed, her forehead pressed to his. 'But it's always been you, Nathaniel. You've *always* had my heart. You're the only one who can hold it together and fix its broken pieces. If that's too heavy a burden, I'll understand, but know that I love you and want to be with you, and it doesn't matter about what Lucas used to be. He's not that now and I think it's time for *us* to find happiness.'

Nate nodded, smiling. 'I agree.'

'What do you say that we go back into that reception and show the happy couple how non-ice-dancers dance?'

Nate stroked her face. 'We will. But first…can you forgive me, for hurting you?'

She kissed him beneath the stars, in the middle of the ocean. 'Of course. Forgiven and forgotten.'

Maddy pressed her lips to his again, the man she loved in her arms at last. There were no secrets between them. All fears had been vanquished by the strength and the power of their love for one another.

EPILOGUE

NATE STOOD WITH his arm around Maddy on the harbour, watching as the large cruise ship *Amore* began its docking procedures. 'Excited?' he asked.

'To see Lucas and Carlos again? I can't wait!' She kissed his lips, gazing up at him.

He smiled. 'Me too. Think they suspect?'

'That we're going to get married whilst they're here? I hope not. I want it to be a surprise.'

'Well, Lucas can be quite wily, and he might wonder as to why I insisted that they both pack their dinner suits.'

She laughed. 'I'm ahead of you. I told them we were taking them to a theatre and then a very expensive and exclusive restaurant for a meal afterwards and they wouldn't be allowed in without black tie.'

'Clever! Are you nervous?' he asked, squeezing her to him, his hand at her waist, still unable to believe that this wonderful woman was going to be his wife in three short days.

'At getting married? Absolutely not. You?'

'Are you kidding me? I'd do it right now if we could.'

She chuckled and turned back to the ship, and waved at the sight of Lucas and Carlos waiting deckside for the gangways to be attached so they could disembark the ship onto Cyprus.

The island had become their home. After cruising around on *Serendipity* for their six-month contract, they had chosen the island as their favourite. Rich with myths and beautiful landscapes, green mountains and turquoise waters, the island was also filled with the sweetest, kindest people. They'd bought a stunning villa in Paphos in which to create their home together, whilst working in a clinic in the town. Here they planned to stay and raise their family, something he hoped they'd begin to work on after the wedding. He was ready and he knew that Maddy was too. It was all she dreamed of, a family of her own, and he'd promised to help her make one.

His idea was that Lucas could walk him up the aisle and Carlos could walk Maddy, as she had no family of her own to do so. It was going to be a small, intimate affair, just Lucas and Carlos, and some of their other friends flying in tomorrow.

Everything was going perfectly. The best revenge to those who had once told him he was nothing was to live well, and he was exceeding that with Maddy by his side. Their relationship had gone from strength to strength.

'Hola!' Lucas ran towards them as he got closer and swung Maddy round in his arms as she squealed with happiness, letting go of her, only to hug his brother, clapping him on the back. 'Looking good, brother dear! Looking good!'

'You too. Hey, Carlos!' He gave his brother-in-law a hug. 'Welcome to Cyprus. How's things?'

'Muy bien! Good to see you. We have missed you!

Madeline...' Carlos stood back to admire her in her beautiful white sundress. 'Stunning! You look amazing.'

Lucas nodded in agreement. 'Now, be honest, we're not just here for a little visit, are we?'

Nate tried to feign innocence. 'I don't know what you mean,' he said, smiling.

'You can't hide anything from me, brother dear! A little birdie tells me that plans are afoot...and it's not only the rock of Gibraltar that is huge, but also that diamond I see on Maddy's finger!' Lucas lifted Maddy's hand to admire the engagement ring Nate had slipped onto her hand months ago.

Nate laughed and shook his head. 'You don't miss a thing, do you?'

'So you are engaged?'

Nate looked at Maddy. 'Yes, we are.'

Lucas squealed with delight and pulled them both in for a hug. Carlos joined in too, determined not to be left out. 'When's the wedding?'

Nate looked at his watch and laughed. 'In three days. Fancy being a best man?'

Lucas let out another sound that possibly only could have been heard by bats and dogs at the upper end and then began flapping his hands in front of his face as he began to cry. 'I'm so happy for you guys! I hoped, of course, but didn't know for sure. You must be so happy!'

'We are,' Maddy said.

Nate turned to face Maddy and pulled her in for a kiss. 'I'm the happiest man alive.'

* * * * *

*If you enjoyed this story,
check out these other great reads
from Lousia Heaton:*

Nurse's Night Before Valentine's
New Year to Nine-Month Surprise
One Night to Twin Miracle
The Surgeon's Relationship Ruse

All available now!

MILLS & BOON®

Coming next month

GREEK HOSPITAL, RED-HOT REUNION
Tina Beckett

Ana shrugged, but curled her fingers around his, not quite ready to break the contact. 'When we first saw each other at the hospital, and I sensed how uncomfortable we both were, I did think it. That I would try to avoid you as much as I could. When Natalia told me I'd have to rotate through surgery, I was horrified. Wasn't sure if I could even do it.'

'And now that you've done it. Are you still horrified?'

'No. I'm actually looking forward to our next time.'

'Our next time.' Dimitry unhooked his hip from the car and took a step closer. 'Are you, Ana?'

God, he evidently felt it too. She swallowed as her senses went on high alert.

'Yes. Very much so.' The words came out as a whisper. Why had she never noticed him like this in school? Hadn't she? She could remember at least one time when she had.

Dangerous. This was moving into territory she had no business exploring. What about working on herself? Wasn't that what she was supposed to be doing?

He took another step and that muscle in his cheek bunched again. This time, though, she knew he wasn't irritated.

She had a feeling it meant something else entirely. That—like her—he was fighting his inner impulses, while being dragged slowly and methodically closer.

'What else are you looking forward to, Ana?'

'Can't you guess?'

His left hand slid behind her nape and he leaned forward until his lips were at her ear. 'Is guessing really what you want me to do?'

'No.' She turned her head so their lips were mere inches apart. 'I want you to kiss me.'

Continue reading

GREEK HOSPITAL, RED-HOT REUNION
Tina Beckett

Available next month
millsandboon.co.uk

Copyright © 2026 Tina Beckett

COMING SOON!

We really hope you enjoyed reading this book.
If you're looking for more romance
be sure to head to the shops when
new books are available on

Thursday 21st May

To see which titles are coming soon, please visit
millsandboon.co.uk/nextmonth

MILLS & BOON

FOUR BRAND NEW BOOKS FROM
MILLS & BOON MODERN

Indulge in desire, drama, and breathtaking romance – where passion knows no bounds!

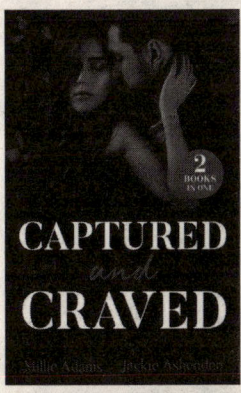

OUT NOW

Eight Modern stories published every month, find them all at:

millsandboon.co.uk

TWO BRAND NEW BOOKS FROM
Love Always

Be prepared to be swept away to incredible worldwide destinations along with our strong, relatable heroines and intensely desirable heroes.

OUT NOW

Four Love Always stories published every month, find them all at:

millsandboon.co.uk

OUT NOW!

Available at
millsandboon.co.uk

MILLS & BOON

LET'S TALK
Romance

For exclusive extracts, competitions and special offers, find us online:

- **f** MillsandBoon
- **X** @MillsandBoon
- **◉** @MillsandBoonUK
- **♪** @MillsandBoonUK

Get in touch on 01413 063 232

For all the latest titles coming soon, visit
millsandboon.co.uk/nextmonth